Among the Ghosts

BY AMBER BENSON

ILLUSTRATED BY SINA GRACE

Aladdin

NEW YORK   LONDON   TORONTO   SYDNEY

ALADDIN

An imprint of Simon & Schuster Children's Publishing Division
1230 Avenue of the Americas, New York, NY 10020
First Aladdin hardcover edition August 2010
Text copyright © 2010 by Amber Benson
Illustrations copyright © 2010 by Sina Grace
All rights reserved, including the right of reproduction in whole or in part in any form.
ALADDIN is a trademark of Simon & Schuster, Inc., and related logo is a registered trademark of Simon & Schuster, Inc.
For information about special discounts for bulk purchases, please contact
Simon & Schuster Special Sales at 1-866-506-1949 or business@simonandschuster.com.
The Simon & Schuster Speakers Bureau can bring authors to your live event.
For more information or to book an event contact the Simon & Schuster Speakers Bureau at 1-866-248-3049 or visit our website at www.simonspeakers.com.
Designed by Lisa Vega
The text of this book was set in Bembo.
The illustrations for this book were rendered digitally.
Manufactured in the United States of America 0710 FFG
10 9 8 7 6 5 4 3 2 1
Library of Congress Cataloging-in-Publication Data
Benson, Amber.
Among the ghosts / Amber Benson. — 1st Aladdin hardcover ed.
p. cm.
Summary: While spending the summer at The New Newbridge Academy where she will soon begin sixth grade, Noleen finds strange things happening and discovers the special talent her aunts saw in her when she was a motherless infant.
ISBN 978-1-4169-9405-3 (hardcover)
[1. Ghosts—Fiction. 2. Boarding schools—Fiction. 3. Schools—Fiction. 4. Aunts—Fiction. 5. Supernatural—Fiction. 6. Mystery and detective stories.] I. Title.
PZ7.B447158Amo 2011
[Fic]—dc22
2009029392
ISBN 978-1-4424-0940-8 (eBook)

For all the "realies" out there who know
that ghosts do indeed exist

Acknowledgments

I want to thank my editor, Liesa Abrams, for helping me make Noh's story as good as it could possibly be.

Contents

Ants and Sweaters

Thomas spied the ants as he waited by the back door to the kitchen. At first he ignored their merry procession, his mind overwhelmed with thoughts of the rich, buttery apple pie that he knew was baking in the oven only a few feet from where he was standing. Once or twice he let his eyes flick away from the window in the kitchen door in order to mark the ants' progression, but it was only *after* he saw Mrs. Marble pull the golden-crusted beauty from the oven that he gave the ants a real looking at.

From what Thomas could tell, it seemed like the ants were on their way home from a military reconnaissance mission in the kitchen. They marched single file down the concrete steps that led to the kitchen door, across the sidewalk, and into the grass. They each carried a small piece of white fluff on their backs, which to Thomas made them all look like they were wearing little angora sweaters. A grin splitting his face at the thought of ants in knitted sweaters, he decided that the white stuff was definitely *not* angora, but something edible that the ants had stolen from Mrs. Marble's kitchen.

Thomas didn't like anyone stealing from Mrs. Marble—even the ants. Mrs. Marble was the nicest lady in the whole world as far as Thomas was concerned, besides which she baked some of the best pies this side of the Mason-Dixon Line . . . or at least, that's what everyone said after they'd sampled one of her delicious desserts.

Feeling like a police detective in search of a crime—a policeman was something Thomas had always wanted to be when he grew up, after being a chef, of course—he decided to follow the ants and see where they were going. He pushed his brown newsboy cap out of his eyes and followed the thieving insects across the school grounds, past the archery field, and back over to the burned-out shell of the West Wing.

There had been a fire in the West Wing a number

of years before, and now most people kept away from the building. Thomas thought those people were silly for being scared of an old, burned-out building, but he guessed that anyone was allowed to feel any way they wanted to about stuff that scared them. Though personally he believed that *just* because something didn't look perfect anymore, didn't mean you had to be scared of it. Sometimes a pie didn't come out looking perfect, but that didn't mean you threw it away—misshapen pie tasted just as good as any other kind of pie, thank you very much!

On the steps that led into the main entrance of the West Wing, Thomas paused to tip his cap to a girl who was sitting on the topmost step. She had her nose pressed firmly into a book, but she looked up and gave him a quick grin as he passed her by. Thomas spent most of his time in the kitchen, which was where he'd worked . . . *before*, but because of this, he didn't really know the other kids at the school very well. He wasn't sure what this particular girl's name was, but he thought it began with the letter *N*—although he couldn't *really* be sure. He was much better at remembering recipes than names.

Before the grin had even left her face, the girl was

back into her book. Thomas saw that she didn't even notice the ants that were marching up the steps beside her. If *he'd* been the one sitting by an army of ants, he'd sure have noticed them.

Thomas went through the door that led into the interior of the building, his eyes trained on the ants' progress. Instantly he saw that the line of ants was making its way across the room before disappearing down into a small hole that sat right underneath the hearth of a large brick fireplace. Thomas got as close to the hole as he could, putting his eyeball right up to it, but it was so dark that he really couldn't see where the ants were going at all.

Suddenly Thomas felt his whole body go stiff as a strange, prickly sensation swept across him. The hairs on the back of his neck stood up at attention. Thomas hadn't felt anything like this in so long that at first he almost didn't recognize what it was.

It was only when his teeth started to chatter that he realized what was happening to him. For the first time in more than eighty years, Thomas was *cold*. He looked up from where he was crouching by the base of the fireplace, and his eyes went wide when he saw what was waiting for him.

He opened his mouth to shout, but only a deep gurgle of fear popped out. It filled the empty room like the hollow sound of the last piece of candy rattling around inside a trick-or-treater's Halloween grab bag.

When the girl with the book came back inside from her perch on the stairs, the room was empty. She scratched a bug bite on her arm and looked around curiously. She was pretty sure that she'd seen the boy from the kitchen come in here only a few minutes before.

She wondered where he'd gone.

In the Beginning

Two minutes after Mabel Maypother gave birth, she looked down into her newborn's steel gray eyes and smiled. Then she lay back on the hospital gurney and died.

Thus began the auspicious life of Noleen-Anne Harris Morgan Maypother, the wee babe clutched tightly in her dead mother's slowly cooling embrace.

Harold Maypother was distraught. Mabel had been the love of his life. He had no idea what he was going to do without her. While he quietly began to lose his grip on reality, his two sisters—and only living relatives—took possession of Noleen-Anne.

Clara was the oldest Maypother and very bossy. She had bossed Harold around from the time he was in diapers all the way up until his marriage to Mabel Harris three years earlier. Aunt Clara thought it was her job to boss. It made her happy and kept the people around her from being messy. And, in truth, by picking up where she had left off on her brother's wedding day, she probably saved his sanity that awful night.

With baby Noleen tucked into the folds of her coat, Aunt Clara marched herself and her two siblings back to Harold's small apartment and, after giving baby Noleen a bottle, sent everyone off to bed with the adage that "things always look better in the morning."

Baby Noleen woke up to find herself wrapped in a pair of warm, strong arms. She trained her gray eyes up into the smiling face of her aunt Sarah. At the time, Sarah was only sixteen, but there was something ancient in her lovely face. When she was older and better read, Noh surmised that Aunt Sarah and Florence Nightingale probably had a few things in common. But at the time, she only saw the glow that emanated from her young aunt, and it made her feel warm and loved.

"Poor little Noh," her aunt cooed. "We'll love you, motherless or not. You're a special little girl . . . even if you don't know it yet."

Noh didn't understand then, but later she would. There was indeed something very special inside the little girl, something passed down through the bloodline of the Maypother women, so that in each generation there was one female child born with a special "talent." This special talent would bide its time, watching and waiting for the day when it could finally show itself—and then, whether she liked it or not, Noh's life would be changed forever.

  9

Noh the Magnificent

The summer had been a mess so far.

Noh was *supposed* to be spending the already messy summer with her father in the Appalachians while he studied the mating habits of the Appalachian Russell Newt. But at the last minute he had decided that his daughter was just too young to go slogging through the muck *In Search Of*, so he shipped her off to Aunt Clara's house for the summer.

When she got there—the note from her father explaining the situation clutched in her small, sweaty hand—she found that Aunt Clara had packed up her family and gone to the beach for the summer. Well, since she wasn't sure exactly what beach her aunt and cousins had decamped to, she didn't think spending the summer with them was going to be a viable solution.

Noh thought about getting back on the train and trying to find Harold, but she decided against it in the end. She thought, quite justly, that he would already be far into the woods and completely unreachable.

She sat on Aunt Clara's stoop for a good two hours, debating her options and eating the lemons (rind, seeds, and all) she had collected from the backyard.

Tired and feeling the onset of an acidy stomach, she walked back to the train station and booked a seat on the night train to New Newbridge. She knew that the only stable person in her family (i.e., guaranteed to be where they were supposed to be) was her aunt Sarah, who taught English literature at the New Newbridge Academy. And anyway, Noh was going to be starting there in the fall for sixth grade, so she figured it was as good a decision as she could make at the time.

She slept the whole way on the train. Her mind was filled with very lucid dreams that tickled her brain. She saw a boy her own age sitting at a tall desk, reading a crumpled and smudged letter. Sensing her presence, he glared angrily at her.

The old lady sitting beside her nudged her awake at the New Newbridge stop. Noh collected her bag and stepped out into a very humid summer day.

In the Cemetery

New Newbridge was not a big town. Noh was able to navigate her way from the train station to the school without much difficulty. She had visited her aunt Sarah three times since she had taken the teaching position there three years before.

Noh's sense of "what was where" was more highly developed than if she had never been there at all, so she only got lost once—when she tried to take a shortcut through the old cemetery.

The cemetery had been in business since the pioneer days. There were graves that had been so exposed to the elements that you could barely read the rudimentary inscriptions. Noh, who was strangely drawn to any and every cemetery she had had the good fortune to come across, clapped her hands happily and opened the creaky iron gate. Pieces of rust came off onto her hands, staining them. But she didn't mind.

No one but Noh knew why she loved cemeteries. And if you had asked her, Noh probably wouldn't have told you, anyway. But, suffice it to say, it had something to do with the word *serenity*. Serenity oozed from the graves and made Noh feel safe and secure. She imagined that when she lay in the grass near a welcoming head-stone, it was like being wrapped in her dead mother's warm embrace.

It was a phantom pain she felt—being motherless. Because how could her feelings of grief be real if she had never even known the person she had lost in the first place? But still . . . it felt pretty real to her, anyway.

Noh had once tried to explain all this to her cousin Jordy, but he had only run and told Aunt Clara, who had promptly told Noh's father, who had sent her to see a psychologist in a drab gray building downtown. So, from that day forth, she had decided to keep any strange leanings to herself.

Noh walked through the old cemetery, picking wild-flowers and reading the inscriptions on the headstones.

She was so intent on what she was doing that she didn't notice that she was back where she had started. The only thing that made her realize she was going in circles was that the headstone inscriptions started repeating themselves.

The next go-around, she paid more attention to where she was going. Yet when she thought she was on the other side of the cemetery, she found herself instead back at the rusty gate. It didn't matter where she started or how slow or fast she walked—Noh just couldn't seem to get to the other side. Finally, she chalked it all up to hunger and low blood sugar and slunk back out the same gate she had happily walked through two hours before.

"What're you doing here, girl? You don't belong here!"

The voice was harsh, tinged with age, and pretty mean-sounding to boot. Noh looked up, startled to find an old woman standing just inside the gate of the cemetery, glaring at her.

Noh may have been lost in thought as she had exited the cemetery only moments ago, but she wasn't blind— Noh knew the old woman hadn't been there before.

"I thought anyone could visit a cemetery," Noh said

defiantly. Usually she was pretty respectful of people older than herself, but there was something about this old woman that made her want to talk back. Maybe it was the cruel turn of the old woman's mouth or the hateful glint in her eye, but it was all Noh could do not to stick out her tongue at her.

"Don't you sass me, girl," the old woman hissed, her bony shoulders shaking beneath the homemade black woolen dress that covered her stick-figure frame. Noh couldn't help thinking that the old woman looked just like a witch. All she needed was a broomstick, a pointy black hat, and a cat.

"It's a free country," Noh said, trying not to be too rude, even though it was very hard not to say what was on her mind. "Anyone should be able to pay their respects, ma'am."

The old woman spit on the ground in front of the cemetery gate.

"This is private property," she hissed again before slamming the gate shut right in front of Noh's face. "We don't want any of your respects—we like it just as it is. We don't need *your* kind coming in and stirring things up!"

The old woman took a small stone from her pocket and threw it through the bars of the cemetery gate, where it landed right at Noh's feet. Noh reached down to pick it up, curious to find a hand-carved eye cut into its polished gray surface.

She knew exactly what this stone was . . . it was an *evil eye*.

Noh looked up, opening her mouth to protest the strange gift, but closed it when she saw that the old woman was gone. She had somehow disappeared among the graves while Noh was picking up the stone. Noh walked over to the cemetery gate and looked inside, but she could find neither hide nor hair of the crazy old woman.

She knew that the old woman probably hadn't meant the stone to be a gift, but that's exactly what Noh decided it was. She wasn't scared of the evil eye—in fact, she kind of liked it. She put it into her pocket, rubbing her fingers against its polished surface. It would be a good reminder that there was always something strange and interesting lurking *just* around the corner.

The New Newbridge Academy

After her strange run-in at the cemetery, Noh spent the rest of her walk to the New Newbridge Academy deep in thought, trying to figure out how an old woman could simply disappear like that.

That was why she smelled the New Newbridge Academy before she saw it. The cook, Mrs. Marble, was known throughout five counties for her apple pie, and she was in baking heaven today. Noh's mouth began to water the minute the school's front drive came into view.

All in all, the school was really a hodgepodge of different architectural styles. The old building itself was Gothic with large pointed windows and ornamental gargoyles sitting benignly at the front entrance and hanging from the roof.

The architect who had designed the building had thought the gargoyles would be sufficiently scary enough to keep even the most daring students from spending too much time climbing around up on the roof.

The inside of the building was voluminous, with two floors of classrooms and another floor for administration purposes. The basement had a therapeutic indoor swimming pool that lay dormant most of the time underneath a mechanized roll-out gym floor. When there was a really mean game of basketball going on down in the gym, you could actually hear the scuff of tennis shoes on wood up in the biology labs.

Except for the basement, all the floors were made from slabs of thick gray stone that in the winter made the place as cold as a mausoleum, even when the furnace was turned way up. Between the drab gray walls, the rough-hewn stone floors, and the school crest and Arthurian-themed tapestries hanging here and there, the place had quite an imposing air. Most sixth graders spent their first semester darting through the halls in mortal fear of ghosts and goblins grabbing them on their way to English class.

  22

To her surprise, Noh saw her aunt sitting on the front steps of the main building, holding a crochet hook.

"Aunt Sarah?" she started inquiringly, but her aunt didn't let her finish. Putting down her hook and yarn, she said, "I went to the station, but I missed you by ten minutes."

"But—," she started, yet once again was stymied by her aunt's honeyed voice.

"Clara's neighbors called when they saw someone lurking about the house. I assured them that it was only an errant niece."

"But—"

Her aunt smiled. "How did I know it was you?"

Noh nodded.

"Because of the harried telegram I got from your father, telling me to go and collect you at Clara's for the start of the school year. I almost borrowed a car to come get you myself, but then the neighbors called and I knew that you were too smart to stick around until Clara got back."

"I didn't want to stay with her, anyway, but my dad said I had to." Noh's eyes filled with tears of exhaustion and hunger. Her aunt smiled and held out her arms.

Noh happily rushed into the proffered hug. For the next few minutes the tears streamed down her face as she recounted her homeless adventure in only slightly exaggerated detail. When she was finally done, she handed her aunt the polished stone from her pocket.

"I think it's an evil eye, don't you?" Noh asked excitedly. She really hoped her aunt would agree. Her aunt turned the polished stone over and over in her hand, deep in thought.

"Maybe you should let me keep this," her aunt said finally, but Noh shook her head.

"It doesn't scare me. I'll just hold on to it for luck," Noh said firmly, taking the stone back and slipping it into her pocket again. Her aunt gave her a funny grin but didn't argue with her. Instead she stood up and took Noh's hand.

"Let's go get my brave girl something to eat." She smiled as she took Noh's bag and led her into the building toward the wonderful smell of newly baked apple pie.

So, She Fancies Herself a Pioneer, Does She?

Noh settled herself into her new room with contented sighs of happiness. The South Wing, which housed all the girls, had been built to look like a villa on the Côte d'Azur. In a very forward-thinking moment the trustees had hired a woman—one of the few women architects in the state—to design the building.

Millicent Farley had grown up in Europe and had been obsessed with the southern coasts of Italy, France, and Spain. When given the commission at New Newbridge, she had been quoted as saying, "I would like to give all the young women of the New Newbridge Academy a taste of what it is like to live in paradise."

It was said that on quiet spring evenings you could

actually hear the roll of the surf from anywhere you happened to be standing in the South Wing. And the smell of suntan oil and cassis was almost palpable every day of the week.

Noh's own small dorm room was warm and cozy. The small twin bed was made up with soft cream-colored sheets and a bright geometric-patterned quilt that her aunt Sarah had made with her own two hands. The floor was smooth vanilla pine and covered with a pink and mauve woven rug. The walls were bare cream, the paint new and unchipped.

All in all, Noh was pleased. It wasn't as nice as her room back home, but it would more than do. She was sure that she could learn to live without her TV and computer. Well, pretty sure.

After a quick nap Noh decided to explore her new surroundings. Her visits to the school in the past had been no more than cursory. She had never had the opportunity to really check the place out. She figured that there was no time like the present to remedy that.

Her room was down the hall from her aunt Sarah's. Since her aunt was one of the dorm supervisors, she lived on the same hall as the youngest girls.

But when Noh got to her aunt's room, she found the door shut and locked. She knocked twice with the back of her fist, but only succeeded in hurting her knuckles. She waited in vain for Sarah to open the door, but her aunt didn't so much as cough behind the thick oak door. Finally, Noh got bored with waiting and decided that Aunt Sarah must be out and about. She shrugged her shoulders and made a quick beeline for the exit.

Once she was outside, Noh felt much better. It wasn't that the girls' dorm gave her the creeps or anything, but Noh had just never much liked being trapped within four walls and a roof. Noh breathed in the fresh air and started to run. Her first order of business was to take a quick jog around the grounds and sort out *what* was *where*.

The wind had started to pick up, and Noh's dark brown hair whipped across her face and tried to find its way into her nose and mouth. She pulled a shiny sterling-silver barrette from her pocket and pulled her hair back into a not-so-neat ponytail.

She was glad that her hair was stick straight and superfine. Otherwise, the thin barrette would never have held

27

her shoulder-length hair in place. The barrette had been a present from her father on her tenth birthday, and she cherished it. Her father never said, but Noh had the distinct impression that the barrette had been her mother's.

As she walked across the grounds of New Newbridge, Noh realized that they were even more picturesque than the buildings.

The football field was huge, with bleachers all around. Everett Smithers, the coach at New Newbridge from 1920 to 1950, was considered to be, by those in the know, one of the greatest high school football coaches of that century. A number of boys, after spending four years under the coach's tutelage, went on to football glory at Notre Dame, Harvard, and Yale. Sadly, after his retirement, football at New Newbridge was never quite the same.

The archery range was beautiful. It had spawned a number of state archery champions and a few "more infamous" students responsible for a number of "unintentional" peer maimings.

The stables were well cared for. The horses were either friendly and eager to please or holy terrors that spent a lot of their time in the paddock, munching grass.

Artemis Lake was wide and calm as Noh stood at its edge. Amateur rowers, swimmers, sailors, and fishermen used it in the spring, summer, and fall. In the winter it was a place to go and mope around when one was feeling depressed over an unrequited crush or bad mark on a paper. Visiting the frigid winter lake was good therapy. It reminded you that even when things looked terrible, spring was just around the corner to cheer everyone up.

Noh couldn't help marveling at just how large the New Newbridge Academy was. She had known that this was the case, but somehow she had needed to see it for herself. When she came to the football field, she climbed to the top of the bleachers and sat down for a quick rest. From her vantage point she could see the whole backside of New Newbridge. She was particularly drawn to the burned-out side of the West Wing.

Noh decided that it looked as if some hungry giant had taken a bite out of the building. The missing and blackened-out parts were in stark contrast to the rest of the building, which was still in pristine condition.

Her aunt Sarah had told her that the school trustees had known how rambunctious boys could be, so they had decided to entrust the design of the East and West

Wings to an ex–army engineer. William Atherton, a twice-decorated Great War veteran, had seen it as his duty to make the place as strong as an elephant. He had reinforced the walls so that they were fist- and foot-proof, put in the hardest woods for the floors and trim, and even put peepholes in every door to instill that little bit of army paranoia that "Big Brother" was watching.

Until the fire that destroyed the West Wing, the boys' dorms were truly thought to be indestructible.

Noh wondered when someone was going to fix the West Wing and make it habitable. Not that she minded the creepiness. In fact, it was quite the reverse—she liked the sadness that she sensed emanating from the burned-out old warhorse of a building. She wondered if maybe, somewhere in its depths, there was a kindred spirit just itching to make her acquaintance.

She left the bleachers and football field behind and found herself standing directly in front of the West Wing's back door. She hadn't meant to go there, but she was unable to make her feet go in any other direction. Out of politeness she knocked on the door and waited the obligatory ten seconds. When no one came to open the door, she opened it herself.

  30

The knob was cold and hard in her hand. She didn't think that the steel would be so cold, with the weather outside as warm as it was. She closed the door softly behind her and shivered. The place was a refrigerator. Noh wished that she had brought her jacket, but how could she know that the West Wing would be a deep freeze? She thought about turning around and going back the way she had come until she could crawl into her nice, warm bed and pull the covers over her head.

But she stayed put. The place wasn't that bad, really, except for the cold.

The sunlight was still alive enough to illuminate Noh's way, so she didn't bother fumbling with the electric lights as she began to explore. Her feet made soft swooshing noises as they echoed their way across the room. Noh decided that the place she had entered must have once been the laundry room. She could almost hear the swishing of the washers and dryers.

She left that room and found herself in a long hallway that eventually dumped her out into the front entrance hall. She walked over to a large painting that hung precariously on the wall. It was placed so that it was the first thing anyone saw when they entered the West Wing from the front door.

Noh studied the drawn, grouchy face of the old man in the picture. The painting was done in oil so that the picture's subject seemed to almost glow with some inner light. *It's a shame that he has such a nasty look on his face,* Noh thought. Otherwise, it would have been a truly magnificent painting.

"He looks like he's got a bug up his butt, huh?"

Noh sucked in her breath and turned around hurriedly at the sound of the voice. The girl was wearing a yellow T-shirt and a pair of hiking boots. The book in her hand was old and dog-eared from reading.

"Yeah, he kinda does, doesn't he?" Noh responded. She had been frightened by the voice, but now was very happy to see that the voice's owner was about her own age and looked friendly.

"Do you go to school here?" the girl asked curiously. She scratched her arm as if something were biting her. Noh wondered if there were lots of mosquitoes because of the lake. Maybe she could entice her dad into visiting her by boasting about all the mosquito larvae that were to be found on the school grounds.

Noh nodded her head. "Not yet, but I *will* be going here when school starts back up again this fall." Noh watched the girl give her arm one final scratch, then leave the bite alone.

"What's your name?" The girl didn't seem to be in the least bothered by the fact that they were all alone in this creepy old building. Noh watched her carefully.

"Noh," she answered smoothly. "My name's Noh, short for Noleen."

The girl thought this was funny. She giggled.

"I'm Nelly. I'm not short for anything." The girl seemed to think that this was funny too, and laughed again.

"I should get back," Noh blurted out. "Maybe I'll see you around."

"Maybe." The girl smiled. She nodded her head up and down as if she were some kind of marionette puppet.

34

Yipes, Noh thought.

They stood in complete silence for over a minute, and then Noh broke the spell.

"Okay. Well . . . er, bye," Noh said quickly, and made a run for the front door. Finally, something—someone—was giving her the creeps.

Nelly watched the new girl run out the door. She looked down at her arm and scratched the sore spot again. It didn't really hurt. She scratched it more from habit than anything else.

She would have to tell Trina about the new girl, she thought.

Back at the girls' dormitory, Noh found the door to her aunt's room unlocked. Noh knew immediately that she should have knocked instead of just barging in, but she was unable to stop herself. Inside she found her aunt Sarah standing over a giant iron cauldron.

"You're just in time for some tea," Aunt Sarah said as she dropped a handful of rose petals into the iron pot.

Noh, Tea in Your Coffee?

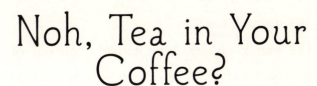

N oh backed into the hallway and, without a word, walked slowly toward her room. When she got there, she opened the door and went inside. Closing the door behind her, she crawled into bed and pulled the covers over her head.

It had been that kind of day.

She stayed under the covers for a long time. She pretended that she was an embryo living in her mother's belly, growing very, very slowly. She played a breathing game in her head—every breath she took was really an echo of her mother's heartbeat.

This continued into the early evening. She finally surfaced from her make-believe world when her stomach started growling. Mrs. Marble was fixing *"something*

and chipped beef"—Noh was certain of it. There was no other smell in the whole world that compared with the smell of good old chipped beef. This made Noh feel better. At the very least, something *normal* was gonna go into her stomach tonight.

The knock on the door startled Noh out of her chipped-beef reverie. When she didn't answer, the door opened and her aunt Sarah came in carrying a tray of tea.

"I thought you might be hungry," Aunt Sarah said in a quiet voice. "Dinner won't be ready for another hour." It was as if she were trying to keep herself from saying other things instead.

"You don't have to have any if you don't want to," Aunt Sarah said even more quietly.

Noh looked down at the tray. There were two scones and a peanut butter cookie arranged elegantly around the teapot and mugs.

"Do you want to have something to eat with me?" Noh said just as quietly. Anyone looking in would have thought they were in a library. Her aunt nodded and began pouring the tea.

"When you were little, Noh, you always tried to drink my tea," Aunt Sarah said as she handed her a mug of honeyed tea. "But you wanted nothing at all to do with your father's cup of coffee."

"Oh," Noh said.

They sipped their tea in silence after that. Noh occasionally stole glances at her aunt from under her lowered eyelashes. She loved her aunt more than almost anyone else, but there was something about her aunt Sarah that—as much as it compelled Noh's love—also very much intimidated her.

"What were you doing? Before, I mean, when I barged into your room without knocking?" Noh blurted out the question, spitting bits of cookie through her lips as she talked.

"I had already had a kinda strange day, and then to see you standing over a big old cauldron like that was even stranger. . . ." Noh trailed off, unsure if she should be saying all this. But she continued on, unchecked. The words slipped from her mouth like slimy old banana slugs.

"You're not a wicked witch, are you? I mean, if you are, that's great, but it's kinda weird. If you are. A wicked witch. I mean . . ." Noh trailed off again. This was just like digging your own grave. Every inch you sank deeper into the earth just kinda creeped you out and made you feel slightly nauseated.

Her aunt put a reassuring arm on Noh's shoulder. "What if I told you that I was going to teach a history class next semester in which one would be pretending to live in the nineteenth century. Well, for the duration of each class, that is, and then one can go back to the rest of one's day living normally in the present. And the giant "cauldron" you saw will be used to show how one did one's laundry—back before the advent of mass electrical consumption and the widespread use of modern washing machines."

Silence, as Aunt Sarah waited for Noh's response. After her own little diatribe Noh felt kind of sheepish.

"Oh," Noh said in a very teeny, tiny voice that she hoped her aunt could hear. It wasn't that she was really *that* worried about her aunt Sarah being a wicked witch. She didn't know why she had made such a big deal out of the whole thing. She supposed that it had something to do with being newly alone and feeling strange about her scholarly surroundings.

"*But* then what if that weren't really the truth? What if I really were a witch? A wicked witch, like you say.

 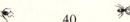 40

Would that bother you, Noh?" Her aunt didn't wait for a response. She stood and patted Noh's head. "You shouldn't judge anyone on what you see with your eyes alone. And just for the record: I'm *not* a wicked witch— at least for the next semester—because I'm going to be a pioneer instead."

Her aunt closed the door on her way out, leaving Noh gape-mouthed. Noh, feeling slightly like a codfish, closed her mouth.

Is this one of those trick-question moments? she wondered. Was she supposed to choose one occupation or the other—wicked witch or pioneer—only to have her aunt laugh and tell her that it was just a joke? Noh thought that if it were a joke, then it was in very poor taste. But if it weren't a joke, then she'd have to make a choice, and soon, because it was almost dinnertime and she'd be seeing her aunt Sarah in the dining room over plates of chipped beef and something or other.

Oh, Henry

ust motes danced happily in the sunlight, streaming in through the two large quarter-paned windows. The dust motes were busy little creatures dancing here and there. They seemed to be having all of their summer in this one hour of sunshine.

Henry stared at them, wondering if when he wasn't there to observe them, did they dance at all? He sighed, thinking that his thoughts were getting silly.

He blinked quickly. Almost as if it were reading his thoughts, one of the dust motes seemed to be waving at him. Well, then that answered it. He *was* being silly. Dust motes didn't wave. They didn't even have arms. It had to be a trick of the light.

Henry growled at himself under his breath. Thinking about the past always made his brain go a little soft and fuzzy around the edges.

Well, what did he want? Fifty years *was* a long time to be alone. *And* memories did tend to get a bit hazy with age, so he was just going to have to learn to deal with the blurriness.

Henry reflected on this as he sat at his old, battered desk trying to reread the letters his mother had sent him while he was away at school.

His mother was a quiet woman who wrote about their farm and what she and his father had had for dinner. It was comforting in a way, but, really, it was that life that Henry had been running away from when he had left for the New Newbridge Academy.

Not that many thirteen-year-old boys were on the lam from their old lives. Well, he wasn't *really* on the lam. He was just a curious, sensitive boy who wasn't born very well suited for life on a farm. He liked getting up early to feed the chickens and hogs, but that was about it.

Actually, he got on well with the animals. He just looked into their large brown eyes and sympathized.

Somehow the animals knew that he understood. But feeding the animals was just a small part of what went on in the "day in the life" of a farm. It was a very visceral thing, with lots of being born and dying in a small span of time. Poor Henry got ill every time anything had to be slaughtered. These were his *friends* that his mother put on the Sunday dinner table.

But Henry wasn't reading the letters to think about all the dead, friendly animals he had eaten in the thirteen years he had been under the rule of his farm-loving parents. No, he was reading the letters because he was feeling sorry for himself. Seeing his mother's large, curly cursive writing somehow made his stomach ache just that little bit more than it already did. Henry found that feeling sorry for oneself could actually be pleasant, in a very strange way. At least once every few months he let himself sink into a dark depression and brood for a week.

Everyone knew to stay out of his way when he was in a funk. Well, everyone, that is, except for Trina. She was a real busybody who always had to have her nose in everyone else's business. When she wasn't being nosy, she was actually very nice. Henry played chess with her when they thought to do it. Which wasn't regularly, but almost.

Now there was a knock on his door. Henry jumped at the sound, then quickly stuffed his mother's letters back into his desk.

The door burst open and Trina came in, her face pinched with worry.

"Why are you up here skulking around like an old ninny," she exclaimed breathlessly, "when you could be downstairs playing cards with the rest of us?"

Henry glared at her, hoping she'd take the hint, but Trina was undeterred.

"You should be ashamed of yourself." She shook her head disgustedly. "I bet you're up here sniffing over those old letters of yours."

Henry continued to glare.

"Mind your own business, Trina," he choked out through tight lips. She rolled her eyes heavenward.

"All right. Fine, be a grump." And with that, she turned on her heel and flounced out. The door slammed behind her. Henry let out a long, exasperated sigh and then took out his letters again. He was not sniffing over them, he thought angrily. It wasn't his fault what had happened to him. It had been an accident. That was the truth. But after fifty years of being cooped up at the school, he thought he was allowed a little bad temper.

Fifty years was a long time to be left on his own—and who knew how much longer?

Trina and Nelly

Once upon a time, Trina was a very pretty girl with red hair and bright blue eyes.

She liked to wear her hair in braids. That was the easiest way to keep it out of her face. When she fell off the horse, her hair was plaited as usual. They carried her out of the ring and up to the infirmary. The doctor had left her as she was because there was really nothing to do for her. There had been no blood. "A very clean break," the doctor said. "A very clean break, indeed."

Trina's parents came to collect the body, and she was still in her riding habit and boots. Her mother thought she looked like a little angel. Her father cried.

And ever since that day, she had been here at New Newbridge. Waiting.

Trina hadn't changed much in death. She still liked to talk a lot and bother people when she felt it was her business to. That's why she got so annoyed at Henry when he was in one of his moods. He behaved like a big old baby. And when she tried to cheer him up, well, he just got nasty.

He didn't want to be cheered up. He liked wallowing. That was the problem, as far as Trina saw it.

The real kids were gone for the summer, and only the ghosts lived there now. Trina liked it better when the realies, as they were called, were around. It made her feel better about things. She could follow the girls around and get all the gossip just like when she had been alive.

But during the long summer months all she had for company were the others like her. It wasn't as bad as it sounded. For the most part, they were very nice. She even counted a few among them as her friends. Nelly, a girl about her age who had gone into anaphylactic shock after a bee stung her during a nature walk, was sweet.

They shared a room together in the disused West Wing dormitory.

The West Wing dormitory had been partially destroyed when a boy who shouldn't have been smoking had fallen asleep with a lit cigarette. Luckily, no one had been killed. But the West Wing was now uninhabitable. The school was always meaning to have it refurbished, but somehow there was never enough money. Sometimes an adventurous student or two would make a hideaway of the place, but so far no one had caught on that a whole gaggle of ghosts was living there.

Nelly was waiting for her at the bottom of the stairs. Her dark hair was cut short and made her look more boy than girl. She had on a pair of hiking boots and a yellow T-shirt that said HAVE A NICE DAY on it. She was reading a book—probably something about bugs. They were her favorite. She had planned to be an entomologist before the bee had killed her.

"So?" Nelly had her head cocked, waiting for an answer.

Trina shook her head. "It was a no-go," she answered.

Trina sat down on the second-to-bottom stair and

dejectedly put her chin in her hands. Nelly patted her shoulder.

"It's all right. Henry will snap out of it in a few days." Trina appreciated Nelly's pragmatism, and usually shared it herself, but she just had this peculiar feeling that Henry was getting worse, not better.

"But every time he gets in a funk, it's always just a little bit worse and lasts a little bit longer." Trina sighed.

She put her chin in her hands and sighed again. This time even louder. Realizing that Nelly wasn't going to answer her, she changed the subject.

"By the way, have you seen Thomas? We were supposed to play chess today, but I can't find him anywhere."

"Who?" Nelly said quizzically.

Unlike Nelly, Trina knew practically everyone at New Newbridge. She made it her business to know everyone else's business, so that way there were never any surprises.

"You've met Thomas a million times. He's the one who likes to hang out in the kitchen and watch Mrs. Marble bake pies," Trina added helpfully.

Nelly began to shrug, and then suddenly her eyes lit up. She had remembered something important about Thomas.

"I saw him come inside the West Wing earlier," she said, then squinted her eyes and bit her lip. "But he never came back out."

"That's strange," Trina replied. Unlike Henry, Thomas was extremely well mannered, never yelled, and was *always* exactly where he said he was going to be. Trina wondered if something bad had happened to him, then quickly put the thought away. Once you were dead, well, there really wasn't that much bad stuff left to happen to you anymore.

"Oh, that reminds me, I met a new girl today," Nelly said casually, her nose partway in her bug book again.

Trina almost hiccupped with excitement, the big news immediately making her forget about Thomas and the missed chess game.

"A new girl! We haven't had a new girl in *forever*," Trina said. "How do you think she died?"

Nelly shrugged her shoulders and went back to her book. Trina opened her mouth to say something else, but realized that Nelly was no longer paying attention.

Suddenly something white and fluffy blew across the lawn, catching Trina's sharp eye.

"What in the world . . . ?" Trina said as she put aside

    53

her excitement about the new girl and floated toward the object. Nelly, her nose still in her book, didn't even notice Trina leave.

But before Trina could get close enough to see what the white fluff was made of, she was interrupted by the unexpected appearance of a tall, lanky man with dark hair, one of the teachers at the school, she remembered. She watched as he ran out from behind the West Wing, passed through Trina like she wasn't there (she wasn't, as far as he was concerned), and stopped short when he reached the place where the white fluff waited. When he was sure no one was watching (Trina didn't count because she was a ghost), he scooped up the fluff, stuffed it into his pocket, and ran back the way he had come.

"Hmm . . . that's strange," Trina said to herself as she watched the teacher's retreating back. When he had finally disappeared behind the burned-out building, she floated back toward the stairs. Sitting down on the step beside Nelly, Trina let her mind return to the important issue at hand: *the new girl.*

A new girl was something special, Trina thought happily, not including Nelly in her thoughts this time. She was going to have to meet the new addition as soon as possible and find out *everything* about her. Nelly might not care that there was a new ghost in town, but *she* certainly did.

"Oh well, it looks like I've got my work cut out for me," she said with excitement to no one in particular.

At least, she thought she did.

Things That
Go Bump

Something not so nice was listening to Trina. It refuses to be named as of yet, but believe me, it's a pretty nasty piece of business. Better not to tangle with it, if you get my drift.

Anyway, as Trina spoke, it listened. Not really digesting what she was saying, just filing it away for later use. It did this because everything can be used at a later date. If you hold on to a bit of information long enough, it will ripen and bear fruit, even if at the moment you receive it, it seems only to be a spare little kernel of unimportant knowledge.

Chipping Away
the Beef

Well, the chipped beef was just as Noh had imagined it. And the something or other she had smelled was steamed broccoli and homemade dinner rolls.

Noh was in heaven as she scooped a huge ball of butter from the butter dish and glopped it on her already partially eaten dinner roll. As she ate, she subtly stole glances at her aunt. She made sure to take her looks discreetly between bites of soft broccoli and fluffy dinner roll. She didn't think her aunt had noticed her careful glances until, as dessert was being served (strawberry short-cake, if you must know), Sarah turned and gave her a wink.

At that moment Noh decided that her aunt was very much like a cat: They both were sleek and smooth and graceful, and as far as Noh knew, they both were gunning for nine lives. Oh, and they both had yellowy green eyes that didn't seem to blink as much as they should.

The dining hall was huge. So it was strange to have only five other people sitting at the table with Noh and her aunt instead of the hundreds of screaming kids the place was used to holding.

To Noh's left were the caretakers, Mr. and Mrs. Finlay. Mrs. Finlay was as straight as a stick—no, a stick bug. That's what her father would have said. He was forever giving people buggie nicknames—even people he didn't know.

It sometimes embarrassed Noh when they would walk down the street and her father would remark—rather too loudly—"Noh, turn around, doesn't that woman look like a giant pill bug?" She didn't mind her father teasing, but she just wished he did it a little more quietly so that no one would give them dirty looks.

Mr. Finlay was shorter than his wife, with a fat red mustache to match his fat red face. *Give him a few more years,* Noh thought, *and he can play Santa Claus at the mall.*

Next to Mr. Finlay was Caleb DeMarck, the physics

teacher for the upper grades. Noh thought he seemed strangely nervous—especially for an adult—and he barely said a word as they ate.

He was a tall, lanky man with a shock of black hair and blue-gray eyes that seemed to be locked on Noh's aunt. Not that her aunt noticed. In fact, she seemed to be purposely "not" noticing. Noh was gonna have to find out what that was all about. She'd never known her aunt to ever be rude to anyone intentionally. *Very strange. Very strange, indeed,* Noh thought.

On the other side of the table, next to her aunt, was the groundskeeper, Jeffrey Hull. Noh knew immediately that she liked Mr. Hull when he had told her to call him "Hullie" and definitely *not* "Mr." anybody. He had a wrinkled countenance and smiling blue eyes. He just seemed happy to be there, period. Plus, he had thirds of the chipped beef, beating Noh's seconds.

The last person at dinner was the cook herself, Mrs. Marble. Even though her husband was long dead, Mrs. Marble talked about him like he was still around. This made Noh feel odd at first, but after a while Noh began to just take for granted that he *wasn't* alive. Maybe this was something Noh herself should try. If she were

to talk about her mother as if she were alive, maybe she would forget that her mother was dead too. Well, it was worth a shot.

"That chipped beef was mighty good eatin'," Hullie said, patting his stomach happily. He was the last one to finish dessert because he had had two helpings. Mrs. Marble was tickled pink that he had enjoyed dinner so much. She kept chattering about what a good appetite he had—of course, not as good as her own husband's, but close.

Noh decided that now was as good a time as any to ask about the girl she had seen earlier in the afternoon.

"Excuse me, but I was wondering where the other kids are tonight?" She said this seriously, but Mr. Finlay laughed. Mrs. Finlay elbowed him.

"Why, the other children don't come to school until the fall," Mr. Finlay said, clearing his throat. Noh knew this and didn't like anyone taking her for a fool.

"I *know* that, but what about the girl I met at that old, burned-out dorm today? Who is she?" No one responded. Silence filled the void.

"What's wrong?" Noh asked haughtily. "Why're you all staring at me like I'm a mealworm?"

Her aunt came to her rescue. "There are no other children here right now, Noh. I don't know whom you saw. Maybe one of the children from the town?"

Noh glared at her aunt. "I don't think so," she countered. She was sure the girl was staying here at New Newbridge. She could feel it in her bones.

"Well, maybe what you saw, my girl, was a ghost," Hullie added seriously. There was something mischievous going on behind his eyes. Noh wasn't sure if he was teasing her or not.

Mrs. Finlay coughed. "Well, Mr. Finlay and I must be turning in for the night." The screech of their chairs made a dent in the silent emptiness of the dining hall. Then, without a backward glance, they were gone.

Noh stared at her remaining dinner companions. Mrs. Marble had gone to the kitchen with the dishes, so this left only her aunt, the physics teacher, and Hullie.

"Do you believe in ghosts, Noh?" Hullie asked, wiping a bit of strawberry shortcake from his bright red beard with his napkin.

"I believe in them," Caleb DeMarck jumped in, before Noh could even open her mouth to respond. "Energy can never be destroyed, only re-formed." Caleb blushed as he realized that all eyes had trained themselves on him. He swallowed hard and looked down at his hands. The fingers were long and tapered like a musician's.

"The energy," he continued, still staring at his hands, "that makes up our person could become trapped in the earthly plane, unable to return to its source—"

"Kinda like damming up a stream," Noh interrupted excitedly. Caleb smiled at her, nodding his head. She realized that Caleb DeMarck might not talk much, but what he did say was pretty neat.

"I think if someone were so inclined, they might come up with an experiment to test this ghost hypothesis—," Caleb began, but stopped when he caught sight of Noh's aunt's disapproving stare.

"Experiments aside, I think that if there are such things as ghosts, Noh, then they are probably more frightened of you than you should be of them." Her aunt said these words as she pushed her chair back and stood up.

"I'm not scared—," Noh started, but her aunt gave her a look. Noh instantly closed her mouth.

"I think it's time to go back to your room, Noh," her aunt said in a soft, lulling voice. "You've had a very

long day, and I'm sure all the traveling has made you very tired."

Aunt Sarah was strangely right. Noh found that she could barely keep her eyes open. She yawned loudly, quickly clapping a hand over her gaping mouth.

"Okay, Aunt Sarah," Noh said sleepily. "Good night, Hullie. Mr. DeMarck."

The two men nodded their good-nights.

"See you in the morning? Bright and chipper?" Hullie smiled.

Noh could only nod sleepily as she followed her aunt across the room, out the door, and into the arms of the waiting night.

Scary Things in the Morning

Nasty situations look brighter in the light of the morning sun.

Now, this assumption is not always a truth. And it is actually quite false in this particular case.

Remember that nasty thing that liked to file away information for later use? Well, it had spent the better part of the morning sitting on a toadstool out by the lake. When it wanted to, the nasty thing could make itself quite small—good for sliding through rabbit holes and into people's ears.

It was pretending to be a toad so that it could eat flies with a long, winding tongue. Not that it couldn't eat flies any time it wanted to, but catching flies just wasn't as much fun without a great big lolling tongue to flick, flop, and twist about.

The nasty thing had no true shape. It had to make do with stealing other creatures' shapes when it wanted to be seen. Mostly it liked being left to its own devices, so it chose to remain shapeless. In this state it was like a clear, undetectable gas.

After filling itself with a number of fly souls, it ceased being toadlike. It returned to the school, settling itself into a crack in one of the exterior walls of the West Wing to take a nap and digest the fly souls.

The nasty thing subsisted on the souls of the creatures it captured—little creatures like flies and beetles and spiders. But once, a long time before it had found its home at the New Newbridge Academy, it had eaten something big. And it had never forgotten the taste—and the *power*. The magnificent power the "something big" had given it.

Now the nasty thing, asleep in its crack, woke up with a start. It smelled something. *Something big*.

It puffed itself up and slipped back out into the midmorning air in search of its newly smelled prey.

  68

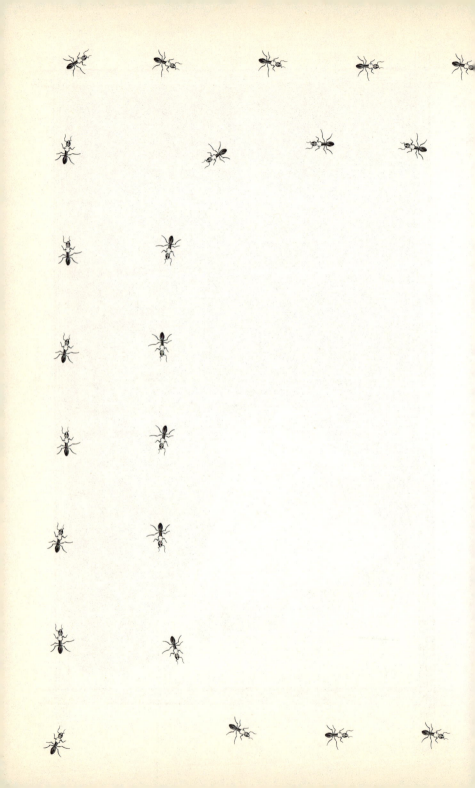

No Noh

N oh woke up and stretched under her blanket. The sunlight streamed in through the window, hitting her right in the face. She didn't mind, though. It was warm and inviting and made her want to smile. She threw off the covers and slipped out of bed. The floor was cold on one foot, the rug warm underneath the other. She quickly brought the other foot onto the rug and wiggled her toes happily.

She looked around her new room and felt happy, happier than she had felt in a long time. Then suddenly she remembered the conversation she'd had at dinner the night before with Hullie and the physics teacher, Mr. DeMarck, and instantly her good mood dissipated.

Two thoughts crossed her mind at the same time:

(1) Had she *really* seen a ghost yesterday? And (2) If so, did that mean there was something wrong with her? From her experience, normal people didn't see ghosts—or at least, the normal people she knew didn't see ghosts.

She was cheered by the scientific part of her brain that said ghosts didn't exist and there had to be a logical explanation for the appearance of the strange girl she'd met at the burned-out dorm. Maybe she was a local girl who was just using the empty building as her secret hide-out. Or maybe Noh had just imagined meeting the girl. She did have a pretty active imagination, and it had been known to get her into trouble in the past.

Growing up, Noh had spent a lot of time on her own, and her imagination had been her only real friend. It wasn't her father's fault, really. He was a good dad. He always made sure that she had food to eat and a nice place to live with nice things inside of it to keep her occupied. And he loved her very much—*that* she was sure of. It was just that he was always so busy.

His work was very important and it took him away for long stretches of time. As a small child, Noh had had a succession of governesses, but once she was old enough

   72

to look after herself, she had asked her father to please let her stay alone. Since Aunt Clara wasn't there to tell him reproachfully that it wasn't a good idea for a child to stay on her own, her father had agreed.

Noh had become a very self-sufficient kid. She could do the laundry, cook breakfast, lunch, and dinner (eggs were her specialty), and make sure that the house was neat and tidy.

But even though she had liked being in charge of herself, now that she didn't have to worry about that stuff anymore, she felt like a giant weight had been lifted from her shoulders. She felt free.

And that's when the happiness quotient kicked in again. So, guilty that she didn't miss her father more (she knew he'd come and visit before the start of the school year) and happy that there was a logical explanation for the "ghost" girl, Noh got her clothes together—making sure that the evil eye stone was safely in her pants pocket for good luck—and trooped off to the bathroom to begin her day.

Her hair slicked back and wet from the shower, Noh stood in front of the mirror brushing her teeth. She

   73

counted to 120 before she stopped twirling the brush around her teeth and spit.

She put her toothbrush back into the small cubbyhole (with her name stenciled on it) in the corner of the bathroom. She had deposited her toiletries there the day before at her aunt's urging. She had grumbled about it then, but she had been so tired when they had gotten back from dinner that she wouldn't have brushed her teeth at all if her toothbrush hadn't already been there waiting for her.

Noh stared at herself in the mirror.

She knew that she wasn't the prettiest girl in the world—her biggish nose and pointy chin made her look rather old-fashioned—but there was really nothing to be ashamed of in her features. They were strong and suited her long face well. Everyone said that she resembled her father, but Noh couldn't help thinking that was because no one had ever met her mother. The only people in the whole world who had known Mabel (Harris) Maypother were her father and his two sisters. Well, Noh was pretty sure that there had been others, but those were the only ones Noh knew about.

Her mother had no other family. Her parents had

died when she was twelve, and she had gone to live with her only other relation, a great-aunt who had been already half-deaf from age. The great-aunt had passed away two years before Mabel had met Noh's father, and that was that. Mabel had been, for all intents and purposes, an orphan.

Thinking absently about her mother, Noh picked up a comb and ran it through her stick-straight hair. There was so much static electricity in the air that her hair stuck to the plastic comb in unruly clumps. She pulled out her barrette, knowing from experience that static electricity hair liked to stick to your face if 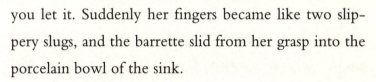 you let it. Suddenly her fingers became like two slippery slugs, and the barrette slid from her grasp into the porcelain bowl of the sink.

As if in slow motion, the silver barrette clattered against the smooth whiteness of the bowl and began to circle around the drain like a race car driver. Noh reached out her hand, groping for the barrette, but she wasn't quick enough. She watched in abject horror as the silver glinted once, then slipped down the drain.

"No!" Noh squeaked and stuck her fingers into the yawning mouth of the drain. It was cold and slimy to the touch, but Noh didn't care. She could just feel the barrette with the very tip of her fingers. She shoved her hand farther down the drain until she heard a small *click* and her fingers scissored around the barrette, dragging it back up into the light.

She grabbed the silvery hair clip with her other hand and moved it far away from the sink.

"I almost lost you," she whispered to the barrette, cradling it. It was a little dirty, but none the worse for wear. She wiped it off with her shirttail and slipped it into her hair. She was so happy to have her mother's barrette back in her possession that she almost didn't notice what the clicking noise had done.

"There, you're all safe now . . . ," she said again to the barrette, but suddenly her words trailed off. With a sharp intake of breath, Noh stared at the mirror. There was absolutely no reflection in it.

"Huh?" Noh gulped as she reached out a hand to touch the smooth sheet of unblemished silvered glass. It rippled as her fingers drew near it. She quickly pulled them away and looked around. She seemed to be alone in the bathroom, but she ran the length of the stalls just to make sure no one was hiding inside one of them. Satisfied, she returned to the mirror.

Instead of sacrificing her hand to the mysterious mirror, she took out her toothbrush and tentatively pushed it into the rippling glass.

It was halfway through the mirror when there was a sharp *crack* and Noh's reflection magically reappeared. She quickly tried to pull the toothbrush back, but the mirror had solidified around it. She grabbed the butt end of the toothbrush with both hands and yanked.

But her efforts were for nothing. The toothbrush was frozen solid.

She gave up her fight with the unyielding mirror and draped a hand towel over the protruding toothbrush. If she was lucky, anyone who came across it would think that she had suction-cupped a tiny hook onto the mirror's face. She didn't think it was a very plausible story, but it was all she had and she was sticking to it.

She quickly finished getting ready, then quietly slunk out of the bathroom hoping no one had seen her going in in the first place.

The Crybaby

Henry was shut up in his room again. Not even Trina's needling would coax him out of his foul mood. As far as Trina and Nelly could see, this black funk had lasted twenty-two days, and the end was nowhere in sight.

Nelly sat on the floor watching a line of worker ants parade across the stone. They each had a tiny parcel of dried, flufflike substance in their pinchers.

"I wonder where they found this stuff," Nelly said as she chewed on the ends of her hair, watching them. She looked up at Trina, expectantly waiting for an answer.

"Looks like asbestos. I saw some earlier in the grass."

Nelly rolled her eyes.

"That's not funny, Trina—," Nelly started, but she

was interrupted by a loud wailing from up above them. Henry had started the final phase of his bad mood: the crying.

Trina sighed. "How many days does this part last again?"

Nelly thought for a moment. "It was three last time, but that's not saying much. The whole thing *only* lasted seventeen days last time. He's five days longer already."

Trina nodded.

Together, they waited for the crying to subside, but it was a futile attempt. Henry had had a strong set of lungs in his human life, and he still loved to use them. It was going to be a long next few days.

Nelly shook her head as the wailing increased and promptly disappeared into the ether. Trina stayed a while longer, hoping that Henry would tire himself out, but finally even she had had enough. The whole thing had given her a terrible headache.

She sighed and slowly faded into nothingness in search of a little peace and quiet.

At that very moment, the front door to the West Wing opened and Noh stepped into the semidarkness. She had armed herself with a flashlight and a sweater. She wasn't going to let the chill in the air keep her from investigating. She was determined to find out who or what the mysterious girl was once and for all.

Noh peered around the space and saw nothing out of place. It looked just like it had the day before. She walked to the staircase and ran a finger over the banister. It came away with a thick head of dust.

"Yuck," Noh squeaked, and wiped the dirt down the front of her sweater. Undeterred, she gingerly put her foot on the bottom step. It creaked with her weight but held firm. When Noh decided that the place wasn't going to fall down around her head, she began the climb to the second floor.

The stairs groaned with every step. She took the last few steps at a jog, happy to be on *almost* solid ground again.

Upstairs was just as unused and dusty as the rest of the place. She started down the hallway but stopped mid-stride when she heard a noise. She froze her muscles and stopped breathing so that she could listen more closely.

There it was again. And it wasn't just the building settling or an animal scampering across the roof. What

Noh heard was the sound of someone crying. It was the tail end of a long crying jag, so there was only a bit of sniffling and a few hiccups, but Noh would have known the sound anywhere.

She had spent many a long night crying herself to sleep. Usually it was when her father was away, but sometimes she found herself crying even when he was just down the hall. She wasn't a hundred percent sure why she did it, but she figured every so often you got so filled up with sadness that tears were the only way to feel any better.

She debated with herself for a few minutes, trying to decide if she should leave the crier in peace or just barge in and demand to know what the heck was going on. Finally, curiosity got the best of her. She walked down the hall and threw open the last door on the left, not knowing *what* she was going to find behind it.

New Friends

"Are you dead too?"

The boy who was occupying the dusty old room she had stepped into was about her age. She guessed that some people might think him handsome, but she found her first impression of him to be that of a big, sulky baby. She took in the red-rimmed eye sockets and tear-stained cheeks long before she noticed the large, well-lashed brown of his eyes, the square jaw, and the thatch of straight brown hair.

"No, I'm not dead," Noh replied. She didn't like having her leg pulled, and this boy was definitely trying to make her look stupid. "If you're dead, then you're not here anymore, and I'm right here," she said tartly, pinching her upper arm hard enough to make her grimace.

"See?" Noh waited for him to answer, but he just stared at her.

Finally, he shook his head and shrugged. "No, I don't see. I'm dead and I can pinch myself too, if I want to."

And he did.

Noh glared at him. "You are *not* dead. I'm not that gullible."

The boy cocked his head curiously. "What's 'gullible'?" At first Noh thought he was being a smart aleck, but then it dawned on her that he was actually being very serious.

"Gullible means that you believe everything that everyone tells you all the time," she said.

The boy scratched his head. "I don't think you're gullible, then. You don't believe *me*, even though I'm telling the truth," he said earnestly. "I wouldn't lie about something this important. Maybe you're dead and you don't know it yet."

Noh shook her head, but the boy didn't look convinced.

"Look, I would *know* if I were dead," Noh began. "I can promise you that—"

The boy interrupted her. "I've seen it happen before. Lots of times. No one really wants to be dead. They're scared of it."

He extended a hand toward Noh.

"I'm Henry."

"Noh. Short for Noleen."

She reached out a hand to shake Henry's but found, to her utter amazement, that her hand slid right through his.

"Oh, goodness!" Noh exclaimed. "You really are dead."

Hasta La Vista
Dead

Noh had never met a dead person before (except for the maybe-ghost girl she'd seen yesterday). She found that it was really no different from meeting a live person—except for the no-physical-contact part.

She and Henry spent the next few hours testing the dead/live waters. Henry made Noh walk through him (which she could do effortlessly), throw an inanimate object at his head (the pen from her pocket went straight through his nose and out the back of his skull), and try to guess a number from one to ten (this would have required a bit of telepathy—which, sadly, Noh did not possess).

"I never knew a living person who could see me before!" Henry exclaimed happily. The tears on his cheeks had long dried, and now his eyes glowed with excitement.

Noh shrugged. "Well, I think I might've seen at least one dead person before."

"Wow, I just wonder how it's possible. Maybe it's a miracle." Henry rubbed his hands together enthusiastically as he said this.

"I don't think it warrants being called a miracle, Henry. Maybe 'amazing' is a more apt word," Noh said thoughtfully. At least she knew that ghosts existed now, and even if that meant there was something different about her, well, she didn't mind it one little bit. It was better to be different and see ghosts than to be normal and not see them at all.

But, like Henry, Noh did wonder what it was exactly that had given her this strange new ability. She was curious to discover if other people could see both the living and the dead too, or if this was a gift that belonged to her alone.

Noh's stomach rumbled and she checked her watch. "It's almost twelve. I better go if I don't want to miss lunch. I think we're having apple pie for dessert."

As Noh started for the door Henry sighed jealously.

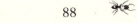
88

"Boy, I wish I were human again. I haven't eaten a piece of pie in forever."

"At least you don't have to worry about your teeth rotting out of your head. I had three cavities the last time I went to the dentist," Noh whispered conspiratorially.

Henry grinned sheepishly at her. "I don't care. I still miss sweets . . ."

As Henry spoke, a strange breeze blew through the room, stirring up eddies of dust that made Noh sneeze twice in quick succession.

"What the—," Noh squeaked, looking around to see where the wind had originated from. She noticed immediately that all the windows and doors were shut up tight as drums.

"All of a sudden it's so cold in here," Noh said as she continued to sweep the room with her eyes.

Henry shook his head in agreement. "This is incredible. I haven't felt *anything* in such a very long time."

As if in response to Henry's words, all the drapes in the room rolled down, covering the windows and blocking out the ambient light. There was another sharp drop in the temperature, and Noh's teeth started to chatter.

"What's going on, Henry?" Noh moved closer to her dead friend, but his company did nothing to relieve the very bad feeling in the pit of her stomach.

"I don't know," he said through chattering teeth.

"Ghosts' teeth aren't supposed to chatter!" Noh said in a shocked voice. "At least, I don't think they are. I mean, I would guess that they shouldn't."

Noh shut her mouth, embarrassed by her nervous babbling. She kept silent as she watched Henry clench his teeth and squeeze his eyes tight. His shape seemed to flicker for a moment, but then he returned to normal.

"Should I try the door?" Noh said, walking toward it.

Henry shook his head. "I wouldn't bother. I just tried to disappear, but I couldn't. And that's never happened to me before."

"You tried to leave me?" shouted Noh. "That's not very nice!"

She stomped over to the door and put her hand on the knob. "We'll just see how you like it!"

She felt a prickly numbing in her hand and released the knob quickly. It was almost as if she'd run her hand under a hot *and* a cold tap at the same time. She held her hand to her chest, cradling it as it throbbed miserably in time to the beat of her pulse. Without thinking, she reached into her pocket. The moment her fingers closed around the evil eye stone, the pain in her hand subsided.

At that very moment the wind picked up in earnest. Dust and pieces of litter, caught up in the wind's orbit, circled around their heads like tiny satellites.

"We've got to get out of here!" Noh shouted over the din.

"I think we're good and trapped!" Henry countered just as loudly.

Suddenly a small orb of light flared into existence in front of them and started to expand until it was as large as a doorway.

Henry sucked in his breath and drifted toward Noh. In a hushed voice he whispered, "It's my time. I have to go now." He dropped his hand on her shoulder in goodbye, but it only slid through her flesh.

"Wait, Henry! What're you talking about?" Noh tried to grab him, but he slipped out of her grasp and floated toward the glowing light.

"I only wish we'd gotten to be *real* friends," he said, his voice faint in the rush of the wind. When he reached

 91

the orb, he gave her a quick wave, then disappeared into the honeyed light.

"Henry!" Noh shouted, but she was too late. The light flared, and then the orb folded in upon itself and was gone.

Noh stared at the place where the light had once been, yet all traces of its existence had fled.

The temperature returned to normal, but Noh's teeth somehow wouldn't stop chattering. She looked down at her clenched fist, and it took her a moment before she realized she was clutching her evil eye stone as if it were a talisman.

Looking around the now empty room, it was as if the past few hours hadn't happened at all.

Noh sighed, upset that she had lost the first friend she had made at the New Newbridge Academy. She was just about to leave when she noticed a sheaf of yellowed paper sitting on the desktop. She picked it up and started to put it into one of the desk drawers when she became filled with curiosity.

Making sure she was unobserved, Noh stuffed the papers into her back pocket. She picked up her flashlight and walked to the door. She made a hesitant grab for the knob, and when it didn't hurt her hand, she threw the door open and stepped out into the hall. Not wanting to spend any more time in the West Wing than she had to, she made a run for the stairway. The thumping of her feet echoed in the empty building, obscuring the sound of Henry's bedroom door being slammed shut by a pair of unseen hands.

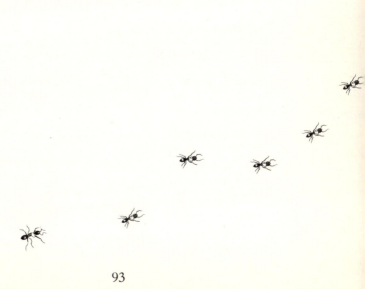

Hullie Says

Noh hit the outside path at a run. She didn't look back at the West Wing as she ran, fearful that she would see something else "amazing" if she did.

She pumped her legs as fast as they would go. She didn't care if she got a stitch in her side or if her lungs collapsed from exertion.

When she got to the football field, Noh slowed to a jog and noticed for the first time how warm the day had become. She decided that going directly back to the dining hall would be a bad idea. She didn't want anyone to see her so spooked. She figured if she were to walk the length of the football field seven times (as seven was a lucky number), she'd be calm enough to return to normalcy.

"I can speak to ghosts, *and* the evil eye stone made my hand stop hurting," Noh said as she walked, even though there was no one around to hear her. "That has to mean something."

Sometimes when Noh was trying to find the answer to an important question, she would talk to herself out loud. Giving voice to her thoughts enabled her to sort out the helpful ones from the not-so-helpful ones. As she mulled over the two seemingly incongruous ideas, she got a tingly feeling all over. Instinctively she pulled the evil eye stone from her pocket and looked at it in the sunlight. It seemed to wink at her, as if to say that the answer she sought was right there in her hand.

Noh grinned as the solution hit her like lightning: *The evil eye stone has to be the catalyst for my new abilities!*

Noh wasn't one hundred percent certain that her hypothesis was correct, but she decided it would be smart to keep her new good luck charm close by just to be safe. She slipped the stone back into her pocket for safekeeping and continued her march around the football field.

Noh had almost finished her seventh lap when she heard a voice calling from the far side of the bleachers. She

squinted into the sun and saw Hullie waving his arms wildly at her to get her attention.

He was too far away for her to hear exactly what he was saying, but Noh thought she could make out the words "lunch" and "hungry."

She picked up her pace and reached the grounds-keeper before he could say "Jack Sprat."

"You weren't waiting for me to get your lunch, were you?" Noh called out as she ran.

Hullie shook his head and smiled.

"Nope, I was just hoping we could have a few min-utes to chat before we went in, that's all. I looked around for you earlier, but you had disappeared."

Noh fell into step with Hullie as they walked toward the dining room.

"Does this belong to you?" Hullie said as he pulled Noh's toothbrush out of his pocket and brandished it about like a sword.

Noh couldn't decide if she should fess up to being the owner of the toothbrush or deny it completely. She decided that honesty was her only choice because she sincerely liked Hullie and didn't want him to think she was a liar. Trust was a lot like lemonade. Once you

stirred in the sugar, it could never be unsweetened again.

"Um, yeah? . . . It's, uh, mine, I guess."

Hullie nodded and handed the toothbrush to her. She quickly pocketed it.

"Where did you get it?" Noh wanted to know. Hullie shrugged.

"Don't worry, my dear, it's our little secret." He gave her a pat on the shoulder, then pulled open the door so Noh could go inside.

"But, Hullie, the toothbrush was—"

Hullie put his finger to his lips to silence her as they rounded the corner and the massive double doors that led to the dining room came into view.

"We'll talk again later," he said. "The walls have ears, you know."

At least I wasn't imagining things, she thought as her nose followed the delicious food smells into the dining room. *There really are some strange and amazing things happening around here.*

Noh and Hullie were the last ones to come in for lunch. Everyone else had already eaten and returned to whatever work they were doing. Noh didn't mind. It meant that she could have seconds and thirds without feeling like a glutton.

She and Hullie tucked into their food in silence, both savoring the taste of the homemade meat loaf and garlic bread. When Mrs. Marble came out with hot apple pie for dessert, Noh and Hullie each had two pieces.

After Hullie had eaten the last bite of his pie, he wiped his mouth gingerly with his napkin and gave a polite burp, which made Noh giggle.

"Why don't we head outside and I'll show you where you can find a five-leaf clover," Hullie announced, setting his napkin on top of his empty plate.

Noh nodded, still remembering his comment about the walls having ears.

Five-Leaf
(or Six- or Seven-Leaf)
Clovers

Noh followed Hullie out the double doors and across the lawn, her smaller feet taking *two* steps for every *one* of Hullie's.

"Where are we going, Hullie?" Noh said curiously.

He looked back at Noh and tapped his ear, reminding her to be quiet. She grinned and he gave her a wink.

After they left the lawn, they crossed the football field (the long way), went up and down the bleachers twice, walked back across the football field (the long way again), and then veered off into the woods. Noh followed Hullie in silence, her mind buzzing with all the questions that she wasn't allowed to ask just yet.

After a few minutes of walking through woods, with twigs and low-hanging branches grabbing at her face and arms, Noh and Hullie emerged by the lake. Noh didn't think she could *ever* retrace the path Hullie had taken— not even with a map that marked all the important places with big red *X*s.

When Hullie got to the edge of the lake, he stopped and squatted by the water. He motioned for Noh to join him. She squatted down beside him, her brain itching to ask questions, but before she could open her mouth, Hullie beat her to the punch.

"This very spot is the safest place in the whole school to have a private conversation," Hullie said, smiling. "Remember that . . . *if* you want to keep your secrets while you're here."

"What makes it so special?" Noh asked. She couldn't even *begin* to imagine what made the spot such a great

place to have a private conversation. And Noh had a *very* good imagination.

Hullie didn't answer. Instead he looked down at the ground, his hand gesturing toward a small patch of green stuff that they just happened to be squatting next to. Noh hadn't even noticed it was there until Hullie pointed it out.

"These little *Trifoliums* are what make this spot so special," Hullie said.

"*Trifolium* is the Latin name for clovers," Noh replied, to Hullie's surprise. "My dad taught me lots of Latin names for plants and stuff. He's *really* a bug specialist, but he loves plants, too."

Noh looked at the green stuff closely, expecting to see a few mutants mixed in with a bunch of normal-looking three-leafers, but instead she found that every plant she saw was an honest-to-goodness five-leaf clover. And some of them even had six or seven leaves—which made them even luckier!

"Wow," Noh said. "This must be the luckiest place in the whole school!"

Hullie laughed.

"I think you just answered your own question, Noh," Hullie said.

It was true. Now Noh knew *exactly* why this was such a good place to tell secrets: It was lucky, and you always wanted luck on your side when you had important things to discuss but wanted to keep them private at the same time.

"Why are there so many of them?" Noh asked.

Hullie shrugged. "Nobody knows why for certain, but there is a legend about this place . . . ," he said.

Noh couldn't contain her excitement. She loved legends and myths. In fact, one of her favorite things to do was to curl up under the covers with a flashlight and *The Arabian Nights,* or a book about King Arthur and Camelot, and read all night long. She actually thought that when she grew up, she might want to write made-up stories exactly like the myths and legends she loved so much now.

"Do *you* know the legend?" Noh said, hoping very much that he did.

Hullie gave her a broad smile, letting her know that he *did* know the legend . . . and that he was going to tell her all about it.

The Legend

It happened during the New Newbridge Academy's first dedication ceremony," Hullie began, taking out a thin, carved toothpick and sticking it in between his teeth.

"The boy's name was Hubert," Hullie continued, "and he was overlarge for his age. This made people assume that he was older than he really was, and since they thought he was older, they treated him like he was older too. Which for some kids would've been the greatest blessing in the world, but for a boy like Hubert, well, it was really a *curse*."

Noh could see Hubert in her mind's eye. Instead of a normal-looking boy, she imagined a giant with fists like meat tenderizers and a head like a gigantic watermelon.

She could see exactly why he got yelled at more, why he got teased more, and why he was expected to behave better more. She completely understood why, as far as Hubert was concerned, everything was *more, more, more, more, more*—and not in a good way.

"As he got older, Hubert became more and more reserved," Hullie said, chewing on the end of his toothpick in exactly the same way that Noh chewed on the ends of her pencils. "He very rarely spoke unless spoken to, and he never yelled. *Never. His* thinking was that if he could just make himself smaller and quieter than everyone else, people would forget he was there and they would leave him alone."

Noh's image of Hubert changed. She now saw a little boy who just wanted to be left alone, hiding behind a giant *shadow* of himself. Noh understood wanting to be left alone. She knew how much easier it was to get by in the world when you pretended like you

didn't exist. Being a shadow lingering on the sidelines was usually how Noh liked to appear when she was around kids her own age. That way no one teased her or poked fun at her name—not that she let that bother her too much—but it also meant that no one asked you to join the kickball team or do a science project with them either.

"How did he do it?" Noh asked curiously.

"Well, when someone told Hubert that the Native Americans had perfected a way to walk without a sound so as not to scare away the animals they were hunting," Hullie said, "he read everything he could about them. And the more Hubert read, the more he wanted to be as silent and invisible as an Indian brave stalking his prey."

Noh wished *she* were an Indian brave. She and Hubert were in direct agreement about how cool *that* would be.

"Pretty soon Hubert had all but vanished," Hullie continued, still chewing on his toothpick. "He could go into any room in his house and no one would even look up. He could walk into any store and take what he wanted, and no one was ever the wiser. In fact, he was so invisible that he stopped showing up to school and

the principal never even called his parents. His curse, he decided, was now a *gift*."

"But was he really invisible?" Noh asked. She'd heard of lots of strange things—and seen lots of strange things too (like her friend Henry!), but she'd never ever heard of anyone learning to become invisible.

Hullie didn't speak immediately. Instead he tilted his head to the side and squinted his eyes, thinking. Finally, he shook his head like he was shifting his thoughts all around inside it and said, "Well, I can't rightly say."

"*I* think he wasn't *really* invisible." Noh shrugged. "I think he just wanted to be so badly that he *made* everyone around him *believe* he was. Kind of like an optical illusion!"

"Maybe so," Hullie said. "Maybe so . . ."

"Invisible or not, what happened to him next?" Noh asked, picking a six-leaf clover and twirling it between her fingers.

Hullie continued, "When Hubert heard about the dedication ceremony for the new school, he decided that this would be the ultimate test of his invisibility. He would attend the ceremony, and at the pivotal moment—when the mayor was *just* about to cut the ribbon officially dedicating the school—Hubert would slip up to the podium, walk right past the mayor, and cut the ribbon himself."

"That's audacious!" Noh said, liking Hubert's plan *very much*.

"Well, if all went as planned, the audience would be so shocked to see a ribbon cutting *itself* that they would think the school was haunted and no one would ever let their children go there," Hullie said, adding, "he would be single-handedly responsible for closing the New Newbridge Academy before it had even opened."

Noh's twelve-year-old mind thought it was the most brilliant and dastardly plan that had ever been conceived. She wished she'd thought of it herself—not that she disliked people enough that she wanted to scare them all so badly.

"Did it work?" Noh asked.

"I'll let you be the judge," Hullie said, biting his toothpick thoughtfully before returning to the story.

"Hubert spent almost two months working on becoming even more silent and invisible than he already was. There was only one problem, one *thing* that Hubert was unaware of, and this one thing would be Hubert's undoing—but we'll get to that part later," Hullie said ominously.

"So, the day for the dedication ceremony came, and Hubert got up bright and early, brushed his teeth, and prepared for his big day. He spent almost two hours in the woods behind the school, practicing his Indian brave walk before he finally made his way over to where the dedication ceremony was being held in front of the new building."

Noh could just see Hubert creeping up to the place where the ceremony was being held. He would be the first person to arrive, of course, except maybe for some old handyman setting up chairs on the lawn for the day's festivities, but Noh figured that the old handyman would never even know that Hubert had ever been there at all.

Noh pictured a small stage where, hung between two wooden stakes, was the pièce de résistance of Hubert's plan: a bright yellow ribbon, rippling in the wind. The setting couldn't have been more perfect for what Hubert had planned, Noh decided. She bet he could hardly wait to put his insidious plot into motion.

Hullie cleared his throat, bringing Noh back to reality.

The stage disappeared from her mind, and Noh looked down to see that she had dropped the little six-leaf clover on the ground at her feet.

"Go on," Noh said. "What happened to Hubert? Did he do it?"

Hullie chewed on his toothpick, clearly enjoying the suspense he was creating. "Hold your horses, girl, give me a moment. It's a long story and I want to make sure I get all the details right."

Noh sighed. She hated waiting. If there was one thing she definitely needed more of, it was patience.

"Now, then," Hullie said, finally continuing the story. "The dedication ceremony went on for a zillion years—or at least, that's what Hubert thought. The mayor droned on about how nice it was to have the New Newbridge Academy in the community, and the man who had given all the money to build the school got up and thanked the mayor and the community for being so nice themselves.

"All the self-congratulating just made Hubert glad he'd come up with his plan in the first place. Finally, when Hubert was absolutely sure the mayor was going to go on *another* twenty zillion years, the mayor's assistant suddenly got up and handed the mayor the biggest pair of gardening shears Hubert had ever seen.

"Instantly Hubert was on the move. If he timed it just right—and luck was on his side—he would get to the stage right before the mayor snipped the ribbon. Hubert moved silently through the crowd, invisible to all the people he passed."

"Did he do it?!" Noh asked. She had been so caught up in the story that she had almost forgotten to breathe.

Hullie shook his head sadly.

"It made Hubert feel very special to be able to do all this right under everyone's noses, and this feeling of 'specialness' was Hubert's downfall. You see, just as Hubert was stepping up onto the lip of the stage, right before he could reach out and yank the ribbon out of the mayor's grasp . . . something *strange* happened.

"The ribbon that had just been quietly rippling in the breeze only moments before suddenly shot up into the air, twitching like a wild snake about to strike. The mayor, who didn't know that Hubert was there, thrust his garden shears right at the rippling ribbon snake, lopping it cleanly in half. The crowd got to its feet and gave the mayor a standing ovation."

"Oh no!" Noh said, fear spreading through her body. Quickly she thrust her hand into her pocket and grasped the evil eye stone. Immediately she felt calmer.

Noh swallowed hard and nodded. "I'm okay, Hullie. Go on."

Hullie sighed. "I'll tell you what happened next, but I don't think you're going to like it very much."

Noh didn't think she was going to like it very much either, but she knew from experience that most stories didn't have a happy ending—no matter how much you wished they did.

"Hubert sat down on the stage between the mayor and the crowd, but nobody saw him," Hullie said quietly. "Nor did anyone see him when he crawled off the stage and across the lawn, cradling his arm to his chest

113

as he tried not to look at where the garden shears had lopped off *all four of the fingers on his right hand.*"

Hullie paused before continuing.

"Hubert made it as far as the lake before he collapsed. Then he just sat there, not sure what to do to make the blood stop leaving his body. He knew he needed help, but he had been invisible for so long that he didn't think he could make anyone see him . . . *even if he wanted to.*

"The hours passed slowly, and Hubert got colder and colder until he stopped being able to feel anything at all. Because of this sad fact, he didn't even notice when the last drop of blood left his body."

Detective Noh

That's a terrible story," Noh said.

No one deserved to die like that, she thought, alone and invisible. Hullie seemed to agree with her.

"It is, but, alas, that's the legend," Hullie said, shaking his head. "They say that because *luck* felt so bad about what had happened to Hubert, it made the very spot where he died the luckiest place in the school."

Noh looked down at all the five-leaf (and six- and seven-leaf) clovers and felt that Hubert's death was a very high price to pay for them.

"It's still a terrible story," she said.

Noh sat in silence, continuing to digest what she had just heard. Even though it was a sad story, it did give credence to all the strange things she had already encountered at the New Newbridge Academy.

She knew there were ghosts inhabiting the school—a bunch of them, actually, but all that was just the tip of the iceberg. There was a whole lot more going on at this school than anybody realized. Well, maybe a couple of people knew what was what—like Hullie, for one—but everyone else mistakenly thought New Newbridge was just a regular old scholarly institution.

"Hullie, have you seen the ghosts?" Noh asked suddenly.

The older man shook his head and Noh sighed thoughtfully.

"Now, wait a minute. I may not have *seen* anything, but I've been the groundskeeper here for more than twenty-five years, and, let me tell you, I've *heard* some pretty funny stuff," Hullie said as he picked out a nice big seven-leaf clover and held it between his large fingers.

This was just more confirmation that Noh was on the right track, that the evil eye stone had special powers. Because, unlike Hullie, she'd *seen* some pretty funny stuff in the past twenty-four hours—like ghosts disappearing forever and toothbrushes stuck in mirrors.

"It's mostly out in the West Wing, but there's lots of strange things happening all over the school," Hullie added, interrupting Noh's thoughts of free-floating toothbrushes.

"This school is special, isn't it, Hullie," Noh said softly. She wasn't asking a question—she was making a statement because she already *knew* the school was special. The evil eye stone had shown her this truth. She just didn't know *why*.

"'Special' is the word." Hullie laughed. "I guess it's just one of those big mysteries you have to go and solve for yourself."

"A *mystery* . . . ," Noh whispered under her breath. That's exactly what it was: a mystery that had Noh's name written all over it. It would be her summer project. She would solve the mystery of the New Newbridge Academy, and her good luck charm would help!

"Thanks, Hullie!" Noh said as she got up and started walking back toward the school, taking the widest steps her legs would make.

"Thanks for what?" Hullie said quizzically.

But Noh was too busy thinking about solving mysteries to reply.

The Something Big

T he nasty thing that does not wish to be named would like you to know that once upon a time—because it has no real recollection of time or space—it ate something big. It doesn't want you to know *what* that something big is right now, but it *would* like to stress the fact that the something big was, well . . . big.

Really, really, really, really, REALLY BIG.

Into the Light

Henry was gone.

Trina had looked *everywhere*, and he was absolutely *nowhere* to be found. She knew she was probably overreacting, that Henry had to be *somewhere* on the school grounds, but since Henry never went *anywhere* under normal circumstances, it did seem a bit strange that he hadn't been in his room in the West Wing when she went looking for him earlier.

And on top of all that, she hadn't seen Thomas, either. She didn't want to think about what *two* missing ghosts might mean.

She had a bad feeling in the pit of her stomach—the kind of feeling that, when you were alive, made you want to go lie down so you wouldn't throw up your lunch. Her tummy felt all bubbly and syrupy inside, like she was a soda can someone had shaken so hard, it was about to burst.

Trina loved adjectives. She could make the juiciest sentences with them, sentences all about how uncomfortable her tummy felt—or really about *anything* she was feeling. She had even won a number of Juicy Sentence Awards in school before she had died. Her parents had been so proud of her that they'd hung the awards in the living room so that everyone who came to visit could get an eyeful of them.

Nelly—who was of the "less is more" school of thought—always made a sour face when Trina launched into her juicy sentences. She said that Trina used too many words. To prove her point, Nelly always tried to use one sentence to describe something that would take Trina three whole pages of notebook paper to explain.

This never bothered Trina, but to make Nelly happy, she took to saying her juicy sentences to herself, using as many similes and metaphors as she could in her head so that no one ever knew she was the queen of juicy sentences at all.

Juicy sentences aside, she really *did* have a bad feeling

in the pit of her stomach. And it wouldn't go away, no matter how much she reassured herself that Henry was perfectly fine, wherever he was. She just didn't believe her own words.

Unable to keep her worries to herself, Trina went looking for Nelly. She found her friend outside, crouched down in front of a large bayberry bush.

"What're you doing?" Trina said as she plopped down beside Nelly and looked over her shoulder.

"Watching ants," Nelly replied, her eyes trained on the snaking line of worker ants, each insect weighted down with a piece of white bread–looking stuff.

"Asbestos again?" Trina asked curiously, forgetting all about Henry's absence for the moment.

"No, something from the cafeteria, probably," Nelly answered. She hadn't looked up at Trina once, but she did scratch her arm three times, Trina noted.

"I guess it does look like bread. They seem to really like

123

the stuff," Trina said, but all Nelly did was shrug. They sat there, staring at the ever-lengthening line of ants for a long time until Trina remembered why she had gone looking for Nelly in the first place.

"Henry's gone!" she shrieked suddenly. "And so is Thomas."

This made Nelly look up from her ants and blink twice, like she'd just seen something that had blinded her.

"They're gone and I think something terrible has happened to them—something *really* bad. I can feel it in the pit of my stomach, like it's a soda can about to burst," Trina finished, glad that she'd told someone else because now her tummy felt slightly better.

"Did you look all over the building?" Nelly asked.

Trina nodded. "I looked everywhere!"

And she really had. When she couldn't find Henry in his room, she'd looked in every corner, every dark spot, every secret place in the West Wing. She'd been dead awhile, so she knew all those places like the back of her hand. She couldn't find a trace of either boy—although she had seen the dark-haired teacher again skulking around outside the West Wing. He didn't have any of the asbestos-bread-fluff with him, but there was still

124

something kind of suspicious about him lurking around the burned-out old building.

"What about the rest of the school grounds?" Nelly asked after Trina had stopped talking.

"Well, um . . . ," Trina stammered. It was the first time in decades that Trina remembered being at a loss for words.

"Yes . . . ?" Nelly said, encouraging Trina to continue.

"I don't really like to leave the West Wing," Trina said sheepishly.

"You're outside now," Nelly said, looking around at their surroundings.

Trina blushed an even deeper shade of red.

"Yeah, but you're with me."

She hated to admit this to her friend—because it made her look like the biggest baby in the whole world—but the truth was that Trina was deathly afraid of being alone outside of the West Wing.

When she'd first died, she'd been entirely carefree, unafraid of anything, but as time had gone on, she'd started to develop the feeling that if she spent too much time away from the West Wing, she'd become one of those ghosts that . . . *disappeared*.

She really hoped something nice happened to you after you disappeared. The ghosts that had gone into the light hadn't seemed scared, but she knew in her heart that she wasn't ready for whatever lay ahead. All she wanted to do was stay at New Newbridge as long as she possibly could.

And if sticking close to home helped make that happen, well, she was just gonna stick as close to home as possible.

Nelly made a sour face and turned back to the ants. She didn't have much use for fears and phobias and definitely didn't think that encouraging Trina's would be a good idea.

"I'm sure they're both around here somewhere," she said finally, her eyes scanning the line of ants for any sign of the queen. She had a feeling that the queen of this busy ant kingdom had to be pretty smart because her worker ants moved with such precision and dedication that it was almost like they were in the military.

"Maybe," Trina said, sensing that she would get no further help on the subject from her friend.

Or maybe not, she thought.

She rather hoped she wasn't right.

Catherine Alexander

Whenever Noh had a problem that she didn't know the answer to, she would ask her dad for help. When *he* didn't know the answer, he would direct Noh to the only place in the whole world that *did* have all the answers to everything: the library.

Noh loved the library in her town. It was bigger than the fire station but smaller than the grocery store. It was made of warm brown brick, and it always seemed to be inviting you inside when you looked at it.

She had spent many a rainy day ensconced in one of the large, overstuffed armchairs that littered the science section, reading up on weird diseases and perusing whatever fiction tome had happened to catch her fancy when she wandered through the literature section. She had made her way through all the Anne of Green Gables books and every Jane Austen novel she could find while sitting in those overstuffed armchairs. Just thinking about their lopsided gray cushions put a smile on her face.

So that's how Noh found herself standing in front of the giant, carved wooden doors that led into the inner sanctum of New Newbridge's library. If she knew anything at all, it was that somewhere inside the library waited her best chance at cracking the mystery.

Noh pushed open the door with a loud *creeeak* that almost gave her a heart attack. She felt like she was in one of those scary black-and-white monster movies her dad liked to watch late at night when he thought she was asleep—except this was *real* life, not TV.

The space was much bigger than she'd imagined—three ominous-looking rooms in total—and chock-full of dusty old books that looked like no one had touched them in a thousand years. She closed the door behind her with another loud *creeeak*, but this time she was prepared for the sound, so it didn't make her heart do somersaults again.

The library seemed empty, with a fine layer of dust on *everything*.

"Hello . . . ?" Noh called out, even though under normal circumstances she wouldn't have made any sounds louder than a whisper in a library.

No one answered her. Not even the squeak of a mouse or the crunch of a shoe sounded in the emptiness. Noh took this as a sign that it was okay to enter. Her thoughts were that if someone wanted the place to be off-limits, then they'd have locked the doors.

Noh tiptoed across the front entryway, her shoes making little *squeak-squeak* noises as they moved across the dark blue marbled floor. Noh thought that there had to be some kind of pattern built into the marble, but the slabs of dark blue and green were so squiggly and strange that she just couldn't make out their code. She wondered if she were to climb the large circular staircase that stood against the back wall up to the second floor, if she would be able to see whatever picture the marble spelled out.

Taking the rickety wrought-iron stairs two at a time, Noh made it to the second-floor landing in less than ten seconds. She walked over to the balustrade and looked down.

What Noh saw made her head hurt and her eyes swim. It was a great big mishmash of color that would

have been at home in the middle of an abstract painting, but seemed *very* wrong for the floor of a school library. Noh put her hand to her head and leaned against the railing. She felt like she was going to be sick right then and there.

"What are you doing?!" called a shrill voice from the first floor.

Noh squinted down at the circulation desk, and sitting squarely behind the counter was the largest woman she had ever laid eyes on. The woman was wearing a bright blue and green muumuu that matched the colors of the floor, making her seem to almost blend in with the pattern. Noh supposed that that was why she hadn't noticed the woman in the first place. Although it did seem strange to Noh that the woman hadn't said a word when she'd first called out her "hello."

Noh's head cleared and she was able to stand up straight again. All the dizziness seemed to have disappeared at the woman's words.

"I was just looking for a book," Noh said, even though that wasn't the complete and utter truth. "And then I wanted to see what the floor looked like from up here, so I climbed up the stairs."

"And how *did* the floor look from up there?" the woman said, cocking an eyebrow with curiosity.

Noh swallowed hard.

"Like an abstract painting."

The woman nodded, then said, "Are you sure about that?"

Noh almost rolled her eyes with frustration. She may have been a kid, but she wasn't blind.

"Why don't you take another look?" the woman said before Noh could say another word.

Noh didn't want to look at the floor. In fact, she would've rather eaten a tub of live cockroaches than look at the floor again, but she also didn't want to seem like she was a scaredy-cat, either.

"Okay," Noh replied, and gulped hard. She took a deep breath and looked down at the floor.

"That's not right!" Noh said loudly. "It wasn't like that before."

What Noh saw now when she looked at the floor was wall-to-wall ugly beige marble. There was no dark blue or dark green anywhere and definitely no pattern that made your brain spin inside your head.

"It's always been this way," the woman said as she picked up a book and stamped it with a big black stamp. "Why don't you come down here and tell me your name."

"But the floor was different—," Noh started to protest, but the woman put a finger to her lips.

"Shush now, girl, you're in a library."

Feeling silly, Noh took the stairs one at a time, dragging out how long it took to reach the bottom. When her toes touched the floor, she realized that it felt very different than it had before. Her shoes no longer made a *squeak-squeak* sound as she crossed the marbled floor, and the layer of dust that had been all over the library seemed to have vanished.

The whole thing was very *suspicious*, as far as Noh was concerned.

The woman was waiting for Noh when she reached

the circulation desk. Even though Noh wanted to dislike the woman for making her feel so stupid, she found herself instantly liking the wide, triple-chinned face; the long, black hair that was so black, it almost looked blue; and the bright violet eyes that seemed to brim with curiosity.

"I'm Catherine Alexander, the head librarian at New Newbridge," the woman said, sticking out her humongous hand. "You must be Noleen-Anne. Your aunt has told me so much about you."

Noh stuck out her own hand and took Catherine's. The skin of the large woman's fingers was soft and warm as she engulfed Noh's hand in her own. She gave Noh a good, strong shake, then let her go. Noh could feel the reverberations of that handshake all the way up her arm and down her spine.

"Now, tell me, Noleen-Anne," the big librarian said in a feathery whisper, "how would you like me to help you decipher that sheaf of papers you have crammed into your back pocket?"

The Lemon Solution

Catherine Alexander took the frayed papers that Noh handed her and spread them out on top of the polished oak circulation desk, where they mixed in with all the rest of the papers on top of the desk.

"Looks like a letter . . . to a fellow called Henry . . . from his mother," Catherine Alexander said thoughtfully. "But this last one's blank." She suddenly lifted the page to her nose and gave it a giant sniff.

"Hmmm," Catherine Alexander said, wiggling her nose and giving the paper a curious glance. This *hmmm* was very thoughtful as well.

Next she took a loupe—Noh knew that this was really just a tiny magnifying glass, because her dad used one for his work—that was attached to a long silver chain from her shirtfront pocket, and she leaned forward to examine the papers, placing the loupe right up to her left eyeball.

Noh, who didn't have her own nifty magnifying glass, squeezed one eye shut (the right one) and put her head down next to Catherine Alexander's. When she got bored with looking at the words that had been painstakingly written across the yellowing sheets of paper in long, looping cursive, she tilted her head so she could watch the librarian.

The magnifying glass made Catherine Alexander's eye seem ten times bigger than it actually was. Noh wanted to laugh at how silly the librarian looked, but since the large woman appeared to be very seriously involved in deciphering the papers, she was afraid to even let out a giggle.

Catherine Alexander cleared her throat twice, then made a low *hmmm*ing sound down in the bottom of her throat. She took the loupe from her eye and offered it to Noh.

"I want your opinion on this," Catherine Alexander said, pulling out the last page, the one that was blank, and helping Noh put the magnifying glass to her own eye. Noh had a feeling her eyeball looked just as big and funny as Catherine Alexander's had only a few moments earlier.

Noh closed her right eye so she wouldn't see double and peered down through the magnifying glass. She blinked twice, expecting to see something strange about the paper, but all she saw was nothing—just a lot bigger.

"I don't see anything," Noh said with disappointment as she lowered the loupe from her eye.

"Exactly!" Catherine Alexander said happily. "*Nothing*. That's exactly what I thought too."

She picked the lone paper up off the desktop, carried it across the room, and stopped at one of the polished oak reading tables. She pulled the lampshade off the table light and laid the paper on top of the bare bulb. Noh trailed a few steps behind her, totally baffled by what the librarian was doing.

"Just as I suspected," Catherine Alexander said, squinting down at the paper. "Come look."

She motioned for Noh to look at the paper as it baked over the lightbulb.

"Wow, that's amazing!" Noh said, shaking her head to make sure she wasn't imagining things, because her

     137

mind was definitely having a hard time believing what her eyes were seeing. Scrawled across the page, completely covering the whole page, was another letter! Only upon closer inspection, Noh realized that it wasn't a letter at all, but a bunch of weird scientific notations. Decimals and fractions littered the page, but there were lots and lots of numbers, too.

"Invisible ink. Lemon juice, I think," the librarian said.

"But why?" Noh asked. "What's so important about a bunch of numbers that someone wanted to hide them like that?"

Catherine Alexander made a tut-tutting sound.

"I believe that this blank piece of paper houses an important secret. I don't know how it got mixed up with your friend Henry's letter, but somehow it did."

"What kind of secret?" Noh said uncertainly. She wished now that she liked numbers *half* as much as she liked words so she could understand the secret too.

"These aren't just numbers, Noh," the librarian said, shaking her head. "They're equations. And if I'm not mistaken, they may turn out to be even more important than I suspect."

Inside Out

The West Wing was awash in ants, and Nelly had been the only one to notice it. All afternoon she'd monitored the ant army as it had amassed its troops in the foyer, and she had waited for them to do something that would explain *why* they had all decided to meet here in the burned-out West Wing.

Her eyes goggled in astonishment as she stared at all the insects marching by her feet. She realized that she had never seen so many of the little suckers in one place at one time in her whole life (or death). Of course, being the avid arthropod lover that she was, she'd had an ant farm back home in Michigan before she'd come to the New Newbridge Academy, but her extra-large plastic terrarium was *nothing* in comparison to this. There were so many ants that she couldn't have counted them all, even if she'd wanted to.

Nelly wasn't sure whom she was supposed to tell this important ant army information to—it wasn't like when she was in school and could just tell a teacher whenever she had a problem. Nope. Now that she was dead, she was on her own.

When she'd tried to point out the ants' strange behavior to Trina, her friend had only made fun of her, teasing her about the hardworking ants eating asbestos—*like they don't know asbestos is poisonous! They're ants, not dummies,* Nelly thought angrily.

But she knew better. She suspected that these ants were up to something . . . something *different*. And she was determined to discover what that something different was.

So while Trina had looked for Henry—he hadn't been in his room, where he normally hid out during his nasty black moods—Nelly had gone off to find the answer to the ant army mystery. Besides, the search for Henry hadn't really interested Nelly all that much, anyway. She'd always liked insects way better than people—and you could go ahead and lump ghosts right into the *people* category, as far as she was concerned.

In the end, Nelly hadn't had to do too much discovering. She'd just followed the line of ants all the way out to where it started by the lake. She'd stood by the edge of the water and watched as more and more ants trooped out of the woods and joined the ever-growing line.

Next she'd followed her own footsteps back to the West Wing, stopping to examine the place where the ant line curved by the archery field, because there seemed to be a smaller line of ants intersecting the bigger line there. She'd wanted to follow the smaller line back to where it started, but something inside her brain told her that it was a dead end, that the ants were going to the New Newbridge Academy, and it didn't matter one little bit where they were coming from.

When she got back to the West Wing, she did what she *should* have done in the first place: She looked to see exactly where the ants were going. She followed the line over to the base of the brick fireplace that stood across from the portrait of the school's first trustee, Eustant P. Druthers, and found that, one by one, the ants were disappearing into a small hole in the hearth just below the fireplace grating.

After that, Nelly could find no trace of the ant line, no matter where she looked.

She was so busy trying to discover exactly where the ants were going that she didn't notice the cold at first, but gradually she realized that she was feeling something she hadn't felt in a long, long time.

"What in the—," she started to say, her teeth beginning to chatter like a pair of windup teeth as all the drapes in the foyer dropped down, blocking out what little light was sneaking into the room through the windows.

It was so cold that when Nelly looked down at the ant army, even the insects seemed to be shivering on their stalklike legs. Suddenly a strange silence filled the empty air. Nelly looked up and saw a shimmering, golden orb materializing by the fireplace. As she stared at it, it grew larger and larger, until the orb was just big enough for Nelly to climb through.

She floated toward it, her mind and body drawn to the glowing thing like a kid to candy. Obviously, it was her turn to enter the light.

She wondered if when she got to the other side, her old dog, Brandy, would be there to greet her. She'd been so heartbroken when a car had hit the big golden

retriever just days before she'd gone off to start her first year at the New Newbridge Academy.

It was a strange last thing to think, she decided, because she hadn't thought about Brandy even *once* in almost fifteen years.

As she felt her essence beginning to merge with the glowing orb, Nelly had another strange thought. And for the death of her, she couldn't have said where it came from.

What if this isn't the real light but a fake light? One that doesn't lead to the other side but to somewhere else entirely?

And then she was gone.

Up and Down the Stairs

Catherine Alexander had declined to go with Noh to Caleb DeMarck's office. She said that she preferred staying in her library, where she always knew what was just around the corner, but she *had* given Noh a note to give to the physics teacher, explaining the urgency with which the librarian hoped he would decipher the equations that she and Noh had discovered.

Feeling like she was finally getting somewhere with her detecting, Noh walked out of the library, making sure to close the giant doors quietly behind her. Catherine Alexander had drawn a map for Noh, pointing out the way to the physics teacher's office, but the more she walked and tried to follow the librarian's directions, the more confusing the map became.

When she had first watched the librarian writing it, the map had looked very simple, a few directions here and there and a drawing or two. Yet every time Noh consulted the map for the next direction, the more directions there seemed to be. No matter what Noh did—whether she took a right turn at the atrium or a left turn at the basketball court, or took three sets of staircases up and two sets of staircases down—she found herself right back at the front entranceway to the main building.

The whole thing made Noh's head hurt.

Finally, after what seemed like hours, Noh opened the front door and went outside. She sat down on the steps that led to the main building and scratched her head. She wanted to crunch the map up into a tiny little ball and eat it. Maybe that way the map would get into her bloodstream and help her go the right way. She was almost tempted to go back to the library and ask the giant librarian why she'd given her a trick map, but she felt silly accusing someone of something that she wasn't sure of. Maybe the map *was* really just a map and the problem was all in Noh's head. She thought back to the cemetery she'd gone into after she'd left the train station. Hadn't she had the same problem there? She'd had to go out the way she'd come in because she couldn't get to the other side—and she definitely hadn't had any kind of map then.

The idea that she might be "directionally impaired" made Noh's tummy feel funny, like she'd eaten too many desserts.

She got up and stretched like a cat, deciding to try to get to the physics teacher's office from another direction. Maybe if she went to the back entrance of the main building, she'd have better luck.

Trina had gone too far from the West Wing. She could feel it in her nonexistent bones. She'd been so busy looking for Henry and Thomas that she'd strayed all the way over to the main building.

"Henry!? Where are you!" she called one more time, her voice as chirpy as a baby bird's. The more nervous she got—and she was starting to feel *very* nervous— the higher and more stretched her ghostly vocal cords became. If she didn't find the boys and get back to the West Wing soon, her voice was probably going to fly away.

"Hey—*who* are you looking for?" a voice said from

behind her, frightening her so badly, she nearly disappeared. She tried to place the owner of the voice, but she couldn't—which was strange because she knew nearly *all* the ghosts at New Newbridge.

Wait a minute, Trina thought. *There's one voice I don't know: the new girl's!* She had been so preoccupied that she had totally forgotten what Nelly had said about there being a new ghost at New Newbridge.

"You're the new girl!" Trina said excitedly as she turned around and found a small, dark-haired girl about the same age as herself standing across from her. This new girl had a jacket wrapped around her waist, even though it was summer.

She'd probably been dead since the fall, Trina thought, and hadn't even known it—hence the jacket.

The two girls stared at each other, a kind, welcoming smile on Trina's face and a curious, pinched look on Noh's.

"How do you know I'm new here?" Noh asked uncertainly. There was something about the redheaded girl in the jodhpurs and riding helmet that seemed *off* to Noh—she just couldn't put her finger on what it was.

"Oh, Nelly told me all about you," Trina said brightly, forgetting how only moments before she had

been so worried about being far away from the West Wing. A new ghost at New Newbridge was an exciting thing. And as far as she was concerned, *this* new girl looked *very* promising, indeed.

"Is that the girl who kept scratching her arm?" Noh asked. She was almost certain that it was.

Trina nodded happily.

"I thought so," Noh said. She had been right. All the kids she'd met so far at New Newbridge were ghosts. That's how this girl knew Henry . . . because she was a ghost too!

"By the way, were you looking for a ghost named Henry?" Noh asked, hoping it was a different Henry from the one she'd met earlier—even though she knew it wasn't.

Trina nodded again, her riding helmet bobbing up and down on her brightly colored head. She was so pale-skinned that Noh could see tiny reddish-brown freckles dotting almost every square inch of exposed skin on the girl's arms and face.

"I hate to have to tell you this, but he's gone," Noh said finally.

"Gone?" the girl said, cocking her head curiously.

The look on her face reminded Noh of a dog: one who'd just been scolded and didn't know why.

"I just met him—he was crying in a room upstairs in the West Wing, and while we were talking, it got really cold and then a glowing orb appeared and he said it was his time," Noh babbled, not sure if the other girl was even listening.

"His time?" the girl repeated. She looked even more confused than before.

"That's what he said," Noh offered. "And then he went into the light and disappeared."

The other girl's eyes got as wide as saucers and she stopped blinking. She opened her mouth to speak, but nothing came out.

"I'm sorry," Noh said, feeling like that last bit of slime at the bottom of a slop bucket. "Are you okay?"

The girl nodded, then suddenly disappeared.

Ghost to Girl

S orry about that," the girl said as she magically reappeared in front of Noh. "I just wanted to check something out."

"Oh," Noh said. She didn't know if she should be annoyed with the girl or not. She *did* think it was kind of rude for someone to simply disappear like that without telling you first.

"I wanted to ask Nelly something, but I couldn't find her anywhere," Trina said. "By the way, my name's Trina. What's yours?"

"Noh."

Trina scrunched her eyebrows together.

"Well, that's a funny-sounding name," Trina said, then clapped her hand over her mouth with embarrassment.

It was only *after* the words were out of her mouth that she realized how rude they sounded.

Noh glared at her. Glaring was something Noh hardly ever did. She was a pretty easygoing girl, but when someone poked fun at her name, it made her so mad that she wanted to scream.

"If my name's funny-sounding, then so is yours," Noh declared, her eyes narrowing. She wanted to say something else, something mean that would put the weird ghost girl in her place, but she knew it was wrong. It was okay to defend yourself, but if you took it any further than that, then you were as bad as the other person.

Trina clasped her hands together and looked squarely into Noh's eyes.

"You're right. We both have strange names."

Noh had been prepared for a fight. Now she didn't know *what* she was supposed to do—she hadn't expected the other girl to agree with her like that.

"I'm sorry I was rude," Trina continued, "but you said something that spooked me and I wasn't really thinking right."

"It's okay," Noh said grudgingly. "I didn't mean to upset you, either."

Trina gave Noh a smile, but her lower lip was quivering.

"I just can't believe Henry's gone. He was kind of mean sometimes, but he was my friend."

Noh felt like she should tell Trina that she was sorry her friend was gone, but no words would come out of her mouth. She decided that words didn't say enough. Instead she pulled the paper that was with Henry's letter from her back pocket and handed it to the ghost girl.

"What's this?" Trina said as her lower lip instantly stopped quivering and her eyes lit up with curiosity.

"It's a secret code," Noh offered mysteriously. "I'm taking it to the physics teacher so he can tell me what it means."

Trina scrunched her eyebrows together. She didn't know how to explain to Noh that the living didn't see the dead. Surely the other girl had realized at least this much . . . but no, if she *thought* she was alive still, well, that put things in a different light entirely.

"I don't know if that's such a good idea," Trina said finally. She decided that honesty was the best policy in this situation.

"Why not?" Noh said. Did the ghost girl know

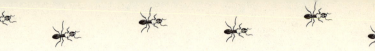

something about the physics teacher that she didn't know?

"Well, I guess the best way to say this is with the truth," Trina said. "You're dead, Noh, and as hard as that is to believe—"

Trina wasn't prepared for the loud *snort* that popped out of Noh's nose. The snort immediately turned into a giggle, then a belly-burning guffaw, and finally, big, wet tears began to roll out of the corners of Noh's eyes and down her cheeks. Trina didn't know what to do. She hadn't meant to make the new girl cry.

"I'm so sorry. I know it's really a terrible thing—"

This just made Noh laugh/cry harder.

"Please . . . ," Noh said between sobs and loud gulps for air. "Don't talk . . ."

"But I—"

"Please . . . no more . . . stomach hurts . . . it's gonna . . . burst . . ."

Trina nodded, working very hard to stop herself from saying anything that would make Noh's stomach burst. This was very hard for her because Trina loved to talk more than anything in the whole world. In fact, asking Trina not to talk was like asking a normal person not to breathe. It was kind of impossible.

"I just—," Trina said, not able to help herself. This made Noh—who'd just begun to calm down—start laughing/crying all over again.

"Sorry!" Trina yelped, feeling awful. She and the new girl had gotten off to a terrible start. She just hoped Noh didn't believe all that hooey about first impressions being the most accurate—otherwise, she would *never* want to be Trina's friend.

Finally, Noh stopped laughing enough to explain to Trina why she had started laughing in the first place.

"It's just that all the ghosts here at New Newbridge seem to think *I'm* a ghost too, just because I can see them," Noh told Trina, who only looked confused. As far as Trina knew, Noh being alive *had* to be an impossibility. Trina had been dead for a *pretty* long time, and *she'd* never met a living person who could see ghosts before.

"I don't know about that," Trina said. "Maybe you *think* you're alive, but you're *really* dead."

Noh shook her head.

"I'll prove it to you," she said.

As Noh reached out to shake Trina's hand, Trina gasped. Noh's fingers went right through her own. Trina took a step backward, and if she hadn't been floating an

inch above the ground, she'd have tripped over a rock and fallen on her butt.

"But . . . but . . . but that's impossible," Trina stammered. "You're not a ghost . . . ?"

Noh shook her head. At last, Trina seemed to be getting the point.

"Oh my goodness," Trina continued, comprehension dawning on her face. "You're a . . . *realie!*"

No Apologies

T he nasty thing that refuses to be named would like to interject something at this point in the story. It wants you to know that when you read the next few chapters, you will not think very well of it . . . *and that the nasty thing feels perfectly fine about this.*

It wants you, the reader, to know that it doesn't care one iota *what* you think of it. It says that "it is what it is" and that you are just going to have to deal with it.

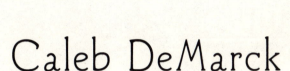

Caleb DeMarck

I'm going with you," Trina said, and no matter what Noh did, the ghost girl wouldn't take no for an answer. That's how Noh ended up at the physics teacher's office, trying to listen to what he was saying about the secret code while she glared at a ghost that no one else could see, who wouldn't stop talking and distracting Noh from the business at hand.

When Noh had knocked on Caleb DeMarck's office door, the physics teacher had immediately opened it and ushered Noh inside. It was a large office with carved wooden panels running up and down the walls.

The place was a mess. There were papers everywhere— on the big wooden desk, on both of the chairs that stood in front of the desk, all over the floor, and covering the

tops of two large metal filing cabinets. Caleb DeMarck had gestured for Noh to take a seat, but she declined, worried that she'd disturb whatever creature might be living underneath all the mess on the chair.

Instead she'd remained standing, handing him the note from Catherine Alexander and waiting for his response. After reading it, he'd wanted to look at the secret paper right then and there. Noh fished it out of her back pocket and handed it to him.

He was so excited by his first glimpse of the mathematical equations that littered the page that he almost tore it in half as he yanked it out of Noh's hand.

"That was weird," Trina said as the physics teacher began to devour the equations like jam on toast—which reminded Noh that it was getting close to dinnertime and her tummy was starting to rumble.

The teacher's hands began to shake as he became more and more engrossed in what he was reading.

"Ask him why he was wandering around the West Wing," Trina said suddenly, but Noh had no idea what she was talking about and ignored her.

Noh knew that she shouldn't feel so annoyed at Trina—the ghost had directed her right to Caleb

DeMarck's office without making her go up or down any flights of stairs at all—but the silly girl wouldn't stop talking. At first Trina just made quiet asides to Noh, commenting on how nervous the physics teacher looked, or how messy his office was, but then she started bugging Noh to ask him questions about his whereabouts, and that's when Noh wanted to strangle her.

Finally, Caleb DeMarck looked up from the letter, and if Noh hadn't known better, she'd have thought he was hiding something. His pupils were larger than they'd been before, and he had a shifty look on his face.

"Well, I think our librarian may have jumped to conclusions . . . ," he began, his hands still clutching the letter like a security blanket.

"Ask him why they used lemon to hide the equations," Trina said, distracting Noh and making her miss the physics teacher's next words. "Just ask him. It might be important. Oh, and don't forget to ask him about the West Wing!"

Noh was trapped between a rock and a hard place. She couldn't tell Trina to be quiet because Caleb DeMarck didn't know the ghost was even there, and she couldn't ask the physics teacher to repeat what he was saying

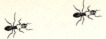

because then it would look like she had the memory retention of a peanut.

"I'm sorry, Mr. DeMarck," Noh said, interrupting Trina *and* the teacher at the same time. "I don't understand. What *does* Ms. Alexander think the equations mean?"

The physics teacher laughed, and it was such a weird, strange laugh that it made the hairs on the back of Noh's neck stand at attention.

"Why, our librarian seems to think that these equations might be part of the lost files of our school's first trustee and cofounder, Eustant P. Druthers. He was an amateur inventor, an inveterate explorer . . . *and a genius*," Caleb DeMarck boomed, his eyes shining.

"He's weird," Trina said in a small voice. "Especially his laugh."

Noh glared at Trina before turning her attention back to the physics teacher.

"Wow, that's cool, but what do the equa—," Noh started to say, but was interrupted halfway through the word "equation."

"You have to understand that he was a great man!" the physics teacher continued. "You wouldn't know

much about him since he was such a private person, but he did amazing things. . . ."

The physics teacher talked for a long time, extolling the numerous feats and virtues of Eustant P. Druthers. Noh started to get the impression that no matter what she did, she was never gonna get the answer to her question.

"Let's get out of here," Trina said with a yawn. "We can go back to the West Wing and find Nelly and maybe go to—"

But Noh quickly shook her head. Caleb DeMarck had just said something that had piqued her interest.

". . . and he also equipped the school with all kinds of secret passageways and hidden rooms," the physics teacher said as he nervously scratched his nose. "But don't tell anyone I told you that. I could get into a lot of trouble."

Noh's stomach rumbled, but she ignored it.

"Secret passageways?" Noh asked. She had a feeling that she might have already come across one of them back in the girl's dormitory bathroom earlier that morning. Which meant that Hullie knew all about the secret passageways and hidden rooms, because he'd found her toothbrush stuck in one of the entranceways.

"There are lots of them sprinkled around the school,

but none of the students are supposed to know about them, so not a word," the physics teacher said quickly, his eyes darting around the room.

"Since you don't think that paper is part of the lost collection, could I have it back?" Noh said suddenly.

"No!" he said loudly, then cleared his throat and said in a much less angry voice, "I think I'd better hold on to this for a while."

"But if it's not important . . . ," Noh said with a sharp smile.

The lanky physics teacher didn't say another word— he just pulled open the top desk drawer, set the paper inside, and shut it with a firm *click*. He took a key from his pants pocket and locked the drawer.

"I'm confiscating this paper," he said, fixing Noh with a steely eye. "And if you make a big stink about it, I'll tell them that I caught you trying to steal it from me in the first place."

That's cheating, Noh thought angrily, but she knew better than to press her luck. Caleb DeMarck was not the sort of a person that he had appeared to be. There was nothing gentle or meek about the rude man sitting behind the wooden desk.

Trina echoed her thoughts.

"Adults shouldn't lie," Trina said hotly. "That's, like, against the law!"

Noh agreed with her. Adults should be setting a good example—especially teachers—for the children around them, but Noh was fast discovering that the world was a very different place from what she had originally thought.

"Do I make myself understood?" Caleb DeMarck said, his eyes fixed on Noh's. She nodded but didn't say a word.

"Good. Now, it's almost time for dinner, so I suggest you go to the cafeteria and forget all about finding that paper."

Once again, Noh only nodded.

From the way she was nodding, most people—this included the spiteful physics teacher Caleb DeMarck—would think that Noh had given up, that she had put the memory of finding the equation-covered paper into a secret drawer in the back of her brain and locked it away, never to be seen again.

But they would be wrong. Noh held her tongue for one reason and one reason only.

She was busy formulating a plan.

A Dip in the Pool

Noh's plan consisted of three things:

1. Missing dinner
2. Being observant
3. Not telling a *living* soul one little thing about her plan.

"But how do we *know* he's not going to dinner?" Trina asked for the third time since Noh had explained the plan to her new friend.

Noh sighed. She hated overexplaining things, especially plans. She imagined that plans were like falling stars. They just happened near you, and if you questioned them, they disappeared. In the past she hadn't had to explain anything to anyone because she had spent most of her time by herself, and when she hadn't been by herself, she had been with her father . . . and he would *never* have asked her to explain anything private like that.

Besides, overexplaining just made everything all muddled inside your brain.

"We *know* he's not going to dinner because he specifically told *me* to go there so I wouldn't be in his way," Noh said for the third time. Trina nodded, but she still didn't look convinced.

"I think he's hiding something for sure," Trina said. "Nelly and I saw him skulking around the West Wing *twice*!"

Suddenly Noh heard a sharp *click* and she sat up expectantly. Her legs were cramped from sitting in the janitor's closet across from the physics teacher's room for so long, but she ignored them, excited to finally put her plan into action. She eased open the door and almost screamed when she saw Trina waiting on the other side.

Sorry, Trina mouthed as Noh glared at her. She wasn't used to ghosts disappearing and reappearing all over the place. Trina pointed down the hall just in time for Noh to see Caleb DeMarck rounding the corner and disappearing into the dark.

"He's getting away," Noh hissed, trying not to make *squeaky* sounds with her sneakers as she jogged down the hall in the same direction the physics teacher had just gone.

Trina disappeared again, but then Noh caught sight of her ghost friend down at the end of the hall, gesturing for Noh to follow her. Noh decided that in the future she wouldn't get so frustrated with Trina's quirks. Without her ghost friend's special abilities—being able to disappear and reappear wherever she liked—Noh would've probably lost the physics teacher's trail, wrecking the whole plan.

Noh followed Trina through three or four long, winding hallways, across a darkened classroom, down two flights of stairs, and into the gym. When she crossed the threshold into the gym, her sneakers squeaking on the polished floor, she saw the safety lights shining onto an empty basketball court. She looked around for her ghost friend, but Trina was nowhere to be found.

Noh was startled by a loud grating sound that filled the empty space, and the whole place began to vibrate.

Noh watched in awe as the gym floor started folding in on itself. She quickly stepped backward, her feet making loud squeaks on the slippery floor as she scampered for the doorway that led out of the gym. She had barely reached firm ground when the mechanized floor evaporated right out from underneath where she'd just been standing.

"Wow," Noh said under her breath as she stared at the Olympic-size swimming pool that had been revealed by the floor's disappearance. She started to take a tentative step toward the empty pool but stopped in her tracks when she spied Caleb DeMarck coming out of the locker room across from her, a gleeful smile plastered on his face.

He walked along the edge of the pool, paused where it was shallowest, and climbed down inside. Noh watched as he crossed the pool floor and crouched beside the exposed drain.

Once again, Noh wondered where Trina had gone.

She found that she was missing the ghost girl's company more than she realized.

When Noh turned her attention back to the physics teacher, she saw that he was on his hands and knees now, pulling hard on the top of the drain. When nothing happened after a few moments, he sat up and scratched his head. He tried a different tack. This time he pressed his fingers against the drain, probing here and there until Noh heard a tiny *crunch*. She watched in amazement as the drain began to sink into the concrete.

"It's one of those secret things," Trina whispered into Noh's ear, making her jump.

"Where were you?" Noh whispered back. Trina frowned.

"I was looking for Nelly, but I can't find her anywhere. And none of the other ghosts I've talked to know where she went," Trina said, her eyes wide with fear. "I think . . . I think she might've *gone*."

"Like Henry?" Noh said, careful to keep her voice low. Trina nodded.

"And my friend Thomas, too," Trina said.

There was another *crunch*, which attracted the girls' attention, and they both looked down to see that the

drain was completely gone and in its place was a massive hole . . . but where was the physics teacher?

"I'll check on him," Trina said, disappearing again. Noh waited for Trina to report back. When the ghost didn't return in a prompt manner, she stepped out of the doorway and walked over to the pool.

She had a funny feeling that whatever Caleb DeMarck was doing down there . . . *it wasn't something good.*

The Machine

There were ants everywhere. If Trina hadn't been a ghost, and therefore safe from having to touch insects and other creepy, crawly things, she would've run screaming from the room. As it was, she wasn't really *happy* about having to make her way through the mass of wriggling, squirming ants, but at least she didn't have a body for them to climb all over.

The hidden room wasn't very large—probably the size of an old World War II bomb shelter, except that it was completely empty (if you didn't count the ants, the physics teacher, and a large metallic machine that stood in the very back). The walls were made of cut stone, and there was one bare lightbulb hanging from the ceiling, illuminating the whole space.

Caleb DeMarck stood in the middle of the room, ants swarming all around him. From what Trina could see, he seemed to be occupying the only ant-free space in the room. For some unknown reason, the ants kept their distance, leaving about a foot of empty space around the physics teacher. It was almost like he was wearing a layer of extra-strength "instant death" bug spray instead of cologne.

Trina moved farther into the room, invisible to Caleb DeMarck and the ants. Even *if* she had been a living, breathing girl, the ants and the teacher were so focused on the large circular machine that took over the entire back part of the hidden room that they wouldn't have noticed her anyway.

Trina had no idea what the machine had been used for, but she decided that it had to have been a dazzling silver color in its youth. Too bad it was so tarnished with age now that it looked dark bronze. It consisted of two large electrodes that sprouted from a squat round frame, and each electrode had three long wires running out of it that reattached down at the base of the machine. There was also a long silver lever soldered to the center of the machine, which Trina figured must be the on/off switch.

  174

The ants seemed to think that the room and what was hidden inside it belonged to them. They swarmed all over the place, making the bottom half of the machine appear alive with movement.

As Trina marveled at the strange sight Caleb DeMarck pulled the secret paper that Noh had given him out of his shirt pocket and opened it. His eyes gazed at the mathematical equations with wonder, with every blink drinking in the lemon-juice ink code that Catherine Alexander had broken.

Trina assumed that the physics teacher had no idea that she was even in the room, so when he started talking, it startled her.

"You don't even know what I've done!" he said, his tone full of excitement.

It took Trina a moment to realize that the physics teacher was talking to himself and not to her, making her giggle with relief. Meeting one realie who could see her was more than enough to last Trina a death-time.

"You left the clues, hidden so ingeniously that only someone as persistent as myself could find them," Caleb DeMarck said, his voice rising in pitch as he spoke. "You were clever, but I was cleverer still."

Trina wasn't sure who or what the physics teacher was talking about, but the whole thing was starting to give her the creeps. She wished Nelly were here with her. Trina had a feeling that her friend would know exactly what to do. After all, Nelly knew way more about insects and science than Trina did.

"Now that I have the final piece of the puzzle," Caleb DeMarck continued, his eyes on the machine again, "we can fulfill your invention's *destiny*."

He scanned the secret paper one more time, then

pulled something white and fluffy from his pants pocket and sprinkled it in front of him. The ants greedily grabbed at the white stuff—the same stuff Trina and Nelly had seen the ants with earlier—and Caleb DeMarck took a step toward the machine. The ants cleared a path for him as quickly as their little legs could carry them. In that instant, Trina realized that the ants were under the physics teacher's thrall!

Whatever that white stuff was, *it was making the ants do anything Caleb DeMarck wanted them to do.*

Trina watched as the physics teacher reached for the wires running out of one of the electrodes. He consulted the secret paper, then pulled two wires out of their sockets and switched them. Satisfied, he stepped back and reached for the silver lever sticking out of the machine's belly. There was a loud *crunch* as he pulled the lever down. The machine roared to life, the two electrodes buzzing with electricity.

Without even realizing what she was doing, Trina took a step backward. There was something about the machine that terrified her, even if she couldn't have said precisely what it was. She just knew instinctively that she needed to get out of that room as fast as she possibly could. She closed her eyes, imagining herself back in the burned-out West Wing's foyer. Then she opened her eyes, expecting to see the portrait of the school's cofounder, Eustant P. Druthers, staring at her.

Instead Trina found herself right back in the hidden room. For the first time in a very long while, Trina's hands felt cold. She looked down at them, but they looked exactly the same: slightly translucent. A shiver ran down her spine—another feeling she hadn't experienced in a very long while—and her eyes widened in fear. There was a giant glowing orb slowly unfolding itself before her eyes. She found herself entranced by the light. It was so beautiful. She didn't know why she'd been afraid of going into it before. If she'd known how pleasant the whole thing was, she might well have welcomed it happening to her.

Trina slowly started to float toward the orb, her thoughts becoming muffled the closer she got to it. She was almost to the edge of the light when she heard someone calling her name. She didn't want to turn around and see who was calling her. She wanted to go *into* the light.

"Trina!" the voice called, louder this time.

She turned her head, her eyes searching for the owner of the voice.

178

"Don't do it! It's a trap!"

Trina's gaze landed on Noh.

"Trina, come back!" Noh screamed, her face pinched with worry. She stood directly behind Caleb DeMarck, who didn't seem to have the least clue to whom Noh was talking. He looked around the room blankly, an expression of befuddlement on his face.

"Turn off the machine!" her new friend cried, pushing past the startled physics teacher and reaching for the silver lever.

"Don't touch that!" Caleb DeMarck shouted, pulling more of the white stuff from his pocket and sprinkling it on the floor. Noh's fingers had just grasped the shiny switch when she started to shriek. Trina looked down and saw that both of Noh's legs were now covered in a swarm of squirming black and red ants.

Since Noh was so busy with the ants, her hold over Trina slackened and the call of the orb overwhelmed the ghost again. Trina turned away from her ant-covered friend, her eyes searching for the beckoning light. She saw that the orb was even larger than it had been before, even more luminescent . . . *and without hesitation she began her journey into its shining depths.*

Explanation: Part 1

N oh had been bitten by ants before, but never so many at the same time. She was tempted to reach down and squish the little buggers with her palms, stopping the nasty ant pinchers from embedding themselves in her skin, but she knew she had bigger fish to fry, and time was of the essence. Ignoring her stinging legs, she again grasped the silver lever sticking out of the base of the machine and pulled it. In the blink of an eye the silvery orb disappeared and Trina turned around, her eyes wide with shock.

Noh let out a loud sigh of relief, but then the pain hit her. She angrily started slapping the biting ants with everything she had. Caleb DeMarck, who up until that very moment might as well have been a statue for all the good he had done, scattered more of the fluffy white stuff at Noh's feet. Almost instantly the ants ceased attacking Noh, and the ones that hadn't gotten mushed crawled off her legs, swarming around the white stuff like it was manna from heaven.

Somehow just knowing that the ants weren't covering her legs anymore made Noh feel a lot better. Her skin still stung from the twenty or so ant bites she'd received, but she knew she'd heal.

"Thank you," Noh said, even though it had been the physics teacher's fault that the ants had attacked her in the first place. She reached down to scratch the most painful bite on her kneecap, knowing all the while that she shouldn't, then returned her gaze to Caleb DeMarck.

"I don't understand your thinking, Noh," the physics teacher said. "What right did you have to interrupt my experiment?"

Noh didn't know where to begin. She was torn between telling the physics teacher *exactly* what he'd almost done and . . . well, there really wasn't any other option than the truth.

"I don't know what that machine does," Noh said,

pointing at the tarnished metal thing in the corner, "but whatever it is . . . I think it sucks up ghost energy."

The physics teacher opened his mouth to speak, then immediately shut it again. He looked *very* confused.

"Ghost energy?" he said finally, his face turning white.

"Ever since I came to New Newbridge, I've been able to see ghosts. I've met three of them personally, and I think there may be a lot more," Noh said, preparing herself for the worst. There was no way in a million years that the physics teacher was gonna believe her story— even if it *was* the absolute truth. She wished she had a truth-telling machine so that she would never have to worry about adults believing her stories. She decided that if this situation was only going to end badly, she might as well tell the physics teacher *everything*.

"Um," Noh continued, "you should also know that there's a ghost here in the room with us right now. Her name is Trina and I think your machine almost ate her."

The physics teacher's face got even whiter.

"You said that the machine almost ate the ghost?" Caleb DeMarck repeated, his eyes searching for some sign of a ghostly presence. "How?"

It had taken a couple of minutes for the effects of the machine to wear off, but now Trina was mad. Since she was feeling more like herself again, she opened her mouth and started doing one of the things she did best: talking.

"Tell him about the orb and the light and the—," Trina began, but Noh held up her hand.

"I'll tell him everything, Trina," Noh said to her friend. "I promise, but just let me think for one minute."

The ghost girl nodded, remembering that she owed Noh her ghostly existence since she had stopped the machine from gobbling her up.

"If you tell me what you think the machine *does*, I might be able to explain how it works," Noh offered after she'd taken a moment to put things in perspective. She didn't have all the pieces to the mystery, but she knew that once Caleb DeMarck gave her a couple more clues, she'd be close.

"Well," the physics teacher began proudly, "many years ago, when I was a student here, I stumbled upon something special, something secret at New Newbridge. I think I have to start there for you—and your friend—to understand."

The Know-It-All

Caleb DeMarck had a hard time making friends. He just couldn't understand why no one liked hanging out with him. He would have been very surprised to discover that it was because the other kids at New Newbridge considered him a know-it-all.

And not only was Caleb a know-it-all, but he was the worst *kind* of know-it-all. He was always the first kid to shake his head and snicker at anyone who admitted that they didn't know something. He made the other kids in his class feel dumb when they got an answer wrong, or when they didn't get an A++ on a test.

The saddest part of the whole thing was that Caleb didn't even know *he* was the cause of his own problems. He just assumed that it was the other kids' faults, that they were mean-spirited or jealous of someone who was smarter than them. He had no idea that that was exactly how the rest of the school saw *him*: mean-spirited and petty.

Since Caleb didn't have any friends, he spent most of his time in his room, reading books and doing science experiments. It was during one of these experiments that he discovered a way to make his own friends.

New Newbridge has always been home to many different kinds of insect life. Every creature that creeps, crawls, or slithers is represented in some capacity at the school. You just have to go off on an insect expedition into the woods and you'll find praying mantises, crickets, ladybugs, lizards, and spiders galore—and that's just the tip of the iceberg.

Yet, by and large, the real kings of New Newbridge have to be the ants.

There are at least nine colonies of black ants and seven colonies of red ants—and that's just on the school grounds. Go into the woods and there are many, many more. They do more business on school property—and give Hullie more trouble—than all the students and faculty combined.

186

In truth, they rule the school.

And that is precisely why, as a student at New Newbridge, Caleb DeMarck found the ants so fascinating.

He loved to sit outside and document their movements, tabulate how productive they were, discover where they made their nests. He found one aspect of their lives to be of particular interest, and this became the thing that he fixated on the most: aphid farming. Ants herded aphids in the exact same way that human beings herded cows and sheep.

Intrigued, Caleb collected specimens to study in his room. He made copious notes and drew numerous sketches. He did all the experiments he could think of to explain the strange relationship between ants and their aphid pets. Of course, it didn't take him long to realize that the ants had an ulterior motive for their aphid care and attention. Ants didn't simply herd aphids for fun, they herded aphids for milk! Just like humans milked cows, ants milked aphids.

More important, Caleb found that when this nutritious aphid milk was administered in high enough concentrations—something Caleb could easily create in the school lab—they became so addicted to the aphid milk concoction that he could basically make the ants do anything he wanted them to.

Thus began Caleb DeMarck's long-standing friendship with the ants, and it was through this relationship that Caleb discovered . . . *the machine.*

Caleb remembered the unusually warm day in March like it was yesterday.

Bored because it was a weekend and no one had asked him to join any of the Frisbee or touch football games outside on the school lawn, Caleb had followed the ants on an expedition into the school. For some reason, the ants ignored the cafeteria (which was their usual destination) and instead made their way through the building and downstairs into the gym. The swim team was preparing for the spring session, so the gym floor had been rolled away and the pool was empty, awaiting a good cleaning before it was refilled with water.

Caleb watched as, one by one, the ants marched down the side of the pool, across the pool floor, and into the shiny silver pool drain. Caleb had no idea where the ants were going, and he desperately wanted to find out, so he climbed into the empty pool after them.

He wasn't small like an ant, so he couldn't fit down the drain, but he had other skills . . . and one of those skills was using scientific reasoning to solve problems. He began pressing on the drain and then pulling on it where he could get a handhold. Suddenly without warning there was a loud *crunch* and the whole bottom of the pool began to descend.

Caleb stepped back away from the pit until he was sure that it was safe, and then he did what any other kid with a scientific mind would do: He followed the ants down into the hole.

Explanation: Part 2

And that's how I found the machine. I don't know *exactly* what it does, but from what I've seen, it appears to create electricity out of thin air."

Caleb DeMarck looked down at his hands. He knew now that what he had said was *very* wrong. The machine *didn't* create electricity out of air . . . it created electricity out of *ghosts*.

"I spent years trying to figure it out, but it wasn't until recently that I discovered this," the physics teacher said, pulling Noh's secret paper out of his pocket.

"That's mine!" Noh said, her hands on her hips.

The physics teacher shook his head.

"No, *this* is your paper," he said, pulling *another*, matching sheet out of his back pocket. "I found the first one in some old papers I checked out of the library. I knew that it didn't contain the whole equation, but it was enough to get the machine up and running."

"Then why did you need that paper?" Noh and Trina said at the same time, overlapping each other. Of course, the physics teacher only heard Noh's question.

"I needed the secret paper you found to calibrate the machine properly," Caleb DeMarck said. "I adjusted a few wires here and there, and this time when I turned it on, I didn't almost freeze myself to death."

Noh didn't doubt his answer one bit. She remembered how terribly cold it had gotten when Henry had been sucked into the orb.

"We have to reverse the machine," Noh said. "You've been using ghost souls to power it and that's not fair!"

Noh expected the physics teacher to agree with her immediately, but instead a stubborn look spread across his features.

"How do I know that what you say is *really* true?" he said, his voice high and reedy like a petulant child's. "I can't see the ghosts, so you might be making the whole thing up. Maybe if you *showed* me the ghosts . . ."

Noh couldn't believe what she was hearing.

It seemed that deep down inside, Caleb DeMarck was still that know-it-all boy who was blind to everything but what *he* wanted.

And what he wanted right now was to see a ghost.

Noh knew the physics teacher wasn't a bad person on purpose, he was just too self-absorbed to see that he was the cause of all the trouble around him. Still, she didn't *really* want him to know about her evil eye stone. Sharing her secret with him might be inviting more trouble than it was worth.

But, she supposed, if she wanted to get Henry and the others back, she was going to have to take the plunge and do it.

"Okay," Noh said, starting to formulate a plan in her mind. "I can make you see the ghosts, but you have to do exactly what I say. No questions asked."

Excited by the prospect, Caleb DeMarck gave Noh an enthusiastic nod. The physics teacher seemed ready to do whatever she asked of him—Noh just hoped she wasn't making the biggest mistake of her life.

The Plan Goes Awry

A nd so that's my plan," Noh finished. "I don't one hundred percent know if it will work, but I think it's worth a try." She had just explained to Trina and Caleb DeMarck how they might polarize the machine's flow of energy and create a reverse black hole, forcing everything inside the orb to come out the way it had gone in.

"Let's do it!" Trina said, ready for action as she floated beside Noh. The physics teacher nodded in agreement, even though he hadn't heard Trina's exclamation because she was still invisible to him.

Noh stuck her hand into her pocket and pulled out the evil eye stone. It felt heavier than usual in her hand. She hadn't actually mentioned the evil eye stone when she had explained her plan, figuring the less the physics teacher knew about her ghost-seeing abilities, the better. Now as he watched her expectantly she decided she wasn't quite ready to share her good luck charm with him just yet. She would wait until the last possible second before she would let him see any ghosts.

Happy with her decision, Noh gestured to Caleb DeMarck and he began to set her plan into motion. He took out the two pieces of matching paper, each covered with equations. Next he pulled both sets of wires out of the electrodes and switched them, so that the wires now crossed each other before going back into the base of the machine.

When the physics teacher gave her the thumbs-up, Noh flipped the switch on the machine. Instead of the room getting colder as it had before, it now started to get hotter and hotter until Noh thought she was going to melt.

"I think it's working," Trina said, and Noh could see that the heat was affecting her ghostly friend, too. Ripples of heat poured from Trina's ghostly essence, making Noh feel even hotter. She looked over at Caleb DeMarck and saw him wiping beads of sweat from his forehead. He gave her another thumbs-up.

Suddenly a flash of light filled the room, making Noh's vision swim with color. When she opened her eyes again, she saw the orb floating in the middle of the room, except now it wasn't glowing anymore. Instead it was the color of the midnight sky.

"Trina! You have to guide him out!" Noh screamed over the rush of air that was being expelled out of the orb. She had been right! Reversing the polarity had created an anti–black hole, sending out energy instead of sucking it in.

"Henry!" Trina called, her arms outstretched. "Follow my voice!"

To her surprise, it wasn't Henry who popped out of the orb but her friend Nelly, holding hands with Thomas!

The other ghosts quickly moved to Trina's side.

"Henry's in there too," Nelly said, her voice high and frightened. Trina thought it was the first time she had ever heard fear in Nelly's voice.

"Henry!" Nelly and Trina called together over the rushing air, their voices blending into one.

"There's not much time left!" Noh cried. She could feel the machine starting to tremble beside her. She was afraid that if she didn't pull the switch soon, it might explode.

"Henry!" Nelly and Trina called again, but still he didn't appear.

"Henry!" Noh cried. "Henry! There's no time!"

Noh let go of the switch and started to move toward the orb. Maybe if she could get close enough, she could make Henry hear her. . . .

She felt a strong hand clasp her shoulder, and she turned to see Caleb DeMarck standing beside her.

"I don't see any ghosts yet!" he shouted over the roar of the machine, his eyes dark with frustration.

"My friend needs my help first—," Noh began, but the words caught in her throat when she felt a surge of heat bloom inside her fist that was clutching the evil eye stone. The heat instantly shot up her arm, pooling at the place where the physics teacher's hand was grasping her shoulder. There was another flash of light, this time so bright it made Noh's eyes double blink, but not before she witnessed something shoot out from inside the orb, bypass her, and slam right into the physics teacher's chest, engulfing him in a pale, golden glow that slowly faded away into nothingness. Still gripping

Noh's arm, he made a funny, gurgling noise low in his throat and then lurched forward, almost causing her to lose her balance.

"Mr. DeMarck!" Noh cried, steadying herself against the wall. It took all her strength to keep them both from being flung backward by the flow of energy the darkened orb was expelling.

The machine let out a loud hiss, and Noh realized that one of the circuits had blown. Now the machine started to tremble even harder, its metallic body clanging so loudly the sound hurt Noh's ears.

"Who are you?" the physics teacher asked, his voice groggy as if he'd just woken up. Noh looked over at him, surprised at his question, but before she could answer, the physics teacher's eyes popped wide open and he pointed at something behind Noh's head. She followed his gaze to where Trina, Nelly, and Thomas were huddled together by the base of the machine. "Two little girls, a boy in a cap . . . and an orb, pitch-black in color. Am I right?" he asked.

"That's right," Noh said, the heat from the stone coursing up her arm. She realized that she was acting as some kind of human conduit. As long as Caleb DeMarck was touching her—and through her the evil eye stone—he was able to see the ghosts.

"Are they . . . *real*?" the physics teacher asked, his voice full of amazement.

Noh nodded, but her attention was quickly pulled back to Henry's plight. "We have to help my friend," Noh said, looking over at the trembling machine. Caleb DeMarck nodded at her words.

Noh knew time was of the essence. She had to get Henry out before the machine exploded. She swallowed hard and took a tentative step forward, ready to call Henry's name again, but before she could go farther, she felt the physics teacher's hand grip her shoulder.

"Let *me* try," he said, pulling her back from the orb. "You're too little. You won't be able to get close enough without being blown away. And the way this machine is behaving, we might only have this one chance."

Noh didn't trust the physics teacher one little bit, but what he said made sense. The orb was sending out so much energy that she could barely stand, let alone fight her way inside it.

Without waiting for an answer, Caleb DeMarck released her arm and began to make his way toward the pitch-black orb. Then Noh remembered that the physics teacher wouldn't be able to see Henry without the stone. She had to give it to him now before it was too late!

She opened her mouth to yell at him to wait, but a dark and slimy thought twisted around inside her head, making her hesitate. It hissed at her, reminding her that if she gave Caleb DeMarck the stone, she might never get it back from him once he understood its power—and that meant she would turn back into a normal girl again, without the special ability to see her new ghost friends.

With a sinking heart, Noh realized this was the hardest decision she had ever been asked to make: She could either save Henry or keep her ghost sight, but she couldn't do both.

The Truth Hits Hard

Wait!" Noh cried, causing the physics teacher to stop in his tracks.

She took a deep breath and stuffed the evil eye stone into Caleb DeMarck's hand. He seemed surprised as his fingers closed over its warmth.

"Are you sure . . . ?" he asked.

"It's how I can see the ghosts," she said.

The physics teacher instantly understood.

"Thank you, my dear. I wouldn't have stood a chance in there without this."

Noh was surprised by the physics teacher's choice of words. Until now he had never called her "my dear," but before she could linger on what this new twist might mean, the machine gave another horrific shudder.

"Just save my friend Henry, please," Noh said, smiling weakly.

Caleb DeMarck nodded.

"If I get stuck inside and can't get back out, pull the lever before the machine explodes," he said as he turned back toward the orb. "It's the only safe way. Promise?"

"Promise," Noh forced herself to reply. She would say it, but that didn't mean she would do it.

Noh felt empty as she watched him go. She had just given away the one thing that made her special. She wanted to cry, but tears would do nothing to get the evil eye stone back. She only hoped her sacrifice had been made in time to save her ghostly friend.

"Henry, my boy?!" Caleb DeMarck yelled. His voice was louder than hers, loud enough to be heard over the rush of energy from the orb.

Suddenly Noh felt a sharp yank on her arm, like she was being pulled forward. She realized that the heat in her arm wasn't dissipating like she had expected, but instead was only getting hotter. It seemed that the closer Caleb DeMarck got to the orb, the more Noh felt the pull on her arm. It was like she was somehow connected to the evil eye stone by an invisible cord of energy, so that wherever it went, part of her went with it.

Transfixed, Noh watched as Caleb DeMarck took a few more steps, getting as close as possible to the orb without actually going inside it. The force of the energy surrounding the thing was so intense that it almost blew the physics teacher off his feet, but he held his ground.

"Son?!" he called. "Can you hear me?"

Still there was no answer. He reached his hands into the heart of the blackened, swirling energy ball. Noh felt the heat in her arm intensify, making her cringe a little from the pain.

"I think I can see him," the physics teacher called. "I'm going in!"

Before Noh understood what he intended, he had disappeared inside the pulsing orb. As soon as he crossed the threshold Noh's arm began to burn like wildfire, forcing her to grit her jaw against the burning ache. She closed her eyes, hoping to make the pain go away, but instead it only got worse with every passing second.

The machine began to shimmy and shake next to her, but Noh's arm hurt too much for her to take any notice.

"Noh, the machine!" Trina cried. "It's smoking!"

Trina's words caught at the edge of Noh's consciousness, and she looked up to find bright orange flames licking the side of the machine. Distracted from her pain by this new dilemma, her brain spun around like a hamster wheel. She could usually figure anything out if she thought hard enough about it, but this problem only had one very impossible answer.

"Pull the lever, Noh!" Trina yelled, leaving Nelly and Thomas cowering on the floor to float over to where Noh stood. That was the exact impossible answer that Noh had been afraid of.

"I know I promised, but I can't," Noh said angrily, tears pricking her eyes. "If I do, they might never be able to come back again!"

Without realizing it, she had made a decision—and there was no going back. She was Henry's friend, and friends didn't leave each other behind at the first sign of trouble.

"We're staying too, then," Trina said with a nervous smile, and Nelly and Thomas nodded their agreement.

"Friends stick together," Nelly said, her voice barely loud enough for Noh to hear, but it was like getting a shot of feel-good juice. It was hard to believe that she

had come to New Newbridge with no friends and in only two days she had made four new wonderful ones. If she hadn't been in such a dire situation, Noh would have said it was the most incredible two days of her entire life.

Right before her eyes, the whole machine was being engulfed in flames. Noh could see them licking around the edges of the machine's metal body. Smoke poured out the top of it, making Noh's eyes water and her throat burn. She tried to cover her face with her shirt to keep the smoke out, but it didn't help one bit.

She thought about her dad and her aunt and how sad they would be when they discovered she'd disappeared. She knew they'd think that she was upset about having to go to New Newbridge and that she had run away to spite them. They would have no way to discover the truth. She doubted anyone else knew about this secret place, so no one would ever think to look for her here. Besides, she'd be a ghost just like Trina and Henry by then, so it wouldn't matter anyway.

Until that moment, Noh had never realized how much she loved her family. Now she felt that love like a fist around her heart, squeezing the muscle so hard her chest ached. Tears pricked her eyes, but she fought against them. If she was going to die and become a ghost, then she was determined not to cry about it: Worse things could and might happen to her than just becoming like her friends.

"Henry!" Trina and Nelly cried in unison, and Noh looked up to find Caleb DeMarck's head re-emerging from within the swirl of the orb.

"Mr. DeMarck!" Noh said as she watched him extricate himself from the pull of the swirling energy, a near comatose Henry in his arms.

Suddenly a loud bell-clang, signaling the ignition of the school's fire alarm, filled the air, and a shower of cold water burst from the sprinklers in the ceiling, instantly putting out the flames that had been threatening to consume the room.

The burning ache in Noh's arm fizzled to a more manageable level, and she sighed with relief, tears of pain and happiness sliding down her already wet cheeks. She ignored the bites on her legs as the ant venom began to make them itch like crazy, everything forgotten in the wake of seeing her ghostly friend in one piece again.

But wait, Noh thought as she peered through the

208

droplets of water cascading from the ceiling, *that can't be right.* There was something strange about Henry. Something she couldn't, at first, put her finger on—and then it dawned on Noh what that something strange was: *Henry wasn't a ghost anymore—he was physically solid!*

Suddenly she understood *exactly* what Eustant P. Druthers had been doing when he had built the mysterious machine: He had been trying to make ghosts real again. Electricity was just the unforeseen by-product of an even more ingenious invention!

With the answer to the machine's true purpose excitedly swimming around in her brain, Noh threw the switch on the machine. Instantly the orb disappeared and Henry became ghostly again, the machine's power no longer exerting a hold over him. He floated down through Caleb DeMarck's solid, living arms just as the machine let out a low growl, spit out a plume of thick gray smoke, and whined to a stop.

As suddenly as the fire alarm had started, it stopped, and the sprinklers slowed down to a trickle. They all stood in silence, waiting for the machine to do something else, but it seemed to be finished. Trina, who was never at a loss for words, spoke first.

"Well, that wasn't *so* bad—," she began brightly, but before she could continue her thought, the lightbulb above their heads unexpectedly fell to the floor and exploded into a million pieces, flooding the room in darkness.

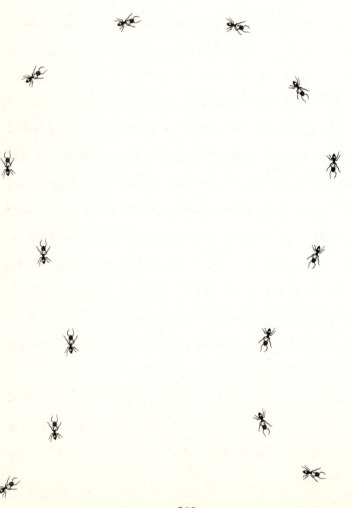

Scary Trouble

The nasty thing that still refuses to be named had been waiting for a long time. It had tasted something *big* once upon a time, and now it was hungry for more.

It had followed the teacher (and the ants) and the two girls (one alive, one dead) down into the hidden room, but it hadn't shown its hand. It had waited patiently while the machine had tried to suck up the ghost's soul, and it waited even more patiently as the machine—rewired now—had *released* the three other ghost souls it had originally sucked up.

It had waited as the teacher—who wasn't what he appeared to be, the nasty thing knew for a fact—pulled the ghost boy to safety, and it had waited as the lightbulb,

the only source of illumination in the room, had shat-
tered into a million pieces on the floor.

Then, with the room in complete darkness, the nasty
thing made its move.

Noh Indigestion

T rina? Is that you?" Noh said, feeling something brush against her shoulder. She whirled around, thrusting her hands out before her, searching for the someone or something that might explain the horrible feeling she was having deep in the pit of her stomach.

It might've been dark in the secret room, but a little darkness had never scared Noh before. What scared Noh now was the terrible sense that something large and scary was trying to swallow her whole. She flung her hands frantically into the air, pushing the bad feeling away, but the more she struggled, the more the feeling took over even more of her body.

She tried to call out for help, but her throat didn't

seem to be working. She wanted to cry, but her tear ducts didn't seem to be working either. She was having trouble breathing, and her body was beginning to feel like it was weighted down with lead.

Then, as quickly as the feeling had overcome her, it got *worse.*

"Help me!" Noh screamed, the darkness increasing her fear. Suddenly she wasn't standing anymore. Instead, she was free-falling through black emptiness, her stomach halfway to her throat, just the way it felt when she was on a roller coaster at the fair. She opened her eyes, but there was only blackness as she continued to fall farther and farther into nothingness.

As she flew through the nothingness Noh had an idea. She reached around in her pocket, her fingers struggling to grasp the smooth surface of the evil eye stone—but then she remembered that it was gone. She had given it to Caleb DeMarck to save Henry.

Help me, she thought, wishing as hard as she could on the evil eye stone that was no longer hers. *Somebody help me!*

Then, abruptly, the free-falling stopped and Noh felt herself suspended in the air, floating. She looked around her, but the only thing she could see was a tiny white light shooting toward her. The closer it got, the larger it got until Noh was able to see that it wasn't a light at all . . . *but a boy.*

"Who are you?" Noh asked, even though she didn't need to. She knew exactly who he was.

The boy didn't reply. He just looked at her with his sad blue eyes, then looked down to where he was holding out his hand for her to take. And that's when she noticed it: *four missing fingers displayed for all to see.*

"Hubert?"

The boy looked up at her and grinned, surprised that she knew his name. Noh realized that he looked exactly how she'd imagined he would look: short blond hair; wide, sad blue eyes; and a cute turned-up nose.

"Where are we?" she asked, but Hubert wouldn't or *couldn't* tell her. Instead, he offered her his hand again, and this time she took it. Instantly she felt her body being pulled up, up, up, and away from the darkness.

As she let the ghost boy guide her toward what she hoped was safety Noh realized something important—something that made her heart sing with joy: She could see Hubert—and she didn't need the evil eye stone's help to do it!

Why Ants Aren't King

Trina and Nelly saw the nasty thing attack Noh. Thomas, scared completely out of his wits, covered his eyes with his cap. Henry was still out like a light, but neither of the girls would have expected him to be of much help even if he *had* been awake.

The nasty thing was huge—the size of a small elephant, with large saber-tooth tiger teeth and great big furry arms that had wrapped themselves around its unsuspecting victim. Unlike Noh and the physics teacher, Trina and Nelly didn't need the lightbulb hanging from the ceiling to see what was going on around them, but they were both so shocked by the sight of the nasty thing trying to eat their friend that it took them a moment to understand what needed doing.

"Something's attacking Noh," Trina cried, but just as the words left her mouth, the nasty thing swallowed Noh whole. "Oh no, it just ate her!"

The nasty thing, its face a corpulent mass of squirming darkness, turned toward Trina and smiled horribly at her, revealing sharp gray teeth and a slavering red tongue.

"The ants!" Nelly said, her voice full of authority. "They can help us."

Trina raced over to the physics teacher and tried to shake him into action, but her ghostly hands slid right through his shoulders.

"How do you make the ants work?" she almost screamed. The nasty thing was slowly moving toward them, its tongue lolling out of its mouth like a big red slug. It watched them with a nasty look on its face, like it wanted to eat all of them whole too.

"I don't know what you mean," the physics teacher said, looking truly mystified by her question.

"Your pockets," Trina yelled. "It's in your pockets! Please, hurry!"

Caleb DeMarck wrinkled his brow, uncertainty flooding his face, but he did as Trina asked, sinking his hands into his pockets.

"My goodness," he said, "you were right!" He held up a handful of the fluffy white stuff, a big smile transforming his face. "Tell me what to do, because I can't see a thing!" he said, getting into the swing of things.

"The monster's at two o'clock," Nelly cried. "Throw it there!"

The physics teacher let loose with the white stuff. It landed almost at the nasty thing's feet. The ants went crazy, squirming all over one another to get to the stuff first, but they didn't stop there. They instantly sensed that there was more for them to feast on than just concentrated aphid milk. They began to climb up the nasty thing, covering it with bites as they tried to make it their evening snack.

The nasty thing let out a gargantuan roar and began to swing its body back and forth like a dog trying to shake the water out of its fur after a bath. It stamped its feet like thunder as it reeled around the room, its steps grinding into the floor and shaking the whole place like an earthquake.

"It's working!" Trina cried, dizzy with happiness, but the happiness didn't last very long.

The ant bites might have made a human girl like

Noh itch with pain, but the nasty thing was anything but a human girl. It continued to hold Noh captive inside its big belly while the ants swarmed all over its furry body, biting away with every ounce of energy they had inside them.

"Noh!" Trina screamed, fear for her friend's safety making her ghostly form shimmer in the darkness.

But it was too late. The ants had failed, and now her friend Noh was going to be the nasty thing's lunch.

Hubert Was Here

Noh opened her eyes to find herself sitting in a familiar place: the special spot by the lake Hullie had shown her earlier in the afternoon. Of course, now that the light had fled for the day and evening was upon them, the woods seemed a whole lot more ominous than they had back then.

The place gave Noh an icky feeling down in the pit of her stomach, but she tried to ignore it so she could focus on more important things.

Like getting back into her body.

She had realized her precarious position almost immediately. Hubert might've saved her spirit, but he'd left her body to molder away inside the monster that had swallowed her. Now all she could do was watch as the wind danced through the canopy of trees above her, scattering a few errant leaves to the ground. It was very disheartening to see the wind blowing around you but not be able to feel it. It made Noh's heart sting to think about never hugging her dad or eating a bowl of yummy tomato soup again.

"You don't like it here?" Noh heard Hubert say, and she turned at the sound of his voice to find him sitting in the grass across from her, picking at the clover, head lowered so she couldn't see his eyes.

"I don't *not* like it," Noh offered. It was the best she could do. If she said anything of a more positive nature, it would be a lie, and she did *not* want to be a liar. To keep herself safe, she decided to change the subject instead. "Why are we here?"

Hubert shrugged. "I dunno. I like it here, and it's safe from prying eyes."

Noh had to agree with him. It *was* safe from prying eyes, but only because it was so creepy at night that she couldn't imagine anyone else wanting to bother with it.

"I appreciate you helping me," Noh continued, "but I really need to get back to my friends before they start worrying about me."

Hubert looked up at her now, his eyes shining, and Noh thought he looked like the saddest boy she had ever seen.

"You don't want to stay here with me?" he asked, wrinkling his brow.

Noh shook her head. "I'm not a ghost yet, so I don't think I'm really allowed."

"But if I don't take you back, then the whatsit will finish eating you, and then you can stay with me forever," Hubert said plainly. "You can be my friend."

Noh realized that if she didn't step in and take charge right then, Hubert might make the choice for her, sealing her fate forever. She could see he was a very lonely ghost, but she didn't think sacrificing herself to make him happy was a smart decision. She knew from experience that the only person you could ever make happy was yourself.

"What if I promise to come visit you every week while I'm here at New Newbridge?" Noh offered. "I could be your alive friend—and that's way better than being a ghost friend."

She could see Hubert thinking about her suggestion, weighing it in his mind.

"Why is it better?"

Noh had her answer down pat.

"It's better because an alive friend can go anywhere and do anything. They aren't stuck in one place like ghosts are. I can be your spy and tell you about all the things that are happening in the world outside of New Newbridge Academy."

Instantly Hubert's face lit up, and he grinned at her.

"You'd do that? You'd be my secret spy?"

Noh nodded.

"And you wouldn't tell anyone about me," Hubert added, the light in his eyes fading a bit as he spoke.

"Not if you don't want me to," Noh agreed, "but I know for a fact that there are a lot of other ghosts at New Newbridge who would love to meet you."

Hubert shook his head vigorously. "Only you know about me, and I want to keep it that way," he said.

Noh didn't argue with him. If he wanted to keep himself hidden away out here by the lake, she wasn't going to rat him out.

"Okay, it's a deal then," Noh said, holding out her hand for Hubert to shake. He reached out to grasp her fingers, but as soon as they touched, she felt a funny prickling sensation all over her body like she'd been plunged into a freezing cold shower.

"Don't forget your promise," Hubert said softly.

And then Noh disappeared.

The Evil Eye Stone

It was still black as night inside the hidden room, so the physics teacher, who couldn't see in the dark, didn't know that the ants had not succeeded. Instead, the man who had once been Caleb DeMarck—but was now someone else entirely—was much more interested in the hot, uncomfortable sensation he was feeling in his right hand—the one that was still clutching the girl's magic stone!

He knew exactly what the stone was and what it wanted from him—and that was because he had helped to create the stone in the first place!

Release me! the stone sang in his head. *Let me fly and save the girl! The ants have failed!*

"Of course, my friend," the man who had once been

Caleb DeMarck whispered to the stone. "But first, I want to see the beast in its true form."

It only took the stone a moment to understand what the man wanted, but when it did the darkness immediately lifted away from the former physics teacher's eyes like a curtain, and he could see the nasty thing in all its glory.

He had never seen anything as strange or ugly as the monster standing in front of him, and he almost yelped in fear. The nasty thing caught him staring, and it hissed at him like an angry house cat.

The nasty thing, which was really nothing more than an accumulation of all the fears of all the children who had ever attended New Newbridge Academy, had spent its whole life hiding away from prying eyes, lingering on the edges of where the living world and the dead world connected, and it was wholly unprepared for the fear it felt at being seen by a real live grown-up human being.

The evil eye stone sensed the nasty thing's terror and began to grow even hotter. The former Caleb DeMarck let the stone sizzle in his hand, the pain a reminder that he was human again after all these years.

Throw me! the stone cried in his head. *Let me fly! Let me save my new friend!*

This time, the words were like a magic spell. They weaved themselves inside the former physics teacher's brain, and with a twinkle in his eye, he wound up his arm, took a step forward, and threw the most perfect fastball the world would never see, shooting the evil eye stone right into the nasty thing's mouth.

The nasty thing yowled with anger and pain as the evil eye stone burned the insides of its gullet. When the stone reached the nasty thing's stomach, it made a loud popping sound and the nasty thing howled in frustration. Eating something big wasn't supposed to be *this* much trouble!

The nasty thing unhappily realized that it was no match for a magical stone that so badly wanted to be back with its mistress. It let go of its hold on Noh, and with its tail between its legs, it scurried out of the hidden room as fast as it could go, shrinking itself to the size of a flea as it made its way out of the building.

Noh blinked, surprised to find herself standing in the middle of the hidden room, holding the evil eye stone tightly in her hand. In the darkness she reached out for Hubert, but she couldn't find him anywhere.

"Hubert?" Noh said weakly, but there was no answer.

Her savior was gone.

"Where did Hubert go . . . ?" she started to say, but then words failed her. The weight of all the crazy things that had happened to Noh since she'd arrived at New Newbridge began to sink in, and she fainted dead away just as a loud banging sound trickled down through the ceiling.

With a discreet *click*, the secret doorway opened to reveal first Hullie, whose bushy hair shone like a halo around his head, and then a tidy young woman who could only be Noh's aunt Sarah, peering into the secret room with only a flashlight to illuminate the darkness.

"Thank goodness I replaced those old sprinkler heads when I did," Hullie said as he shone the beam of his flashlight down onto the charred wreckage of the machine. "It could've gotten pretty hot down here, otherwise."

He moved the light away from the machine, letting it slide across the floor and over to the spot where Noh's unconscious form lay. The man who had once been Caleb DeMarck was kneeling on the ground beside her, looking very worried.

Following the beam of the flashlight, Aunt Sarah scampered into the secret room and crouched down beside her unconscious niece. Hullie was fast on her heels, pulling a brand-spanking-new lightbulb from his pocket at the same time.

"Thank you so much for looking after her, Caleb," Aunt Sarah said, smiling up at the former Caleb DeMarck. She might've acted differently had she known the man before her wasn't the *real* physics teacher anymore, but she didn't, so gratitude was all he got.

"She was very brave," the former physics teacher managed to say before looking down at his hands so no one would see the scarlet blush creeping up his cheeks.

Luckily, Aunt Sarah didn't notice his embarrassment because she was too involved in her own thoughts.

"Oh, Hullie, I know it's important to let her find her own way, but what if something truly terrible had happened," she said, her voice thick with worry.

Hullie finished putting the new bulb in place, then turned the light back on, letting a warm glow expose the mess that was once the secret room.

"You know the rules, Sarah," he said, popping a fresh toothpick into his mouth as he moved to stand beside her, placing a reassuring arm on her shoulder. "No interference, unless it's specifically asked for."

Aunt Sarah nodded, but it was apparent she didn't wholly agree with his words.

"Besides," Hullie added, giving her a wink, "that's why I keep both my eyes wide open. So creatures like that old *nasty thing* don't get too out of hand at New Newbridge Academy."

And with that, Hullie reached down and picked Noh up, lifting her over his shoulder as if she was the lightest thing in the world.

"Let's get this girl cleaned up and off to bed before she catches cold," he continued, making his way back to the secret door with Aunt Sarah right behind him.

Trina and Nelly watched silently as the procession of realies left the room. To their surprise, (the former) Caleb DeMarck stopped in the doorway and gave them a small wave good-bye. He couldn't see them anymore, but somehow it didn't matter. In his heart he knew they were there, waving good-bye to him in return.

It's All in the Soup

Noh sat up in bed with a tray of tomato soup and grilled cheese sandwich squares resting gently on her lap. The tomato soup was better than amazing, Noh decided as she took another spoonful. It had just the right amount of cream in it so that it wasn't too tomatoey. She picked up one of the grilled cheese squares—it was made with a hefty amount of American cheese and toasted white bread, no crusts—and took a gigantic bite.

"Yummy," Noh said to herself after she'd swallowed the bite.

There was a knock on her

door, and Noh sat up straighter, almost spilling her soup.

"Come in!" she called, but just exerting that amount of energy wiped her out. Whatever nasty creature had attacked her, it had succeeded in stealing a good chunk of her energy. She figured she was gonna need at least two weeks—and lots of good, hearty food—to recuperate, and by then summer would almost be over. Just a few more weeks and she'd be in the library studying for tests, not chasing after secret papers and solving mysterious occurrences . . . and nearly getting eaten by hungry monsters.

Of course, everyone *else* believed that there'd been a freak electrical fire down in the basement and that, luckily, the physics teacher had been passing by and had smelled the smoke and rushed in to save her.

Noh figured maybe that was for the best. She didn't want to frighten anyone by letting out the fact that monsters and ghosts existed at New Newbridge—at least until she could figure out what to do about the monster part.

The door opened and her aunt Sarah, followed by a sheepish-looking Caleb DeMarck, came into the room.

"I hope you don't mind company, but Mr. DeMarck

wanted to say good-bye before he left," her aunt said as she pulled the chair out from underneath Noh's desk and moved it closer to the bed.

"Good-bye?" Noh said, looking up at the physics teacher, who indeed was wearing a traveling coat and a gray fedora. He also had a large briefcase under his arm, which he set on the floor beside the chair before sitting down. It had been almost twenty-four hours since the attack—most of which Noh had spent in a dark and dreamless sleep that the town physician said was likely due to the shock she had suffered from so many ant bites—but Caleb DeMarck looked like a different person.

Gone was the know-it-all boy, and in his place was what seemed like a wiser, more thoughtful man. Noh watched as her aunt Sarah gently shut the door on her way out, giving them a bit of privacy.

"Yes, I'm afraid that I have to go away on a very important mission," he said, taking off his hat and placing it in his lap so he could play with its brim as he spoke. "But I wanted to share something with you before I left."

Noh nodded.

"You see, I am not who I appear to be," he began.

This made Noh sit up straighter in her bed, the soup almost spilling into her lap.

"When you reversed the polarity on the Matter Re-Former—"

"Is that what the machine's called?" Noh asked, curiosity getting the better of her.

He nodded. "Yes, that is its given name. Sadly, I cannot take credit for its name *or* its design because I am not the machine's inventor," he continued. "That title belongs to my mentor, Professor Eustant P. Druthers."

It only took Noh a moment to remember where she had heard that name before.

"Wasn't he the man who built this school?" she said, her brain sizzling with this new piece of information.

The former physics teacher nodded.

"So, if you're not Caleb DeMarck, then who are you?" Noh asked, this time actually knocking some of her soup onto the bedcover in her excitement.

The man looked down at his hands as if he were deciding how much information to divulge. Finally, having made his decision, he looked back up at Noh and smiled. "On pain of death you must never tell anyone what I am about to tell you," he said.

Noh nodded so hard it hurt. "I promise."

The former physics teacher nervously scratched his chin and then began. "My real name is Karl Freund. I was once a student here at the New Newbridge Academy, but when Professor Druthers realized my talent for inventing, he took me on as one of his five assistants."

"Wow!" Noh said, loving Karl Freund's story immediately.

"Yes," he said, becoming bashful, "it was amazing for me. All the incredible inventions I imagined in my brain were given life under Professor Druthers's tutelage. I spent years honing my talent for scientific invention under his watchful eye while we built many machines together, and I even had a hand in the creation of the Power Magnifier you carry with you—"

"The Power Magnifier?" Noh repeated. "Wait, do you mean my evil eye stone?"

Karl Freund nodded, pleased she had made the connection so quickly. "The Power Magnifier takes on whatever special power it is exposed to, magnifying it a hundredfold. It is a very useful tool," Karl added, "so long as it does not fall into the wrong hands."

His words made Noh shiver.

"It bestows the last power it has magnified on the next person who possesses it—even those who would use it for evil."

Noh swallowed hard.

"Yes, my dear, it is *you* who are gifted with the ability to see and interact with the dead—and the stone only magnified your power," Karl said gravely. "I was able to view your ghostly friends while I held the stone, and so now I, too, know your secret. You must be very careful with whom you share this information. There are many, like the dastardly Caleb DeMarck, who would steal your gift and use it to further their own means."

"He *was* pretty dastardly, wasn't he?" Noh whispered.

"Yes, he is," Karl agreed.

"Wait, you just used the present tense," Noh wondered out loud. No sooner had the words flown from her lips than she realized what this might mean: Caleb DeMarck was still here among them!

"I know what I am about to tell you will seem highly improbable, but it is the truth," Karl Freund said.

"After all the strange things I've seen over the past few days, I'd pretty much believe anything," Noh said.

This seemed to give Karl Freund more confidence.

"Caleb DeMarck and I share the same body—"

"Wow," was all Noh could manage.

"Even now he seethes because he is trapped in here with me and cannot steal the Power Magnifier," Karl Freund added. "For now, I can control him, but not forever. That is why I must go and find one of Professor Druthers's other assistants—wherever they may be after all these years—so that I might be cured of this strange and unsettling dilemma."

His story finished, Karl Freund got up and put his fedora back on his head.

"Well, at least we are safe from Mr. DeMarck for now—and I am very pleased that you are feeling better," he continued. He tipped his hat and moved toward the door. "You gave your poor aunt a horrible scare. I am afraid she will be watching you like a hawk for a long while to come," he added, his hand on the doorknob.

"Wait!" Noh cried, stopping him. "You never said how you got in the machine in the first place."

Karl Freund gave her a pleased grin as he stepped away from the door. "A freak accident. We were testing the Matter Re-Former and something went wrong. I was sucked into the machine and remained there, frozen in time, until you rescued me from my prison. Upon my release, my spirit attached itself to the first body it came in contact with: your physics teacher."

As crazy as the whole thing might sound to someone else, it made perfect sense to Noh.

"But how come no one ever tried to get you back?" Noh asked, concerned.

Karl Freund shook his head sadly. "That I do not know—"

"But how long were you trapped in the machine?" Noh interrupted, trying to get all the facts.

Karl Freund thought about this question for a moment before answering. "The year was 1951 . . . and I was seventeen."

Noh quickly did the math in her head, the number causing her to cringe inside.

"It was a very long time to be left alone. And I hope, in my travels, to discover why it was so," Karl Freund said as he picked up his briefcase again and returned to the door. He stopped in the doorway and turned back around, pulling a folder from the briefcase and handing it to Noh.

"Until we meet again, Noleen Maypother."

Then he tipped his hat to Noh one final time, opened the door, and was gone.

"He's like a different person," her aunt Sarah said as she came back into the room, marveling at the change in her coworker. "I bet you didn't know that Mr. DeMarck and I went to school together—"

Noh almost toppled her tray onto the floor.

"*You* went to New Newbridge?" she said, staring at her aunt.

"Of course I did," her aunt said. "On scholarship, mind you."

"No one ever told me that," Noh said. She couldn't believe that she hadn't known her aunt had gone to school here. It was weird, like finding out that your parents weren't your parents, or something.

"New Newbridge has always had a place in its heart for *special* children," her aunt began. "In fact, it seems to call to them, inviting them to learn and explore their talents here."

"What do you mean by the word 'special'?" Noh asked curiously.

"I think you know exactly what I mean, Noh.

You're a scholarship student like I was," her aunt said mysteriously. "That means New Newbridge called you here—and it's why the evil eye stone found you. Special things are attracted to special people."

Noh asked her aunt Sarah to explain more, but her aunt shook her head.

"You need to rest now. I'll be back later to check on you." That was all her aunt would say. Noh nodded, closing her eyes to show that she wanted to get some rest too. Her aunt gave her a kiss on the forehead and gently shut the door behind her on the way out.

Noh waited until she couldn't hear her aunt's footsteps in the hall anymore, and then she opened her eyes and slid open the folder that Karl Freund had given her.

"What's that?" Trina said, popping up beside the bed, her riding helmet askew on her head. She'd been in the middle of refereeing a chess game between Henry and Thomas when she had remembered that she'd promised to check on Noh.

"Look," Noh said as she held up the two secret lemon-inked papers covered in spidery equations.

"I wonder how many other secret papers are hidden in the school," Trina said.

Noh shrugged, her eyes finding the evil eye stone where it was sitting in a place of honor on her dresser top. Just knowing the stone was nearby made her feel stronger and braver . . . ready to take on as many mysteries as the world saw fit to throw her way. The evil eye stone wasn't the key to Noh's ghost sight, it only enhanced it.

"I know another secret place," Trina offered. "Behind the mirrors in the girls' bathroom. I bet there's lots of cool stuff there."

"Yeah?" Noh said, thinking about her toothbrush that got stuck in the bathroom mirror.

"It's pretty neat," Trina said. "I can show you, if you want."

Noh didn't have to think twice about her answer.

"Count me in, but first, let's find the nasty thing that tried to eat me," she said. "The other students will be coming back to New Newbridge really soon, and we can't let it hurt anyone else!"

"Deal!" Trina said, excited by the idea of another adventure coming so soon after their first. Without thinking, she held up her pinkie so they could pinkie swear and seal the deal, but it wasn't until Noh grinned sheepishly at her that Trina remembered her friend was a realie—and realies and ghosts couldn't touch.

"Deal," Noh replied instead. And then the two girls—one a ghost and the other living—hunkered down and began to make their plans.

My Singing Teachers

MY
SINGING
TEACHERS

MEL TORMÉ

■ ■ ■

New York   Oxford
OXFORD UNIVERSITY PRESS
1994

Oxford University Press

Oxford   New York   Toronto
Delhi   Bombay   Calcutta   Madras   Karachi
Kuala Lumpur   Singapore   Hong Kong   Tokyo
Nairobi   Dar es Salaam   Cape Town
Melbourne   Auckland

and associated companies in
Berlin   Ibadan

Published by Oxford University Press, Inc.,
200 Madison Avenue, New York, New York 10016

Oxford is a registered trademark of Oxford University Press

Library of Congress Cataloging-in-Publication Data
Tormé, Mel, 1925–
My singing teachers / Mel Tormé.
p.   cm   Includes index.
ISBN 0-19-509095-0
1. Tormé, Mel, 1925- —Knowledge—Singing.
2. Tormé, Mel, 1925- —Views on singing.
3. Singers—United States—Biography.
4. Singing teachers.
I. Title.
ML420. T69A3   1994   782.42164'092'2—dc20   93-42408

9 8 7 6 5 4 3 2 1

Printed in the United States of America
on acid-free paper

■
―――――

Preface

It was one of Sinatra's biggest hits, and as the last stanza came through—

> *For what is a man, what has he got?*
> *If not himself, then he has not*
> *To say the things he truly feels*
> *And not the words of one who kneels*
> *The record shows I took the blows*
> *And did it my way—*

you couldn't help but notice that art was imitating life. Frank, with his three "c's" in place (consistency, concentration, credibility), was singing about the way he did it, and who could fault him?

Sinatra, a true original, seemed to have no role model. Singers who came before him seemed to have had

no effect on his work. It was as if he held the patent, the
original blueprint on singing the popular song, a man who
would have thousands of imitators but who, himself,
would never stoop to draw from or be influenced by a single solitary person. It has been written that he learned a
lot from the megaphoned mewlings of (wait for it) Rudy
Vallee! I can't hear it. For me, there was Bing, a true original in his own right, and then Frank Sinatra's easy delivery, his sense of the lyric, his phrasing, his intonation,
and, most especially, his role as "everyman," a singer
whose style touched a chord in the broadest part of the
American psyche. He was the ultimate balladeer, and
there is no tracing his roots.

   Now I, on the other hand, had role models almost too
numerous to mention. They came from all walks of the
entertainment business: band singers, bandleaders, movie
performers, instrumentalists, vocal group members, songwriters—well, like I said, the list is almost endless. From
my very beginnings, people from every walk of the music
business affected me, molded me, and, inadvertently,
taught me what there was to know about performing,
phrasing, breath control, singing in tune, enunciation, and
all the elements essential in becoming a successful singer.
There isn't enough space to properly thank all of them,
but, here and now, I'll take a shot at it.

Acknowledgments

I would like to thank my wife, Ali Tormé, for "sticking with" the long, lonely nights of writing and researching this project.

Plus my manager, Dale Sheets, my children, and various friends and family members who saw me through this undertaking with encouragement and suggestions.

Finally, a tip of my hat to Oxford University Press for their interest, input, and insight in the editing and publishing of this book.

Contents

My Singing Teachers

BESSIE ——————
AND CONNEE

■ ■ ■

It began with Bessie Smith.

My father and his two brothers were enthusiastic (make that "obsessive") moviegoers. In the early Thirties, the South Side of Chicago was liberally sprinkled with picture palaces of every size, shape, and description. The tony Avalon with its Moorish architecture, the big, brassy Tivoli at 63rd and Cottage Grove, the Stratford, the Capitol, the Art Deco Southtown complete with multi-fountains. And the smaller "nabes": the Jeffrey, the Picadilly, the Frolic, the Vista, the Ray, the Shore, and the Oakland.

One fine spring evening in 1930, my father and my uncles, Art and Al, took me to the Oakland, located at 39th and Drexel, to see a cowboy picture. Prior to the feature film, a fifteen-minute short unfolded. It was called

"The St. Louis Blues." The musical director was W. C. Handy himself. He was also listed as having led the choir. The orchestra came under the baton of James P. Johnson, although the personnel was actually a large part of the Fletcher Henderson band.

What made this little film memorable was the appearance of a woman, dressed inconspicuously in what looked like hand-me-downs, standing at the bar of this "colored" club, singing her heart out about hating to see the evening sun go down, " 'cause her baby done left this town."

The woman was Bessie Smith in her only film appearance. And her vocal performance was filled with all the frustrations, the sorrow, and the weariness of her people and their lot in life. How did I know how marvelous her rendition of this classic song was? I didn't. I was five years old, and even though I had broken into show business the previous year, singing downtown at the Blackhawk restaurant with the Coon-Sanders orchestra, the short subject in question was merely a preamble to the Western that followed, as far as I was concerned.

"The St. Louis Blues" is really a mini-movie. Bessie plays a betrayed woman, whose man, "Jim," is messing around with another girl. Bessie wrestles with this girl in the room she shares with Jim; the girl leaves, and so does Jim. Now Bessie is seen in a bar. She orders a beer and proceeds to sing "St. Louis Blues," accompanied by the patrons, who sing in complex harmonies. Suddenly, Jim appears again, does a short dance routine on his own, pretends to reconcile with Bessie, removes a wad of money from her stocking, and disappears, whereupon Bessie turns back to the bar and resumes singing "St. Louis Blues" until the picture fades to black.

In recent years, I have unearthed that Radio short and run it again and again. It's easy to see why Bessie was such an inspiration and influence on the singers who came after her. Essentially a blues singer, she infused into her work a kind of earthy quality that is seldom heard these days. Perhaps she was a product of her time. The Twenties roared with its own special rhythm, and the black musical community was part of the scene.

Duke Ellington and Cab Calloway held forth at the Cotton Club in Harlem, and territory bands played "selected" ballrooms and theaters throughout the country. But outside of Ethel Waters and Bill Robinson, the Twenties belonged to the white majority of musicians, dancers, and singers. Paul Whiteman, Ruth Etting, Rudy Vallee, and hundreds of other white performers dominated show business, and the artists of color took what they could get in the way of bookings.

Enter Bessie. A protégé of Ma Rainey's, she began making a dent in the business in the early Twenties. She started recording in 1923 and numbered among her accompanists on record Louis Armstrong, Fletcher Henderson, Benny Goodman, and Chu Berry. Some of her more interesting recordings included "Jailhouse Blues," "Ticket Agent, Ease Your Window Down," and "Empty Bed Blues."

By 1929, when she made "The St. Louis Blues" for RKO Radio, she was riding high, a name to be reckoned with. The Depression, however, was right around the corner, and almost overnight her success was a thing of the past. She still headlined but was forced by circumstance to play second-rate theaters and clubs.

By the mid-Thirties she was singing songs she wasn't meant to sing: pop tunes. She finally latched onto "The Rastus Show" and fell back on the material that had made her famous: the blues. On September 25, 1937, en route to Memphis, she was involved in an automobile accident that claimed her life. She was forty-two.

Bessie Smith was a large, slightly overweight woman with a sweet face. Her singing, of course, is what interests me, and on that score she was peerless. She shouted the blues and exhibited a style that was way ahead of her time. I have occasion to sing the blues, and I can't help but mentally refer to Bessie when I do. She nourished that aspect of my work.

In 1931, a Vitaphone short (nine minutes) in which the Boswell Sisters were featured played theaters from coast to coast. It was called "Rambling Round Radio Row," and the Boswells—Connee, Martha, and Vet—were on the rise and cookin'. These New Orleans girls (actually Martha and Connee were born in Kansas City, Missouri, and Helvetia, "Vet," was born in Birmingham, Alabama) had brought something entirely new to the art of singing, a kind of close harmony rarely heard coming out of three mouths, a singular sense of syncopation, scat singing to rival Louis Armstrong's or the Rhythm Boys', and an over-all feeling for jazz that was unique to them.

When she was three years old, Connee suddenly became afflicted with infantile paralysis. Although the family was not Christian Scientist in their beliefs, Connee's mother refused to buy her daughter braces or crutches and set about massaging Connee's paralyzed lower body in an effort to help her recover. She never did, but that didn't stop her from going on to become one of the really great singers and an inspiration to the likes of Ella Fitzgerald and Sarah Vaughan, among many others.

The girls worked as a trio throughout the Twenties, made dozens of records and appeared in feature films like *Moulin Rouge* (1934) and *Transatlantic Merry-go-round* (1934), played the Paramount theater in New York, where they broke it up, and guested on "The Fleischmann

Hour" with Rudy Vallee. They made their first records for Brunswick on March 19, 1931, and engaged the services of some of the finest musicians of the day, including Tommy and Jimmy Dorsey, Eddie Lang, Joe Venuti, Carl Kress, and Perry Botkin.

The Boswells were seen in *The Big Broadcast* with Bing Crosby, Stuart Erwin, and the Mills Brothers in '32 and made two enormously successful trips to Europe, the first in 1933, the second in 1935. They made their final records as a trio in January and February of 1936 (Artie Shaw played clarinet on this pair of dates), and then Connee headed out on her own.

Her solo recordings were matchless. "Martha," which she recorded with Bob Crosby's Bob Cats, is one of my all-time favorite sides. She sings it with that slightly southern accent, and her time and pitch are flawless. Throughout her singing career she continued to surprise her listeners by changing keys abruptly, imitating jazz horns, and singing scat superbly. What sets her scat singing apart from that of so many others is that she sang absolutely in tune. It is difficult to hold pitch when the notes form in your head at lightning speed and come tumbling out of your mouth in scat syllables a micro-second later. With Connee, that was never a problem.

She made dozens of radio appearances and guest-starred in *Artists and Models* with Jack Benny. In *Kiss the Boys Goodbye* she sat in a terraced area and made "Sand in My Shoes" her own special song. When she sang, you were totally unaware that she was wheelchair bound. In fact, she never succumbed to a wheelchair on stage; she sat on a stool, almost upright, and never looked back.

After a full and rewarding career, she died of cancer October 11, 1976. Tributes to her talents were boundless, and I, for one, was saddened at her passing, despite the fact that I never met her. Her singing was so pure, so free of tricks, that every exposure to her work was a joy. Ella Fitzgerald exclaimed: "Who influenced me? Only one singer, and that girl was Connee Boswell."

The Andrews Sisters made no secret of copying the Boswells, and Patti, a great singer in her own right, followed the lead laid down by Connee.

There is no question that Connee Boswell formed and shaped my early singing style. She was among the first scat singers, and I found that side of her art very attractive. Her ballads were gently realized, with wonderful enunciation, patent attention to phrasing, and, once again, perfect pitch. She was genuinely one of a kind.

LOUIS ———
AND BILLIE

■ ■ ■

When I first began to sing, I did not like Louis Armstrong's singing. (Imagine that!) When I became old enough to understand that the heart was not merely an organ which pumps blood to all parts of the human body, I got the message. Louis sang with more heart than any ten vocalists. Blessed (yes, blessed) with a gravelly throat, he delighted a gang of front-row admirers, of which I was a part, at the State-Lake theater in Chicago.

The year was 1942, and when he sang "What Is This Thing Called Swing?" and "Ain't Misbehavin'," we were blown away. We sat through the inevitable "B" movie four times to hear Satch sing and play the same tunes differently every show.

Besides being a singer with heart, Louis was also a figurehead vocally. He was proof that the public wanted something besides the usual staid rendition of a song. His singing was a pure extension of his playing. If his initial role model was King Oliver, Louis took it from there and improved on the playing. His trumpeting was, above all else, comprehensible. No frills; he took the melody of a given tune and worked his way around it, with just enough embellishment to make it interesting. The same thing applied to his singing.

In addition to running his tongue lovingly over the words, he was among the first scat singers, and that element of his vocalizing brought him as much attention as his playing. Every syllable to come out of Satch's mouth could be traced right back to his horn playing. He had a habit of turning the corners of his mouth down and rolling his eyes to one side when he scat-sang. The musical content was simple, not gaudy, and easily understandable by the millions who worshipped him.

Louis joined King Oliver in mid-1922, toured with him, and married his pianist, Lil Hardin. When he joined Fletcher Henderson's crew in 1924, he became the toast of New York. He fronted a big band from 1935 into the mid-Forties, then led an all-star group with such stalwarts as Jack Teagarden, Trummy Young, Barney Bigard, and Earl Hines. He appeared in numerous films, including *Cabin in the Sky, Pennies from Heaven, The Glenn Miller Story,* and *High Society.* He died July 6, 1971.

I got to know Louis over the years and found him to be a warmhearted, loving man. He had great pride in himself and his accomplishments, particularly his role as unofficial goodwill ambassador from America to the world.

He had a great sense of humor, sometimes biting, sometimes self-deprecating. I remember once, when I was playing the Paramount theater in New York, he came bounding up the stairs to say hello to some musicians on the floor above my dressing room. I yelled at him: "Hey Louis, what's happening?"

He bounced back into my doorway, grinned that Chinese grin of his, and said: "White folks still in the lead."

He was an unforgettable character, and I learned a lot listening to him sing. George T. Simon, the editor of the now-defunct *Metronome* magazine, once approached me as I got off the stand at Bop City in New York. I was appearing with Dizzy Gillespie's ground-breaking big band, and I had just sung several choruses of scat with Diz and his vocalist, Joe Carroll.

"Mel," Simon said, "you know, just because you're a Mercedes-Benz doesn't mean you have to go a hundred and fifty miles an hour all the time."

That critique was a lesson to me, and for a long time afterward I tried to model my scat singing after Louis. Simple, to the point and swinging.

Louis's influence on all manner of jazz musicians in the Twenties and Thirties is unmistakable. His fiery solos infected trumpet players from the Atlantic to the Pacific.

Here was a man who broke new ground, who dispensed with the stiff, old way of playing a horn. Louis's ideas were as fresh as today's fish, and many musicians (not only trumpet players) latched onto his swinging sound, his driving solo flights, his warm tone, and his predilection for high notes.

Ample examples of what made Louis the trendsetter can be found on his recorded accompaniments of Ma Rainey (Milestone M-47021), Bessie Smith (Columbia CL 855), and Bertha "Chippie" Hill (Raretone RTR 24009).

His RCA Victor recordings (1932–33) labeled *Young Louis Armstrong* (Bluebird AXM 2-5519) offer the man in complete control, and on Decca (issued in the MCA Jazz Heritage Series) Louis's big band romps behind him.

All in all, snatches of Louis can be discerned in the

work of virtually every trumpet player extant, from Roy Eldridge to Dizzy Gillespie, from Miles Davis to Wynton Marsalis. No one came away from listening to and ingesting Louis without being affected. In the long, convoluted history of jazz, Armstrong stands out as one of the two or three greatest influences on subsequent practitioners of the art.

Someone once said of Billie Holiday: "She's like spinach; it doesn't always taste good, but it's always good for you."

Billie did have a raw, moaning sound that wasn't for every ear. But for those who marched to her musical drum, she was heaven with a gardenia in her hair. She was the illegitimate daughter of a guitar player, Clarence Holiday. She arrived in New York in the late 1920s with nothing but the clothes on her back. Unemployment led to a period of prostitution, but she began getting work in clubs around New York and, in 1933, made her vocal debut on record with Benny Goodman.

She recorded under a pseudonym until 1936, when she decided to use her own name. She sang with Basie in 1937, with Artie Shaw most of 1938—until the color problem drove her from the Shaw bandstand. Promoters could not tolerate a black singer with a white band. Her golden years were from 1939 through the end of WW II, when she appeared at Café Society and made some of her most noteworthy records.

God Bless the Child is a hard look at what it means to be on your own, and Billie's plaintive singing on this record is philosophic and brittle. *Strange Fruit,* a 12″ Commodore recording, is a brave incursion into the underworld of the lynch mob.

> *Black bodies swingin' in the southern breeze*
> *Strange fruit hangin' from the poplar trees*

It was one of those records you either loved or hated. Not surprisingly, Southerners detested it and made futile moves to suppress it. But the jazz community hailed it as a landmark disc, and the northern stations, particularly the jazz-oriented ones, gave it a lot of airtime.

Like other great singers before her, she surrounded herself with some of the best jazz players around. Drugs got her into deep trouble in the Forties, and she served time in jail. She worked her way back in the early Fifties, but her deteriorating health showed up in her singing. She died July 17, 1959, in New York.

That she was one of the two or three greatest female jazz singers goes without saying. She was a stylist in the true sense of the word, and her intimate approach was widely imitated. She had a small voice, but she sang with great warmth and emotion. At times she dropped well behind the beat, and she had a distinctive way of forming her words.

I got to know Billie toward the end of WW II. I used to see her at Billy Berg's, a jazz club in Hollywood. There is a picture of Billie and myself that appears in my autobiography (*It Wasn't All Velvet*; Viking Press, 1989) taken at Billy Berg's toward the end of the war. She was frankly "out of it" and later wrote, in her own autobiography, that she used to watch me dancing at Berg's with Lana Turner. P.S. I never dated Lana Turner.

It didn't matter. Just being with Billie was an honor, and when she got up to sing, her hair pulled tightly behind her ears, a gardenia framing her face, it was a singing lesson I absorbed and learned from.

BING ■■■

It is difficult to categorize Bing Crosby. Was he the king of the crooners? An able scat singer with the Rhythm Boys? A matinee idol? A superb actor? A linguist with a formidable vocabulary? In fact, he was all of the above. Crosby was the complete man. He played hard and worked hard, although he made singing and acting look easy.

A native of Tacoma, Washington, born in May of 1903, Bing grew up in Spokane, went to school there, and appeared in amateur dramatic productions. He hooked up with Al Rinker, and in 1925 the two friends made their way to Los Angeles, where they stayed with Rinker's sister, Mildred Bailey. They played vaudeville theaters in and around Los Angeles until 1926, when Paul Whiteman dis-

covered them and added them to his roster of talented
musicians and singers.

They appeared with Whiteman at the Cocoanut
Grove in Hollywood and were seen in RKO and Pathé
shorts as well as *The King of Jazz,* a Universal picture in
two-strip Technicolor, teamed with Harry Barris, another
Whiteman musician-songwriter-singer. Called "The
Rhythm Boys," they proceeded to revolutionize the art of
group singing by doing scat choruses in perfect three-part
harmony. A prime example of their art was "Mississippi
Mud," and that arrangement, as much as anything else,
catapulted the Rhythm Boys into national prominence.

Bing had other fish to fry, though. In addition to being newly married to Dixie Lee, he was paged by Mack
Sennett to play himself in a series of two-reelers. He left
Whiteman and made ten of these short films that estab-
lished him as a new romantic singing idol.

After "I Surrender Dear," one of the Sennett shorts,
was released in June of 1931 with astonishing success,
Bing went to New York and appeared at the Paramount
theater. The crowds lined up for blocks to hear this new
phenomenon. At the same time, CBS signed him for a
weekly radio series.

In 1932, he headed west again, this time to appear
in *The Big Broadcast,* the first of his long list of films for
Paramount. In 1936, he moved from CBS to NBC to do
"The Kraft Music Hall," a show that lasted ten years, finally ending in 1945. John Scott Trotter was the musical
director of that program, and Bob "Bazooka" Burns was
a regular.

Bing's early movies included *College Humor, Too
Much Harmony,* and *Rhythm on the Range.* His private life
was turbulent. Dixie had developed a drinking problem,
which finally led to her death. Bing had four sons to raise,

and, as much as he could, he spent quality time with them. He had a passion for horses and horse racing, and he loved nothing better than to go hunting with his great friend Phil Harris. He won the Academy Award for his portrayal of the laid-back priest in *Going My Way* and was nominated twice more for his acting roles. Of course, his main interest was singing, and in that he excelled to a degree that no other singer, with the exception of Sinatra, could match.

One of the best moves Bing ever made was to marry Kathryn Grant. A budding actress, she gave up her career to become Mrs. Crosby, and that was a loving alliance that lasted until the end of Bing's life.

What I have written is merely the tip of the iceberg. Bing's career was so busy, so varied, that it is almost impossible to do justice to the man in a few short paragraphs. He had the advantage of being handsome (even though his protruding ears gave Paramount execs a headache for a time). His acting was so natural that it seemed matter-of-fact in most instances. His singing is what brought him everlasting fame. Before Bing, most singers were stiff and predictable. Russ Columbo and Rudy Vallee were the reigning vocalists of the day, but Columbo, whose career was cut short in a shooting accident, was never really loose enough to put the audience at ease, and his acting left a lot to be desired. Rudy Vallee, who later went on to become a fine comedic actor, was, back in the Twenties, a bandleader with funny hair and a megaphone. His nasal offerings captivated the ladies for a time, but he faded in the stretch.

Bing, on the other hand, exuded charm, ease, and a nice tenor quality that instantly endeared him not only to the female population but to a much broader audience that included men as well. In the Mack Sennett two-reelers, his voice was somewhat high-pitched, but as time went on, the lower end of his range boomed out and took hold.

With each successive record and movie he relaxed more into a gaze-at-the-stars, dreamy kind of approach to singing the popular song, and the glossy close-ups of him, provided by a slew of Paramount cameramen, didn't hurt him one little bit.

He wasn't always the soul of sartorial splendor, given to outrageous Hawaiian print shirts and straw fedoras, but I believe much of that look was calculated to give him "color." His bantering with Bob Hope is legendary by now, and his language, particularly on the old "Kraft Music Hall," would have been envied by Bernard Shaw. When he received his Oscar for *Going My Way* from Gary Cooper, his thank-you speech went: "A lot is said about the quality of opportunity in these United States, and you're certainly witnessing a practical demonstration of it in my receiving this award, because if Leo McCarey can take a broken-down crooner like me and lead me through a picture so deftly that I come up with this happy property here, well, there's a chance for anyone."

Bing's most endearing quality was his off-the-elbow approach to life. He never took his success "big"; he remained human, accessible, and unaffected. In later years, golf became his passion, and, like everything else he did, he attacked the game with zest and determination. Likewise, his hunting activities. Along with Phil Harris, he would sit forever in a duck blind waiting for the birds to fly. His pigeon-grade shotguns were tools he prized above anything else he owned.

In 1977, on a golf course in Spain, Bing died of a heart attack. Most of the people who knew and loved him felt it was a perfect way for him to go, doing something he dearly loved to do. *Newsweek* magazine called me for a quote, and I'm sure what I gave them was puerile and inadequate. What could I say about Bing?

In 1945, my Mel-Tones and I walked into Decca recording studios in Hollywood to cut our very first record with Bing. We didn't know what to expect. Bing Crosby. A terror? Haughty? Difficult? When he walked in, grinning, relaxed, and friendly, we relaxed as well and proceeded to make what I feel was a very good record. Bing treated us as though we were old friends, making, not forcing, suggestions. There were a few solo spots for me, and I sang them hesitantly. Bing encouraged me to "sing out" and egged me on during the actual making of the record.

Then, in 1975, he invited me and my family to lunch at his home just outside of San Francisco. Mary Frances and Harry, Bing's kids, were on hand as well as Kathryn, and it was a funny, jolly, loving luncheon, full of stories and remembrances. After lunch, Bing, sans hairpiece, asked Harry to go get his guitar. We adjourned to the music room, and, just like that, Bing sat down and began to sing. He did about eight tunes, invited me to join him, which I did, and that's the way the afternoon went.

It was New Year's Eve, and as we got into the car to go back to the Fairmont hotel where I was appearing, Bing said, casually: "See you tonight."

Flabbergasted, I said: "Bing, you've got to be kidding. It's New Year's Eve. You'll get mobbed."

"Not to worry," came the reply. "See you tonight."

Sure enough, that night he brought the whole family to the Fairmont, sat at a front table (still sans toupe), and stayed through my whole performance. I never quite got over that.

Or the fact that he was enormously human. Or that he sang with unmatched resonance and control. His vibrato became warmer through the passing of years, and his low notes could make your bass woofer beg for mercy.

If there is anyone I have modeled myself after over the years, I would have to say it is Bing Crosby.

FRED

∎ ∎ ∎

He was thin and short with rather large ears. When Paramount screen-tested him for *Funny Face* in 1928, rumor has it that one executive sent a memo around that went: "Can't act. Can't sing. Balding. Can dance a little."

Vaudeville spawned him. He did an act with his sister Adele, and for all practical purposes she was the dominant element. She was a great dancer, the best partner he ever had. After hit after hit on Broadway, she left him to marry into British aristocracy.

He was crushed and scared. He had always maintained that Adele was the real star of the duo, and now here he was, out in the cold, facing an unknown career as a single. He was far from a romantic type. His forte was comedy, that's the way he and his sister had played it, and now he had to fend for himself, to function as a leading man—and that included making love to his leading lady.

In 1932, he accepted the lead in *Gay Divorce*. His dancing partner was Clare Luce. The critics weren't impressed. He left Broadway and went out to Hollywood, where he was cast in *Dancing Lady*, an MGM musical. He performed two numbers with Joan Crawford. The critics still weren't impressed, but he didn't care; he had already signed with RKO.

His first RKO film, released at the end of 1933, was *Flying Down to Rio*. He received fifth billing, behind Dolores Del Rio, Gene Raymond, Raul Roulien, and Ginger Rogers. By the time the film was released, the RKO execs realized what a potential gold mine they had in Fred Astaire.

As luck would have it, he was teamed with Ginger Rogers. It wasn't calculated; it just happened. They made nine RKO films together. My personal favorite is their sixth, *Swing Time*. Astaire also had the advantage of introducing some of the greatest songs this country ever heard.

Jerome Kern, George Gershwin, Irving Berlin, and Cole Porter wrote the scores for his films, and, as engaging a dancer as he was, his singing (at least for me) overshadowed his terpsichory. His voice was high and melodic, and his hands, expressive and eloquent, punctuated the lyrics.

From the lushly beautiful "Night and Day" in *The Gay Divorcée* to the obstreperous "I Won't Dance" in *Roberta* to the elegant "Top Hat" and "Cheek to Cheek" in *Top Hat;* from the jaunty "I'd Rather Lead a Band" and the poignant "Let's Face the Music and Dance" in *Follow the Fleet* to the romantic "The Way You Look Tonight" to the grumbling "A Fine Romance" and the soliloquizing of "Never Gonna Dance"—Astaire was in complete control of each mood, each nuance, each lyric.

And that was what his singing was all about, the lyric. His voice, as an instrument, left much to be desired. But his way with the words to a song was sophisticated and moving, especially the love songs. Those songs are a feat in themselves, since Astaire was considered anything but a romantic figure. And yet he did possess the ability to be appealing and sexy in his own inimitable way. Surely the audiences would not have bought a delicious girl like Ginger falling for him if he had not had that certain something that attracted her.

And while, admittedly, a great deal of his attractiveness manifested itself in his dancing, I maintain that his singing is what drew Ginger (and Joan Fontaine and Cyd Charisse and Leslie Caron, among others) into his arms.

Ruby Braff once made an album I loved. It was called *Adoration of the Melody*. Astaire might have made a similar album called "Adoration of the Lyric." His early records, with Johnny Green, Leo Reisman, and Ray Noble, bear proof that he met the acid test and survived it. Without the visual image of Astaire, in his tailored slacks and fedora, a tie rather than a belt encircling his waist, the records had to stand on their own. And they did.

His singing on these discs is gemlike. His pronunciation and pitch are perfect, and he performs with a joie de vivre that is singular and rare. Much later in life, he did *The Astaire Story* for Norman Granz. On these records we find a more mature Astaire, firmly in control of his material, singing with strength and assurance.

One aspect of Astaire's singing that always impressed me was his handling of torch songs, the ones about lost or unrequited love. Unlike any other singer in memory, Fred approached these tunes with an air of self-ridicule. Instead of wearing a hair shirt during the performance of "One for My Baby" (from *The Sky's the Limit*), instead of a hand-

wringing version of the lyrics to "They Can't Take That
Away from Me" (from *Shall We Dance*), he adopted a
gosh-look-what's-happened-to-me—oh, well . . . kind of
attitude that served the songs far better than a maudlin
approach might have.

Far and away, my favorite Astaire film of them all is
The Band Wagon. Early in the film, Astaire descends from
a train and casually walks the length of the platform singing "By Myself." That song alone and the way he sang it
could stand as a benchmark for all the lost-and-lonely
Fred Astaire songs that preceded it.

> *I'll face the unknown*
> *I'll build a world of my own*
> *No one knows better than I myself*
> *I'm by myself, alone.*

Self-sufficient and independent; one got the feeling
that he could survive anything and do without anyone.
That was Astaire in real life. He went his own way, almost
reclusive, certainly shy and somewhat introverted. He
lived for his dancing (and singing, although he once told
me I shouldn't go around shouting his praises as a singer),
and the time spent perfecting his art in a variety of movies
showed him to be the true professional he was.

There was an insouciance about his work that was almost European, belying his Nebraska upbringing. His
hands were large and well formed, and the graceful way
he moved, in either a ballroom mode or in the many tap-
dance numbers he created, was never equaled by anyone
in films.

The ultimate tap-dance routine was realized in
Broadway Melody of 1940, opposite Eleanor Powell. No
matter how beautifully he danced with Ginger, with Cyd
Charisse, with Leslie Caron, the pairing of Astaire and
Powell was made in heaven. In the final production num-

ber of *Broadway Melody*, they dance together to the strains of "Begin the Beguine." It is a sheer delight, two champions challenging each other in what is probably the greatest single tap-dancing sequence ever. Astaire doesn't sing in this number, but I felt it was worth mentioning.

It is wrong to dismiss his dancing in favor of his singing; that is something I have had no intention of doing. Yet, as a singer, I think he was as close to representing what the composer and lyricist had in mind as anyone who ever sang the popular song.

I knew him slightly. I wanted to get close to him, but very few people were, and I had to content myself with his films and his records and everything about him in print that I could lay my hands on. Sometimes when I sing, a phrase, a note here and there, a gesture, will remind me that Astaire was one of my most predominant teachers.

ETHEL

Ethel Waters was once widely quoted as having said that I was the only white man who sang with the soul of a black man. That remark was enormously flattering, and there may be an element of truth in it.

I was born in the black (they called it "colored" in those days) section of Chicago, and my initial influences were the customs, history, and music of the black people. From my earliest recollections, my senses were imbued with the songs and the stories of the people around me.

When I was four years of age, my parents took me downtown to the Blackhawk restaurant to hear the Coon-Sanders orchestra. That night I got up and sang with the band (the song was "You're Drivin' Me Crazy"). I became a Monday-night special attraction at the restaurant.

While I certainly cannot be accused of having a

"style" at the time, my leanings musically were definitely steeped in the music I listened to throughout the day at home. Since the Coon-Sanders Nighthawks were an integral part of the Jazz Age (1929), I suppose it followed that my mini-mite-mewlings rolled off my tongue with a degree of syncopation as well a soupçon of black jazz.

Of the early records my parents played for me, Ethel Waters's offerings were among the most influential. Born in Chester, Pennsylvania, in 1900, she grew up in Philadelphia and Baltimore, working as a teenage dancer and singer. She moved to New York in 1917 and toured with her first show, *Hello,* in 1919. In the early Twenties, she became a major vaudeville act, and, beginning in 1921, when she made her first recording, her reputation soared.

The Twenties and Thirties, more than any other decades, belonged to Ethel Waters. She was a welcome participant in several Broadway shows: *Africana* (1927), *Blackbirds of 1930, Rhapsody in Black* (1931). Then, in 1933, she was a runaway hit at the Cotton Club. The main reason was a song, written by a young writer named Harold Arlen. "Stormy Weather" lifted Ethel out of the ordinary and into the special world reserved for stars.

Her early Broadway appearances were short-lived, but "Stormy Weather" changed all that. Soon she was featured in major Broadway hits: *As Thousands Cheer* (1933), *At Home Abroad* (1935), and the mega-hit *Cabin in the Sky* in 1940.

In 1943, she repeated her role in *Cabin* in the movie version for 20th Century–Fox. This time her old sidekick Harold Arlen, together with lyricist Yip Harburg, penned a great song called "Happiness Is Just a Thing Called Joe." Ethel's rendition of this tune was positively beatific. Her smile was radiant; it could light a darkened hallway, and all the pain and joy of that song was included in her reading of the touching lyric.

She was married to Eddie Matthews but worked (and lived with) a different Eddie—Mallory, a bandleader, and from 1935 to 1939 she toured with his band in her own show.

Broadway beckoned once more in '39, and she appeared in *Mamba's Daughters* that year. It wasn't until 1950 that she again trod the boards, this time in the highly regarded *Member of the Wedding.*

She was no stranger to films, beginning with *On with the Show* in 1929, then *Check and Double Check* in '30 with Amos and Andy and the Duke Ellington band. *Gift of Gab* was a 1934 entry. In 1942, she appeared in both *Tales of Manhattan* and *Cairo.* The aforementioned *Cabin in the Sky* and *Stage Door Canteen* rounded out her filmic activities in 1943, and she gave a stirring performance in *Pinky* in '49, having split her time by touring with the Fletcher Henderson orchestra—as a pianist! Between her singing, acting, and piano playing, Ethel had one of the most diversified careers in show business. In 1951, she sat down to write her best-selling autobiography, *His Eye Is on the Sparrow.*

If anyone was qualified to do a one-woman show, it was this lady. In 1957, she appeared once again on Broadway in the appropriately titled *An Evening with Ethel Waters.* The reviews were sparkling. It was a night filled with the music that she had made famous throughout four decades, and every performance ended with cheers and standing ovations.

Later in life, she fell ill and sharply curtailed her performing activities. In the 1960s and on into the 1970s, she made an alliance with evangelist Billy Graham, speaking as well as singing on his many crusades and TV programs.

In her early career, she sang the blues. Her wide vibrato, her closed eyes as she sang, her expressiveness, all made for some of the best renderings of the tried and true form. "Georgia Blues," "Midnight Blues," and "St. Louis Blues" were part of her early repertoire. Later on, she opted for more traditional pop tune entries like "Don't Blame Me," "Jeepers Creepers," "Takin' a Chance on Love," and "Moonglow."

Mahalia Jackson once remarked, "They all come from Ethel: Sarah and Ella and Billie." That seemed to be true of a whole parade of singers who were affected by Waters's singing. Thelma Carpenter was unabashedly influenced by Ethel and even went so far as to emulate her singing style.

Who influenced Ethel? Louis Armstrong, for one. But then, so many people were affected by Louis's singing that it is far from surprising Ethel should take several leaves from his book. Other than Louis, though, she seems to have had no role models. She just went out and started singing in her unique way; whatever she made of herself, she made on her own.

At various times in her career her weight fluctuated, and it was not unusual for her to soar to two hundred pounds or more. She hated herself when this happened, and her poundage went up and down like a yo-yo.

She was not very wise about men. She bought a wide variety of men everything from jewelry to Cadillacs. From all reports, she was not an easy woman to get along with, but she could sing. I never met her, but my admiration for her work is intact to this day.

THE CANARIES

In 1937, my uncle Art, a well-respected Chicago lawyer, introduced me to a squat, swarthy man named Danny Pulagi. This man ran all the jukeboxes in town. Was he mob-connected? Probably. I remember him as a jovial, warm guy who, when I visited his place of business, waved his arm in the direction of a ton of records and said: "Take. Go and look and listen and take."

I took. Charlie Barnet and Jimmie Lunceford and the Duke of Ellington, Benny Goodman and Artie Shaw and Count Basie, and oh so many more. A whole new world opened up for me, a world of swinging bands and their attendant singers. My tutelage was about to begin in earnest. Day after day, night after night, I listened to those 78 rpm goodies until I wore them out. Then I went and bought more. In the course of the next few years, I practiced and copied and gleaned. And learned.

One of the first lessons I took was from Helen Forrest. To my way of thinking, she was the best band vocalist of the Swing Era, particularly when she appeared with the Artie Shaw orchestra. Later, she went on to sing with Harry James and Benny Goodman.

She maintains that her best singing was done with the James band. I disagree. She stretched her notes out with James, and, to use an old Yiddish expression, she "qvetched" a lot with Harry.

With Artie, in 1938–39, she was lean and clean. Her vocals were of the purest quality. In a pair of Warner Bros. short subjects, she appeared, simple and unaffected, and sang the life out of "Deep Purple" and "Let's Stop the Clock." In a similar short for Paramount that same year, she sang "I Have Eyes." With minimal hand movements, her head slightly tilted back, she was the epitome of what a band singer should be: attentive to the lyric, attractive, and unobtrusive. She sang her chorus (brilliantly), then stepped aside and let the band carry the final moments of the tune.

As time went on, she became more mannered and less positive about pitch. Even so, she still has it at this writing and remains my favorite vocalist of the period. A good comparison is her vocal on "Any Old Time" vis-à-vis Billie Holiday's working of that song. Billie's version is wonderful but moderately whiny. Helen's is straightforward.

Helen also shines on "I'm in Love with the Honorable Mr. So and So." Her treatment of that lyric makes you feel for the girl in the song, a back-street baby who waits in a stuffy hotel room for "the moment so rare that's convenient for him to spare."

All through her Shaw days, she made momentous

records with the band, and she admitted enjoying working for Artie. On the other hand, she hated working for Benny Goodman. She claimed he was rude, insensitive, and obstructive. Nonetheless, Benny had a great ear for singers and employed some damned good ones.

Helen Ward was his first singer of note. She fit his band and the Fletcher Henderson arrangements like a glove. Her vocals were jazz-oriented, a necessity for the swinging Goodman organization. When she married Albert Marx, a wealthy record exec, Benny replaced her with Martha Tilton.

Tilton was as fresh as a breath mint. She had a girl-next-door quality that the college boys responded to. Pert and pretty, her blonde good looks were a great asset to the band, but she was more than just a pretty face. She could sing and sing well (even though, at the famous Carnegie Hall concert of 1938, the critics were unkind to her).

Her record with Benny of "And the Angels Sing," as well as her rendition of "Loch Lomond," helped make the Goodman band, in 1938–39, a huge record-selling operation.

Next in line was Helen Forrest. She called Benny "a cold, inconsiderate character—self-absorbed, rude, impossibly tight-fisted." Nevertheless, she made some fine records with him, among which "The Man I Love," a 12″ Columbia disc with a gorgeous Eddie Sauter arrangement, stands out.

Helen constantly threatened to quit and finally did. Benny was staying at the Ambassador hotel in Chicago. He heard a girl singing in the lounge and hired her on the spot. Nineteen-year-old Peggy Lee, a native of North Dakota, went from singing with a little group called The Four of Us onto the bandstand of one of the biggest bands in the country. She was naturally nervous as a cat. Her initial vocals with Goodman were halting at best. Gradually, she rose to the occasion and produced some of her best work. Her plaintive rendition of "How Long Has This Been Going On?" is in direct contrast to the rollicking "That Did It, Marie." She functions beautifully in both instances. Likewise, her vocal on "My Old Flame" is a lesson in control.

Many critics of the period thought she was a cold singer, delivering the notes with unerring pitch but little else. Peggy was finding her way, and those critics were forced to eat their words when she broke away from Goodman and went out on her own. She developed a sly, almost mocking style, a secret inner grin that told you she knew "a little bit about a lot of things."

In 1951, we took over the Perry Como Chesterfield show on CBS. It was a summer replacement, but, in the eight weeks or so that we performed together, I learned a lot about keeping my cool and performing with restraint from Peg.

In 1992, we appeared together at the Hollywood Bowl. I stood in the wings and watched her. Confined to a wheelchair, she held that vast audience in the palm of her hand, and I learned something else from her that night. It's called courage.

Tommy Dorsey had his share of fine vocalists, but no other was so "right on" as Jo Stafford. Initially the lead singer with the Pied Pipers vocal group, she stepped out and did many solo vocals with the Dorsey organization. She was utterly incapable of singing out of tune. She had a built-in tuning fork inside that lovely throat of hers; when she sang, every single note was, well, "right on." Nothing rattled her, and her crystalline vocals were one of the highlights of the Dorsey experience.

Of all the singers Duke Ellington ever presented, none surpassed the swing, the syrup, the sass of Ivy Anderson, who had a long tenure with the Ellington orches-

tra. She sang with an exuberance that Duke found wanting in subsequent girl vocalists. In addition to being a
world-class belter with a slightly nasal approach to the
tunes Duke wrote, she was a great performer. She would
snap her fingers, whirl around on the stand, dance, and in
general add a dimension of performing that was right in
keeping with the show band Duke led in the Thirties and
Forties.

When MGM made *A Day at the Races* with the Marx
Brothers, Ivy was chosen to do Bronislau Kaper's "All
God's Chillun Got Rhythm." It could have degenerated
into an "Uncle Tom" kind of production number, but Ivy,
singing and scatting, overcame the tune and its title, and
the result is a joyous romp. She was something else.

June Richmond, with Andy Kirk's Clouds of Joy,
weighed three hundred pounds, and every single one of
those pounds showed up in her vocals. "Robust" might be
a good way to describe her singing. She virtually shouted
her songs, but with great feeling, and, to my way of thinking, she laid down some of the best performances on wax
that I ever heard.

Outstanding are back-to-back efforts on "Fine and
Mellow" and "A Fifteen-Minute Intermission." She never
got the recognition she deserved, but she hung in there,
turning out some really fine sides with the Kirk band.

There were others, of course, who moved me and
taught me during the Swing Era. Bea Wain with Larry
Clinton, Helen O'Connell with Jimmy Dorsey, Mary Ann
McCall and a very young Lena Horne with Charlie Bar-
net, Kitty Kallen with Harry James, Fran Warren with
Claude Thornhill, and Irene Daye and Anita O'Day with
Gene Krupa.

And Ella.

ELLA

What can I say about Ella?

Well, how about: She's the greatest singer in the world.

Ella Fitzgerald has been affecting and inspiring my singing since I first heard her with Chick Webb's band in the late 1930s. In 1934, she entered an amateur contest at the Apollo theater in Harlem. She was a rapid sixteen, and she came to dance. Always a nervous girl, she decided to sing instead. What she sang is a matter of who heard what, but Bardu Ali, a surrogate leader for the Chick Webb band that evening, was impressed.

He brought her to Webb, and the diminuitive drummer not only signed her to sing with the band; he made her his ward. The first records she made with Webb were "Are You Here to Stay?" and "Love and Kisses." A few years later she recorded "A-Tisket, A-Tasket," which brought her to national prominence. One of my favorite "Ella" sides with that band is "F.D.R. Jones." She sings it with great humor, while the band answers her vocally with "Yes, indeed, yes, indeed." It is out of the jazz mainstream, a pop tune, really; yet she makes the most of it, and it remains one of her most affecting performances.

Suddenly, tragically, in 1939, little Chick Webb died. He was a mere twenty-nine years of age, a great drummer who suffered with spinal tuberculosis. He sat hunched over his Gretsch-Gladstone specially constructed drums, and much of the time he was in agony. You'd never know it to hear him play. He was the forerunner of Gene Krupa and a whole host of drummers who aped his cymbal work and his snare-drum technique.

Ella was left to front the band. It was never as successful as it had been when Chick powered it, and it eventually collapsed in 1942. Now Ella was on her own. And terrified. Every night, in front of Chick's orchestra, she had sung under duress. Her stomach hurt. She fidgeted with her dress. Her eyes darted around the old Savoy ballroom where the Webb band had held forth for so many years. Now here she was, beginning a solo career. It was daunting, to say the least.

Somehow, she managed. She got married, divorced two years later, and remarried to bassist Ray Brown, who was playing with Dizzy Gillespie. Along the way, she graduated from mere singing to scat singing. Ella is not a musician in the pure sense of the word. She doesn't play an instrument; she doesn't read music. It doesn't matter. Her finely tuned ear picked up Dizzy's swinging perambulations on trumpet, Lester Young's smooth, silken tenor sax variations, Ray Brown's rhythmic patterns on bass, and more, and turned them into a rollicking free-for-all on Decca called "Lady Be Good."

No one had ever heard a complete record done in scat. Ella had broken new ground, syllabalizing as she went along, quoting from Connee Boswell's "Martha," from "Love in Bloom," from "Oo Bop Sh' Bam," and infusing the whole number with original phrases and riffs of her own. The result was stunning, and the record was a huge hit, prompting Ella to follow it up with "Air Mail Special" and "How High the Moon," solidifying her reputation as "the Queen of Scat" and, more significantly, "the First Lady of Song."

Ella's marriage to Ray Brown ended in 1952, but now she was stronger, surer of herself. She made a couple of movies *(Pete Kelly's Blues, St. Louis Blues)* and played the Paramount theater in New York in the early Fifties. I was on that bill, and I have lost track of how many times I stood in the wings and watched her perform her magic. She came on before me, and, as I waited to do my thing, I stood rooted to the spot backstage as she wove in and out of her repertoire with seeming ease, going from the lush ballads to the fetching "jump" tunes to the outright excursions in scatting.

She was miraculous, and I think that the Paramount engagement convinced me to convert from the bobby-sox, teenage career I was carving out for myself, into the world of jazz and scat singing. I remember that during that engagement Ella was extremely shy, sticking close to her dressing room, emerging only to go onstage and kill the people. Essentially uneducated, she retained that little-girl persona that not only reflected itself in her singing but contributed to her charm and likability.

What Ella needed at that time of her life was direction. She was in danger of falling into the "cult singer" trap, an abyss wherein only jazz fans and musicians appreciated her. This was not the way to the gold, and, even though she was solidly committed to singing in her jazz-

oriented, jazz-influenced manner, she wanted more out of
life and a career than smoky joints and out-of-the-way
venues in which to ply her trade.

Help came in the form of Norman Granz, the owner
of Verve Records. Let me say at the outset that I am not a
Norman Granz fan. However, his Svengali-like handling
of Ella produced astounding results.

He had her embark on a series of "songbooks" that
elevated her into a new category: a "pop-jazz" singer, ex-
ploring the music of the Gershwins, Duke Ellington, Jerome Kern, Cole Porter, and Rodgers and Hart. These
songbooks were landmark recordings and led to Ella being persona grata in every part of the civilized world. Her
fame spread to the four corners of the earth, and in this
country she played where she wanted to.

What is amazing about Ella is that she transcends
styles, fads, and changes in music. Every new era seems
to belong to her, and now, in her seventy-sixth year, she
is still going—well, if not strong, certainly with that same
girl-woman enthusiasm she exhibited with Chick Webb's
band, back in the mid-Thirties.

Ella's health has been tenuous at best for the past
several years. There are times when she seems to be her
old self, singing with a richness and a verve that makes
you want to jump out of your seat and smother her with
kisses for the great artist that she is. There have been
other times when she has faltered, and that is sad. But
after all, she is seventy-six. How many people of that
many years can still walk on the stage and function at all?

I think that one of the two or three greatest nights of
my life occurred in February of 1976. The occasion was
the Grammy Awards, held at the Palladium ballroom in
Hollywood. Ella and I were chosen to duet on "Lady Be
Good." I didn't do much. I just followed her lead, extem-
porizing on what she sang, and the result was, according

to a letter I received from the NARAS president of the time, "the single longest standing ovation in Grammy history."

On another evening, in Beverly Hills in 1992, Ella and I performed together at an affair honoring Burt Reynolds. Needless to say, we did the time-honored "Lady Be Good" together. You'd think by now it would have become stale, but Ella sprinkled it with new phrases and quotes from more contemporary tunes, and we were treated to a rousing, long-lasting round of applause and whistles when we finished singing.

Ella seemed frail that evening. My heart went out to her, but I must say, even though she wasn't up to par, she still sang better and with more feeling than anyone else could have.

She lives quietly on a shaded street in Beverly Hills. She sees few people, but not because she is a recluse or anti-social. She is merely uncomfortable with people she doesn't know. A few close friends make up her retinue. Her eyes are failing, and much of the time she is wheelchair bound. But her great heart, unflagging sense of music, and that sweet voice are intact. She is a walking blessing.

There are times when she forgets the words to a song. I love those times. She improvises lyrics, catches a sentence or a phrase, builds on it—and what comes out is a joyous, freewheeling performance full of originality. Catch her vocal on "Old MacDonald." She honks, oinks, grunts, and pulls out the stops in one of the freshest vocal exercises ever recorded.

Ella is eclectic, there's no getting around it. She draws from musicians, from a few (a very few) singers, from big-band charts. One of her influences is certainly a trombone player named Leo Watson, one of the early Swing Era practitioners of scat. Watson didn't have the range or even the ear that Ella has, but he was a ground-breaker, and his scatting, although somewhat crude, was a model for what came after.

She has the purest tone in music. In either a ballad or an up-tune mode, her voice is crystal clear. Add to that her great sense of timing, her undisputed feeling for swing, her effervescent demeanor on the concert stage, bubbling with rhythm, and it is easy to understand why Ella, above all other lady singers, stands alone, at the head of the pack.

Ella has embraced the widest variety of songs imaginable. She has covered all the bases. She recorded Beatles tunes like "Michelle" and "Yesterday" and even learned "Ode to Billy Joe" to please a fan. Her heart, however, is deeply rooted in jazz. As I once remarked, if there was a pill or a potion for jazz, Ella probably swallowed it at birth.

MABEL
AND LEE

■ ■ ■

Mabel Mercer sat in her high-backed chair, straight as a ramrod, her hands folded in her lap, her hair swept up atop her head. She wore a simple white gown. Her eyes were closed as she nodded, almost imperceptibly, to her accompanist. In her rich English accent she began to sing:

> *Just a year from today*
> *Will be the first anniversary*
> *Of the day you went away*

She then launched into one of the prize pieces of special material that limned her repertoire. Every inch a person of regal bearing, she half sang, half talked the lyric:

> *Seasons greetings, Merry Christmas*
> *And a Happy New Year*

Have a pleasant Arbor Day
Don't forget Pearl Harbor Day

The song, about a lost love, proceeded to inform the listener that the singer would not be undone, that she would rise above the melancholy of this broken romance and go on to bigger and better things. Such was the stuff Mabel's material was made of; longing for a lost love, rising above it all, stiff upper lip, together with tragic consequences and new alliances.

Occasionally she would twist a handkerchief between her hands, as she looked first right, then left, then center at her audience. Sometimes, to express a deeply felt emotion, she would close her eyes as she sang, and the words, so carefully enunciated, would tumble out with an extra ounce of feeling.

In addition to her storehouse of special songs, Mabel Mercer investigated the works of Noël Coward, Rodgers and Hart, and all the other songwriters of her time who delivered the kind of material she could sing like no other woman of the period: "I'll See You Again" and "Have You Met Miss Jones," the bittersweet message contained in "When the World Was Young," Johnny Mercer's poignant words to "How Do You Say Auf Wiedersehen?," the lovely Alec Wilder evergreen "I'll Be Around," and, most significantly, the Schwartz and Dietz 1937 Declaration of Independence, "By Myself."

Mabel was something of an iconoclast. She kept to herself, with just a few loyal friends serving as a clique. This isn't to say she wasn't gregarious and friendly. But she was a total professional. She played close attention to her work, and she didn't have a great amount of time for socializing or recreational activity. Born in the north of England to a musical family, she appeared in vaudeville (they call it "variety" in Britain) until after WW I, thereafter traveling abroad, singing in small cafés and any other venues available that would enable her to earn a living.

She sang initially with her three cousins and an aunt, but in 1920 she went out on her own. The town was Paris, and she discovered that she could sustain herself singing obscure material, unknown tunes from the pens of unheralded writers, songs that had been cut from Broadway and London shows. In an interview with the late Alec Wilder, she said: "A lot of excellent songs were cut from shows, were never even published and just pushed aside. No one bothered with these. I began to get a reputation for singing songs no one else sang or knew."

She made her reputation at Bricktop's club in Paris. She was the rage there. Texas Guinan and Cole Porter were only two of the innumerable people of note who, night after night, listened to the amazing Mabel.

Never the possessor of a great vocal instrument, she made her mark singing the lyrics meaningfully and with great feeling. With a shawl around her shoulders, she would gently run through the words to "While We're Young" or "These Foolish Things" and bring tears to your eyes.

"When I came to America," Mabel explained, "I continued to sing all those orphaned songs. The music publishers would come to me and give me songs, deleted show tunes, which often happened to be the type of song I could sing successfully."

Tony's, in Manhattan, became Mabel's club. People from all over town as well as visitors from London and Paris flocked to the little club to hear this woman sing songs of love in bloom and love locked out.

I remember hearing her one night at the St. Regis hotel. I had brought her a song of mine called "I'm Gonna Miss You." That night she sang it, and I have never been the same since. What I wrote was transformed into a message of despair, a lament for a lost love, by this unprepossessing woman, sitting quietly in the St. Regis Astor Bar, singing her heart out, moving the audience with her power.

Sylvia Syms, Anita Ellis, and just about every singer of note listened and learned from Mabel. Why was she so special? In an interview with noted music critic Whitney Balliett she said: "It's just a matter of reading a book out loud and with sense, with full stops and commas and the sense of what you're singing about. And more reading and elocution and enunciation. And it's experience, too.

"Then there's the choice of songs. Don't sing anything you can't make sense out of. Some people use sound more than sense. I don't."

She lived out in the country, in upstate New York. She retired in 1978, but it was more like the farewell of many farewells. She was seduced out of retirement time and again, singing at Lincoln Center and at the 1982 Kool Jazz Festival in Carnegie Hall as well as appearing in benefit concerts around the Manhattan area.

Her material was sometimes arcane, but she was always in control of what she sang. Her warmth, her arch delivery, and her great sense of humor made her the grande dame of song. I loved her and learned from her.

I was born in Chicago and yearned for New York. Ever since I can remember, New York was, for me, the promised land. Sophistication, glamour, excitement, Broadway, 52nd street, the uptown clubs and the downtown boîtes, all were fodder for my imagination. When I heard remote broadcasts from somewhere in Manhattan, my mind would conjure up the scene: people dancing, glasses tinkling, women in furs and men in tuxedos, dining and drinking, soaking up the pleasures to be had at the Mad-hattan Room, the Café Rouge, Le Ruben Bleu, and the Blue Angel. I wanted, more than anything else, to be a "New York" singer.

Lee Wiley was a New York singer, even though she hailed from Oklahoma. She claimed 1915 as her birthdate (actual date, 1910). She ran away from home when she was fifteen and sang on a radio show on KNOX in St. Louis briefly before moving on to Chicago and finally New York.

She had a throaty quality that was instantly associated with jazz, and even though Leo Reisman, a bandleader of the period, was far removed from the jazz scene, he signed her to sing with his orchestra as well as record for RCA Victor.

All at once, it seemed as though she could do nothing wrong. The Pond's Cold Cream company took her on, starring her on radio; she sang with Paul Whiteman's large organization; she signed with Decca to make records on which she was backed by excellent musicians of the day, not the least of whom were Johnny Green's crew and the Dorsey Brothers.

New York was her parish, and she rapidly became a favorite in the Big Town. She sounded somewhat like her great friend Mildred Bailey, with a tinge of southern accent, possibly a holdover from her Oklahoma upbringing. She was a true stylist, and her blonde good looks didn't hurt her popularity one bit.

Strange, that blonde hair, since she was reputed to have Cherokee Indian blood. She did have great bone structure in her face and was considered one of the best-looking of the lady singers of her time.

Her time was the Thirties, that period of the Great Depression that also brought forth from the songwriters of the day some of the best music America ever listened or danced to. Lee's ear was acute; she gravitated to the best available tunes and made her reputation by singing the songs of Gershwin, Rodgers and Hart, Berlin, and Vincent Youmans.

Her pitch was not always "right on," and she had a tendency to "drop off" at the end of a held note, but these are picayune considerations. She looked great and sang in a manner that prompted tenor saxophonist Bud Freeman to remark to her: "When you sing, it reminds me of the way Bix played." Max Kaminsky, a fine Dixieland-style trumpet and cornet player, once said in praise of Wiley: "Lee set the style for years to come with her marvelous phrasing and the haunting timbre of her voice."

One of Lee Wiley's greatest attributes was her penchant for verses. In these days of rock tunes, country ditties, and rap, verses to songs are as extinct as the dodo bird. In the Thirties and Forties, the verse to a song sometimes set the chorus up so that, without that frontispiece, the tune was actually incomplete. Certain songs, sans verse, sometimes gave an entirely erroneous impression of what the song was all about.

A perfect example is "I Guess I'll Have to Change My Plan" by Schwartz and Dietz. Without the verse, the song merely conveys the impression that the singer is in love with a woman who, in turn, is in love with another man and, consequently, forces Man Number One to "change his plan." When sung with the verse preceding the chorus, the song takes on a completely new meaning:

> *I beheld her and was conquered at the start*
> *And placed her on a pedestal apart*
> *We planned a little hideaway*
> *That we could share one day*
> *Then I held her and enfolded all my dreams*
> *And told her how she fit into my schemes*

Of what bliss is
Then the blow came
When she gave her name as "Mrs."

Now, all of a sudden, we're dealing with a married woman who has, perhaps, dallied with a single man but chooses to remain with her husband, prompting the single man to "change his plan."

Lee Wiley was a great delineator of verses. She was usually accompanied on them by piano or a small string-and-woodwind ensemble. She would sing these "set-ups" rubato, going into tempo at the chorus. Consequently, the songs were complete, the meaning of the lyrics clear. In this respect, she was a major contributor to the inventory of the popular song and its performance on record and in person.

Early on, she had her share of problems, mostly with her health. At one point, she was thrown from a horse and blinded. It took a year of treatment to restore her eyesight. Then she was diagnosed as having tuberculosis. The doctors were wrong, but she wasted a year of her life recuperating in Arizona. These were setbacks over which she had no control, but they slowed her progress and caused interruptions in her career.

Her most meaningful work was done in the late Thirties, when she performed at Eddie Condon's club with a clutch of superior Dixieland musicians, among them the aforementioned Max Kaminsky, Bobby Hackett, Bud Freeman, and George Wettling. Her voice was particularly suited to this kind of accompaniment. It was smoky and subtle, but with a fine edge. The words came out of her mouth slightly slurred, but they were understandable and insistent. And—she sang the verses.

In the Forties, she married pianist Jess Stacy and went on the road with a big band that he fronted. Their

marriage lasted five years. Then it was back to her beloved
New York and engagements at various clubs in and
around town.

In 1963, Piper Laurie played Lee in a teleplay based
on her life. You would have thought such a venture would
invigorate Wiley's career, but by that time the parade had
passed her by. Not that she wasn't welcome in most of the
smaller night spots and jazz clubs that dotted the Manhattan landscape. It's just that she never really got a foothold
on fame in the fast lane.

She had her own constituency, though. For as long as
she cared to sing, her fans came to see her and went away
satisfied with her "chic, sleek, slim good looks" (as Dick
Phipps observed) and her ability to sing songs that
touched their hearts. New Yorkers are a clannish lot; they
cling to their own. And Lee Wiley, by way of Port Gibson,
Oklahoma, St. Louis, and Chicago, was, for all intents
and purposes, a New York singer.

WOODY
AND JOHNNY

■ ■ ■

There is a "live" broadcast of the Chico Marx band. The location is the Blackhawk restaurant in Chicago. The time: December of 1942. On this LP, young Melvin Howard Tormé sings "Abraham" from *Holiday Inn.*

I was seventeen years old, and I sounded like a cross between Woody Herman and Johnny Mercer. Properly so, since Mercer and Herman were two of my greatest heroes. My vibrato was terrible ("nanny goat", if the truth be known), but the will to sing like these two men was unshakable in me and evident in every number I did with the band.

Johnny Mercer was nothing less than a titan. He was, quite simply, the best lyric writer in America. He could conjure up words that tickled and touched you. His range was extraordinary. From down-home lyrics like "Blues in the Night" and "Jamboree Jones," to the sophisticated couplets of "Laura" and "That Old Black Magic," to the humor of "With My Baby on the Swing Shift" and the poignancy of "Mandy Is Two," to the wonderfully descriptive "Song of India."

"Song of India"?

One day, as I was driving around in my car in southern California, a voice from my Becker-Mexico radio announced that Mario Lanza was about to sing "Song of India." Now, Lanza was an okay singer, but not really my cup of musical tea. I reached for the knob to switch stations, then, for some reason, left KFAC on.

What came out of that speaker enthralled me, a lyric of such scope, such dimension that I thought to myself: I never have to go to India—Lanza just brought it to me. I pulled into a service station, hurried to the phone booth, and called KFAC.

"Who, for God's sake, wrote those words?" I asked.

"Johnny Mercer," came the reply.

I should have known. For as long as I could remember, Mercer had been turning out the niftiest words on the planet. This pixie from Savannah, Georgia, had written over one thousand songs. Occasionally, he wrote the music as well, but his forte was lyrics. His list of collaborators read like a "Who's Who" of songdom. Harry Warren, Hoagy Carmichael, Richard Whiting, Jimmy McHugh, Jimmy Van Heusen, Jerome Kern, and an unending cadre of tunesmiths had lyrics by Mercer woven around their melodies.

For my money, his finest partner was Harold Arlen. Together they turned out some of the "finest" music in the history of the popular song.

Mercer was educated at Woodbury Forest Prep in Orange, Virginia. Like so many other songwriters, he served his time on Tin Pan Alley, improving his craft. By 1934, he was off and running. He was in a couple of films *(Old Man Rhythm,* To *Beat the Band),* and he became one of the most prolific writers of songs for the movies by the mid-1930s.

The roster is virtually endless: "I'm an Old Cow Hand," "Goody, Goody," "Jeepers Creepers," "Hooray for Hollywood," "Tangerine," "One for My Baby," and "G.I. Jive," to name but a very few. This last tune became one of his biggest hit records as a singer. More about that in a moment.

What really brought Mercer to the attention of the general public, with particular emphasis on the teen community, were his appearances as "Vice President" of the "Camel Caravan" radio show that featured Benny Goodman and his orchestra. The weekly program was aimed at the young dancers (and smokers!) of America, and Mercer's bubbly personality lent just the right touch to the proceedings.

On top of that, he introduced many of his songs on that show. One week in 1939, Benny exhorted Mercer to write words to a Ziggy Elman piece called "Fralich in Swing." Ziggy played it that week, and on the very next broadcast Mercer turned up with "And the Angels Sing," complete with a vocal by Martha Tilton.

The lyrics to the bridge of that song are worth quoting:

> *Suddenly, the setting is strange*
> *I can see water and moonlight beaming*
> *Silver waves*
> *That break on some undiscovered shore.*
> *Then*
> *Suddenly, I see it all change.*

Long winter nights
With the candles gleaming
Through it all, your face that I adore.

Those lyrics were a miracle. They brought pictures to the mind. They were miles ahead of the average song-writer's output of "moon-june-spoon" trivia. The song was a runaway hit, and Mercer moved up a few notches in the collective mind of the pros and the public. He also sang on "The Camel Caravan"—pop tunes of the day, his own creations, and, in particular, a charming segment that he called "Newsie Bluesies."

The story goes that Johnny would arrive at the studio minutes before airtime, with a few items taken from the news of the day. It could be FDR defending his dog, Fala. It could be a miners' strike in West Virginia, or the latest craze in women's hats. Johnny would fit lyrics to the tune of "Loveless Love" that were witty, topical, and imaginative. The "Newsie Bluesie" feature became one of the most anticipated on that show, and everyone marveled at how Mercer, time and again, would come forth with line after line, rhyme after rhyme, that set the studio audience and the radio listeners on their respective ears.

His singing of these (and other) tunes was right out of the South. He had an impish way with a song. He rarely, if ever, sang ballads. But his rhythm singing was contagious and laced with humor.

"G.I. Jive" was a paean to the dogfaces of WW II. Like Bill Mauldin, the writer-cartoonist who was the voice and the spirit of the American soldier, Mercer painted phrases with his words that went directly to the heart of the GI experience. The song was a huge success, and Johnny's singing had a lot to do with it.

He had a connection with the soldiers, sailors, marines, and airmen that struck respondent chords in them.

He sang like a "good 'ol boy," and the GIs understood
that. One other thing: his voice "fit" most of his songs,
like "Atcheson, Topeka and the Santa Fe" and "You Must
Have Been a Beautiful Baby," which he recorded with Bob
Crosby's Bob Cats in the late Thirties. Those songs were
so endemic to Mercer that almost anyone else who sang
them sounded uncomfortable.

I met him during the war. I had the Mel-Tones, my
vocal group, and we did several Armed Forces Radio
shows with him. With a fedora perched on the back of
his head, this leprechaun-like man captivated me and my
group, and I unashamedly picked up a lot from his singing style.

On Sundays, many of the top songwriters in Hollywood used to gather at tea time at the Encore, a small
club on La Cienega Boulevard. The name of the game
was "instant lyrics." Each one of these tunesmiths would
endeavor to write and sing words in the blink of an eye. A
rhythm section was usually on hand, and some of the best
of the songwriters of the day would perform impromptu, a
kind of "Newsie Bluesie" experience, Hollywood style.

Once Mercer began his stint, it would be all over for
the day. He would reel off line after line, all cogent, with
inner rhymes galore and great payoffs or punchlines. He
was the Champ, and, Sunday after Sunday, his mastery
was acknowledged with cheers, whistles, and huge applause. I was privileged to be part of those gatherings, and
I sat and listened and learned.

In the early 1940s, along with B. G. DeSylva and
Glen Wallichs, owner of Music City in Hollywood, Mercer
founded Capitol Records. Early artists on the fledgling label included Stan Kenton, Nat Cole, Peggy Lee, and Jo
Stafford.

Mercer was also a recording artist on Capitol, and
many of his hit records saved the company in its early

years of trial. Some of Johnny's greatest vocal hits were "Accentuate the Positive," "Personality," and "Candy" (with Jo Stafford).

He even tried his songwriter's hand at Broadway, with mixed results. *Walk with Music, Texas, L'il Darlin',* and *Foxy* were mildly successful. *L'il Abner,* however, was a hit, as was *Top Banana,* for which he wrote both the words and the music.

His singing improved as time went on. The rapid vibrato, a product of nervousness more than anything else, was more under control, and he even tried his hand at a few ballads ("Memphis in June" and "One for My Baby").

In the Sixties and Seventies, Johnny became depressed. More and more, rock singers were writing their own songs, and Mercer found himself in a dried-up market. It hurt. He had brought lyric writing to such a high peak, only to have it denigrated by far lesser talents penning suggestive words to banal melodies, heedless of the rhyming patterns, sometimes making little or no sense at all.

He had almost completely stopped singing by this time. The airwaves were dominated by the very young, and Mercer was fast becoming the forgotten man. He had a lot of company. Many middle-of-the-road-singers were finding it hard to get their records played, since rock was permeating radio.

Mercer came to see me at the Maisonette Room of the St. Regis hotel in New York. He was his gracious self that night, but he could see that I was down in the mouth. When he asked me why, I told him that I was fed up with the music business and was seriously considering becoming an airline pilot. (No kidding!) I was having trouble finding good songs to sing in the junk-music-dominated seventies, and I felt it was time to pack it in.

Mercer held forth for the best part of that evening,

encouraging me to "hang in there" and wait for the pendulum to swing back as, according to him, it certainly would. Thanks to Johnny, I gritted my teeth and sang my songs, and, sure enough, jazz had a renaissance the very next year, 1976. I appeared with George Shearing and Gerry Mulligan at Carnegie Hall, and things turned completely around for me. I credit Mercer for stopping me in my tracks and talking some sense into me, just when I thought of chucking it all.

I remember his grin, with that boyish space between his front teeth, his wry southern humor, and his humanity. When he died, in 1976, I was part of a tribute to him at the Music Box theater in New York on July 22 of that year. Jimmy Rowles, Margaret Whiting (an especially close friend of both Johnny and Ginger, his wife), Harold Arlen, Alec Wilder, and myself, among others, celebrated the songs of the Master.

It would have taken three days of continuous singing to get through his repertoire. We did our best with the time alloted to us. "Day In, Day Out," "Fools Rush In," "Hit the Road to Dreamland," "Come Rain or Come Shine"—we sang them all and wept at the thought of no more Mercer.

In an era of mediocrity, it's nice to remember a man like Johnny Mercer. I, for one, will never forget him.

It was March of 1949, and I was on my honeymoon. We had driven from Baltimore to New York. The plan was to stay at the Astor for a few days, then motor up to Hartford in time to play the State theater there for the weekend. The bandleader graciously loaned us his station wagon to make the trip. In addition to our clothes, we carried his wardrobe and that of his manager.

On Thursday evening, we left the hotel and pro-

ceeded up Broadway. When we got to 97th Street, I noticed a British film playing at one of the theaters there.
Being the number one movie fanatic of all time, I insisted
that we (my bride and I) park the car and see the film
before we continued on to Connecticut.

We sat through *Corridor of Mirrors* and exited the
theater. The car, parked directly across from the movie
house, had been broken into. Our suitcases and the bandleader's suitcases were gone. I panicked. I jumped into the
car and promptly ran it into a fire hydrant, tearing the
right front fender to pieces.

Now, it was my unhappy lot to find the bandleader
and inform him of our joint losses. I finally made contact
with him at Birdland.

"My God," I blurted. "I don't know how to tell you
this, but—we've been robbed. My clothes and Candy's
clothes and—and your clothes are all gone!"

On the other end of the line, there was a sigh, and
then Woody Herman said: "Hey, it's happened before and
it will happen again. See you in Hartford."

That was typical of Woody, the most laid-back guy I
ever ran into or worked with. He was an absolute
pussycat, but that didn't mean he was a fool. He was a
strong bandleader, albeit patient and understanding
where his sidemen were concerned. That's why they all,
to a man, loved him. They knew, however, never to cross
him or to commit a breach of professionalism on the
stand.

Scant days before the robbery, we were in Toledo,
Ohio, playing a split week at the Paramount theater there.
I was enjoying the band, which sported such heavyweights
as Serge Chaloff, Shorty Rogers, Red Rodney, and Zoot
Sims. Zoot was like a great big kid, and his magnificent
tenor playing had the entire band business buzzing.

On closing night at the Paramount, Woody and I

were duetting on his time-tested arrangement of "Golden Wedding." As we came to the drum-clarinet feature, Zoot audibly began yelling, "Yeah! Yeah! Yeah!" No doubt about it, it was a taunting put-down. I couldn't have cared less. Playing drums in my act was purely an adjunct, not the main event, but, as I looked at Woody, I saw the veins stick out on his forehead.

The number concluded, the curtain came down. Woody turned, walked over to Zoot, and slapped him in the face. "Get out," he said tersely. "You're fired."

The guys in the band descended on me and begged me to talk to "the old man" and prevail upon him to reconsider Zoot's firing. Woody was adamant.

"No, Melvin," he said to me. "He committed the cardinal sin: he was unprofessional onstage. I won't tolerate that from anybody, I don't care how well he plays."

Zoot stayed fired for several months, then was hired back. He was essentially a sweet guy, and I think he learned an object lesson that night in Toledo: never put the bandleader on, especially if that leader is Woody Herman.

Woody had been down the pike and back again. He had seen it, done it, been there. He was born May 16, 1913, in Milwaukee, Wisconsin. Early in his career he was billed as "the Boy Wonder of the Clarinet." He also did a song-and-dance routine. He played with Harry Sosnik and Gus Arnheim in 1932–33. During those days, the band business was rough. Woody once told me that, early on, he had refused to join the newly-formed Musicians' Union. At that time, the union was nothing more than a racket, perpetuated by thugs whose sole purpose was to bleed revenue out of the sidemen and bandleaders of America.

Woody steadfastly avoided joining up until one night, as he was driving on a lonely road on the way to a gig, a car pulled alongside him and forced him off the road. Two men got out, dragged Woody out of his car, and shot him in the leg. He joined the union the very next day. He showed me the scar the bullet left on his right calf. It was ugly.

Woody's big break came when he joined the Isham Jones band in 1934 as sideman-vocalist. He stayed with the band for two years; then, when Jones temporarily retired, Woody formed a co-op band with several of Jones's sidemen. They opened in New York in 1936.

With arrangers like Dean Kincaid and Gordon Jenkins and key sidemen like Frankie Carlson and Saxie Mansfield, the band developed into "the Band That Plays the Blues." That appellation wasn't exactly accurate. They also played pop tunes like "Say Si Si," "You're a Sweetheart," and "Lullaby in Rhythm," but the basic format was the playing of the blues. "Woodchopper's Ball" and "Blues on Parade" were only two of the instrumentals that secured the band's reputation.

A major element in keeping the band at the forefront of the orchestras that dominated the mid- to late Thirties was Woody's singing. Initially, Woody had planned on a singing career. His clarinet and alto sax playing had been secondary to his vocals. But fate, in the form of the Swing Era, changed all that, and he saw bandleading as the best way to reach the public.

His singing didn't suffer. He possessed a smooth voice with a decided jazz inflection permeating everything he sang. He was versatile; he could sing the ballads beautifully, with much heart and fine pronunciation, then turn around and shout the blues, bending the melody into "blue" notes, adding a "buzz" to his tone and generally swinging. In his Decca days with the "Blues" band, he warbled a particularly fetching ballad called "Blue Evening," then turned around and growled "Blues Upstairs" ("When my baby left me, she left me a mule to ride").

"The Band That Played the Blues" was essentially a hybrid, a Dixieland band with swing band roots. Steady Nelson and Cappy Lewis held down the first two trumpet chairs; Tommy Linehan was Woody's longtime pianist; and Walter Yoder not only played bass, he managed the band. The personnel changed from year to year, but Herman was able to keep these constants in the band, and the result was one of the best orchestras of the period. An interesting addition to his crew was a female trumpet player named Billie Rogers, who joined up in the summer of 1942.

He employed a variety of good singers, among them Mary Ann McCall (an early vocalist who later came back to sing with the band in the late Forties), Dillagene (who married Frankie Carlson), Frances Wayne (who married Neal Hefti), Anita O'Day (who married no one), and even a "boy" singer, Sonny Skylar.

But Woody was the principal singer. When he abandoned "the Band That Played the Blues" and jumped into the modern world of music with his First Herd, the gifted arranger Ralph Burns wrote a lovely chart on "Laura" that Woody sang with much feeling. It was a resounding hit, and it encouraged Woody to perform more and more ballads. "I'm Always Chasing Rainbows," "Everybody Knew but Me," "I'll Get By," and "It's Anybody's Spring" are just a few of the slower tunes that he attempted.

They worked, but his real forte were the "up" tunes, the jazz-oriented blues numbers. "Panacea," "Caledonia," "There's Good Blues Tonight," and "Mabel! Mabel!" were all cookers that Woody handled with humor and ease.

His great strength lay in his ability to recognize young

new talents and to incorporate them in his various bands. Right through his First, Second, and Third Herds, the level of musicianship was outstanding, and the credit goes directly to Herman for his keen eye and ear in the employment of his sidemen.

He also reveled in his role as "Daddy." (A set of stands he used on the road carried the legend "Road Father.") He was paternalistic; after all, he was considerably older than his young charges, and he kept an open ear and an open door for anyone in the band who had problems. Probably more than any other bandleader, Woody really cared about his men, and, more than once, he bailed them out of marriage problems, money worries, and even drug-related hassles.

Early on, I tried to sing like him. I liked his gentle delivery on ballads and his fierce, sometimes strident readings of the swifter numbers. In my earlier recorded efforts, Woody's influence is plainly noticeable. We worked together on many occasions, at Basin Street East in New York City in 1966 and at several jazz festivals. He was unfailingly buoyant, friendly, and optimistic about the future.

It was sad to see what happened to him in later life. It began with a near-fatal accident. He loved cars, particularly Corvettes. One night, out on the road, he lost it and was mangled in the process. He spent several weeks in a hospital and came away shaken and never quite the same.

And then he discovered that his business manager of many years had swindled him out of hundreds of thousands of dollars. It was a bitter blow, particularly since a monumental amount of taxes were left unpaid. He had to work out a deal with the government. It came down to his being given an allowance to live on. The rest of his money went to the IRS. Even his home went down the tubes, and it was sad to see him work, night after night, at his age, just to satisfy the Internal Revenue Service.

He died in 1987. It was a blessing, really, since his beloved Charlotte had preceded him by several years and, other than standing in front of the band, struggling to play his horn and remember the words to the songs he sang, he really had nothing to live for.

I owe a lot to Woody. In addition to being one of my main singing teachers, he was responsible for launching my vocal career.

At the end of 1946, Woody and Les Brown jointly called the famous manager Carlos Gastel and told him that my efforts on the Musicraft Artie Shaw records indicated my potential as a solo singer. Gastel called me from his office, having listened to those records with Les and Woody, and talked me into disbanding my vocal group and going out on my own, with himself as manager.

That recommendation was typical of Woody Herman. He was a selfless man, a sweet soul with a totally unselfish attitude where the business of talent was concerned. I think about him a lot. I miss him.

NAT

■ ■ ■

I have many recollections of Nat Cole, but none so vivid as the day Bob Wells and I brought our "Christmas Song" to him. At that time, Carlos Gastel, a three-hundred-pound Honduran, was the hottest manager in show business. The year was 1945. Gastel guided the destinies of Stan Kenton, Peggy Lee, and Nat "King" Cole. He was a music appreciator first and foremost, and his stable of performers glistened under his direction and tender, loving care.

Wells and I were a songwriting team. Every day, either at my parents' home in the Hollywood Hills or at Wells's sumptous house in Toluca Lake, we would sit at the piano and try to fashion melodies and lyrics. The publishing firm of Burke and Van Heusen had placed us under contract. We wrote some movie music (for *Abie's Irish*

Rose, Magic Town, So Dear to My Heart) and busied our-selves turning out tunes for the consideration of the reign-ing pop and jazz singers of the day.

One day, in July of 1945, I entered Bob's house, went to the piano, and found a spiral pad sitting on the music board. Scrawled in pencil on the pad were the words:

> *Chestnuts roasting on an open fire*
> *Jack Frost nipping at your nose*
> *Yuletide carols being sung by a choir*
> *And folks dressed up like Eskimos*

When I asked Bob about this little poem, he replied: "I am so hot today. I jumped in the pool, took a cold shower, and tried everything I could think of to cool off. Nothing worked. So I sat down and wrote those few lines as an experiment to see if thinking about winter scenes would do the job."

"Hmmm," I said. "You know, this might just be a song." Forty-some-odd minutes later, "The Christmas Song" was born.

Who to give it to? Almost simultaneously we both re-marked: "Nat Cole." Nat and Carlos had become two of our greatest friends. It just seemed natural for us to expose this tune to Nat before showing it to anyone else.

First, though, we took the song to the offices of Burke and Van Heusen and played it for our mentors.

"No, fellas," Johnny Burke said, upon hearing it. "No good. The minute you say 'They know that Santa's on his way,' you make it a 'one-day' song; Christmas Eve. No one's going to buy a tune that's only good one day of the year." No matter what we did to assure him this was more than just a one-day song, he remained unconvinced.

Somewhat dejected, we brought the song to Nat. He listened to it once. He listened to it twice. He stood up and pointed at us. "That song is mine," he intoned. "Nobody gets that song except me."

We were giddy with delight. We brought the song back to Burke and Van Heusen and told them we had secured a Nat Cole record. Reluctantly—RELUCTANTLY—they bought it. As it turned out, Nat's record came out the following year, 1946, and took off. At this writing, it is the single biggest-selling record he ever made and one of Capitol's all-time monsters.

A funny sidebar to this story: when Nat first recorded "The Christmas Song," he sang the words to the bridge like this:

> *They know that Santa's on his way*
> *He's loaded lots of toys and goodies*
> *On his sleigh*
> *And every mother's child is gonna spy*
> *To see if REINDEERS really know how to fly*

Almost as soon as the record was released, Nat realized his error. He was mortified and apologized profusely to Bob and me. Now then, how to rectify this mistake in grammar? Several months later, at the end of one of his recording sessions, Nat Cole hauled out the arrangement of "The Christmas Song" and recorded it again. This version was almost identical to the original, except, of course, he sang "REINDEER really know how to fly."

In 1947, Carlos Gastel became my manager as well, and my relationship with Nat became closer than ever.

Nat "King" Cole was one of the finest gentlemen it has been my pleasure to know. Although he was born in Montgomery, Alabama, March 17, 1917, he grew up in Chicago, something else we had in common. His brothers, Eddie, Fred, and Isaac, were also musicians. In 1934, Nat led his own big band, toured the country in a show called

Shuffle Along, and then, eventually, settled in southern California.

He played solo piano in clubs for a while. Then, in 1939, he formed his famous King Cole Trio with Oscar Moore on guitar and Wesley Prince on bass (later replaced by Johnny Miller). Originally, there were unison vocals with an occasional solo segment by Nat himself. More and more, Nat jumped into the spotlight, doing vocals on such tunes as "Straighten Up and Fly Right" and "It's Only a Paper Moon."

Now the public was taking notice of Nat's singular song styling. He dominated the act. It is interesting to note that Nat's singing, during this period in which he was seated at the piano, was pleasantly flat. Not very flat, mind you, but, in many instances, a quarter of a tone off the mark. He was embarrassed by it and once told me that singing and playing the piano at the same time was tantamount to patting his head and rubbing his stomach. He was split down the middle and couldn't concentrate on his intonation as much as he would have liked to. Later, when he broke away from the trio to become one of the greatest singing stars of this century, his pitch was right on target, but by then he was standing up.

In 1948, Nat recorded "Nature Boy," a minor-keyed oddity written by Eden Ahbez. It sailed to the top of the charts, and Nat saw the handwriting on the wall. His trio had been used on record in recent months mainly in support of a large orchestra. It was time to break away, to try his wings in a solo flight.

Late in 1951, the Trio was no more. Nat became a major star in the ranks of male artists. Almost anything he touched with his deep, semi-raspy voice became a Hit Parade staple. All through the 1950s, he churned out hit after hit. "Mona Lisa," "Too Young," "Ramblin' Rose," and scores of other pop tunes all enjoyed Nat's magic touch.

He toured Europe and headlined in Vegas, New York, and Chicago, where he was given a hero's welcome. His marriage to Marie Ellington was a good, solid union. Marie, a beautiful girl who had once sung with Duke Ellington (no relation), had poise, class, and savvy. Together they made an unbeatable couple.

I once bounced Natalie Cole on my knee. The offspring of Nat and Marie, she grew up to become a fine singer in her own right. Singing in unison and harmony with her illustrious father was an inspiration that stamped her version of "Unforgettable" as one of the most original and unusual records of all time. It won the Grammy, and that award was never more deserved.

Nat appeared in a slew of movies in the Fifties, including *China Gate, St. Louis Blues,* and *Cat Ballou.* He had everything going for him until 1964, when he was diagnosed as having lung cancer. He came to see me at the Crescendo on the Sunset Strip and somberly informed me of his illness. I was shocked and saddened. He was philosophical about it. "Nothing is forever," he grinned sadly.

I will not soon forget that night. A bunch of drunken hillbillies heckled me all through my performance. After I finished, Nat came down to my dressing room to inform me that they were lying in wait for me upstairs. Calmly, Nat picked up an empty bottle and recommended that I arm myself as well and that we go upstairs and meet these morons head-on.

I timidly followed his advice and cautiously followed him up the backstairs. He was as calm as a lagoon. I know now that he was thinking, what with his lung cancer eating him alive, that he had very little to lose. As it happened, when we got upstairs, the hecklers had gone, but I will never forget the look on Nat's face as he prepared to do battle. It seemed to say: "Come on, come on." Months later, on February 15, 1965, at St. John's hospital in Santa Monica, Nat was dead. He was forty-eight years old, way too young to die.

Jazz purists have always complained about Nat deserting the piano. In the large sense of the word, I don't really blame them. He was an outstanding jazz pianist, full of originality. His locked-hand method of playing was a breath of fresh air. He had developed that style early on with his Trio, playing big, block chords, surrogates, no doubt, for the big band that was absent. His technique was virtually flawless. His right hand darted out and around the keys, developing scintillating patterns and riffs that were positively rib-tickling.

One of my favorite outings of Nat's was a record that he made for Eddie Laguna on a tiny label called Sunset Records. With him on this record were Buddy Rich, Charlie Shavers, Herbie Haymer, and John Simmons. Nat was billed simply as "the King," and/or "Sam Schmaltz" and/or "Eddie Laguna," depending on which edition of this disc you got. "Laguna Leap" is one of the most exciting small-band sides ever recorded, and Nat's solo is breathtaking in its virtuosity. The exchanges between Nat and Buddy are in the best tradition of "humor in jazz," and, even though Tommy Dorsey gave Buddy hell for appearing on this record without his express permission, it remains one of the great jazz adventures of all time.

His playing aside, it would have been wrong for Nat not to pursue a solo vocal career. He had all the ingredients it took: sleek, good looks, a tall, lanky frame, and a larynx like pure honey.

With each successive recording, he simply got better and better. With the onset of years, his voice mellowed, growing warmer and more vibrant. He sang softly, especially on ballads, and I think that quality endeared him to the millions of fans (particularly women) who marched to his vocal drum.

As he caressed the lyrics to the love songs he sang, his voice seemed to seep right out of the speaker into the hearts of a generation of music lovers who recognized his specialness and supported him.

In later life, it could be argued that his smoking contributed to his husky tones, making his work, well, sexier than ever. Nat was an obsessive smoker, and I'm sure he would have had the good sense to stop immediately had he known what tobacco was doing to his body. In those days, however, the evils of cigarettes were cloaked in clever ad campaigns designed to impart an aura of sophistication and hipness to the habit. Nat wouldn't stop, couldn't stop, and the habit killed him.

Nat's taste in music was exemplary. He not only sang the songs; he listened. On many an evening, we would sit in Carlos Gastel's office on the Sunset Strip, listening to Kenton, Barnet, Lunceford, and a myriad group of singers Nat admired. His sense of humor bordered on the fey, and his memory for jokes, dirty and otherwise, was prodigious.

In the Fifties, despite his fame, he suffered racial slurs. I was privy to one of these. I was playing the Oriental theater in Chicago. My wife and I had gone around the corner with Nat and Marie to a steak house to have dinner between shows. As we were ordering, in walked a bunch of rednecks, who stood at the bar a short distance from our table and proceeded to make insulting remarks. Nat took it as long as he could. Then he beckoned me to follow him to the bar. Understand: I am 5'7", and at the time I weighed a strapping 135. What I was supposed to do against these bull-necked hulks at the bar was beyond me. Nonetheless, Nat was my friend. I followed him.

Nat sat down next to one of these noble creatures and

commenced making small talk. The guy was uncomfortable and squirmed on his bar stool. The situation became tense and intense. Just when I thought a full-blown fight was about to erupt, in walked Big John, Nat's aide-de-camp cum bodyguard. He was six-five, without an ounce of fat on his huge-muscled frame. When the rednecks saw him, their spirits were dampened, to say the least. The confrontation was defused, but I won't forget Nat's willingness to mix it up with those cretins.

Another kind of prejudice bedeviled Nat. In the late 1950s, the Wildroot company chose to sponsor him on NBC in a musical series. He had famous guests, and he made a fine host—easy, relaxed, and in command. It didn't matter. In the climate of the times, he simply could not attract an audience.

At various times in the long history of Capitol, the company was in trouble financially. Several of Nat's hit records bailed that company out, time and time again. He and a few other artists on the label were what kept Capitol going, increasing its solvency and firming up its position in the recording industry. Therefore, you can imagine his chagrin when he picked up the phone to call an old associate at Capitol and the operator greeted him with: "Good afternoon. Capitol Records. Home of the Beatles."

"Home of the fucking Beatles?" he stormed. "What about all those records of mine that kept Capitol from drowning? How dare they! 'Home of the Beatles,' for chrissakes!"

He had a point. In a world of "how soon they forget," that salutation from an operator working for a company he helped save was grinding. What Nat was indisposed to recognize was: things change. The Capitol record company he once loved and worked for is no more. It is a company pandering mainly to very young tastes, and, at the time of this incident, the Beatles meant more to Capitol than Nat Cole. A hard pill to swallow.

In the same vein, there has been a predilection in recent times, by the press, TV, and radio media, to refer to Elvis Presley as "the King." Don't you believe it.

Nathaniel Adams Cole was the King.

THE BOYS ———
IN THE BANDS

■ ■ ■

In the Thirties and Forties, it was de rigeur for bands to carry male vocalists. Female singers, of course, were also a feature of the big bands, but the male contingent of singers was the element that melted young female hearts. Girls of all sizes, shapes, and descriptions crowded around the bandstands of the country, gazing dreamily at the young men who stepped forward and sang the love ballads of the day.

Bandleaders were canny; the boys who sang in their bands brought in business, and business was the name of the game. As a record buyer, I paid close attention to the guys who warbled, crooned, and shouted with the various organizations.

Many of them were influential, teaching me poise, attitude, presence, and phrasing. Some were less than spectacular; some were awesome. They sang the tunes submitted by song pluggers and music publishers, a broad variety of sameness.

The subject matter inherent in the popular songs of the day was limited, to say the least. Male singers were essentially balladeers, and the songs they sang fell mainly into three categories: I love you and you love me; I loved you and lost you to another; I loved you and lost you, and now I have to win you back.

The grinding repetition of these three themes must have driven those fellows up the wall. It is to their great credit that they managed to sing these songs ad infinitum and still retain a freshness in the performances. Their concentration is nothing short of admirable, since night after night the words and music came out of their mouths until some of them actually sang the songs by rote.

There were a few, however, who viewed the singing of the popular song as a profession and a challenge. In their cases, every single rendition carried with it an understanding of the lyrics, close attention to the melodic structure, and an investment of feeling that marked those few singers as giants.

Bob Eberly, who sang with Jimmy Dorsey's crew, was one such singer. Genuinely handsome, with full lips and high, arching eyebrows, Eberly was the epitome of what band singers were all about. Nightly he would sing the Dorsey hits, "Tangerine," "Marie Elena," and "Green Eyes," without the slightest trace of artifice, hands at his side or clasped together in front of him. His rich baritone would boom out over the loudspeakers, and girls' knees would go weak.

Born in 1916 in Mechanicsville, New York, he first gained attention as the vocalist with the Dorsey Brothers orchestra in 1935. When the Dorseys separated, Eberly (changed from Eberle) elected to stay with Jimmy and became a mainstay of the band. He traveled the length and breadth of the country, dispensing his robust brand of singing in ballrooms, theaters, and nightclubs. Dorsey landed in Hollywood in 1942, and Eberly was prominently featured with the band in Paramount's *The Fleet's In* that year, as well as in MGM's *I Dood It* (1943) and, finally, *The Fabulous Dorseys* (1947).

Bob Eberly was strangely reticent to pursue a solo career. He certainly had the looks, the voice, and the presence to succeed on his own, but he chose to remain with the Dorsey band until he went into the service in 1943. Out of sight, out of mind, he never regained the popularity he had won with the Jimmy Dorsey band. When he mustered out of the military, he worked infrequently, but whatever momentum he had faded away.

It is arguable whether he would have made it on his own. On the other hand, he seemed to have all the equipment necessary for success in the parade of singers who emerged right after WW II.

There is a moment in *The Fleet's In* in which Eberly, wearing a yachting cap, sits on the beach with Dorothy Lamour and sings "I Remember You." It is one of those gentle interludes that touches the heart, and one could just picture the Paramount execs watching it in a screening room, noting Eberly's good looks and flawless vocalizing and saying, "Let's sign this guy up."

It was not to be. Except for a few brief appearances on TV shows and random gigs in the New York area, his star dimmed, and soon he was no more than a memory.

His younger brother Ray achieved fame with the Glenn Miller orchestra. That fame was proportionate to the popularity of the Miller band, far and away the most listened to and loved aggregation of the late Thirties and early Forties. While Jimmy Dorsey's orchestra had its large following, that band could not match the overwhelming celebrity of the Miller clan. Consequently, Ray was more visible and accessible to the public than Bob had been.

Ray was a "spotty" singer. His voice was pitched higher than his older brother's, and his vibrato was sometimes unstable. He did have a nice quality on several of the Miller discs, principally "Indian Summer," "Blue Evening," "A Handful of Stars," and "Serenade in Blue."

Born in 1919 in Hoosick Falls, New York, he was totally inexperienced when he joined the Miller band in 1938, thanks to a recommendation from his brother Bob. He learned how to sing on the job, and soon he was a major asset to Glenn's up-and-coming orchestra. He was featured on Miller's famous Chesterfield radio show as well as in the two Fox movies the band made: *Sun Valley Serenade* (1941) and *Orchestra Wives* (1942).

In mid-1942, something happened. Rumor had it that Ray was drinking too much, showing up late for rehearsals, and missing performances. Whether these rumors had any foundation in fact is anyone's guess. Glenn promptly fired him and paged Skip Nelson to replace him. (More about Skip shortly.)

Ray sang for a short time with Gene Krupa, then went out to Hollywood and appeared in a few Universal pictures. He got into the service toward the end of the war. When he was discharged he put together a band that featured the Miller sound. Finally, he joined Tex Beneke's West Coast–based band in the early Seventies and toured the country with him, delivering the same brand of ballad singing he had been famous for with Glenn Miller.

I joined the Chico Marx band in August of 1942, fresh out of Hyde Park High School in Chicago. I was a rapid seventeen years old, and Skip Nelson was my roommate. He hailed from Pittsburgh, and I must admit I looked up to him for a lot of reasons. He was tall, good-looking, of Italian descent, and he could sing. The timbre of his voice was gorgeous, full, round, and commanding. He sang the ballads while I sang the "jump" tunes. Any pretensions I might have had toward ballad singing with the Marx band were quickly stifled as soon as I heard Skip sing.

He was very much a lady's man, and several nights I had to occupy myself in a coffee shop or movie theater while Skip used our room for his nocturnal pleasures. He called me "Junior" and gave me myriad pointers on the fine art of singing ballads.

Incidentally, the Chico Marx band wasn't Chico Marx's band at all. It was put together by Ben Pollack, a 1920s drummer-bandleader whose orchestra spawned some of the greatest musicians in the history of jazz. Benny Goodman, Tommy Dorsey, and many other stalwarts of the Big Band Era emerged out of the Pollack orchestra.

When Chico Marx decided to put a band together and go on the road, he got in touch with Pollack, who organized a dandy, swinging ensemble. The personnel included Marty Marsala on trumpet, George Wettling on drums, and Barney Kessel on guitar, as well as the arranging talents of Freddie Norman and Paul Wetstein, later known as Paul Weston. Word got around that the Marx band was a "killer," and I remember nights when most of the Ellington band as well as the Charlie Barnet crew came to hear us.

Skip was restless, longing to go on to bigger and better things. He deserved to, and when Glenn Miller singled him out, he jumped at the chance. Unfortunately, Miller was Army-bound shortly after Skip joined the band. However, he made some lovely records with Glenn, my favorites among them being "Moonlight Mood" and a definitive reading of "That Old Black Magic."

When the Miller band broke up and Glenn went off to war, Skip literally disappeared, after a short stint with Tommy Dorsey. I heard that he had returned to Pittsburgh and was singing locally there, but he never again enjoyed high visibility, his moment in the sun being those few short months with Glenn Miller. What a shame.

Another singer I admired during the Big Band Era was Bob Carroll. Essentially a Bing Crosby sing-alike, he nonetheless managed to impart originality in 1940, singing with Charlie Barnet's roaring ensemble. The Barnet band was Ellington-influenced, and the Wild Man (Charlie) brought to the ballrooms and theaters of America a kicking, romping group of musicians who lit up the stages with great arrangements and solid solo instrumentalists. There were lovely charts in the ballad mode as well, and Bob Carroll functioned handily in that department.

Along with "Pompton Turnpike" and "Cherokee," Barnet wound up with a hit record of a beautiful tune called "I Hear a Rhapsody." Carroll's vocal on that side is classic. It is a virile rendition, sung with great warmth. Although Bob was only with Barnet for most of 1941, he made several fine records with the band. Then Pearl Harbor happened, and he went into the service.

When the war was over, he tried going solo with mixed success, then graduated into the theater and more legit singing. In 1971, he traveled with the road company of *Fiddler on the Roof,* playing Tevye to very good notices. I remember him best, though, with Charlie Barnet; Bob was certainly one of the finest singers of that time in American music.

Dick Haymes started in the business with a distinct advantage; his mother, Marguerite Haymes, was one of the leading singing teachers in the country. After an itinerant childhood, he brought some songs he had written to Harry James. James signed him as a singer (he replaced

Frank Sinatra), and he stayed with the band almost two years.

Oddly enough, I brought some of my songs to Harry James in 1941. He had me play drums for him and stated his intention to sign me as a featured drummer-singer. Dick Haymes was, at that time, James's singing star. I'll never forget how warm Haymes was with me. As I walked out of the State-Lake theater that day, Haymes encouraged me and said that, when I came with the band, we would room together.

The Harry James job never came to pass, but I followed Dick Haymes's career closely after that. He recorded my song "Lament to Love" with the band and sang it beautifully in that rich, wide-vibratoed voice of his.

Interestingly enough, he also replaced Sinatra with the Tommy Dorsey orchestra, appearing briefly with the band in *Du Barry Was a Lady* (MGM, 1943). Haymes took a look at what Sinatra was up to and decided to try and make it on his own. It was a wise decision. In subsequent movie appearances he was given good songs to sing, among them "How Blue the Night," "The More I See You," and "I Wish I Knew."

In my opinion, his finest hour came in the form of a 20th Century–Fox film, *State Fair* (1945). Rodgers and Hammerstein fashioned this charming movie, and Haymes, co-starring with Dana Andrews, Jeanne Crain, and Vivian Blaine, sang "Isn't It Kind of Fun," "A Grand Night for Singing," and "All I Owe I Owe I-o-way." His easy delivery and natural acting style boded well for the snub-nosed singer, but his Hollywood career went downhill in the early Fifties.

Money problems, wife problems, and deportation problems (He wasn't a U.S. citizen) laid him low, and he never quite recovered from these setbacks. While he still worked, playing various clubs and appearing occasionally

on TV, his career had stalled. He was a wonderful singer
and a very good guy, and just listening to his records or
watching him on film did me a world of good.

A totally different kind of band singer was a roly-poly
tenor sax player named Tony Pastor. Born Antonio Pes-
tritto in Middletown, Connecticut, he appeared with a variety of bands before becoming one of the mainstays of
Artie Shaw's wonderfully musical organization in the late
1930s. Pastor was the featured tenor saxist with the Shaw
band, but his vibrato was too fast on his solos, and Artie
foraged around until he came up with Georgie Auld, who
thereafter handled all the tenor sax solo work.

Tony didn't care. He was a happy-go-lucky musician,
a jolly individual who was content to be the featured vocalist with the band (along with Helen Forrest). During
the year 1939 (the magical year for Shaw's band, with
players like Buddy Rich, Auld, and Bernie Privin, as well
as Shaw himself), Tony Pastor turned in some amazing
performances, many of which were captured live at the
Café Rouge of the Hotel Pennsylvania and the Blue Room
of Maria Kramer's Lincoln hotel in Manhattan.

Pastor's ebullient vocals on "Jeepers Creepers," "The
Old Stamping Grounds," and "El Rancho Grande,"
breathless and exciting, are treasures of the time. Remi-
niscent of Louis Armstrong, and not unlike the singing of
Louis Prima, Tony's vocals evoke the happiness of the
years before WW II, the carefree spirit that pervaded the
music of those days.

When Shaw deserted his band and went to Mexico in
November of '39, Tony formed his own band, which featured the Clooney sisters, Betty and Rosemary. His work
continued to please the American public, but the spirit,
the musicality, and the feeling of the Shaw band simply
weren't there.

After the war, Pastor held onto his band by the very

skin of his teeth. He disbanded in the early 1960s and did an act with his sons, Guy and Tony Jr. Pastor died in 1969, and, although I never met him, his singing left an indelible mark on me.

Jimmy Rushing, the original Mr. Five by Five, held the vocal spotlight with the Count Basie band for at least a decade. He was a blues shouter in the best sense of the word, bellicose and exuberant. He was short, he was fat, and he swung.

Prior to working for Basie, he had appeared with Walter Page and Benny Moten, the latter in Kansas City. When Moten died, Basie, who had been his piano player, formed a combo that featured Rushing. That combo evolved into the Basie big band, and Rushing stayed on, singing and swinging the blues.

Rushing's contribution to the Basie library cannot be discounted. In addition to singing with the band, he wrote many of the blues tunes it featured, including "Sent for You Yesterday," "I'm Gonna Move to the Outskirts of Town," "Take Me Back, Baby," and "You Can't Run Around." Rushing's blues lyrics were gutty, nitty-gritty poetry that successfully portrayed the loneliness and the longings of the black man, wailing for his lost woman, crying out in the night.

He left Basie in 1948, led his own band for a while, worked as a single in theaters and clubs, and appeared with Benny Goodman in Brussels at the World's Fair in 1958. From the mid-Sixties into the Seventies, he performed many times at New York's Half Note. He sang his last song there before dying in June of 1972. He was a little giant, unique in his art. No one ever sounded quite like him, and, within the range of his narrow but meaningful catalogue of songs, he stood alone.

In the early Sixties, I made a record for Verve called *I Dig the Duke; I Dig the Count.* In that album I sang

"Sent for You Yesterday" and "Outskirts of Town." I did my best to espouse the Rushing style, but let's face it, there was only one Jimmy Rushing.

Unusual was the pairing of Dave Lambert and Buddy Stewart with the Gene Krupa band. They sang with the edition of the Krupa orchestra known as the "Be-Bop Band." Gene's band had turned a corner and, since late in 1945, had embraced bop as the standard regimen of the Krupa library.

Stewart and Lambert were leaders of this movement, and many of their vocal duets were steeped in the bebop mode. Best known among these was a knock-down, drag-out exercise called "What's This?" Both Lambert and Stewart were extremely facile, syllabizing these fly melodies and, Lambert in particular, wailing in the scat department.

In Lambert's case, the Krupa employment was a presage of things to come. Along with Jon Hendricks and Annie Ross, he became part of a trio that broke ground in the field of appending special lyrics to some of the great instrumentals of those days, as well as harmonizing on an extremely hip scale and doing some breakaway scatting in the process.

Buddy Stewart, tall and blondly handsome, had been a vaudeville baby, touring with his parents from the age of eight for seven years. He married singer Martha Wayne, and together they worked with Claude Thornhill in a vocal group called the Snowflakes. Martha Stewart went on to make several movies and eventually married Joe E. Lewis, the gravel-throated comedian.

Buddy, upon leaving Krupa's band in 1946, worked with Charlie Ventura in 1947, Kai Winding in '48, and Charlie Barnet in 1949. In 1950, he was killed in a freak auto accident in Deming, New Mexico. With the Krupa band he was equally at home singing ballads as well as the bop vocals. Heaven only knows what he might have accomplished had he lived. A very talented young man; a very untimely death.

Of course, there were many other singers gracing the bands of that irregular decade between '35 and '45. Herb Jeffries and Al Hibbler come to mind. They both sang with Duke Ellington; they both made excellent records with that band. Hibbler's singing of "I Like the Sunrise," from "The Liberian Suite" by the Duke, is one of the gentlest, most moving vocals ever put on wax. Jeffries shone on a number of sides, but "Flamingo" still stands as his best-loved piece of work. Tall, slim, mustachioed, and handsome, Herb was an imposing presence in front of the Ellington crew. A wonderful singer.

Tex Beneke sang as he played, with verve and originality. His strong Texas accent, formed around his prominent front teeth, graced several songs in the Miller band. He was a simple singer. He stuck to the melody, served the tunes well, and had the distinction of having a sound that was his own. There was no escaping the Beneke trademark, a slightly nasal, fast-vibratoed style that was infectious.

Joe Thomas, Trummy Young, and Willie Smith all sang with the Lunceford band. On a two-sided 78-rpm record of "Dinah," Thomas's breathless vocal is a winging, soaring performance. When he abandons melody to remark, "Now, Dinah," it is the essence of hipness.

Trummy sings "I Got It" as if his jaw is wired. His taut, strained vocal swings like crazy, and as he sings you can just visualize him, hands at his side, fingers snapping, strutting across the stage, his head jutting out in front of his body, his eyes closed. Catch him on "I Wanna Sing Swing Songs" or "I'm in an Awful Mood." Too much!

Willie Smith sang with the Lunceford trio and did occasional solo vocals, but he was mainly known for his alto sax work with the Lunceford band and, later, with Harry James.

Kay Kyser presented a whole host of singers, the best of whom were Ginny Simms and Harry Babbit. The latter is an unsung hero, a clean, in-tune, sprightly singer whose enunciation was perfect and who sang the songs with more heart than he has ever been given credit for.

Art Lund sang for a time with Benny Goodman. He had a good, masculine sound, but I felt his phrasing and melody bending were corny. On "Blue Skies," with Benny, he sings "Blue days/ A-a-a-a-all of them gone," and he sounds for all the world like a schoolkid trying to sing "hip." Just my opinion.

Last, Sinatra. So much has been written about him that I feel I could add no new insights into either his personal life or his singing. In 1991, I hosted a PBS special, "Frank Sinatra: The Voice of Our Time." Let that title stand as the hallmark for Sinatra's impact on the business of singing.

MY FELLOW AMERICANS

■ ■ ■

The year was 1947. There we all were, all the fine young cannibals, marching into the arena, snapping at Sinatra's heels, looking for our place in the sun.

Frank had led the way; he was the trailblazer. Now it was our turn to navigate the treacherous shoals that would take us to (1) stardom or (2) anonymity. In those days, the way to the gold was through the bobby-soxers. Huge bands of young girls chose their champions, formed fan clubs, wore T-shirts bearing the imprimatur of their particular hero, and in general showed up at the venues screaming, whistling, cheering, and causing an inordinate amount of chaos in support of the singer of their choice.

The singers were plentiful: Alan Dale, Vic Damone, Bill Farrell, Guy Mitchell, Tony Bennett, Jerry Vale, myself, and Eddie Fisher.

Eddie Fisher was an interesting case. He had a voice as clear as a mountain spring. He was a handsome young man. He had presence. In short, he had all the requisites—except one. He could not keep time. In any given eight-bar phrase, he would get lost, wander, and never recover.

When I played the Copa in 1947, he was pointed out to me by one of the maitre d's. "See that kid," he remarked. "Name's Eddie Fisher. Good singer. He worked here as a production singer for the Copa girls until last week. Then they fired him. Couldn't sing in meter. Threw the girls off every time he got up to sing."

When Eddie got his radio and TV shows, he had a man facing him, mouthing the words to every song he sang, leading him on the righteous path to correct time. It didn't hurt him one bit. He went on to become a major singing star. His unfortunate alliance with Liz Taylor did him in, but he remains one of the better singers of that period.

Vic Damone (Vito Farinola) had the best vocal chords of anyone in the business. He rivaled Frank Sinatra for tone quality, enunciation, and power. In the beginning, like so many other neophyte crooners, he aped Sinatra, and there are records of his that are so close to the Sinatra sound, you can't tell them apart.

Wisely, he abandoned that course and began to sing in his own particular fashion. The result is some of the best singing these, or any other, ears have ever heard. Vic is also blessed with agelessness. He looks as good today as he did forty-five years ago. No, better! He has matured and remains, for my dough, one of the great singers.

As do Jack Jones and Jerry Vale. I lump these two guys together because their vocal instruments are nonpareil. Jack and Jerry sing with a purity that is a joy to listen to.

Jerry is a real gent; quiet, thoughtful, and a pleasure to be around. He doesn't take his fame too seriously; he leans back and enjoys it. And whether he is singing songs in his native Italian or doing fine pop material, the results are the same. Beautiful, unalloyed, and clear as a bell.

Incidentally, when Jerry auditioned for the Copa, Jules Podell, the iron-fisted boss of the club, growled to his lieutenant, Jack Entratter, "Tell that kid he can stay as long as he wants." Jerry stayed twenty-two weeks.

Jack Jones is a real chip off the old Jones block. His father, Allan Jones, was a singer of the first water, having starred on the MGM lot, then at other studios, on radio, and in concerts, nightclubs, and stage productions.

Jack went his own way and developed a range that is the envy of every singer around. His breath control is nothing short of spectacular; he can hold a note from nine o'clock until midnight.

He has the added advantage of being a genuinely handsome young man, with prematurely grey hair and a mischievous smile. Additionally, he is a clever writer of lyrics, a talent he has not pursued, at least so far, and he is witty to a fault.

Jack's forte is the singing of contemporary songs, and in these choices I do not always agree with him. He does them better than anyone else around, but it is when he puts his talents on the line with renditions of songs like "Deep in a Dream" that he positively glows. He is a serious singer, professional to a fault, and I admire him greatly.

Andy Williams is yet another of the guys who started right about the time that I threw my hat into the ring. His choices of material were lucky, to say the least. He couldn't seem to sing anything that didn't turn into a roaring hit record. He is extremely easy to listen to, a voice that is soothing and mellow.

His experiences with Kay Thompson and his singing brothers had a lot to do with his eventual solo singing style. That act was one of the finest to ever hit the boards. Andy also dubbed his voice in on a couple of production numbers in *Good News*, in which I played a role at MGM in 1947. He has endured to become a staple in the business.

Tony Bennett (Anthony Benedetto) made his bones with Columbia Records. "Because of You" and "Rags to Riches" got him off the ground. Having a hit record is an absolute necessity in achieving star status. In 1962, Bennett found and recorded "I Left My Heart in San Francisco" and was forevermore part of the Golden Circle of hitmakers. He picks his tunes very carefully, and many of them are obscure but highly listenable. Likewise, his coterie of musicians is wonderful; the backgrounds for his singing, especially in the hands of the redoubtable Ralph Sharon, give him a platform upon which he shines vocally.

Bill Farrell sang with a growl, emulating Bing Crosby. He was very popular with the young girls for a while, then, suddenly, he faded from sight. This was the case with many of the singers who came along at that precise moment in time.

One surprising casualty was Guy Mitchell, who lingered on the charts for the longest time with hits like "Pittsburgh, Pennsylvania," "Belle, Belle, My Liberty Belle," and "My Truly, Truly Fair." He was a sunny, outgoing guy, and you would have thought he would have lasted in the business forever. It was not to be. Even though he appeared in a couple of movies (*Those Red Heads from Seattle*, 1953; *Red Garters*, 1954), his career waned in the late Fifties, and he dropped into obscurity.

As did Alan Dale. He had sung with Carmen Cavellero's band in 1943 and with George Paxton in 1944–46. Sinatra's defection from the ranks of the Tommy Dorsey orchestra to go solo affected Alan, as it did so many of us, and in late 1946 he struck out on his own.

He also was blessed with a couple of record hits, "Oh, Marie" and "Darktown Strutters' Ball," and subsequently made the usual rounds of clubs and theaters. He became weary of the constant traveling and chose to retire early on. Too bad. He was a good singer.

And so was Bobby Darin. Not only did he sing up a storm, he was a fine actor. Two of his films come to mind; he played the psychotic soldier in *Captain Newman U.S.A.* with Gregory Peck and one of the love interests in Richard Brooks's bittersweet *The Happy Ending*. He was natural and effective in both parts.

Mainly, though, he was noted for his singing, and that was very, very good. Besides the obvious ("Mack the Knife"), Bobby illuminated a lot of ballads. The results were a mixed bag but, generally, very good to excellent.

He dabbled in every genre, satisfying the bubble-gum brigade with "Splish Splash," his older listeners with "This Nearly Was Mine," and those pretenders to the swing and rhythm-and-blues bag with "Beyond the Sea." He was a swinger in the truest sense of the word.

Unfortunately, he was a childhood victim of rheumatic fever. When he went in for corrective surgery, his body couldn't take the stress. He died on the operating table, far too young. Had he lived, I believe he would have been one of the lasting breed of singers.

Many singers tried; a few survived. The demands on one's time and energy are devastating at times in the rat race called show business, and it is not uncommon for singers to prematurely quit performing.

Several ladies also fared well and not so well in those days. Gogi Grant is still around and singing, although not really active in the business. Likewise, Kitty Kallen, married to ex-publicist Bud Granoff. At a recent Society of

Singers function, she got up and sang with warmth and control, but her high-visibility days are behind her.

Bea Wain, wife of the late distinguished announcer André Barusch, began singing with Larry Clinton's orchestra and then went on to try a solo career. Her singing voice is intact, although she only performs these days at benefits and special events.

Fran Warren was the girl singer with Claude Thornhill. She began in the chorus line at the Roxy theater in New York. She joined Thornhill in 1946 and had a hit record in "A Sunday Kind of Love." Her voice has held up remarkably well, and she still appears in theaters, clubs, and summer stock companies.

Perky Helen O'Connell was a good reason for the boys to crowd around the bandstand when she sang with Jimmy Dorsey's orchestra during the Thirties and Forties. She had more than her share of hits, including "Amapola," "Tangerine," "Green Eyes," and "Yours." She remained active right up to her death from cancer in 1993. She played theaters and nightclubs and appeared on talk shows, sometimes with a slightly acerbic tongue. An amazing gal.

Steve Lawrence and Edie Gormé have intertwined their careers, even though, originally, they were separate entities. They've been singing together for so long that the blend of their voices is as one.

Steve is a smooth and creamy singer; Edie belts 'em out. There is a fine balance between them, and when Edie chooses to forego her iron tonsils, she can sing a ballad that will melt your heart.

In their Vegas stints, they specialize in extended medleys, honoring the Gershwins and other excellent songwriters. These medleys are cleverly crafted, with one song weaving in and out of the previous tune. Steve and Edie

are easily among the best of the nightclub performers currently working.

The singing community is a huge one. These days it
is divided between the young rock performers and the
older, standard kinds of singers who follow the paths of
righteousness in the namesakes of Berlin, Kern, and
Gershwin.

" . . . AND FROM — OVERSEAS . . . "

There is absolutely no doubt in my mind that if Al Bowlly had lived he would be one of the top two or three singers in the world today. If the word "heartfelt" ever applied to any vocalist, then the likely recipient of that word would be Bowlly.

Hugh Hefner is a close friend. On Monday evenings, I join him and a few more of his intimate buddies at his mansion in Holmby Hills, California. We have dinner, listen to the music that nourishes us, and then retire to his projection room to run an old movie. More than any other single band's or singer's, the music of Al Bowlly dominates these evenings.

We sit and listen and talk about him and his work and decry the fact that he died an early, tragic death. Bowlly was a product of the Twenties and Thirties, and the songs he recorded reflect his taste in singing, tunes that stick to your ribs. "The Day You Came Along," "I Never Had a Chance," "You're My Everything," and "It Must Be True" are all redolent of a bygone era, when the melodies were strong and the words wrenched at you with a vengeance.

Luckily, Bowlly made lots of records, and they can be heard and enjoyed by anyone interested in really fine singing. He had a tenor's range, and he sang directly from the left ventricle in a pure, piping, clear tone that made him one of the most beloved performers of his time. Strangely, as in the case of many English singers, his accent is undetectable on these records; he could be American. His singing, though, is delicate, straightforward, and delicious.

He was born in, of all places, Mozambique, in 1898. He grew up in Johannesburg, playing the guitar and singing his heart out. He got to England in 1928 and was instantly accepted as a singer of exceptional ability. He recorded with a wide variety of orchestras including the New Mayfair orchestra, conducted by Ray Noble. He also worked with the Roy Fox band and continued with it when it was taken over by Lew Stone.

Ray Noble sailed for America in 1934, bringing Bowlly and his drummer Bill Harty with him. They put together a fine orchestra and began to record for RCA Victor in 1935. The Rainbow Room in New York was Al's first major engagement in the States, and, instantly, it was a love affair between Bowlly and Manhattan.

He stayed in America until 1936, then returned to England, where he continued his recording activities with several of the best English bands including the famous Geraldo ensemble.

He was active through 1939, then he recorded less

and less. Don't ask me why; his voice actually improved
and became stronger with age.

He looked after his voice with great care, and when,
in early 1941, he began to sense throat problems, he consulted with several doctors to be sure that he wasn't in
serious vocal trouble; he wasn't.

The Blitz was on, and he felt he led a charmed life.
But he told his friend Jimmy Mesene: "If anything hap-
pens to me, remember the Greek spirit." (Bowlly's father
was Greek, his mother Lebanese.)

On the night of April 16, 1941, London was in for it.
One of the most devastating of the air raids was going on.
Al was oblivious to these raids and rarely went to the shel-
ters. On this night, he retired to his bedroom as the raid
continued.

When the bombing finally stopped in the early hours
of the 17th, the hall porter checked the rooms of the flat
to be sure everyone was safe. He opened Bowlly's door to
find him dead on the floor.

Bowlly and Lord Auckland occupied rooms in the
same block of flats, with Judge Gerald de la Pryme in between them. De la Pryme escaped with minor injuries, but
both Auckland and Bowlly were dead. It is said that Auckland was killed by the concussion of a bomb that fell in
Duke's Court and that Bowlly died of a heart attack,
caused by the same bomb.

There were tributes to Bowlly throughout the English
press and the music magazines. His passing was a great
loss, and I can't think of a single English singer who has
come along since who has the style, the voice, and the
panache that Bowlly had.

His discography is voluminous—page after page in
his biography (by Ray Pallett) of the wonderful songs of
the Twenties and Thirties. Bowlly was a handsome man,

with a soulful countenance, heavy eyebrows, a strong chin, thick, dark hair, and a sympathetic mien that was attractive in the extreme.

A great singer; an untimely loss.

The only singer who comes close to approximating what Bowlly created in the decades before the war was Matt Munro, a former lorry driver, whose creamy way with a ballad was popular with British music lovers in post-war England. He sang in a rich baritone, not unlike Perry Como, and is remembered for his rendering of "Born Free" in the movie of the same name.

Munro, in fact, became the prime singer of movie songs for years. He sang the title tunes for *From Russia with Love, Go Go Mania, The Italian Job, A Matter of Innocence, The Quiller Memorandum,* and *The Southern Star.*

Born Terry Parsons, he had interesting beginnings. He became a tank instructor in the Army when he was seventeen years old. For a while he drove a truck, then switched to the wheel of a London transport bus on the Highgate-Teddington route. At various other times, he was a tobacco worker, a plasterer's laborer, and a plumber's assistant.

Slowly, his singing career took shape, with a recording made in conjunction with Peter Sellers, a jingle for the Pepsi-Cola company in America, and then some eastern nightclub appearances and a few shots on the Ed Sullivan show. His singing of the movie themes helped him gain a foothold in both the European and North American markets.

He carried on, singing and recording, appearing in Vegas and other venues in this country, and finally settled in Florida. His last movie assignment was to cut the title theme for *The Sea Wolves*, a WW II adventure starring Gregory Peck and David Niven. The song was an adaptation of Richard Addinsell's "Warsaw Concerto" with lyrics by Leslie Bricusse.

In 1985, at the age of fifty-four, Munro died in London of liver cancer. He was a first-rate singer, and his records still sell in those markets where people are interested in good music.

Caterina Valente is one of the most astonishing singers of this or any age. Her range is incredible, and her pitch is precisely on the button. Her vocal power is unmatched by any of her contemporaries; she sings in four languages and is fluent in five. From "Malagueña" to the pop tunes of the day, she is comfortable and effective.

She was born in Paris of a Spanish father and an Italian mother. They were all seething with music; not only Caterina but her siblings, brothers and sisters alike, who sang and danced. Her father was a virtuoso accordionist, and her brother Silvano was famed for his guitar playing.

Early on, the whole family was engaged in a successful vaudeville act, incorporating all six Valentes. Eventually, Caterina broke away from the family and went out on her own. She began to record European songs and even dabbled in a little scat on occasion, although that aspect of her singing was structured and mainly written out.

For a while, she was enormously popular in the States, headlining the venues in Las Vegas and doing a multitude of concerts. She was actually a German citizen by marriage, and when that marriage went by the wayside, she married Roy Budd, an English composer. That marriage also failed, and she took up residence in Switzerland, continuing her busy career, flying to every city and country on the Continent to do as many concerts as she could handle in a given year.

She is a charming lady—funny, loving, and extremely professional. From time to time we have made plans to work together. It would be a delight for me just to sit and listen to that voice night after night. So far, those plans have not come to fruition, but hope springs eternal, and someday I might have the pleasure of singing in tandem with the great Valente.

Vera Lynn was dubbed "the Sweetheart of the Forces" during WW II. Born Vera Margaret Welsh, she began singing at the age of seven and never stopped. She worked with the popular Ambrose orchestra from 1938 to 1941 and then decided on a solo career.

The war was in progress, and Vera became as much a part of the Battle of Britain as barrage balloons and Spitfires. There was an unquenchable admiration for her, not only by the armed forces but by the English public at large. Her singing of the nostalgic song "We'll Meet Again" earned her the undying love of the entire British continent. She was indefatigable where entertaining the troops was concerned, tirelessly appearing in every possible location where "the boys" were stationed.

She retired briefly in 1946, then resumed her career, headlining a radio series and gracing many TV shows. In 1952, she broke wide open once again with a major record hit, "Auf Wiedersehen, Sweetheart."

She remained active throughout the Sixties and even added another hit to her stellar list of accomplishments. In 1967, she recorded "It Hurts to Say Goodbye," and the English public ate it up.

She sang with a catch in her throat, sentimentally and

essie Smith.

Connee Boswell.

Bing Crosby with The Rhythm Boy

d Astaire rehearsing with Judy Garland.

Ella Fitzgerald.

Sarah Vaughan.

Peggy Lee.

Woody Herman. *Credit:* Ray Avery's Jazz Archives, Los Angeles.

he Andrews Sisters.
redit: Universal Pictures Co., Inc.

Sigmund Romberg.
Credit: RCA/Victor.

Bea Wain.
Credit: CBS Photo.

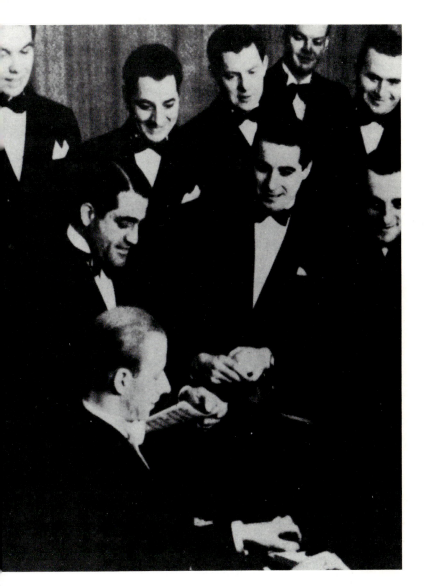

Al Bowlly, standing behind Ray Noble.

Helen O'Connell.

The Mills Brothers at the Cotton Club, 1934.

theme song of
SIX HITS AND A MISS
featured on Bob Hope's Program

ix Hits and a Miss.

The Modernaires with Paul Whiteman.

mbert, Hendricks, and Ross.

Jackie Cain and Roy Kral.

Jane Frazee.

Helen Forrest.
Credit: Ray Avery's
Jazz Archives,
Los Angeles.

Jimmy Rushing.

with a very personal message for her listeners. She was a genuinely beloved figure in England.

Another good singer was Anne Shelton, who, like Miss Lynn, began her career singing with the Ambrose orchestra. She was also popular during the war, appearing in 1944 with Bing Crosby, when he went to England for a visit and a series of broadcasts and camp shows. Her voice was pleasant if undistinguished, but she enjoyed a goodly amount of fame.

In France, the king of the balladeers was Jean Sablon, who was known as "the Bing Crosby of France." He sang in the appropriate crooner style and won many a female heart.

Charles Trenet likewise was a French icon, although I did not very much care for his work. He had a big hit in "Beyond the Sea," but his vocal properties were somewhat lost on me. Different strokes, I guess.

Another French "crooner" was Yves Montand— again, a cooing kind of singer, performing his songs with half-lidded eyes, nonchalant and distant. He always seemed to me to be more of an actor than a singer, starring in *The Wages of Fear* and, in America, *On a Clear Day You Can See Forever* and the Marilyn Monroe epic *Let's Make Love*.

The most effective and talented of all the products of France is Charles Aznavour. Actor, writer, lover, he is a Renaissance man in the true sense of the phrase. Aznavour's gritty charm and hoarse singing (once, when questioned about his hoarseness, he replied, "I've never been much of a singer") made him the toast of three continents. When he played Carnegie Hall, 150 people flew from France to witness the event.

Each song he sings is a little playlet, a vignette, an experience in itself. He is rail-thin, with sad eyes, thinning hair, and a wiry frame. He has been called the Frank Sinatra of France. He gets into the core of each of his songs, most of which he wrote himself (he has written over five hundred tunes). "Yesterday, When I Was Young" ranks as one of the great soliloquies of all time, with a brilliant lyric by the man himself. Every ounce of pain, self-examination, contrition, and redemption imaginable is here for the naked ear to listen to, as performed by the one and only Charles.

I continue to study him. The little Armenian's acting prowess is almost as formidable as his singing and writing. He starred in *Shoot the Piano Player,* directed by François Truffaut and scored hauntingly by Georges Delarue. Aznavour elicits our sympathy as a piano player in a café who unwittingly becomes embroiled in gangster activities. This was Truffaut's homage to American gangster films, with Charles playing the lead commandingly.

He once came to see me at Marty's in New York and professed an affinity for my work. That blew me away. If there is anyone whose admiration I covet, it is certainly Charles Aznavour.

There are no jazz singers to speak of in France, which is something of a surprise, considering France's preoccupation with jazz. The country that gave birth to Django Reinhardt and Stephane Grappelly has failed to produce a viable jazz singer.

Re: France's love affair with the jazz idiom. It has always been suspect where I am concerned. I don't think the French really "get it." I feel their enthusiasm for the music of our jazzmasters is a faddist's preoccupation with a form that is not native to their shores. I could be wrong, but, in one instance, I feel my suspicions are justified.

There is a scene in *'Round Midnight* in which Dexter

Gordon is making a "comeback," playing in a small club in Paris. A man brings his son to hear Gordon. Dexter's playing in this particular scene is execrable; yet, at the end of his solo, the audience applauds wildly and the man turns to his son and says, "Didn't I tell you? The man's a genius!"

I believe that the French propensity for jazz is a pose and that a clear grasp of the genre is sorely lacking in that country. I can't help thinking that jazz is understood and evaluated far better by Americans than by the French.

THE SONGWRITERS

■ ■ ■

In a recent interview, I was asked how many songs I know. I blithely answered: "Oh, around five thousand." I would here and now like to change that estimate to a couple of thousand. Maybe even three thousand. That figure shouldn't really surprise anyone. I have been singing professionally since I was four years old. During the course of my lifetime, I have learned and sung songs from the movies, Broadway, Tin Pan Alley, from the big bands and vocal groups and individual singers and . . . oh, just about everyone.

Obviously, without songs to sing, where would singers be? In an old Henry Morgan sketch, investigating the discovery of air, the announcer intoned: "Air! Without it, smoke would lie around on the sidewalk!" By the same token, singers, without songs, would lie around on their derrieres, eating bon-bons, reading the *Sporting News* or merely staring blankly into space.

The retention of songs, especially lyrics, is important in the pursuit of a singing career. The finest musicians develop a huge laundry list of tunes—all kinds—to play as accompaniment for singers or to improvise upon while appearing with a small instrumental group or a big band. So do singers, if they are worth their salt, commit to memory every single song of every shape and description their brains can lay hands on.

I began learning songs at a very early age. Growing up, I became more and more selective as to which songs I would simply learn and storehouse, and which tunes I would sing in performance. The next step was to differentiate between the hacks—the plethora of songwriters who churned out reams of forgettable fodder—and the golden few who were artists, craftsmen, poets, and genuine composers.

From the beginning of memory, my favorite composer has been Jerome Kern. Prior to Kern, what passed for the popular song was, in actuality, light opera, operetta, or semi-classical. The field was limited to a few men: Sigmund Romberg, Victor Herbert, and Rudolf Friml.

Herbert, born in Dublin, Ireland, in 1859, provided many enduring songs, operatic in form and style. "Ah, Sweet Mystery of Life," "Gypsy Love Song," and "I'm Falling in Love with Someone" are typical of Herbert's output. His shows enjoyed substantial runs on Broadway, and Jeanette MacDonald and Nelson Eddy immortalized him in their motion picture debut together, *Naughty Marietta*. He died in 1924, having given the world an impressive galaxy of music.

Sigmund Romberg showed up a bit later, having been

born in Hungary in 1887. He composed over fifty Broadway operettas, including *Maytime, The New Moon, Blossom Time*, and *The Student Prince*. His best-remembered songs—"When I Grow Too Old to Dream," "One Alone," "Wanting You," "Lover, Come Back to Me," "Softly, as in a Morning Sunrise"—were closer to the mark of what we have come to view as The Popular Song, and his "Close as Pages in a Book," even more so. He is still looked upon, though, as a writer of operettas, and a biopic entitled *Deep in My Heart* with José Ferrer playing Romberg verifies that fact.

Rudolf Friml was born within a few years of Romberg in Prague, Czechoslovakia. Like Herbert and Romberg, Friml was steeped in the romanticism of the operetta. His greatest successes were *Rose-Marie* and *The Vagabond King*. His scores were especially adaptable to the screen, and MGM made great use of his work not only with Eddy and MacDonald *(Rose-Marie)* but with Allan Jones in *The Firefly*, in which "The Donkey Serenade" emerged as a major hit.

All of the above were fine composers, and they left a lasting legacy of music that will live forever. But it wasn't until the coming of Kern that we saw a new kind of music take form. The melodies were more modern, the chord formations fresher and more challenging, and the harmonies broke away from the traditional structure of the Herbert-Romberg-Friml mold and explored new horizons.

Jerome Kern was born in New York in 1885. By age and by birth he was a contemporary of both Romberg and Friml. But where they pursued more conventional approaches to music, typified by Victor Herbert, Kern went in search of a newer, lighter brand of songwriting and, unwittingly, invented the popular song.

Which is not to say he wasn't a serious composer. His landmark score for *Show Boat* stands as one of the greatest compilations of music the world will ever know and is, to a degree, closely connected to the work of his predecessor Herbert and his contemporaries Romberg and Friml. However, as a writer of songs for the consumption of the general public, he had no peer.

He started early. When he was barely nineteen, he revised an English score for a Broadway show, *Mr. Wix of Wickham.* By 1911, he completed the entire score for *La Belle Paree;* in 1914, he had a winner in "They Didn't Believe Me" from *The Girl from Utah.* From that moment until 1933, Kern's string of successes is distinguished by the fact that almost every show he wrote had at least one or two major song hits. For example:

Oh, Boy: Till the Clouds Roll By

Sally: Look for the Silver Lining

Sunny: Sunny; Who?

Show Boat: Can't Help Lovin' Dat Man; Old Man River; Why Do I Love You?; Make Believe

Sweet Adeline: Why Was I Born?; Don't Ever Leave Me

The Cat and the Fiddle: The Night Was Made for Love; She Didn't Say Yes

Music in the Air: The Song Is You; I've Told Every Little Star

Roberta: Smoke Gets in Your Eyes; Yesterdays; The Touch of Your Hand

From 1935 on, he wrote almost exclusively for the movies, with one exception. In 1939, he ventured back to Broadway with a show called *Very Warm for May.* The show itself was feeble; one song in that show became what I, and many other Kern fanatics, believe to be the finest single song of his illustrious career. "All the Things You

Are" is simply perfect in all respects, with a poetic set of lyrics by Oscar Hammerstein and a venturesome melody that pushes the envelope to well beyond its limits. It is the perfect wedding of words and music and a hallmark for many other songs to emulate.

Kern was not beyond making some mistakes. Perhaps the rashest of these was to provide the score for a Paramount picture in 1936 that went from comparative obscurity to total oblivion in about four weeks. *High, Wide and Handsome* was a musical whose star was—wait for it— Randolph Scott. In fairness, Irene Dunne also starred in this ill-fated affair, and, turkey or not, the film boasted yet another of Kern's loveliest creations.

"The Folks Who Live on the Hill" is perhaps the most stirring of Kern's songs, a "family" love song that runs the gamut from building "A home on a hilltop high" to "And when the kids grow up and leave us." More than once as I sang that song, especially with my musical alter ego, George Shearing, audience members and we performers on the stage welled up and shed unashamed tears.

The songs that Kern wrote for *Swing Time, Lady Be Good, You Were Never Lovelier,* and *Cover Girl* are among his finest efforts. You would think that, having become the writer of the strongest melodies of all time, he would have rested on his laurels, not taken chances. This was not Jerome Kern.

In 1945, he reworked his beloved *Show Boat* into a sparkling revival. He composed a new song for the show, "Nobody Else but Me." In the first eight bars, the song goes from the key of C to the key of B. Those changes had heads snapping. His device to get the song back into C by the end of the sixteenth bar was inventive and totally original. His colleagues shook their heads in wonder; Kern had done it again.

He died late in 1945, and with him died one of the

most creative and original minds the popular-song field
has ever known.

His closest competitor was Richard Rodgers, who was
born seventeen years after Kern but who, like Kern, specialized in the writing of iron-clad melodies that stuck to
your ribs. It is almost impossible to chronicle all of Rodgers's work; he was one of the most aggressive composers
this country ever gave birth to, and his collaborations with
Lorenz Hart (from 1919 to 1943) and Oscar Hammerstein
II (from 1943 to 1959) marked pairings that changed the
face of Broadway as well as motion pictures.

Rodgers strove for success but had tough sledding for
the first several years of his career. He actually walked
away from songwriting for a time. Then, in 1925, he finally struck pay dirt with *The Garrick Gaieties,* and from
that time forward he and Hart made Broadway their personal thoroughfare.

Lorenz Hart was an eccentric, disturbed young man
who was also one of the great poets, writing prodigiously
clever lyrics to Rodgers's melodies. As a young man, Hart
had been a counseler at a boys' camp, along with another
songwriting great, Arthur Schwartz. Together they wrote a
camp song that endures to this day. It went:

> *I love to lie awake in bed*
> *Right after "Taps"*
> *I pull the flaps above my head*
> *And let the stars shine on my pillow*
> *Oh, what a light the moonbeams shed*
> *I feel so happy, I could cry*
> *And tears are born*
> *Within the corner of my eye*

To be at home with Ma was never like this
I could live forever like this
I love to lie awake awhile
And go to sleep with—a smile.

Years later, a group of boys who had gone to that camp sat in the balcony of a movie theater, watching MGM's *The Band Wagon.* As Fred Astaire and Jack Buchanan danced to a certain melody, the lads in the balcony jumped to their feet and yelled: "Hey! That's our camp song!" Hart and Schwartz had written the camp song to the tune of what would later become "I Guess I'll Have to Change My Plan."

Hart's lyrics were brilliantly crafted. Many of them contained inner rhymes, a process that was limited to a few clever minds then writing words to music. In "Mountain Greenery," for instance, he writes: "While you love your lover let—blue skies be your coverlet"; and in "Blue Room" he advises: "You sew—your trousseau—and Robinson Crusoe," etc. Hart's ear was phenomenal. Many tried to imitate him, to put together sentences with those extraordinary inner rhymes, but he was the master, and all the other lyricists of his time could do was listen and learn.

When he died of pneumonia in 1943, Rodgers turned to Hammerstein, a writer of an entirely different stripe. He was not nearly the rhyme king Hart was, but he wrote solid, fundamental lyrics that carried great import. In short, he was a far more serious lyricist than Hart had ever been, and he brought to Rodgers the making of an entirely new form of theater.

"*Oklahoma!,*" adapted from Lynn Riggs's *Green Grow the Lilacs,* was essentially a play with music. Broadway had never seen anything like it before, and its coming

brought to the theater a new form—a drama with attendant music and lyrics. It was a smash and brought about
what is, for me, the finest of the Rodgers and Hammerstein efforts, *Carousel,* another play with music adapted
from the classic *Liliom* by Ferenc Molnar.

I remember playing the Copacabana in 1947, as *Carousel* was enjoying its record-shattering run on Broadway.
Many evenings, after my first show, I would run up the
stairs of the Copa, hail a cab, and make my way to the
Majestic theater, to stand at the rear of the theater and
catch most of the second act.

One evening, as I stood there spellbound, I detected a
tall presence next to me. I turned slowly and looked into
the face of Richard Rodgers! He was concentrating on
what was going on on the stage, and I hated to intrude
upon him, but I simply had to.

"Mr. Rodgers," I said softly. "This is the ninth time I
have seen this masterpiece of yours, and every time I see
it I walk out of this theater in tears."

Rodgers looked at me and said: "Well, when you stop
crying, stop coming."

He was tall, autocratic, and a bit cold, but, my God,
he could write.

And then, of course, there were the Gershwins.

I always thought Ira got the short end of the stick. He
seemed stuck in the shadow of his younger brother
George, who garnered all the plaudits and the glory.
George undoubtedly deserved every kudo; he was a genius
of the first stripe, the closest thing to a jazz composer (with
the exception of Harold Arlen) we had in the Twenties
and Thirties.

There sat Ira, chomping on a cigar, avoiding the lime-
light, churning out some of the most engaging lyrics to be

heard and sung. Ira not only collaborated with his illustrious brother; he wrote the words for songs and shows in partnership with other composers, including Vernon Duke and Jerome Kern.

Ira's lyrics were wrought from his own life experiences. He was born in New York in 1896, two years before George. He had a strong family background, a set of parents who immigrated from Russia, nurturing souls who molded George and Ira into work-ethic individuals during their formative years.

George became a song plugger for Remick Music Publishers at age fifteen. Shortly thereafter, he was the accompanist for Nora Bayes and Louise Dresser. Then he signed on as staff composer at Harms Music. In 1918, he enjoyed his first hit, "Swanee," featured by Al Jolson in the Broadway hit *Sinbad.*

George collaborated with a select group of lyricists, including Irving Caesar, Gus Kahn, Oscar Hammerstein, and Otto Harbach. Ira was waiting in the wings, but, the minute he began contributing words to George's melodies, he clearly became his brother's lyric-writing alter ego.

The list of Ira's accomplishments is endless. From his first published effort with George ("Waiting for the Sun to Come Out," from *The Sweetheart Shop,* 1920) to his final lyric with his brother ("Our Love Is Here to Stay," from *Goldwyn Follies,* 1937) and beyond, Ira's portfolio is staggering.

When George died in '37, of a cerebral hemorrhage, Ira allied himself with Johnny Green, Kurt Weill, Arthur Schwartz, Burton Lane, and Harry Warren, among others. Even before the death of his brother, he was in demand. In 1920, he wrote a show called *Piccadilly to Broadway* with Vincent Youmans. In 1922, using the pseudonym "Arthur Francis," he penned *Pins and Needles,* and he continued the "Arthur Francis" deception that same year for three more shows, *For Goodness Sake*, *Molly Darling*, and *Fascination*.

Why Ira insisted on this nom de plume is anyone's guess. The best explanation is that he did not want to trade on his brother's name. He kept up the ruse in 1923 with *Greenwich Village Follies* and *Nifties of 1923*, finally reverting to his own name in 1924 with *Top Hole*, *Be Yourself*, and *The Firebrand*.

It is interesting that the Gershwins each followed his own star for a time, finally coming into full partnership in 1924 with *Lady Be Good*, a vehicle they crafted for Fred and Adele Astaire, which featured, among other songs, "Oh, Lady Be Good" and "Fascinating Rhythm."

George's ambitions lay well beyond the writing of show tunes and popular songs. He had concert pretensions, and they were fully realized in the number of extended pieces he wrote for symphony orchestras: "Rhapsody in Blue," "Concerto in F," "An American in Paris."

Porgy and Bess, the only true American folk opera, was yet another feather in George's already expanding cap. Ira shared lyric-writing honors with the show's librettist, Du Bose Heyward.

As an eleven-year-old, I saw the original company, with Todd Duncan, Anne Brown, and one substitute, Avon Long for John Bubbles, at the World theater in Chicago. It was one of the most moving experiences of my life, and the process was repeated in 1953 at the Ziegfeld theater in New York and once again in Houston in July of 1976, this time performed by the Houston Opera company.

I must say that, for me, the most affecting of all the companies I saw and heard was the 1953 troupe, with Cab Calloway as Sportin' Life and William Warfield and Leontyne Price as Porgy and Bess. The tragedy of these two ill-matched yet perfectly star-crossed lovers was never as poignant or touching as it was in the hands (and voices) of Warfield and Price. The timeless melodies and the riveting, sometimes shocking lyrics were handled with grace and knowledge by these two peerless performers, and the result, on opening night, was an experience I carry with me to this day.

Attempting an evaluation of the brothers Gershwin is almost futile. When you look at the body of their work together, the sum total subverts any kind of value you can place on it. The songs—"Love Walked In," "Someone to Watch over Me," "I Got Rhythm" (the most imitated and copied song in the jazz world), "'S Wonderful," "I've Got a Crush on You," countless others—are evergreens that will last until the stars fade and the heavens erupt.

Porgy and Bess is, once and for all, the quintessential folk opera that will periodically be revived and revered.

George's concert pieces elevated him into a stratosphere he never dreamed of when he first began plugging songs at Remick.

And Ira?

He remains, today, one of the great lyricists of his or any other time, quiet, almost reclusive, yet bursting with a talent that transcended his affiliation with his brother, offering up a wide variety of rhymes to a broad spectrum of composers who appreciated him for his work and himself.

Irving Berlin had the common touch. Perhaps more than any other songwriter, he was able to write words and music that everyone could understand and sing. He was the single most prolific of all the tunesmiths associated with Tin Pan Alley.

Born Israel Baline in Russia in 1888, he came to America at a very young age, changed his name to Irving Berlin, worked as a singing waiter when he was still in his teens, and, in 1911, sat down and wrote "Alexander's Ragtime Band," which was an immediate hit. From then on, everything he touched turned to pure gold.

He started his own music publishing company after his discharge from the Army in the First World War and, in 1921, built the Music Box theater with Sam Harris. That theater stands today as one of the finest venues on Broadway.

He wrote many shows, including the *Ziegfeld Follies* of 1919, '20, and '27, *Watch Your Step* (1914), *Stop! Look! Listen!* (1916), *Face the Music* (1932), *Annie Get Your Gun* (1946), and *Call Me Madam* (1950). In addition, he wrote extensively for films, from *The Cocoanuts* (for the Marx Brothers) to *Follow the Fleet* (Astaire and Rogers), *Alexander's Ragtime Band* (with Tyrone Power and Alice Faye) and *Holiday Inn* (Crosby and Astaire).

The list of his songs would fill this book twice over. Most significantly, he authored patriotic songs that have become virtual anthems in this country. "God Bless America," "Oh, How I Hate to Get Up in the Morning," "This Is a Great Country," and "This Is the Army, Mr. Jones" represent Berlin at his patriotic best.

With a wide variety of all kinds of songs, he was able to touch the hearts of every man and woman, and even children, and is certainly looked upon as one of the two or three greatest songsmiths who ever lived.

Cole Porter was the soul of sophistication. He, along with Berlin, was one of the few men who wrote both words and music. He came from a wealthy family, having been born on a farm near Peru, Indiana. For a while, he attended both Yale and Harvard law schools, then abruptly switched to Harvard School of Music and finally studied music at Schola Cantorium in Paris.

When World War I began, he enlisted in the French

Foreign Legion. In addition to his duties as an artillery officer, he entertained his fellow Legionnaires by playing a small, portable piano.

He inherited a fortune after the war and spent most of the 1920s in Europe. Then he returned to America and began his songwriting career. His first hit song was "Let's Do It", from the Broadway show Paris, and he went on to write an incredible number of hit shows and hit songs.

His legs were broken in a freak accident while riding a horse, and after several operations he suffered the loss of his right leg. But that did not slow him down, and over the years he became one of the best-known songwriters in the world.

I have probably sung more Cole Porter songs than those of any other composer. In 1946, Artie Shaw made an album for Musicraft records called *Artie Shaw Plays Cole Porter*. Shaw chose me to sing Porter's "Get Out of Town," thus effectively launching my solo singing career. Consequently, I feel I owe a lot to the man from Peru, and I continue to celebrate his extraordinary talent each time I walk on the stage.

Harold Arlen, born Hyman Arluck, enjoyed a songwriting career that spanned at least two decades. He was born in 1905 in Buffalo, New York, and, like so many of his contemporaries, he was a professional pianist at the age of fifteen. He composed his first hit, "Get Happy," in 1930 and, in 1933, wrote a song for the ages, "Stormy Weather," for a Cotton Club revue.

He, more than any other songwriter within memory, was steeped in jazz, and his output reflected that fact. There were always "blue" notes in Arlen's melodies. Think about it: "I've Got a Right to Sing the Blues," "I've Got the World on a String," "Last Night When We Were Young," "Blues in the Night," "Sleepin' Bee," "One for

My Baby." All of these, and more, had a jazz influence, a jazz orientation, that is rarely found in the catalogues of other popular-song composers.

In addition, Arlen was a wonderful singer. Time and again, when you hear songwriters demonstrate their wares vocally, the results are disappointing and, in some cases, downright dismal. Arlen sang with great robustness, in tune, and his voice had a slight cantorial pitch to it that tore at your heart. (His father was a cantor.)

While he collaborated with a number of lyricists, including Ted Kohler, Yip Harburg, Ira Gershwin, and Leo Robin, his most felicitous pairing occurred with Johnny Mercer. Together they wrote "This Time the Dream's on Me," "That Old Black Magic," "Come Rain or Come Shine," "Accen-tu-ate the Positive," "Out of This World," and a little song they scribbled for Paramount's *Star Spangled Rhythm* that is a personal favorite of mine, "With My Baby on the Swing Shift."

In the 1960s, several TV specials honored the music and the man. I was privileged to be a part of such a tribute, seated at the piano on the old "Today" show, with Dave Garroway in charge.

At one point, though, Garroway asked Arlen an embarrassing question: "Why did you never become a household name? Why did you never achieve the status of, say, Cole Porter or Richard Rodgers?"

Arlen was nonplussed. He stammered for an answer and came up empty. Dave Garroway was a kind, thoughtful man. I am certain that the question came tumbling out of his mouth before he had a chance to think about it. In fact, it was a question that many of us pondered. Outside of the entertainment business, Harold Arlen's name was relatively unknown to the general public. It is one of those mysteries that is unsolvable, unanswerable.

The very moment one of his songs is played or sung,

however, there is instant recognition and warm appreciation. He was one of the best.

Another gentleman who never achieved "star status" was Harry Warren. He was one half of the team of Warren and Dubin that wrote many of the Dick Powell starrers for Warner Bros. in the Thirties. He had a truly interesting upbringing; at the (apparently magic) age of fifteen, he was drumming in a carnival band, playing piano and accordion, and appearing in road shows as both stagehand and actor.

In 1922, he wrote "Rose of the Rio Grande." While it was a hit, he really didn't get going until the late 1920s, when he hit Broadway with *Sweet and Low*, *The Laugh Parade*, and Billy Rose's *Crazy Quilt.*

From there it was the Brothers Warner and a long list of movie musicals, although his talent wasn't confined to Warner Bros. alone. For the Goldwyn company he wrote the music for *Roman Scandals*, starring Eddie Cantor, and for *Moulin Rouge* (Paramount, 1934) he gave Constance Bennett "The Boulevard of Broken Dreams" to sing.

Mainly, though, he toiled for WB, contributing to *42nd Street*, *Gold Diggers of 1933*, *Wonder Bar*, *Twenty Million Sweethearts*, *Footlight Parade*, and *Dames*. His songs ranged from "Shuffle Off to Buffalo" to "We're in the Money," "Shanghai Lil," "I'll String Along with You," "I Only Have Eyes for You," and a multitude of tunes of every description. "Versatile" is the perfect word for Warren, who, like so many of the previously mentioned composers, turned out a wealth of material for three decades. Because he essentially wrote for the movies, he performed "on assignment," and the vast disparity of his work attests to his incredible diversity.

In 1950, for instance, he wrote the music for a Judy

Garland–Gene Kelly film called *Summer Stock*. One of my favorite songs in that film is "Happy Harvest." Judy sings it as she drives a tractor down a country lane. It is carefree and wonderfully musical.

Back during the war years, he moved over to the Fox lot and had Betty Grable, Alice Faye, Carmen Miranda, John Payne, and Don Ameche to work with. His output for these performers is nothing short of miraculous. He wrote in tandem with Mack Gordon, a roly-poly ball of fire.

Gordon, who early on teamed with Harry Revel at Fox, appears in a short subject promoting a Paramount picture called *College Rhythm* (1934). Gordon sings, dances, and clowns in this little one-reeler and handily steals the show from such experienced actors as Jack Oakie and Lyda Roberti.

When Gordon teamed with Harry Warren, they wrote "Down Argentine Way," "I Know Why," "Chatanooga Choo-Choo," "(I Got a Gal in) Kalamazoo," "Serenade in Blue," "I Had the Craziest Dream," "There Will Never Be Another You," "I Wish I Knew," "The More I See You"— well, the list goes on and on.

Why Harry Warren never became as celebrated as so many of his contemporaries is one of those enigmas that will go echoing down the corridors of time. Again, it was perhaps because of his allegiance to the movies that he never gained the luster of his Broadway-based confreres. Who knows?

He has certainly provided me with enough great material to sing; so much, in fact, that I could almost forego singing anyone else's songs. Harry Warren is one of my heroes.

The only other composer I can think of who shared a love of jazz and incorporated it in his songs was Hoagy Carmichael. Remember: he performed at an early age with the immortal Bix Beiderbecke and was greatly influenced by him.

Hoagy's greatest triumph (and possibly the single best-known, best-loved popular song of all time), "Star Dust," was originally written with Bix in mind, way back in 1927. The verse, in particular, rambles up the scale and down, resembling nothing so much as an improvisational cornet solo. The song remained lyric-less until Mitchell Parrish put words to it in 1931. It leapt forward to become an overwhelming hit. It put Hoagy on the map, but he had more than one song in him.

Over the years, he not only produced some of the finest music we have heard and loved; he also emerged as a credible actor and TV-show host. He worked with a number of superb lyric writers, including Frank Loesser, Paul Francis Webster, and Ned Washington.

Incidentally, "Star Dust" has now become a permanent fixture in my act. I know it has been done to death—but there's something about that song that is so moving I can't resist it. I sing it every time as though it were the first time, and the words and music are a constant source of interest to me. Far from being a "love" song, it is one of the most bittersweet examples of "lost love" ever written. I'll sing it till I die.

So many songwriters; so many great songs.

Frank Loesser, a tough, street-wise guy from New York City, whose *Guys and Dolls* alone should have won him the Congressional Medal of Honor.

E. Y. "Yip" Harburg, who wrote the lyrics to "Over the Rainbow," "Down with Love," "Happiness Is Just a Thing Called Joe," "How Are Things in Glocca Morra," and thousands of words in between.

De Sylva, Brown, and Henderson, stalwarts of the

Jazz Age, who managed to typify the mood and the madness of the Roaring Twenties. Their main metier was Broadway, and in their time they turned out *Good News, George White's Scandals of 1926, Follow Through,* and *Flying High,* as well as several movie scores.

Bert Kalmar and Harry Ruby were also tunesmiths who began churning out words and music with their first Broadway show, *Helen of Troy* (1923), and gave the world, among many other songs, "Three Little Words," heard in the Amos and Andy–Duke Ellington film *Check and Double Check* (1930). Over the years, their songs included "Thinking of You," "Nevertheless," and "I Want to Be Loved by You."

Sammy Cahn and Jule Styne were two of the most facile writers of songs ever to grace the songwriting scene. Sammy could write a parody on virtually any given subject, to any melody, in about three minutes.

He had a wonderful way with words; as a matter of fact, his biggest love affair was with lyrics. He was a master of similes, and, diminuitive, mustachioed man that he was, he was a runaway romantic. All of his lyrics reflected that fact, from "I Fall in Love Too Easily" and "Time After Time" to:

> *You sigh, the song begins*
> *You speak, and I hear violins*
> *It's magic!*

Jule Styne went from tunesmith to serious composer, once Cahn moved away from him to team up with Jimmy Van Heusen (Chester Babcock), another world-class melody writer.

Styne joined with Stephen Sondheim to bring *Gypsy* to the stage, and the soliloquy he wrote for Ethel Merman in that show transcends popular-song writing and makes its way into the classical form of composition.

For many years, Van Heusen was partner to a bright, incisive lyricist named Johnny Burke. They were Bing Crosby's team, writing much of what he sang in the Thirties and Forties. They were based at Paramount, and from 1936, when they did the score for *Pennies from Heaven*, to 1953 and *Little Boy Lost*, Crosby crooned their tunes and championed them tirelessly.

When Johnny Burke died in 1964, Jimmy Van Heusen joined forces with Sammy Cahn. Their combined talents produced some excellent songs, but Johnny's lyrics were special, and a kind of magic existed when he collaborated with Jimmy.

Ralph Rainger was another Paramount writer, who died in a plane crash near Palm Springs in 1942, forty-one scant years after he was born. He preceded Van Heusen as Bing's composer, writing songs for some of Crosby's earliest efforts *(Here Is My Heart, Big Broadcast of 1936, She Loves Me Not, Rhythm on the Range, Waikiki Wedding,* and *Paris Honeymoon.)* Among his best-known songs are "June in January," "I Wished on the Moon," "Blue Hawaii," "What Goes On Here in My Heart," and dozens of others, many of which were written with wordsmith Leo Robin.

In 1943, Ralph Blaine and Hugh Martin were newcomers to Hollywood, fresh from their Broadway smash, *Best Foot Forward.* They went west to write the movie version of the show and stayed on at MGM to adorn *Meet Me in St. Louis* with some of the most outstanding songs of this century. "The Boy Next Door," "The Trolley Song," and especially the glorious "Have Yourself a Merry Little Christmas" are perfect candidates for the Songwriters Hall of Fame. They wrote "Love" for *Ziegfeld Follies* (1946), and it has become one of the most-performed songs of all time. Strangely enough, their later efforts were not as well received as the foregoing, but they were (and are) still among the finest talents to ever put words and music to paper.

Vernon Duke (Vladimir Dukelsky) was born in Russia in 1903. In 1920, his family emigrated to America, and he began writing music at an early age. He is best remembered for two lovely creations, "Autumn in New York" and "April in Paris," but he also penned "Takin' a Chance on Love" and Bunny Berigan's signature song, "I Can't Get Started." In 1940, he wrote "Cabin in the Sky." He also composed serious music, and one of his songs, "The Silver Shield," became the U.S. Coast Guard fighting song. He died in Santa Monica, California, in 1969.

Arthur Schwartz and Howard Dietz were a pair of disparate souls who clicked as a team of songwriters. Dietz worked in the publicity department at MGM. Schwartz was an elegant man, educated at NYU and Columbia universities; he taught English in New York high schools in the 1920s and practiced law from 1924 through 1928.

In 1929, he began writing in earnest. In the course of the next three and one half decades, he turned out some of the most enthralling melodies ever concocted, in tandem with Howard Dietz, Dorothy Fields, Johnny Mercer, Ira Gershwin, and Oscar Hammerstein.

Dietz was his main man, though. While he labored at MGM, he almost casually wrote the words to "Dancing in the Dark," "By Myself," "I Guess I'll Have to Change My Plan," "Alone Together," and dozens more of the kinds of songs that standards are made of.

A notable exception is the score Schwartz wrote with Dorothy Fields for the Broadway play with music *A Tree Grows in Brooklyn*. It is tough and tender and touching, one of the best musicals ever conceived.

In more recent times, heavyweights like Henry Mancini, Johnny Mandel, Michel Legrand, Stephen Sondheim, Cy

Coleman, John Barry, Burt Bacharach, Donald Fagen, Barry Manilow, Janis Ian, Paul Williams, Billy Joel, and Stevie Wonder have contributed to the roll of American popular songs. Some of these tunes have lasting qualities, but the masters are the masters, and it is a safe bet that the music of the Gershwins, Porter, Kern, Berlin, Rodgers and Hart, et al. will be around until Armageddon.

What I owe those men and women is immeasurable. Comedians are trapped by the talents of their joke writers. It is a hit and miss proposition. But singers like myself (and the long list of practitioners who are my contemporaries) have the pick of the pack, a never-ending panoply of great songs to choose from and pursue careers with.

In recent times, the public has been lulled into a senseless round of three-chord tunes, plunked on a guitar or bashed away at with electronic gear and drum machines. The glorious music of the talented people mentioned herein, the wit, intellect, ingenuity, and craftsmanship of the writers of words practicing their trade in the Twenties, Thirties, and Forties, reached a pinnacle we will never see or hear again.

God bless the songwriting profession and all those who sail her.

THE ARRANGERS

■ ■ ■

Early in my career, I knew that I would become an arranger. Singing was fun (and easy), but arranging the music was something that fascinated me. It was going to be tough, I knew that. First of all, I had never studied music. Not in any way, shape, or form. No singing lessons, no piano lessons, and certainly nothing academic in the way of the study of theory, harmony, or the application of notes to paper.

But listening to the big bands, absorbing what the arrangers had to say by way of melodic structure, harmonies, and figures, tantalized me. Arrangers virtually formed the character of the bands. Orchestras were usually identifiable by the charts they played, and the unmistakable signature of individual arrangers was indelibly stamped on the output of the bands.

My awareness of the role arrangers played began in 1937. I would have been hard pressed to identify the work of the men who wrote for Whiteman or Vallee or Gene Goldkette. Fletcher Henderson caught my attention and held it with those early gems he did for Benny Goodman. As a kid, going to Hyde Park High, I spent my afternoons listening in rapt attention to "Sometimes I'm Happy," "King Porter Stomp," "When Buddha Smiles," and "Down South Camp Meeting."

Henderson's output seemed so right for that band. Fletcher's even division between the saxes and the brass was characteristic of the Goodman charts of those days. The light, airy backgrounds he wrote for the four saxophones to underline Benny's solo flights were the perfect filigree to enhance the King's clarinet playing. Benny once said that his single favorite arrangement of all time was "Sometimes I'm Happy." It is understandable. What emerges is a lazy, sweet-natured chart that dares the listener to not feel good.

Benny, through the course of his career, had many great arrangers contribute to his library: Eddie Sauter, with his Space Age mentality; Jimmy Mundy, who wrote what some believe to be the greatest swing classic of all time, "Sing, Sing, Sing"; the redoubtable Mel Powell, who brought "Clarinade," "Mission to Moscow," and "The Earl" to the Goodman organization; and even Harry James, who arranged, among other things, "Life Goes to a Party."

Yet Fletcher predominates. In 1982, I sat down with Benny between my sets at Marty's, a club on Third Avenue and 72nd Street in New York City. I specifically asked him about the various arrangers he had employed throughout the years. Without hesitation, Benny told me: "There was only one, really, Fletcher. He was the best arranger I ever had."

One might call Benny a "mouldy figge" for favoring

his earliest arranging compatriot, but when you look back on the body of Henderson's work, it's difficult not to agree with BG. Fletcher was really the first big-band arranger of note. An amazing number of writers followed his early lead, and for that alone he must be given full marks.

I now have to eat my words. Duke Ellington, long before Fletcher came on the scene, was writing wonderful arrangements for his Famous Orchestra. If there is a single individual who has had an effect upon me as an arranger, it is most certainly the Duke.

One of the first records I obtained as I left puberty and entered adolescence was Duke's four-part mood piece to the memory of his mother, "Reminiscing in Tempo." I played that extended work until I wore the grooves thin.

At that time, we still lived on the border of the "colored" neighborhood. What I heard in "Reminiscing in Tempo" was every heartache the black people ever suffered; the beauty, as well. The struggle, the futility, and, finally, the hope for the future. All of this in a jazz dirge by Ellington. It is still one of my favorite recordings.

You could hear Duke grow by the year. When the Swing Era came into being, he upgraded several of his earlier charts. "Black and Tan Fantasy," "East St. Louis Toodle-oo," and "Creole Love Call" are a few of his earlier compositions that he brought up to speed in the 1950s. His method of arranging was unlike anyone else's. He wrote in thick clusters, and, more often than not, his work took on a dissonance that was challenging and yet not unpleasant to the ear.

His arranging and composing covered an enormous range, from pop tunes and ballads to swinging instrumentals and effective tone poems ("Mood Indigo" and "Blue Light" come to mind.)

Most Ellington aficionados favor his 1940–41 band as

being the best cluster of musicians in his long tenure as a bandleader. With Johnny Hodges, Lawrence Brown, Jimmy Blanton, Cootie Williams, and Ben Webster in tow, it isn't hard to understand why this edition of the Ellington band was the most lauded, the most praised.

His recordings of this golden era in the band's history more than support the critical acclaim heaped upon his "famous orchestra." "Ko-ko," "The Flaming Sword," "Jumpin' Punkins," "Blue Serge," "A Portrait of Bert Williams," "Sepia Panorama," "Main Stem," "Moonmist," "Harlem Air Shaft," "Cottontail," "In a Mellotone," "Jack the Bear," and "Concerto for Cootie" are RCA cuttings to be savored and treasured as the best of Ellington.

And then there were the concert pieces, "Black, Brown and Beige," "The Liberian Suite," "The Perfume Suite," and "Such Sweet Thunder." And the non-secular works, an undertaking Duke experimented with late in his illustrious career.

He even "monkeyed" with classical music. Ellington and Strayhorn (Billy, that is, Duke's arranging alter ego) and Tchaikovsky all combined to bring you the "Nutcracker" in all its resplendent glory, except this time Carney and Hamilton and Cat Anderson were the suite's protagonists.

There is no evaluating what Duke Ellington brought to popular music and to jazz. He was a fine piano player and a competent if lackadaisical leader, but his arranging was paramount, and as an arranger he stood alone.

Charlie Barnet's band was the white equivalent of the Ellington ensemble. Barnet was committed to Duke's music, and it dominated his band's repertoire.

Charlie employed a staff of arrangers, not the least of whom was himself. Sometimes he would quirkily bill himself as "Tom Billings" or "Dale Bennett," but more often than not his name would appear on such meaningful charts as "The Duke's Idea," "The Count's Idea," "Lament for May," "Blue Juice," and "Leapin' at the Lincoln."

Barnet had the measure of his band, and his arranging was "spot on." A friend of mine in my high school days was particularly fond of the Barnet band, especially the saxophone section, which he called "decidedly feminine" in sound. I know what he meant. Just as Wilbur Schwartz led the Glenn Miller sax section with his resounding clarinet lead, so did Charlie Barnet stand in front of his saxes, playing soprano sax with beauty and great clarity. The combination of his lead line and the rest of his saxophone players made for a sweet, mellow, or "feminine" motif where that section was concerned.

His arranging staff included William "Billy" Moore Jr., who was wasted with Barnet, writing ballads for the band ("When the Sun Comes Out," "Be Fair," "Wasn't It You") and only occasionally shining with a rollicking "Spanish Kick," "Southern Fried," or "Redskin Rhumba." Moore was to find prominence a bit further down the road with the Jimmie Lunceford orchestra.

Andy Gibson was on Barnet's staff, churning out "Echoes Of Harlem" (excellent) and "Scotch and Soda" (not so excellent). "The Gal from Joe's" was more like it, and so was "Ebony Rhapsody," utilizing the power of the Barnet trumpet section and the rhythm section, which at that time boasted Wes Dean on drums, Phil Stephens on bass, Bus Etri on guitar, and Sinatra's longtime pianist, Bill Miller.

The really great find was trumpeter-arranger Billy May, who joined the band in mid-1940 and turned in some dazzling charts, one of which, "Pompton Turnpike," became a huge hit for the Barnet band. Billy also penned

Duke's "The Sergeant Was Shy" and "Ring Dem Bells" for Barnet, and on a July 26, 1940, air check he introduced his "Aviation Suite," which, by September of that year, became "Wings over Manhattan." Ellington's influence on Billy May is clearly evident here.

"Wings" owes a lot to "Reminiscing in Tempo," particularly in the slower section, in which the saxes move downward in chromatic diminished chords in much the same way Duke's 1935 saxophone section did in "Reminiscing." It's a beautiful work, jammed with bright colors and wistful ballad passages. Barnet not only recorded it on two sides of a Bluebird disc; he used it on his transcription dates, and it became one of his most-played charts. Indeed, it was the only extended work Charlie ever attempted.

Billy May is some sort of genius. In the early Sixties, I made a record with Billy called "Olé, Tormé." One night, he picked me up at my house, on the way to the recording session at Radio Recorders.

As I came down the stairs, he slid over into the passenger seat and asked, "Would you mind driving?" I got behind the wheel and headed for the studio. Billy sat next to me, writing furiously on a score pad.

"What's that?" I asked. "Something for another session?"

"No," he replied. "This is for tonight."

After I got my jaw rehinged, I stammered, "B-b-but we're going to be recording in fifteen minutes."

"No problem," he said laconically. "While we're doing the first few tunes, my copyist will get this one done, and we'll do it last."

I sat there amazed. He was writing an arrangement, completely transposed for every instrument, without a piano! Sure enough, we got to the studio, recorded three songs, and then his "automobile" chart was placed before the musicians and we proceeded to put it on wax. P.S. It was excellent! Fully realized, brilliantly written, and a joy to sing with.

Billy finally got his own band and his own style after serving time with the Glenn Miller orchestra, for which he also arranged. "Sweeter than the Sweetest" with Marion Hutton and the Modernaires is one of the cookingest confections on record, but my vote goes to his wondrous introduction to "Serenade in Blue."

The story goes that Miller was not happy with the opening segment that Bill Finnegan had turned in. He crooked his finger in Billy May's direction, and the result is one of the most remarkable twelve-bar gambits on record. The intro is semi-classical in content, dark and brooding, and it sets up "Serenade in Blue" in a unique fashion that is unlike any other Glenn Miller recording.

I still love the things Billy wrote for Barnet best of all, but he really is a man for all seasons, one of the most gifted men with a music pen on earth.

Another talented man was Jerry Gray. Born Jerry Graziano on July 3, 1915, in Boston, he came to prominence with the Artie Shaw band of 1938–39. Shaw was known as the man who played the show tunes, and Jerry Gray fit neatly into Artie's scheme of things.

For one thing, Shaw had what was arguably the single best saxophone section ever assembled in a Swing Era band to work with. In those days, four saxophones were "the thing." The baritone sax had not yet come into its own, and many sax sections were equally divided between the altos and the tenors. Shaw's sax section consisted of Les Robinson, Hank Freeman, Tony Pastor, and Georgie Auld. They played as one man, and the results were stunning.

The harmonies employed were mainly of the close variety. The section used just the right amount of dynamics, and Gray's writing showed off not only the saxes but the whole band. Jerry judiciously used mutes, derbys, and plungers in the brass section. His arranging was clean and musical, and he was particularly clever when writing backgrounds for Helen Forrest and Tony Pastor vocals.

He arranged what became one of the most enduring hit records of all time, "Begin the Beguine," but that was only the tip of the iceberg. "Softly, as in a Morning Sunrise," "Jungle Drums," "What Is This Thing Called Love?," "Copenhagen," "Serenade to a Savage," "One Foot in the Groove," and "Octoroon" were some of the charts Gray turned out for the Shaw band. There was a smoothness about Jerry's arranging that touched the heart, a romanticism that was rare.

When Shaw abandoned his band in November of 1939, Jerry went on to arrange for the Glenn Miller orchestra. In a strange kind of turnaround, his Miller arrangements bear no resemblance whatsoever to his previous work with Shaw. They are full-blown (remember: he went from a six-brass, four-saxophone band to an eight-brass, five-sax ensemble) and even raucous on occasion. This is in no way a condemnation of Jerry's work with Miller; it is merely a realistic evaluation of how he changed in the Miller milieu.

One of Jerry's greatest talents was his bent for composing. He did little original work for Artie; mainly, he wrote charts that were vocal backgrounds for the pop tunes of the time, or outlined known instrumentals ("Copenhagen," "Softly, as in . . ."). When he was occasionally permitted to vent his composing talents, it was only in conjunction with Artie Shaw—directed melodies ("One Foot in the Groove," etc.).

With the Miller band, Jerry emerged as a full-fledged

composer. "A String of Pearls," "I Dreamt I Dwelt in Harlem," and "Caribbean Clipper" make up a small part of the originals Gray submitted to the Miller library. While these offerings didn't have the subtlety or beauty of the Shaw pieces, they were very effective and placed Jerry high at the top of the list of arranger-composers then plying their trade.

When Miller went into the Army during WW II, Jerry's services were in demand on the Bob Crosby radio show, as well as the Phillip Morris show. In the early Fifties, when the Glenn Miller style was in full bloom with the orchestras of Ralph Flanagan, Tex Beneke, and Ray Anthony, Gray formed a band with Wilbur Schwartz, Miller's great lead clarinetist, in tow.

That band, more than any other of the Miller imitators, captured the true Miller sound. At one point, Jerry was musical director for the Fairmont hotel in Dallas, Texas. I worked with him on many occasions there, and I must say, he was a true inspiration to me where arranging was concerned.

William "Billy" Moore Jr. left the Barnet band to join Jimmie Lunceford in 1939. He had been nominated by Sy Oliver, who left his longtime mentor, Lunceford, to write for the high-powered Tommy Dorsey band.

Moore was a class act from the very beginning. One of his first charts for the Lunceford band was "Belgium Stomp," and it was clear from this entry that he was an arranger's arranger. His backgrounds for Trummy Young, especially "Rock It for Me" and "I'm in an Awful Mood," are radiant, but he was really impressive with original instrumentals like "Bugs Parade" and "Monotony in Four Flats."

My favorite Moore arrangements are "What's Your

Story, Mornin' Glory" and, especially, "Chopin's Prelude No. 7," which I always list as one of my five favorite records of all time.

In 1940, a lackluster arranger named Roger Segure joined Lunceford, and the band was never the same, declining into eventual disbandment. Billy Moore became an expatriate, emigrating to Sweden.

One day, listening to "Chopin's Prelude" for the umpteenth time, I wrote him a fan letter. He replied almost instantly, and we kept up a correspondence until his death. His charts were suave and unerringly musical, and, once in a while, I find myself writing a phrase in one of my arrangements that is a throwback to the work of Billy Moore Jr.

Perhaps the king of the Swing Era arrangers was Sy Oliver (real name, Melvin James Oliver). He grew up in Zanesville, Ohio, played trumpet professionally in Columbus for a time, and then, in 1933, joined the Jimmie Lunceford band and became one of the most influential and imitated arrangers of the period.

His charts for the Lunceford band were riff-filled, kicking adventures in swing. He literally created the unique style that set the Lunceford band apart from all its competitors. The long list of arrangements he wrote for the band includes "Margie," "My Blue Heaven," "Cheatin' on Me," and an almost endless parade of derby-waving, saxophone-slurring goodies. In addition to the foregoing, Oliver wrote "Organ Grinder's Swing," "For Dancers Only," and a long legacy of instrumentals and vocal backgrounds that placed him in the forefront of the league of arrangers prominent during the Swing Era.

He left Lunceford in 1939 to join Tommy Dorsey's higher-paying organization. Ensconced in the Dorsey family, he gave that band many original instrumentals, in-

cluding "Well, Git It!," "Easy Does It," and "Opus No.
One." On occasion, he sang vocals with the band, and
"Yes, Indeed" was an immense jukebox favorite when it
appeared, with Jo Stafford and Sy sharing the vocal
honors.

Oliver also penned "That's It," "Not So Quiet Please"
and "Quiet Please," a pair of Buddy Rich–featured drum
solos, "So What," which spotlighted Don Lodice's tenor
sax, "Another One of Those Things," "Serenade to the
Spot," and "Swingin' on Nothin'." This last was not only
a kicking vehicle for Sy and Jo Stafford but was also
picked up and recorded by other bands, Charlie Barnet's
version with a Ford Leary vocal and a great Bus Etri guitar solo being among the most prominent of the lot.

One of my favorite Oliver jobs is "I'll Take Tallulah"
from *Ship Ahoy*. After the vocals are dispensed with,
Sy launches into an instrumental section that clearly
shows his versatility. Not merely a jazz arrangement, it
fills the bill as movie music, broad and wonderfully
conceived.

He led his own band with a collection of great sidemen in 1946–47, then broke the band up to write for
nearly every major singer on the scene. We made a couple
of singles together for Coral Records in the late Forties,
one of which was an extended version of "Yes, Indeed,"
with extra lyrics and a minor-keyed section. It was a good
record, one I'm proud of, and, of course, Sy's knocked-out
arrangement is the reason.

Oliver is gone now, but his impact on the arranging
world lives on. There is scarcely a person writing today
who doesn't cull something from the Oliver bag of tricks.
I know: I'm one of them.

Right after WW II, I had the opportunity to record with
Artie Shaw's studio orchestra. This was a group that fea-

tured not only some of the best sidemen Hollywood had
to offer in the way of jazz musicians but a superb string
section, made up of the finest studio men and women.
Shaw's first record for Musicraft, a budding label that had
signed both Artie and my vocal group, the Mel-Tones, was
a tribute to Cole Porter.

The Mel-Tones and I sang "What Is This Thing
Called Love?," and, alone, I warbled "Get Out of Town."
The arranger was Sonny Burke. Sonny had seemingly
been arranging forever. His charts were heard within
the confines of the Buddy Rogers band, with Joe Venuti,
Xavier Cugat, and, from 1940 to 1942, with the Charlie
Spivak crew.

He wrote especially fetching tomes for Spivak, including an absolutely beautiful rendering of "When the Sun
Comes Out." By the time he went to work for Artie Shaw
in 1946, he was as seasoned an arranger as one could find
in the galaxy of Hollywood writers,

I learned a lot about arranging, just hanging around
Sonny and watching him work. He was another one of
those tireless guys who took on more than you felt he
could chew; then he chewed it up and spit it out, and the
results were not only some of the finest arrangements of
their kind but the most versatile as well.

Sonny wrote for strings with the same ease he tackled
the big-band sound. His range was enormous; there was
nothing he couldn't write, and write with authority and
originality. Strangely, he couldn't READ music worth a
damn! Of course, he wrote everything, laboriously com-
mitting his pen to music-score paper, but when it came
time to have those charts of his played, he pfumfed and
fumbled through the rehearsal, squinting at the score,
peering hopelessly at what he had written.

"I'm not a schooled musician," he would say defen-
sively. "Writing these things a note at a time is easy, but
reading them! I'm hopeless."

I know what he meant. I am in precisely the same boat. My writing now takes me from my trio to the symphony orchestra. I labor over those symphony charts like a mother hen, and—contrary to, say, Billy May, who churns out reams of arrangements without benefit of piano, expeditiously, with great rapidity—my arranging efforts are slow, tedious, time-consuming. It is the lack of formal musical training that waylays me and confounded Sonny Burke. No matter. He was one of the greats, and chances are I would not have become an arranger if I hadn't been stimulated by his work.

In recent years, I have had the pleasure of having some of the best arrangers in the world write for me. Dick Hazard, Shorty Rogers, Hal Mooney, Nelson Riddle, Chris Gunning, Russ Garcia, Neal Hefti, Paul Villepigue, Jimmy Jones, Johnny Mandel, John Williams: the list goes on.

I have benefited greatly from my association with these men, both as a singer and arranger. I have asked questions (interminably) and gotten, in return, advice, help, collaboration. While all of them have affected me in my pursuit of the arranging craft, two stand out.

In 1955, I traveled to England for my first tour of that country. During my stay, I went into a Phillips recording studio to make an LP called *Tormé Meets the British*. On the podium, in front of the sizable orchestra assembled, stood a slight, blond young man named Wally Stott.

From the first downbeat, I knew I was in the presence of a major talent. What he fashioned for that orchestra, particularly the woodwinds and strings, is beyond description. The closest I can come to explaining his method of arranging is to commend you to the glorious writing of Robert Farnon. Wally was cast in the Farnon mold, and, in a way, he outdid Farnon, with some of the richest, loveliest charts I have ever had written for me.

His manipulation of chords, his substitutions, giving this melody and that a fresh, new perspective, is something I will always treasure. Frankly, I don't sing well on this album, and I think the fault lies directly with Wally's arranging. The charts overwhelmed me. They were so perfect, so beautiful, that I became emotional just listening to them, and those emotions colored my singing and my control.

Years ago, Wally went to Denmark, had a sex-change operation, and emerged as Angela Morley. She wrote all the original music for the popular TV shows "Knot's Landing" and "Dallas," turning her back on arranging.

In 1992, I was about to make my very first Christmas album. Because I wrote, with Bob Wells, "The Christmas Song," way back in 1945, my followers have been astounded to find that I had never done a Christmas album prior to this one.

On the off-chance that she might just acquiesce, this one time, I called Angela, and, to my total delight, she agreed to write four arrangements for the album. When the rehearsal with the Cincinnati Pops orchestra came to pass, I was once again taken back to that Phillips recording session in London, so many years before.

When Angela's arrangement of "The Christmas Waltz" concluded, I was shaken. The sheer gorgeousness of her writing caught me off guard. And not just me; the entire corps of musicians sort of halted in mid-air after the last notes were played. Then breaths were expelled, and everyone in the orchestra applauded. Wally/Angela certainly hadn't "lost it." We all felt we had performed a Pulitzer-Nobel-Prize-winning arrangement.

The other arranger is Marty Paich.

Initially, he arranged many of my vocal efforts for Bethlehem Records and beyond. I had heard an arrangement he made for Shelley Manne and his men. The tune was "You're My Thrill." I was caught up in the West

Coast jazz scene, and it seemed to me, in hearing this chart, written for four saxophones and a rhythm section, that Marty resided plumb dead center within the West Coast musical mentality.

Joining Bethlehem was an important move for me. I had had enough of the majors and their strictures. Every one and his uncle was telling me how to sing and what to sing. I had tried to be pliable and, in the process, made some of the worst records in the memory of modern man.

Red Clyde of Bethlehem called. He heard something in me that Columbia and Capitol missed: the ability to sing jazz. I signed, and we were prepared to do our first album, a ballad affair called *It's a Blue World*.

"I've found an arranger," I told Red, "who knocks me out. I'd like to use him on this first album."

"Name?"

"Marty Paich."

"Yeah, I know him. Good jazz writer. But this is a ballad album."

"I know that. But I've got a feeling about this guy . . ."

"Mel, this is a BALLAD album."

"Trust me, Red."

Marty was given four of the twelve tunes to do on the album. The orchestra was smallish but effective: fourteen strings, harp, French horn, trumpet, and a rhythm section. Paich's four arrangements were total jewels. The way he wrote for that mini-orchestra made them sound like the Cleveland Symphony.

In particular, "All This and Heaven Too" stands out as an example of Marty's immense talent. He had studied at the Los Angeles Conservatory of Music under the tutelage of the famous Mario Castelnuovo-Tedesco, graduating from that school in 1951 with a Master of Music degree in composition.

His bent was jazz, essentially, and he went right to work, writing for the likes of Shorty Rogers, Dave Pell, the Stan Kenton orchestra, Count Basie, Peggy Lee, and Woody Herman. By the time we got together, he was a seasoned chart writer. In our first jazz album, we put together a group called the Marty Paich Dektette, so named because there were ten men in the band.

Our third effort was a Bethlehem album called *Mel Tormé Sings Fred Astaire*, and once again Marty's colorful writing was right on target. He placed the tuba, the low end of the Dektette, in many positions other than the obligatory bass note. Sometimes he would write a unison line for the trumpet and alto, using the rest of the band as a bed under them. The results were sensational.

Over the years, we collaborated on several albums, as well as performing together in a number of venues. Ultimately, it was Marty, more than any other single person, who was responsible for my becoming an arranger.

One of the albums we did was an updated version of a suite of music I had composed in 1949 called "The California Suite." It was a kind of alter ego to Gordon Jenkins's "Manhattan Tower," and while, in '49, it had been done originally with a full orchestra and chorus, this new version, recorded in March of 1957, featured the Dektette, a string section, a regrouped Mel-Tones, and a rhythm section.

One of the songs that I had written for the suite was something called "Poor Little Extra Girl." I had based the tune on Dizzy Gillespie's closing gambit on "I Can't Get Started." It went like this:

When Marty arranged it, he decided that he didn't like the final chord in this quote, so he changed it. While it was beautiful, it simply did not follow the Gillespie pattern, and it became something else. There and then, I decided that the only way I would ever get precisely what I wanted in any given arrangement was to do it myself.

I began conservatively, writing for four horns and a rhythm section. Gradually, I moved up to a small big-band grouping: three trumpets, trombone, three saxes, and rhythm, not unlike the Dektette. Finally, I got my feet wet by graduating to a full big band: seven brass and a tuba, five saxes, three rhythm.

Remember, I had written for the Mel-Tones for years, and in a way that was like writing for a saxophone section, with two altos, two tenors, and a baritone. In the course of my budding arranging career, I asked a ton of questions.

Marty was enormously helpful, supplying information on the effective range of the horns, the lowest notes accomplished by the bass trombone and the baritone sax, and how to write block figures for the band, with the trumpets on top, the saxes a third below the trumpets, the trombones in the middle to lower register, and the tuba in the basement.

Eventually, I experimented with symphony charts, drawing much from a loose-leaf book given to me by Angela Morley. She called it "Mel's String Book," and I devoured it. The mystery of writing for strings evaporated, and I gained confidence with each new arrangement I wrote. To date, I have turned out over fifty symphonic charts, and they seem to work quite well.

What I owe to all the foregoing arrangers is immeasurable. In listening to what I have done as an arranger, you will undoubtedly hear quotes from Marty Paich, Angela Morley, Shorty Rogers, and so many more. When somebody recently pointed out my proclivity for using figures and chords attributable to the above, I shrugged my shoulders, raised my hands palms upward to the heavens, and exclaimed: "Hey! I only steal from the best!"

THE ——————————— INSTRUMENTALISTS

■ ■ ■

In a thousand and one interviews, I have been asked how I came to sing scat and who my influences were. Naturally, I spoke of Ella Fitzgerald, Leo Watson, Louis Armstrong, and many more. The truth is: I learned more listening to instrumentalists than to other singers.

Whenever people see me in person, they notice that, as I scat my way through this song or that, my right hand is approximating a trombone slide, or held close to my mouth as I simulate a trumpet solo with my fingers. Or I may place both my hands down low, in front of my chest, in imitation of a tenor sax.

Scat, of course, is the alter ego of instrumental work, a vocalizing of improvised notes that might be played on a horn. Consequently, I lean more toward cloning the work of the musicians I admire than aping the syllables and vocal perambulations of other singers.

Early on, my favorite musicians were those of the Swing Era. Their solos were comprehensible and uncontrived. Later, the bebop gang caught my ear, and, in several outings of mine, I mimed what I had heard out of the horns of Dizzy Gillespie and Charlie Parker.

George Shearing once said: "I only incorporate bop in my work to the degree of digestibility." Good advice. Bebop confused the average listener with its complex, multi-noted figures and whirlwind execution by its protagonists. When I am singing bop figures, I keep them as simple and "digestible" as I can.

Duke Ellington and his parade of remarkable musicians were my earliest influences. Ben Webster is far and away my favorite tenor saxist. His deep, low tones and his propensity for melodic passages were thrilling to hear. When I started venturing into the scat department, he was one of the players upon whom I hung my hat.

Rex Stewart likewise. His playing was tentative at times, and he certainly did not have the best vibrato in the business, but he played with such feeling that I found him irresistible. "Morning Glory" is one beautiful piece of work, and Rex makes the Duke Ellington composition breathe.

Lawrence Brown's mellow trombone and Johnny Hodges's creamy alto sax also played a part in my learning to scat-sing. Both were longtime veterans of the Ellington band. Both could string out their solos into beautiful works of art, and in the ballad area they were not to be equaled.

Roy Eldridge was and is my favorite trumpet player. His high-note work with the Gene Krupa band of the Forties is not to be believed. He would hunch his shoulders up, point his horn at the audience, and breathe fire and brimstone through it. He had wonderful facility and a tone as wide as Fifth Avenue. I find myself emulating his horn technique many times when I am singing scat.

The Lunceford band was chock full of musicians to admire. Snooky Young, Joe Thomas, Trummy Young, and Willie Smith were all, in their individual ways, pacesetters. The band itself was a marvelous amalgam of stupendous arrangements and pinpoint-accurate playing, with the above-mentioned soloists shining within. All through my high school days, I played their records and sang along with the solos until the platters collapsed. Then I'd go out and buy them again.

My most intense period of "listening" occurred in high school. My record collection was vast, an investment in the future. Singing with the records was my way of learning my craft. There were shining examples everywhere. Basie's boys, Erskine Hawkins's band, Earl "Fatha" Hines, Andy Kirk's Clouds of Joy—all harbored musicians whose styles and playing affected and inspired me.

On the white-band or "ofay" side of the ledger, myriad men molded me. Artie Shaw is a perfect example of the player I keyed into at an early age. His taste in music was in a class by itself. He played the clarinet with more of a "saxophone" tone than a clarinetist's approach. During my days at Hyde Park High, the battle raged constantly: who was the better player—Goodman or Shaw? I was firmly entrenched in the Shavian camp.

There are so many examples of his playing, it is hard to single out just one, but on his record of "I'm in Love with the Honorable Mr. So and So," as Helen Forrest sings the last line of the second stanza, Artie plays a run that defies description, it's that exciting.

Whenever I call him, I never say hello. As he picks up the phone to answer it, I sing the "So and So" phrase into the mouthpiece. There is a pause. Then he says, "Oh, hello, Mel." His stamp is upon me to this day.

Georgie Auld was the featured tenor man in Artie's record-breaking 1939 band. Auld took over from Tony Pastor and gave new meaning to the word "swinging." Originally an alto saxist, he switched to tenor in the mid-Thirties and proceeded to make history, holding down the jazz chair with Bunny Berigan, then Shaw, then Jan Savitt, and ultimately Benny Goodman.

He made the transition to bop when that form took over the music scene and had a busy career thereafter, appearing on Broadway in *The Rat Race* and later playing one of the leading roles in the Robert De Niro–Liza Minnelli starrer *New York, New York*.

Georgie's chorus with Shaw on "One Foot in the Groove" has fostered many a scat chorus out of me.

There is no denying Benny Goodman's influence on me. We were both from Chicago, so I naturally bought his records, listened to him on "The Camel Caravan," attended his in-person stands at the Chicago theater, and enjoyed him in the movies. Strange guy, Benny. A mixture of genius and vulgarian. He was tactless in the extreme, and one wag put it succinctly: "Benny should never— NEVER—take the clarinet out of his mouth."

With all this, though, he was quicksilver with his horn, and in recent times I have put together a quintet, with myself as the sixth part of the BG Sextet. We do several tributes to the man, and I particularly like to get into "Three Little Words," with excerpts from "Slipped Disc" and "A Smooth One" and several "out" choruses. This number is mainly "vocalese," using syllables to maintain my role in the six-man group. It's fun, and I never fail to lean heavily on Benny's ideas when I perform that medley.

I admired Tommy Dorsey's breath control. Dorsey was a protagonist of "circular" breathing. That means that he could play a note and continue to blow into his horn while, at the same time, taking in air through the side of his mouth. The note would go on ad infinitum, seamless and unending.

Harry Carney with Duke Ellington was another man who could hold notes, on his baritone sax, until the stars faded. Since breath control is an integral part of singing, I listened closely to both of these musicians, trying to figure out how they did it. I never did. I finally devised my own system for holding long notes, which I will discuss shortly.

Woody Herman always threw together some of the best corps of musicians the jazz world ever fostered. Stan Getz, Zoot Sims, the Condoli brothers, and Bill Harris were inspirational to me as I grew and learned.

Harris, in particular, stood out, easily outclassing all other trombone players. Nobody had ever heard the kind of sound he made on that horn. It was raunchy, impassioned, and bold. Harris, more than any other musician I can think of, "sang" into his trombone, and the results were positively startling.

There is a Woody Herman vocal on a song called "If It's Love You Want, Baby." After Woody sings the first chorus, Harris takes over the bridge and last eight bars in a display of strident, dynamic playing that is nothing short of breathtaking.

When I did my CBS afternoon show in 1951-53, I insisted on having Bill on the show, since he had left Woody's employ. Every single day was a celebration of wonderful listening. He was the genuine article, and when I do my scat singing, with my hand imitating a trombone, my mind is strictly on Bill Harris.

For smooth, sweet meanderings on their respective saxophones, Stan Getz and Zoot Sims cannot be beaten. After the gutty, abrasive (but brilliantly musical) sounds of

Coleman Hawkins, Chu Berry, Charlie Ventura, and Illinois Jacquet, Stan and Zoot were a breath of spring, playing cleanly, with no evidence of anything other than a pure, uncluttered tone and flawless technique. They both pioneered the bossa nova when that form of music came into vogue, and their records of the Brazilian music stand as the foremost efforts of the genre.

One of my heroes is Gerry Mulligan. Baritone saxist, pianist, composer, and arranger, Gerry was at the forefront of the Bebop Era. He played with and arranged for Gene Krupa in 1946. "Disc Jockey Jump" was one of Krupa's favorite instrumentals.

He appeared on the Miles Davis *Birth of the Cool* sides in 1948. He contributed "Jeru," "Boplicity," and "Rocker" to Miles's library. After short stints with Elliot Lawrence and Claude Thornhill, he formed the Gerry Mulligan quartet (Chet Baker, Chico Hamilton, Bob Whitlock, and Gerry).

It was an unusual foursome, with no piano; just trumpet, baritone sax, bass, and drums. Gerry's arranging skills let the listener imagine the piano. He managed to write the bass and himself in tenths, while Chet Baker soloed, and his two-part harmony lines with Baker left nothing to the imagination.

Shortly thereafter, he put together the Gerry Mulligan Tentet, a group comprised of two trumpets, trombone, French horn, and tuba; alto, tenor, and baritone saxes; and bass and drums. Once again, it omitted the piano except for a few instances in which Gerry played it.

The records he made with this band on Capitol are the most advanced, sophisticated arrangements ever written. They predated the entire West Coast jazz scene, and dozens of groups sprang up on the heels of these recordings, in imitation of the real thing. The one element all these combos had in common was a lack of Gerry Mulligan's considerable arranging skills. Only Gerry had the talent and foresight to write for the Tentet with restraint and shading. I still play that record once or twice a month. The music never palls.

Gerry himself found an entirely new way to play the baritone. Where Serge Chaloff (Woody Herman's star baritonist), for instance, would play with the usual guttural, raw sound we have all come to expect from that instrument, Mulligan caressed his notes, sounding more like a tenor saxophonist on his horn than a baritone player. In all the time I have listened to Mulligan—(and we have worked together on several occasions)—I never once heard him fluff a phrase or be at a loss for an idea in any given tune. He is one of the true originals, a very special musician.

And George Shearing.

What can I say?

In 1976, entrepreneur George Wein put Mulligan, Shearing, and me together in Carnegie Hall. It was a night I will never forget. Both Mulligan and Shearing outdid themselves, delivering to the packed house a perfectly balanced program of some of the best music anyone ever heard. I sang along, and together the three of us were compatibility personified.

From that night onward, Shearing and I teamed in a series of concerts and nightclub engagements that are among the highlights of my musical life. The man is amazing. He sees things a lot more clearly than almost anyone I can think of. He has built-in radar going for him. In a hair's breadth, he can insert a substitution chord or entire phrase that changes your perspective on what you are singing and alters the very fabric of the song.

We used to say, in interviews, that we were "two bodies with but a single musical mind." I hope that's true. He instantaneously conformed to my alterations on tunes we did together, and I, alternately, adjusted to his chord patterns and transpositions. What came out were certainly, from my point of view, the most creative performances (and records, for Concord Jazz) I have ever done.

George has the best sense of humor I have ever come across. He is self-deprecating where his blindness is concerned. We worked together so many times that I found myself forgetting he had that disability, and that's the way he lives his life. In a world of seeing people, his attitude is: I'm blind. So what? He goes about his business, "watching" movies and TV and, in one instance I recall, driving a car under the watchful eye of his loving wife, Ellie.

He is my friend and one of the greatest sources of inspiration to me. His ballad playing is, incontestably, the finest, most delicate ever practiced on his instrument. He has a vast storehouse of songs in his noggin and an even greater knowledge of classical music. On almost any song we did together, he would weave a classical quote into the material, giving our performance an entirely new dimension.

Like Mulligan, he is one of a kind.

From Harry "Sweets" Edison, I gathered a kicky "right on the beat" kind of stance where my scat singing is concerned.

From "Cat" Anderson, I simulated the high notes, sometimes with "head" tones, occasionally in falsetto.

From Lester Young, I picked up ideas, which, after all, are the most important element in jazz.

The instrumentalists. They shaped my thinking and my singing and were my greatest influences.

BANDLEADERS ——
WHO SING

■ ■ ■

Buddy Rich always wanted to be a singer. With all that immense talent for drumming, his fondest wish was to make with the vocal cords. When we were in Vegas together, he would constantly ask me to come to his house and give him singing lessons. (Who was going to give ME lessons?)

Rich sang with the Tommy Dorsey band on occasion, even more with the Harry James band, and much more with his own outfit. He had an off-the-elbow kind of approach to singing that was extremely pleasant. His one bugaboo was intonation; he had none. But he could sing, make no mistake, with a rhythmic sense of time that was the envy of many a genuine singer.

In October of 1959, Buddy made a "singing" record for Mercury. It was called *The Voice Is Rich*, and it was nice if not outstanding. When he worked with the Tommy Dorsey band, he was always complaining about the number of ballads being forged for Frank Sinatra. "They're boring," he would grumble. "This is supposed to be a jazz band. Dammit! Enough with those slow tunes. Let's cook!"

The truth was, he loved the ballads, and particularly Frank's singing of same. Once he told me: "You know, when Sinatra sings 'Star Dust,' I have to turn away from the audience so they won't see the tears rolling down my cheeks. Gets me every time."

In late 1959, he had an angina attack that left him shaken and worried. The doctors told him his drumming days were over. He brooded about the news for a while, then decided he would take up a singing career.

On a cold autumn evening, I went over to catch his act at the Living Room, a small boîte on Second Avenue in New York City. I sat there, nursing a Coke, while he sang for an hour. Later, we strolled silently toward 52nd Street. Finally, he could bear it no longer. He turned to me challengingly and asked: "Well? What'd you think?"

I looked at him and replied: "Well, let me put it this way; I'm not your favorite drummer and you're not my favorite singer." He grunted once, and we walked the rest of the way in silence.

When we got to 52nd, we walked into one of those narrow clubs that line the street. Buddy sat down in a booth, lost in thought. Allan Eager and his crew were wailing away on the bandstand. Now Allan spotted Buddy. "Come on up here, Buddy, and sit in," he invited Rich. Buddy waved him off, but he was not to be denied. "Come on, come on," he insisted, beckoning with his hand. "Knock us out."

Rich looked at me.

"You know you want to play," I said. "Do it!"

He got up behind Max Roach's drums. Roach hates me to this day because, in another telling of this story (*American Way* magazine, December 1974), I said his drums sounded like they were filled with water. Plop plop. Sorry, Max, that is exactly what they sounded like.

It didn't matter. Rich began to play, and that club, which had only a handful of customers when we came in, was suddenly full to overflowing. The word had gotten around the Street. "Buddy Rich is playing drums with Allan Eager."

Rich played an eight-minute solo that evening that had the customers gasping, crying, cheering, whistling, and stompinng. As we walked back to his flat, he said: "Screw singing. I'm a drummer!"

Still and all, he loved to sing. In an eight-minute short that he made for Vitaphone in 1929, he not only sang but scatted as well, and he was good. During his early teens, when he emceed shows on riverboats going up and down the Hudson, he sang. And once, when we both guested on the Merv Griffin show, I sat at the drums while he sang, and Merv complimented him on his "hip" style.

In his last appearance, on a PBS special that we shot in January of 1987, I once again took over the drums while he worked his way through "Whatcha Know, Joe?" He was relaxed and happy and, as usual, swinging. He died shortly afterward.

Bobby Sherwood was a fine singer. His "God" was Willard Robison, the man who wrote "Old Folks," "Cottage for Sale," and "Guess I'll Go Back Home This Summer." Robison was also a singer of sorts, performing with a decided twang, almost a country singer but softer and gentler. (Robison can be heard in a vocal album called *Deep River Music* on Capitol, 1948.)

Sherwood emulated Robison and added some twists of his own to come up as a singer of note. He was a quadruple-threat man, playing trumpet, trombone, guitar (with beautiful chording), and piano. He also wrote excellent arrangements.

Born in 1914 in Indianapolis, he worked in his parents' vaudeville act as a child. He became a professional musician in the late 1920s, and when Eddie Lang died he took over as Bing Crosby's accompanist. He had a busy time in his younger days, playing for the Burns and Allen show, on "The Lucky Strike Hit Parade" with Lennie Hayton's band, on "The Camel Caravan," and conducting and performing on the Eddie Cantor show from 1939 to 1941.

He was a staff musician at MGM until 1942, when he formed his own band, wrote "Elk's Parade," and became enormously popular, particularly on the West Coast. In 1950, he headed for New York, where he worked many radio and TV shows as actor and emcee as well as singer. He was also in demand on the various panel shows that dotted early television in the 1950s. He was seen to good advantage in *Pal Joey* (Columbia, 1957) as Sinatra's sidekick.

It was during his personal appearances with his band that he sang a great deal. He was a singularly soothing singer. When I lived in New York, we became close friends. On the weekends, we would go up to Timberlane Ranch in the Catskills. Bobby was an avid horseman, and he rode a buckskin like he was born to the saddle.

In the evenings, he would haul out his guitar and play and sing. Those moments were something to remember. He knew all of Willard Robison's songs, especially the obscure ones, and sitting around a campfire, in the hush of a summer's evening, listening to Bobby sing was about the closest thing to heaven imaginable.

Bing Crosby's little brother, Bob, wasn't a great

singer, but when he stood in front of his Dixieland band (actually a "co-operative" orchestra led by Gil Rodin) he had a nice, easy manner, a winning smile, and acceptable vocal qualities if not exceptional ones.

The Crosby band (and the Bob Cats) were among the most written-about, highly respected organizations in the band business. Bob made himself useful, singing in a kind of ersatz "Bing" style, low and soft and croony. One thing that distinguished him from the pack was his choice of songs.

He always picked good tunes with interesting lyrics. "I Never Knew Heaven Could Speak," "What's the Name of That Song," and "At Your Service, Madame" are typical of the kind of songs Crosby sang. The lyrics were chiefly cosmopolitan, and he was highly effective.

In 1953, he took up where I left off, heading a CBS-TV afternoon show five times a week. He made an engaging host on this series and went on to become one of the really durable bandleader-vocalists of the Sixties and Seventies.

In *The Gang's All Here* (20th-Fox, 1943), Benny Goodman sang "Paducah" and "Minnie's in the Money." Not unusual. Benny had a long history of singing as well as being the King of Swing. As early as 1936, Benny is listed as "apologetically" singing " 'Tain't No Use" on an RCA Victor record made in November of that year.

Throughout his tenure as a bandleader, he took to the mike to sing various tunes. On a "Camel Caravan" broadcast, August 10, 1937, Benny sang "Me, Myself and I." Johnny Mercer contributed special lyrics each week to the "Camel Caravan" broadcasts. Benny was prominently featured vocally in these numbers.

In 1943, in a broadcast from the Hollywood Palladium, Benny warbled "Rosie the Riveter"; in yet another broadcast from the same location, Benny sang "Drip Drop." He recorded "Oh, Baby" in 1946 and vocalized extensively on that one for the next few years.

Benny always sounded as though he had a deviated septum. He sang and spoke in that peculiar way, almost as if he were pinching his nose or suffering from a cold. He was far from being a credible vocalist, but he did sing with considerable swing, his vibrato coarse and rough, unlike his vibrato on clarinet. Somehow, he sounded right with his own band, and his vocals are to be admired for what they are: an instrumentalist attempting to sing and being partially successful at it.

Vaughan Monroe was the subject of considerable criticism when he brought his brand of singing to the music business. He had a "legit" quality to his singing, an attribute that would have been more at home on the Broadway stage than in front of a big band. Much fun was made of his voice, and many imitators considered him fodder for their acts. His vocals were strident at times but effective nonetheless. He had a major hit in "Racing with the Moon." (He also played good trumpet, and his band was quite popular during the Big Band Era.)

He took a crack at the movies as a Western star (*Singing Guns*, 1950) and even abandoned his band to become a publicity man for RCA Victor in 1955. His popularity faded in the late Fifties, and he was semi-retired thereafter.

He had a huge voice (he was called the "Iron Lung" by many reviewers). He had to tone down his power for the pop tunes he sang with his band. The results were not always successful, but he remains a major figure of that era.

Cab Calloway, the king of "hi-de-ho," had a band almost exclusively organized for the purpose of featuring himself on the vocals. In a subsequent chapter, I will discuss his singing.

Louis Jordan led a fine little combo, the Tympani Five, organized in 1938. He was a good alto sax man, and his vocals were clean and pure. The group specialized in novelty numbers like "Knock Me a Kiss" and "Is You Is or Is You Ain't My Baby," which Louis sang with zest and humor. He made several movies, toured the length and breadth of America, and led the Tympani Five through quite a few rhythm-and-blues numbers that exemplified good jazz qualities.

There were other bandleaders who sang, among them Will Osborne and Russ Morgan, but the prime mover in those circles was certainly Rudy Vallee. From 1929 through 1931, Vallee reigned supreme as the most popular singing bandleader in the country.

In '29 he began an NBC weekly radio show for the Fleischmann's Yeast company. In addition, he made a film, *The Vagabond Lover*, in which he sang the title tune to the delight of the entire U.S. population. "My Time Is Your Time" and "The Maine Stein Song" are just a pair of his enormous hits during this period.

He sang into a megaphone in a nasal tenor-baritone voice and, for all intents and purposes, was the first real singing matinee idol. With his crinkly hair, his quizzical eyebrows, and his pearly teeth, he captured the hearts of the entire female contingent.

He faded for awhile in the mid-Thirties but came back strong as a rich prude in *The Palm Beach Story*, Preston Sturges's romp about a disaffected married couple (Paramount, 1942). Thereafter, he espoused roles of this nature, scoring heavily in *How to Succeed in Business Without Really Trying* on the Broadway stage and then repeating that triumph in the movie version (1967).

Interesting note: Frank Sinatra once said that his main role model was Rudy Vallee. This remark may be apocryphal, since Sinatra was in the habit of doing it "his way" and his way alone, but it wouldn't be that surprising to me. Vallee's singing was clean, his enunciation perfect, his intonation right on the button, and, after all, that's Sinatra to a "T."

THE ———————
VOCAL GROUPS

■ ■ ■

In 1942, Ben Pollack dragged me out of Hyde Park High School in Chicago, put me on the El Capitan, bound for Los Angeles, and threw me together with the Chico Marx orchestra, then rehearsing, with a nationwide tour in front of them. The main reason for my being there was to form a vocal group out of members of the band and write for them.

I had been experimenting with vocal-group writing while I was still in high school. Hyde Park was a cornucopia of talented kids; kids who played instruments, kids who sang and danced, kids who acted, and kids who, like myself, had a "thing" about vocal groups.

Four- and five- and even seven-voice units were all over the place. The Merry Macs, the Pied Pipers, the Modernaires, Six Hits and a Miss, the Skylarks, the Town

Criers, the Mills Brothers, the Andrews Sisters, the Dinning Sisters, the Mellolarks, Four Jacks and a Jill, and the best couple to ever sing and play music, Jackie Cain and Roy Kral.

I put together a group out of the band, with Johnny Frigo, Elise Cooper (soon to be replaced by Kim Kimberly), Bobby Clark, out of the trumpet section, and myself. It was good. Not spectacular but certainly more than passable. With each rehearsal we improved until, finally, the Revellies (named after Chico's character in movies) were ready to be competitive with all comers.

When the band broke up in November of 1943, I headed for Hollywood. I had been signed to play the juvenile lead in an RKO picture called *Higher and Higher*, with Frank Sinatra, Michele Morgan, and Jack Haley. Once that film was completed, I elected to remain in Hollywood. My family made the trek from Chicago, and we all settled on the West Coast.

One problem: I had nothing to do.

Ben Pollack became my manager. One day he told me about a vocal group called the School Kids, a quartet that had gotten together at L.A. City College. They sang well, head arrangements mostly, but they needed an arranger. I needed a vocal group. We fit like a glove.

We did camp shows, AFRS broadcasts, entertained at the Hollywood Canteen, made a couple of "B" pictures (*Pardon My Rhythm* at Universal, *Let's Go Steady* at Columbia), and in general busied ourselves learning new arrangements and becoming involved in the war effort.

And listening.

There was a lot to listen to.

The Modernaires (Chuck Goldstein, Ralph Brewster, Bill Conway, and Hal Dickenson) had left Paul Whiteman and gone with the Glenn Miller organization. I admired their singing to the point of copying much of what they did in arrangements I wrote for the School Kids. (Shortly after I took over the School Kids, Bernie Parke, one of the group, suggested we change our name to Mel Tormé and his Mel-Tones).

One of the main reasons for the Mods' distinctive sound was the lead singing of Chuck Goldstein. He had a high, piercing quality to his voice, and the group's sound hinged on his leading the way.

Bill Conway was the arranger. A rather shy, diffident man, he made up in sheer talent what he lacked in personality. His arranging was tight and original. The Mods were at home with ballads or up-tempo tunes.

One of my favorite records by that group was "Sweeter than the Sweetest." The orchestration was by Billy May, the vocal chart by Conway. There is a light, swinging feeling to the record that builds and builds. Easily, one of the best vocal-group scores of all time.

Marion Hutton, then Paula Kelly, and occasionally Tex Beneke and Ernie Cacares joined in with the Modernaires, as did Ray Eberle on the slower tunes, and those ballad moments, particularly "Serenade in Blue," are special experiences to be cherished.

I have one record of the Modernaires that I treasure. It is a side they made with Paul Whiteman in 1938 called "Mutiny in the Nursery." That record was a presage of things to come. The writing was close harmony, and they sang it perfectly, without a flaw. Most of Conway's work was based on close harmonization. Occasionally, with other voices added, he would stretch out into more open voicing, but he excelled in the close-harmony method.

The Pied Pipers, on the other hand, almost always sang in open stance. Jo Stafford, that paragon of perfect pitch, led the Pipers through many Tommy Dorsey charts, with Chuck Lowrey, Verne Yokum, and John Huddelston, who, for a while, was Stafford's husband.

Originally, the Pied Pipers consisted of seven guys, and the group burgeoned to eight when Jo Stafford joined them. In 1940, upon joining the Dorsey band, they trimmed down to four and proceeded to make some of the most remarkable recordings in the history of the big-band days.

They were aided and abetted by arranger Sy Oliver, the hippest of the hip, whose writing for the group created an image of awareness and topicality that was unmatched by any of their contemporaries.

Sy had his finger on the latest "street" patois of Harlem, and he incorporated the language into many of the Pipers' charts. In his original "Swingin' on Nothin'," Jo says to Sy: "You don't have to tell me, pops. I know that that'll get it."

In "East of the Sun," an arrangement he made for Sinatra, the band answers Frank's lines with "We'll mix the square," "A righteous pad," and "Where you can really lay it on me."

Sy's vocal charts were not always the best defined, but they moved along with an impetus all their own, making the Pipers, Connie Haines, and Sinatra the best-backed singers in the business.

As influential as the Modernaires were in shaping the Mel-Tones, no group had more of an impact on my writing than Six Hits and a Miss. They were the first septet (outside of Kay Thompson's singers) to approximate a band. They sang in block figures, they sang segmented, four of them the brass section, three of them the saxes.

They supplied "boo wahs," like trumpets and trombones would do, under the vocals of their lead singer, Pauline Byrne. Vince Deegan was one of the driving forces behind this magnificent troupe of singers, and the seven voices produced a thick, rich sound that grabbed you and held onto you.

Pauline was a painfully shy lady who reluctantly sang solos not only with the Six Hits but with Artie Shaw's orchestra. Shaw was adroit at recognizing vocal talent. When he heard Pauline sing, he recorded her with his band, doing, among other things, "Gloomy Sunday."

It is a milestone of a record. Byrne sings it with heart, simply, with a great understanding of the lyric. She made only a few sides with his orchestra, then withdrew to sing within the sheltered confines of the Six Hits.

Kay Thompson's Rhythm Singers were heard weekly on a popular radio show with André Kostelanetz during the late Thirties. Kay knows more about vocal-group writing than any other person alive. In addition, she was a fine writer of special material. It shone in her work with her singers and, later on, at MGM, where she became one of the leading lights in writing words and music for Judy Garland, Mickey Rooney, and for the cast of *Good News,* of which I was a member.

Kay's tag endings to her arrangements were a hoot. She made a specialty of starting a line, adding to it, adding a bit more to it, then saying the whole line. Example: In "Back in Your Own Backyard," she would wind up the arrangement with

> *Back*
> *Back in*
> *Back in your*
> *Back in your own*
> *Back in your own back yard*

Her act with the Williams Brothers, organized in 1947, was one of the biggest attractions in show business for that period.

The Merry Macs were more of a novelty group than a swinging foursome ("The Hut Sut Song," "Pop Goes the Weasel"), but they could swing on occasion, and they certainly pioneered four-part harmony at a time when three-part was the vogue.

The reason for their extraordinary blend was their kinship; three brothers (Judd, Ted, and Joe McMichael) formed three-fourths of the group. Cherry Mackay sang lead with them.

They began recording in the late Thirties, often incorporating vibes, piano, and guitar. They were featured in several movies and were considered one of the top groups of their kind when Joe died in 1944, during his military service.

The remaining brothers brought in a variety of girls to try and shore up the hole left by their dead brother. Helen Carroll, Marge Garland, Imogene Lynn, and Judy's sister, Jimmie Garland, all had a crack at reshaping the Macs. Eventually, the group disbanded.

Other groups came and went. The Town Criers, a family affair with the Polk brothers and sisters, held forth for a time with Will Osborne's band. The Skylarks toiled with a variety of bands and on their own. The Pastels were a hastily formed quintet, singing with Stan Kenton's orchestra; and the Mellolarks did various gigs until they landed on my old CBS afternoon show, emanating from New York five times a week in 1951–52.

A pair of great singers emerged from their respective vocal groups. The Andrews Sisters were one of the most successful trios in the business. They had more hit records to their credit than you could count, and one of the main reasons for their popularity was Patti Andrews.

She stood in the middle of her sisters, planted her feet apart, and belted out solos as well as singing the lead parts with zest and confidence. Whether doing one of the girls' many novelty hits ("Bei Mir Bist Du Schoen," "The Boogie Woogie Bugle Boy of Company B") or singing on her own ("I Can Dream, Can't I?"), Patti exuded an eyes-closed, smile-on-her-face persona that was irresistible. The kind of singing she did cannot be taught; it can't be studied in books, it can't be written down. Long experience as a singer and wide-open ears were her only teachers, and she learned her lessons well.

The sisters were not particularly attractive. Laverne (who died fairly young) was presentable if not beautiful. Maxine was the best looking of the three sisters, with regular features, a petite nose, and a good figure. Patti was cute, that's all there is to it. She had a gamin kind of personality, a piquant face, and expressive eyes. All in all, one of the great acts, with fine three-part harmony, clever staging, and, above all, the singing voice of Patti Andrews.

One of the most relaxed quartets of all time was the Mills Brothers, whose star continued to ascend from the Thirties right into the Seventies. Three brothers, Herbert, Don, and Harry, formed the nucleus of the group, with their fourth brother, John, singing vocal bass notes and playing guitar.

With John's death in 1935, the brothers' father took over the fourth position as bass singer, retiring in 1965 and passing away in 1967.

Their singing was cool and smooth. No histrionics; they stood and sang with pleasant countenances and excellent three-part vocals. Occasionally, Harry cupped his hands to his mouth and imitated a trumpet. In fact, they all, at one time or another, simulated a trumpet section very effectively.

Harry was a super singer. I used to listen to him for hours as he soloed on "Paper Doll," "Lazy River," and "The Glow Worm." Harry sang scat the way I like to hear it sung: laid-back, not too intricately, with special attention paid to incorporating the melody in most of his improvising. Again, not the kind of singing you learn in music class. You're born with it. Harry Mills certainly was.

A word about Jackie and Roy. While they do not qualify as a "vocal group," the arrangements Roy Kral turned out for himself and his partner-for-life wife, Jackie Cain, smack of the kind of special lyric, two-part harmony, unison singing associated with the best of the groups.

Jackie Cain is one of the finest female singers I have ever heard. One night, at the Hungry I, in San Francisco, she brought tears to my eyes, singing a moving "I Didn't Know What Time It Was," backed brilliantly by her husband.

Jackie sings directly from the heart, in a clear, perfectly-in-tune voice that sends shivers up and down your spine. Her choice of material is spotless: she chooses to sing not only the great standards but tunes that are not heard every day of the week, and she is one of the few singers who makes a song her very own the moment she wraps her talented tonsils around it.

She is wonderfully attractive, in a special New York way, dressing smartly and keeping her figure exactly as she kept it when she was seventeen, singing (along with Roy) with Charlie Ventura's little combo. Their record of "I'm Forever Blowing Bee-ob-ity Bobbity Bubbles" is required listening for anyone interested in early bebop.

Roy is the foundation upon which "Jackie and Roy" is built. Besides being a fine singer, he is the practitioner of the best "substitutions" in the music business. He sits at the piano, enhancing well-known tunes with his own "substitute" changes that, more often than not, improve upon the original. Many times I have heard him accompany Jackie with delicacy and taste, wishing it were me standing in front of his piano singing, with Roy gently playing behind me.

In November of 1946, the Mel-Tones, in a week-long emotional stand at the Golden Gate theater in San Francisco, disbanded, all of us going our separate ways. In January of 1947, I embarked on a solo career at the Bocage Room in Hollywood.

Since then, I have reorganized the Mel-Tones for various special events: my old Phillip Morris radio show in 1948, my "California Suite" on Capitol Records in 1949, and a "reunion" LP, made for Verve in the early Sixties, called *Back in Town; Mel Tormé and His Mel-Tones.*

All of these projects were fun, if short-lived. But every once in a while I think back, with great affection and not a little longing, to the days when the Mel-Tones were a daily part of my life, rehearsing at my house in the Hollywood Hills, having picnics in a cave in Bronson Canyon and singing our hearts out there, appearing on "The Fitch Bandwagon" every week with Dick Powell in 1945–46, working constantly on new arrangements, the kids learning them super-quick, having parties thrown for us by actor John Carroll and the Wells sisters . . .

They were unforgettable times, full of hope and fun and learning and being part of a Hollywood long gone in these days of high-rises, endless traffic, and smog-laden skies.

Mainly, it was being part of a vocal group that gave me the most happiness. Vocal groups are still my first love.

There I stood, at the back of the Majestic theater. The year was 1947. I was appearing at the Copacabana in New York. On several nights, I would finish my first show, take the stairs two at a time to the street level, hail a cab, and make my way to the Majestic in time to hear John Raitt sing the "Soliloquy" in *Carousel.*

Of all the moments in the theater I can remember, his singing of that monumental piece of music inspired and affected me—to the point where I saw *Carousel* nine times in four weeks. Raitt was an unusual man. Large and muscular, he could sing with the sweetest quality imaginable, making head tones that wafted out over the footlights and enveloped the mesmerized audience.

Conversely, when he sang "The Highest Judge of All," his voice was forceful and commanding, filling the theater with power that came from his diaphragm. His breath control was stunning; he could hold a note for the longest time, going from piano to forte effortlessly.

One of the great things about John Raitt was his approach to legitimate singing. He had a tenor/baritone range, and, unlike many of his contemporaries who sang their notes formally and sometimes pompously, Raitt was Everyman. He pronounced his words (at least in *Carousel*) with the slightest of twangs. At once, he became a star in a Broadway musical drama who delivered his music in an almost "popular" vein. The result was real empathy between Raitt and his audience.

These days, you have to qualify who John is by adding: "You know; Bonnie Raitt's father." That's a shame, because he certainly qualifies as a star in his own right. The trouble was, after *Carousel*, he was burdened with lesser properties that eventually took him out of the public eye.

He did have success in the Broadway musical *The Pajama Game* (1954). He repeated that success with the movie version (1957). He guested on TV and did many concerts in the Fifties and Sixties. He was slightly wooden as an actor, which may have something to do with his faltered career, but, for me, the magical moments he spent on the stage, creating the role of Billy Bigelow, the carnival barker in *Carousel*, were among the most riveting I have ever witnessed.

If *Carousel* is my favorite play with music, then certainly *Guys and Dolls* stands out as my favorite musical comedy. I was fortunate enough to see the original cast, with Robert Alda, Vivian Blaine, Sam Levene, and Stubby Kaye.

Stubby Kaye.

Now, there is a singer.

I held my breath and waited for those moments in that show that featured the rotund Kaye. "Fugue for Tin Horns" and especially "Sit Down, You're Rockin' the Boat" are a pair of numbers that show off the power and the purity of Stubby's singing.

He held that company together like Krazy Glue. Alda was more of an actor than a singer. Vivian Blaine's brassy "Adelaide" pierced your ears, but the singing was more endemic to the character she played than her true vocal qualities. (She sang beautifully in *State Fair*, Fox, 1945)

Sam Levene talked most of his songs, "Sue Me" being one of the better duets (with Blaine) in the long roster of man versus woman in the theater.

But Stubby Kaye! His girth had everything to do with the way he sang. Possessed of a sweet face, he simply opened up and out poured that golden voice.

For a man of his proportions, he was nimble and light-footed. He moved around on that stage fluidly, playing Nicely Nicely Johnson, in Damon Runyon's epic about a gambler and a Salvation Army girl. And when he sang "Sit Down, You're Rockin' the Boat," the house came down. In a musical with many show-stopping moments, Stubby stood out as, quite simply, the best singer in the company.

Alfred Drake was a little guy, but when he took the stage he was ten feet tall. An exceptionally handsome man, he had created the role of Curly in *Oklahoma!* as well as the lead in *Kiss Me, Kate*. His crowning glory was *Kismet*, adapted by Charles Lederer and Luther Davis. It made its debut on Broadway on December 3, 1953, and was an immediate success.

Drake's personality was geared to the Great White Way as opposed to films. Outside of a minor effort called *Tars and Spars*, (Columbia, 1946), which co-starred him with Janet Blair, and which was actually a debut vehicle for Sid Caesar, Drake confined himself to the stage, acting in *As You Like It* and *Joy to the World.*

As his career wore on, he was seen in several Shakespeare plays *(Othello, Hamlet, Much Ado About Nothing)* and appeared on TV in *The Adventures of Marco Polo, Volpone, Naughty Marietta,* and *The Yeomen of the Guard.*

He had an exceedingly warm manner and a wonderful presence on the stage. His leading lady in *Kismet* (she played his daughter) was Doretta Morrow, a young soprano who "went to school" on Drake. He took her under his wing (actually had a well-publicized romance with her) and taught her the mechanics of stagecraft. She emerged a good actress and a better singer, thanks to Drake's tutelage.

Len Cariou, a superb actor-singer from Canada, rocked Broadway with his title-role characterization of Stephen Sondheim's *Sweeney Todd.* The idea of making a musical out of so gruesome a subject as Todd was unthinkable to a number of Broadway mavens, but they did not reckon with the courageous and blindingly talented Sondheim, who threw caution to the wind and created a masterpiece about the Demon Barber of Fleet Street and his ground-up victims.

To get just the right "tone" to the Todd character—cold and unfeeling, tortured by his past, passionate in his zeal to provide his customers with "meat pies" that were succulence personified—involved a monumental job of casting. Cariou was exactly right for the part.

Sweeney Todd is really an opera, and it is a tribute to Cariou's diverse range of talents that he sang the role with authority and shading. His rendition of "Pretty Women" is wrenching; he becomes a monster of a man singing tenderly about the beauty of the opposite sex.

In recent years, Cariou has done stage work, appeared many times with Angela Lansbury (his co-star in *Sweeney Todd*) on "Murder, She Wrote," and sung with symphony orchestras. His lovely wife, Heather, herself an actress of great range, has appeared alongside her husband in several stage productions.

Cariou is a Man for All Seasons (now, there's an idea; Cariou as Sir Thomas More. I'll look forward to that one).

Inspiration, in my case, does not come from jazz alone; nor is it rooted in pop music or the movies or even the classical forms. I find it in many avenues, not the least of which is the Broadway stage, from Price and Warfield's *Porgy and Bess*, to Jan Clayton's tender singing of "What's the Use of Wonderin' " from *Carousel*, to Johnny Johnston's hopeful "New Broom" from *A Tree Grows in Brooklyn*, to Julie Andrews's splendid work in *The Boy Friend* and *Camelot* and Zero Mostel's impassioned Tevye in *Fiddler on the Roof.*

There are many great moments from the Broadway stage. There is still something about seeing a "live" show that is more immediate and compelling than watching a movie.

And you know I *love* movies.

THE ——————————
MOVIE SINGERS

■ ■ ■

Forget about the Martha Raye of the buxom build, forget about the big-mouthed gal whose trademark was "Mmmm-n-n-n-OH BOY!" Think of her, instead, as the wife of composer David Rose. In 1938, she walked into Columbia recording studios and sang with Rose's orchestra. The results were a delight to the ear.

Her supporting role in Bing Crosby's *Rhythm on the Range* (Paramount, 1936) catapulted her into star status. She became a Paramount regular in such films as *Waikiki Wedding, College Swing, Double or Nothing* and *Artists and Models*.

Her forte was comedy, and she milked it to the hilt in these and other movies in which she appeared. She was also an excellent singer, with ballads, of all things, her special love. With her husband's help (and considerable arranging skills), she wistfully sang "Melancholy Mood" and "My Reverie" on the aforementioned Columbia date, and the tear in her voice tore your heart out. "Once in a While" and "Stairway to the Stars" were yet two more examples of why she was a vastly underrated vocalist.

She could, of course, also turn around and swing like crazy. "How'd Ya Like to Love Me?" is a riot of raucous phrases and hip-shaking. Around a pool in Olsen and Johnson's *Hellzapoppin* (Universal, 1941), backed by the Six Hits (without the "Miss"), she romped through "Watch the Birdie." For sheer high-spiritedness, it is unbeatable.

But she loved the ballads.

During the war, the Mel-Tones and I appeared as regulars on an Armed Forces Radio show called "Swingtime," with Martha as the host. She sang more than her share of ballads on that show, and I am sure unlimited numbers of GIs had their fantasies fulfilled listening to her sing the songs of the hour in her high, breathless fashion.

She entertained our troops, just as Vera Lynn had done for the English Tommies, in a ceaseless round of camp shows, Red Cross concerts, and, out of a jeep, up-at-the-front appearances. She was brave and tireless and earned many honors for her unswerving devotion to the plight of the dogfaced soldier.

She is currently in poor health, confined to a wheelchair. She still has that gleam in her eye and that radiant smile. And she remembers the old days, married not only to David Rose, but to Nick Condos, who, with his brother Steve, was one of the best of the tap dancers. She still enjoys music and listens to it constantly.

And she loved the ballads.

Jane Frazee always looked as though she had just brushed her teeth. She had a clean, crisp look about her, with the whitest teeth in the movie game.

She was a Universal contract player, and they used her in just about everything you can think of during the war. Her real name was Mary Jane Frahse. She appeared in films from 1940 to 1951, most of them Universal pictures.

She was also in *Hellzapoppin*. She sang "You Were There" with Robert Paige looking on adoringly. She was a lovely girl, resembling Lana Turner to a degree, and she was a more than capable singer.

At the age of six, she and her sister Ruth began performing in vaudeville and in nightclubs. When they split (Ruth took a screen test and flunked), Jane was signed by Universal and began a long list of Westerns and "B" musicals.

Hollywood is weird. Here was a girl with more on the ball than half the women in Hollywood. Had the right studio taken an interest, she might have become one of the major musical stars; she sang that well.

Instead, she was relegated to minor movies with midget budgets. She excelled in these, but the clout was elsewhere, and, eventually, she faded to black. She was married to cowboy star Glenn Tryon until 1947. When they divorced, she went into real estate. Boo! Hiss!

Another Universal player in the 1940s was Gloria Jean. (The rest of her name was Schoonover.) She was signed in 1939, to take up where Deanna Durbin left off, since the studio was grooming Durbin to play more mature roles.

She was a soprano, with a pleasing personality and voice to match. Her pitch was very good; her vibrato was uncertain and somewhat rapid, but she was very impressive, appearing in teen-oriented films opposite Donald O'Connor, W. C. Fields, and, in one instance (ahem!), me.

We did a little film together in 1944 called *Pardon My Rhythm*. I played her boyfriend, the drumming leader of a school band, eager to get into a radio contest for high school orchestras. Sound familiar? Mickey and Judy did it time and again, but Universal wasn't above appropriating plots and using them to their own advantage.

Gloria was a delightful young girl. Her films had done much to stabilize Universal's shaky financial condition, but she was down-to-earth, modest, and as unaffected as anyone I have ever met in this business.

When it it was over for her, she took a job as a hostess in a San Fernando Valley restaurant and then as a receptionist and switchboard operator for a California cosmetics company. The transition to civilian life has never seemed to faze her. She is comfortable and happy in her new career.

The real heavyweight at Universal was Deanna Durbin. She was born Edna Mae Durbin in Winnipeg, Canada, and showed early signs of ability as a singer. At fourteen, she was recommended to MGM by a talent scout.

Metro put her in a short called *Every Sunday*. She was pitted opposite Judy Garland in this virtual audition trifle, and when the smoke cleared, despite Durbin's having sung beautifully, MGM chose to go with Garland. Durbin not only could sing; she was a good, natural actress. Universal recognized these qualities and signed her immediately.

If Gloria Jean's pictures helped stabilize Universal, Deanna Durbin films saved the company from bankruptcy. Durbin's first movie, *Three Smart Girls*, put Universal in the black and shored up its crumbling fortunes for many years to come.

Durbin was phenomenal. Possessed of a glorious operatic voice, she could and did sing anything put in front of her to perfection. In one of her 1937 efforts, *That Certain Age*, she is seen in a cabaret setting, with kids all around her, singing "Les Filles de Cadiz" by Delibes.

The sixteen-year-old diva suddenly attains maturity and confidence, singing this minor-keyed work, and you realize, in watching her, that she is more, much more, than a mere child star; she will go on to bigger, better, more fruitful roles as time goes by.

In *Lady on a Train* (Universal, 1945), she turns in a fine job of acting and shows us, once again, the broad range of her talents. She had a fresh-faced beauty that was piquant and appealing. One of her arms (the left, I think) was slightly crooked, and she carried it with her elbow out.

In 1938, she and Mickey Rooney were awarded "special" Oscars for "bringing to the screen the spirit and personification of youth."

As she matured, she went on to become the highest-paid woman working in films at that time. Suddenly, unaccountably, she quit the movies and moved to France.

A few years ago, I looked at *That Certain Age* once more and fell in love with Deanna Durbin all over again. I secured her address in France and wrote her a fan letter. She answered my letter almost immediately, and I was thrilled to make contact with her. One of these days, I will go to France, meet the lady, and have one of my fondest desires fulfilled.

Donald O'Connor is remarkable. A top-calibre dancer, he also sang in his myriad films, and sang well. Donald has a Bing Crosby–like approach to singing. The notes are rounded and deep, the tone quality and vibrato outstanding. As he progressed, so did his vocal work, until, at this stage of the game, he is easily one of the best song-and-dance men who ever lived.

Donald, like so many of his contemporaries, began with his family in vaudeville (and the circus). He was eleven months old when he appeared onstage for the first time, and eleven years old when he made his film debut in something called *Melody for Two*, sharing the screen with his two brothers in a specialty act.

Paramount signed him in 1938, but it wasn't until 1942 that his star began to rise. Under contract to Universal, he played the lead in a series of low-budget, high-visibility movies, opposite gifted Peggy Ryan. Again, Universal depended on young talent to bring in the money. Donald didn't disappoint them. His pictures were among the top-grossing features of 1942–45.

He played Buster Keaton to perfection in *The Buster Keaton Story*. His most enduring film was *Singin' in the Rain*, and his featured number "Make 'Em Laugh" is still regarded as one of the great cinematic tour de forces of all time. All in all, a splendid performer.

Born Alice Jeanne Leppert, Alice Faye was seen by Rudy Vallee in the chorus line of *George White's Scandals* on Broadway. He signed her to sing with his band, and they commenced a relationship that resulted in divorce for Mr. Vallee, with Faye named as corespondent.

Fox signed her, liking her sultry looks and husky voice. She made a series of musicals for the company (*On the Avenue, Alexander's Ragtime Band, Rose of Washington Square*, and *Lillian Russell*, to name a few of the many.)

She warred with Darryl F. Zanuck, the mogul in charge of Fox's cinematic output, and she was eventually replaced as the top musical star on the lot by Betty Grable.

From 1936 to 1940, she was married to Tony Martin,

who made Fox musicals as well. Tony, an ex–reed player with several California bands, was photogenic to say the least. He also had a beautiful tenor voice, and it was put to good use in several movies, not only at Fox but at MGM as well.

He appeared in *Ziegfeld Girl*, *The Big Store*, *Till the Clouds Roll By*, *Easy to Love*, *Hit the Deck*, and *Two Tickets to Broadway*, all MGM musicals. He looked good and sang masterfully in all of them. His version of "Tenement Symphony" from *The Big Store* is one of the best-sung pieces in any movie, ever.

Betty Grable was primarily a hoofer, and a good one. She sang many songs in her starring vehicles at Fox. Her vocals were always slightly under pitch, but she had a nice sound, and she went on to become the Queen of the Fox lot as well as the favorite of the GIs during WW II.

At MGM, it was Judy all the way. Singers would come and go. A few would make their mark to greater or lesser degrees, but no one could match Garland's luster, her swingy singing style, her acting abilities, or her star quality.

Born Frances Gumm in Grand Rapids, Michigan, on June 10, 1922, she appeared with her two sisters in the "Gumm Sisters Kiddie Act" when she was five years old. She was billed as "the little girl with the great big voice," and every time she stepped onto a stage she proved it.

At thirteen, Louis B. Mayer signed her at Metro "without a screen test," but we have seen, from her appearance in the short *Every Sunday*, that this wasn't quite true.

Singing "Dear Mr. Gable" in *Broadway Melody of 1938*, she ran away with the picture, and Mayer set the wheels in motion. Garland was to be one of the top stars on the MGM lot.

In *The Wizard of Oz*, she sang "The Jitterbug," which was cut, and "Over the Rainbow," which wasn't. The tremulous performance of that song endeared her to the hearts of the entire country. She made a variety of films, starring with Mickey Rooney in many of them. As she got older, she had problems, but she always remained in that select circle of performers who are bigger than life, beyond the pale of ordinary mortals: stars.

I wrote a book about my relationship with Judy on her CBS television show (from May of 1963 until February of 1964.). The book was honest and, in some quarters, was reviled. Mickey Rooney had the last word on this book, however.

He came to my house one day to give me a quote for the dust jacket. Before he left, he looked me square in the eye and said: "Mel, Judy would have thanked you for this book." That's the best review I got on *The Other Side of the Rainbow*.

Mickey, the Renaissance man of all time, sang in many of his films, particularly with Judy. His voice was gravelly, but he understood the rudiments of singing, and, for me, he was a joy to watch and listen to.

In *Girl Crazy* (MGM, 1943), he sings "Treat Me Rough" with style and wit. In *Strike Up the Band* (MGM, 1940) he duets with Judy on "Our Love Affair." This is a sweet song, made all the more palatable by the blend of their two voices, seemingly incompatible and yet perfect together.

Paramount, of course, belonged to Bing. He was the "Paramount singer," and, yes, that is supposed to have a double meaning. He stood at the head of the Paramount studios' list of musical personages. He was also the paramount singer among all the other singers of his time, and he held that exalted position for a long time, until Sinatra came along and unseated him.

Bing has been dealt with elsewhere on these pages. Suffice it to say: he had no peer (my opinion) as an actor and a singer.

Columbia was low man on the totem pole. That studio's "thing" was dramas and comedies. With the emergence of Rita Hayworth, Columbia attempted to cash in on her dancing talents by presenting her in a drama with "music." She sang "Put the Blame on Mame" in *Gilda* (Columbia, 1945.) Well, no . . . she didn't sing it at all. Her voice was dubbed by Anita Ellis, but Hayworth was a master (mistress?) of the art of lip-synching, and as far as the public knew, she was the singer.

Cover Girl (Columbia, 1944) presented Rita paired with Gene Kelly, with Phil Silvers along for comedy relief. The score was by Jerome Kern and Ira Gershwin. There were some great songs in this film ("Long Ago and Far Away," "Sure Thing"). When Rita sang, you were listening to the sexy voice of Nan Wynn.

As a matter of fact, over-dubbing the "voices of the stars" has been a cottage industry in Hollywood, from the advent of sound right up to today. A star actor or actress who couldn't sing? No problem. Bring in the second team, a parade of guys and gals who planted their feet on the recording stages of the various studios and "filled in" for the luminaries.

There were some excellent singers involved in this practice, and, while their faces were never seen on the silver screen, they were heroes and heroines to me.

For instance: a lucky blending of picture and sound

came in the form of Louanne Hogan, who was signed to sing for Jeanne Crain in *State Fair* (Fox, 1945). Leaning out of the window of her Iowa farmhouse, Crain mouthed, while Hogan sang, a bittersweet "It Might as Well Be Spring." Crain's restlessness, her search for something meaningful in her life in the way of a man-woman relationship, was perfectly executed by Louanne, whose voice had a tender quality that made you feel for Jeanne and her "problems."

In *Poor Little Rich Girl* (Fox, 1936), Tony Martin (believe it or not) sings "When I'm with You." He is unbilled in this, his first film, and his voice is dubbed by Dick Webster, a band vocalist of the era.

As Dennis Morgan descends the long spiral staircase in *The Great Ziegfeld* (MGM, 1936) singing "A Pretty Girl Is Like a Melody," the voice you actually hear is Allan Jones.

Martha Mears was the busiest off-screen singer in Hollywood. Her voice was highly adaptable to almost any female on-screen image. She sang for Michele Morgan in *Higher and Higher* (RKO, 1943), for Lucille Ball in *Du Barry Was a Lady* (MGM, 1943), and for Veronica Lake in *Star Spangled Rhythm* (Paramount, 1942), a partial list of her credits.

In *Wake Up and Live* (Fox, 1937), Jack Haley wakes up to find he can sing, and the story progresses from there. His alter-ego voice belongs to Buddy Clark, a world-class singer, who died tragically in a plane crash on Beverly Boulevard in Hollywood, returning from a Stanford football game. Buddy also sang for Mark Stevens in *I Wonder Who's Kissing Her Now* (Fox, 1947).

Cyd Charisse had Carole Richards sing for her in *Silk Stockings* (MGM, 1956) and in *Brigadoon* (MGM, 1955), but she (or the studio) switched to India Adams for *The*

Band Wagon (MGM, 1953). The public, as usual, was unaware of the disparity of voices.

Nor were they bothered by the fact that Lynn Bari's vocals in *Sun Valley Serenade* and *Orchestra Wives* were handled by Pat Friday.

The beat goes on.

In *Three Little Words* (MGM, 1950), Anita Ellis dubbed for Vera-Ellen, and Helen Kane sang for Debbie Reynolds.

In *Carmen Jones* (Fox, 1954), it was Marilyn Horne for Dorothy Dandridge and Laverne Hutchinson for Harry Belafonte.

In *Centennial Summer* (Fox, 1946), Louanne Hogan repeated her stand-in vocals for Jeanne Crain.

In *The Five Pennies* (Paramount, 1959), Eileen Wilson dubbed Barbara Bel Geddes's voice.

In *Gentlemen Marry Brunettes* (UA, 1955), Jeanne Crain's singing is done by Anita Ellis.

In *Gigi* (MGM, 1958), Betty Wand stands in for Leslie Caron.

In *Gypsy* (Warners, 1962), Rosalind Russell's songs were partially dubbed by Lisa Kirk.

In *The Harvey Girls* (MGM, 1945), vocals for Cyd Charisse were dubbed by Marion Doenges.

In *The King and I* (Fox, 1956), Marni Nixon filled in for Deborah Kerr.

In *Meet Me in St. Louis* (MGM, 1944), Leon Ames had no less than the producer of the picture, Arthur Freed, dub in his voice.

In *The Merry Widow* (MGM, 1952), Trudy Ewen dubbed Lana Turner's songs.

In *My Fair Lady* (Warners, 1964), Marni Nixon did all of Audrey Hepburn's singing.

In *Pal Joey* (Columbia, 1957), Rita Hayworth's voice

was dubbed by Jo Ann Greer and Kim Novak's by Trudy Ewen.

In *Porgy and Bess* (Goldwyn, 1959), Dorothy Dandridge had Adele Addison fill in for her. Sidney Poitier was covered by Robert McFerrin, father of Bobby McFerrin.

In *Rhapsody in Blue* (Warners, 1945), Sally Sweetland did Joan Leslie's singing.

In *Show Boat* (MGM, 1951), Ava Gardner's voice was dubbed by Annette Warren.

In *A Song Is Born* (Goldwyn, 1948), Virginia Mayo sings, but the voice belongs to Jeri Sullivan.

In the remake of *State Fair* (Fox, 1962), Pamela Tiffin's songs are recorded by Anita Gordon.

The record holder of these off-screen substitutions is undoubtedly Vera-Ellen. She made many films and was dubbed by a different voice in each of these, with the exception of *Three Little Words* and *The Belle of New York*, in both of which Anita Ellis was on hand to dub for the dancer.

Otherwise, she sang in several diverse voices. *Call Me Madam* (Fox, 1953): Carole Richards. *White Christmas* (Paramount, 1954): Trudy Stevens. In *The Kid from Brooklyn* it was Dorothy Ellers; in *Carnival in Costa Rica* the singer was Pat Friday. *Three Little Girls in Blue* had Carol Stewart doing Vera-Ellen's songs, and in *Let's Be Happy* her surrogate was Joan Small. Whew!

A word about the singing cowboys. Their domain was mainly Republic Pictures. They held forth in the movies from the inception of sound through the Thirties and Forties. The films were small-budget "B's," and the cast of characters was almost always the same. The heroes were Hoot Gibson, Bob Steel, Tom Tyler, Ken Maynard, Buck

Jones, and Tom Mix. The villains were Dick Alexander, Ed Cobb, Roy Barcroft, Harry Woods, and Dick Curtis.

Then, in the early Thirties, along came Gene Autry, singing cowboy. *Tumbling Tumbleweeds* marked his entry into the movie game, and he immediately became the rage among kids who went to the movies on Saturday afternoon.

He was a melodious singer, as was Roy Rogers, his successor. Rogers's real name was Leonard Slye, but how would that look on a marquee? His first starring movie was *Under Western Stars* (1938). His horse was Trigger; his "gal" was Dale Evans, whom he later married.

With the Sons of the Pioneers, he recorded "A Melody from the Sky" (from *Trail of the Lonesome Pine*, Paramount, 1936) and "The Hills of Old Wyoming" (from *Palm Springs*, Paramount, 1936), which proved he could operate in the "pop" vein as well as sing cowboy songs. He is still going strong.

Other singing cowboys include Tex Ritter of *High Noon* fame; Jimmy Wakely, an old pal of mine and a damned good singer; Dick Foran, who crooned a sweet song called "My Little Buckaroo" to tiny Tommy Bupp in *Cherokee Strip* (1937); and Smith Ballew, who starred in a series of Westerns beginning with *Western Gold* (1937) and ending with *Panamint's Bad Man* (1938).

Ballew bore a startling resemblance to Gary Cooper, but his film appearances were short-lived, although he made five Westerns in two years. He sang with a deep, rumbling baritone and, I think, could have done more with his career if conditions had been more favorable to him.

Bob Baker was also a singing cowboy who deserved a better fate than the one he was dealt. Universal signed Baker, and he was quickly saddled with inept scripts and tepid action. Even the sets used in his films had the look of having been used before—in his other films. He sang very well, but he couldn't overcome the poor plotting of his movies, and he died on the vine.

John Wayne sang in three of his movies, *Riders of Destiny*, (Monogram, 1933), *The Man from Utah* (Monogram, 1934), and *Westward Ho!* (Republic, 1935). Although the word is that Smith Ballew dubbed in his voice, several documentaries on Wayne have portrayed him as having done his own singing. We'll never know.

I liked the cowboy singers. Their songs were simple and to the point. For the most part, they sang mellifluously and without pretense, and there is a lot to be said for that.

SCAT! ———————————

His bailiwick was Birdland. He hung out in front, dressed in an overcoat, shades, and a beret. Always a beret. His name was Babs Gonzales, and he operated on the fringe of the scat singers. He worked on occasion at Birdland itself. It seemed to me more of a favor on the part of the owners than in recognition of his talents.

He was Mr. Bebop. His scat singing was crude and slightly out of tune. But he had something. He was unreservedly cheerful. No matter what bad fortune may have come his way, he wore a perpetual grin. And in his own, special way, his scat singing made sense.

He used a lot of quotes. Quotes from Dizzy Gillespie and Bird (Charlie Parker) and Cannonball Adderly and Clifford Brown. He knew a goodly amount of tunes, but his mainstays were the original instrumental stuff of the bebop boys. When bop ran its gamut and slowly evolved into something else, he simply disappeared.

Before that disappearance, though, he dabbled in a wide variety of endeavors: managing a Paris nightclub, writing a book (which he himself published) called "I Paid My Dues," and occasionally writing bebop tunes like "Oop-Pop-a-Da."

His singing generally was toneless, and, as Will Friedwald says in his excellent book *Jazz Singing*, Babs was "a comedian, a professional hipster and a music businessman." Still . . . he had something.

Jon Hendricks is a totally professional jazz singer-composer. Born in Newark and raised in Toledo, Ohio, Hendricks, at fourteen, began singing at a local nightclub, billed as "the Sepia Bobby Breen."

He stayed in Toledo until the draft caught up with him in 1942. After his discharge, he returned to Ohio and entered the University of Toledo by day and the jazz clubs of the town by night, playing drums, singing, and writing songs.

Briefly, he considered a career in the law, but powerful forces were drawing him toward another career. He went to New York, ran into Charlie Parker at the Apollo bar in Harlem, got up and sang with him, and was never, ever the same.

Jon had written witty, rapid-paced lyrics to "Four Brothers," Woody Herman's saxophone soliloquy. He sang them for a casual friend named Dave Lambert, who flipped. They began working together. They gathered a group of singers, most of whom couldn't sing at all.

Annie Ross (more about her later) was the exception, and the boys amalgamated with her to become Lambert, Hendricks and Ross. When they recorded "Sing a Song of

Basie," they emerged as the hottest jazz vocal group in the country. Jon continued to write, and his work became more polished and topical.

The group broke apart in 1962. Annie Ross failed to return to the United States, and suddenly Lambert and Hendricks were faced with replacing her. Anne Marie Moss stayed on for a bit, then was replaced by Yolande Bavan, who was Ceylonese.

What really broke up the group was the death of Dave Lambert. He got out of his car to change a tire one night for a total stranger. A car swerved into him, killing him instantly. (Strange. His erstwhile singing partner in the Gene Krupa band, Buddy Stewart, was also killed in a traffic accident.)

Jon gigged around England for a while after Lambert's death, then returned to the States, this time to San Francisco, where he taught a jazz history class at the University of California.

He settled in Mill Valley, wrote reviews for the *San Francisco Chronicle,* and sang where he could find work. He wrote a show called *Evolution of the Blues* and, with his family and some friends, kept it going for five years.

Currently, he sings and writes and is a credit to jazz singing. Jon's one failing is his intonation; he, like so many people who sing scat, sings slightly out of tune. It doesn't bother me, because his ideas as a scat singer are marvelous. He has great charm and charisma, and he is the supreme enthusiast. Nothing can stop him.

Joe Carroll was a cool little cat who sang, for a time, with Dizzy Gillespie's big band. We all worked Bop City together. It was on the corner of 49th and Broadway, and Diz, with Chano Pozo on conga drums, plus a roaring ensemble of musicians, came in and blew the walls down.

Joe Carroll was his singer, and I remember our all "getting into it" with something called "Hey Pete! Let's Eat! More Meat!"

Joe was a sharp little scatter, shuffling about on the stage, dancing as well as singing. I have read that he wore outlandish bebop-style outfits with Diz. When we played Bop City, his normal attire was . . . normal attire.

He was a disciple of Leo Watson, and much of what he sang in the way of scat approximated Watson's frantic mouthings. When Diz pared his band down to a combo, Carroll took a cab and was seldom heard from again.

Speaking of Diz, he was one of the great scat singers. Whenever we sang "Hey Pete," Diz would jump in and cut Carroll and me. He sang like he played, and it doesn't get any better than that.

Leo Watson, for a long time, was the best of the scatmen. Born in Kansas City in 1898, he sang at an early age with a group called the Spirits of Rhythm and then decided to make it on his own. Along the way he was given a scat chorus on Artie Shaw's 1937 record of "I've a Strange New Rhythm in My Heart."

For eight months, he was Gene Krupa's vocalist. He made a knock-down, drag-out record with Gene on "Nagasaki." Then the Andrews Sisters got Decca to take him on as a solo vocalist.

His scat singing was highly original, a bit crazed, and decidedly out of the mainstream, even for scat singers. He was an eccentric, running naked through hotel lobbies and generally making a nuisance of himself. Too bad, because when it came to singing scat he was in a class by himself for quite a while.

He died of pneumonia in 1950.

Cab Calloway is hard to categorize. Some would have you believe he was a first-rate scat singer. Others are not so sure. They see him as a showman-bandleader whose vocal gyrations were almost corny, nearly "so hip it hurt."

I'm caught somewhere in the middle of the controversy. There is no denying he had a powerful, musical voice, or that his "hi-de-ho" bordered on improvisational singing. But I am hard-pressed to acknowledge him as an out-and-out scat singer.

He was the brother of Blanche Calloway, an entertainer working in the Twenties and Thirties. Born in Rochester, New York, on Christmas Day, 1907, he led several bands before becoming—Cab Calloway and his orchestra.

The Cotton Club was his base, and, with his long, dark hair, his rolling eyes, his wild gyrations, and his "hi-de-ho," he managed to capture the attention and admiration of the clientele, most of whom were white, traveling from downtown to uptown to hear and see the great black performers.

Cab had a wonderful band, comprised of some of the best musicians in the land, among them Chu Berry, Jonah Jones, Tyree Glenn, and Dizzy Gillespie. He also composed many songs that he sang in front of his orchestra. "The Jumpin' Jive," "Are You All Reet?," "Boog It," and "The Scat Song" were all part of his roster of "hip" tunes.

But was it really scat?

I don't think so. He never explored any songs that had a great variety of chord changes, sticking to simpler stuff that was undemanding yet attention-getting.

There was one Calloway outing that I enjoyed immensely. In 1936, he made a Warner Bros. movie called *The Singing Kid.* In the opening sequence, he stands on the roof of a New York skyscraper, in front of his band, his pencil mustache framing impossibly white teeth, and shouts out a Harold Arlen song called "I Love to Sing-a" across the way to Al Jolson, standing on the roof of a neighboring skyscraper. Calloway's frenetic movements

and singing are in perfect contrast to Jolson's more re-
strained finger-snapping presence. Together they make a
terrific pair, singing back and forth across the high-rises.

Calloway could sing ballads with feeling. In a long-
forgotten short subject, he sings "I've Got a Right to Sing
the Blues" with fervor and passion. He is wonderful in this
groove, and he was superb in *Porgy and Bess* on Broadway
as Sportin' Life, but I don't think he qualifies as a pure
scat singer.

Bon Bon (George Tunnell), on the other hand, was the
real article, and so was Jan Savitt, who was among the
first white bandleaders to employ a black singer.

Bon Bon's vocals, particularly "720 in the Books" and
"Rose of the Rio Grande," both Savitt cuttings, were pure,
smooth singing, with the accent on swing. He stayed with
Savitt until 1941, when he went out on his own and became a force in the business of jazz singing.

He worked with Tommy Reynolds for a while in the
early Fifties and was an inspiration and influence on
many singers who came after him and a few who were his
contemporaries. Ella Fitzgerald was one of these.

Sarah Vaughan could sing scat with the best of them.
Years ago, we co-starred at the Claridge hotel in Atlantic
City. She came out scatting on "Autumn Leaves." I
thought it was very brave of her to open her set with scat
syllables as opposed to singing the lyrics of the song, but
that was Sarah.

She was a product of the Bebop Era, just as Ella grew
up with swing. Sarah's earliest influence was Billy Eck-
stine, and she modeled her singing after his. But she also
played piano, a big plus for her, and she kept her ears

open to Bird, Diz, and the other bop mavens from whom she gleaned a computer-brain-full of phrases and riffs.

Sarah sang jazz and scat in the most modern fashion imaginable, and, while her singing was occasionally incomprehensible to the average listener, her musicality was right on. Her vocal equipment was probably the most "legit" in the business. I used to call her "the Diva," to her great delight, and she was, in fact, a singer who could have easily taken a turn into classical music and a career on the stage of the Metropolitan.

She was a childlike, joyful woman, with bad habits and a God-given voice. One thing is for sure: like a few others of her kind, she was one of the totally original singers in a world full of imitators.

Johnny "Scat" Davis was a roly-poly little man who adopted the name "Scat" but was not a scat singer in any real sense of the word. He was a happy soul, with a cherubic grin, devilish eyes, and a metallic sort of voice. He was not without merit as a "swinging" singer; just listen to his work on "Hooray for Hollywood" from *Hollywood Hotel* (Warner Bros., 1938), and you know he had the right idea.

He worked with a variety of bands, made a few films, led his own big band in 1939, but faded with the passing of years.

Bing, covered in an previous chapter, was an early singer of scat. In his first feature film, *Reaching for the Moon*, he sang one song, "When the Folks High-Up Do the Mean Low-Down!," and his sense of jazz was firmly in evidence.

Throughout his career, whether singing with the Rhythm Boys or on his own, he extemporized on many occasions. Considering his early days, working alongside

Bix and Eddie Lang, it is no wonder he was imbued with a solid sense of syncopation and a penchant for "blue" notes.

Incidentally, Harry Barris was a good piano-playing scat singer in his own right. He was essentially a musician-songwriter, with "I Surrender, Dear" and "Wrap Your Troubles in Dreams" to his credit.

In 1926, he joined Paul Whiteman as a member of the Rhythm Boys and proceeded to write the group's special material. This included "Mississippi Mud," one of the classics of the Jazz Age. On occasion, he scatted with good results.

George Benson is a scat singer of sorts. His unison singing, accompanied by single-string guitar playing, has made him one of the country's leading performers.

Slim Gaillard, with his "vout-o-roonie" brand of scat, was popular during the war. A clown in many respects, Gaillard was actually an accomplished musician and could sing creditably when called upon to render a swinging tune or even a ballad.

Joe Williams is best known for his renditions of the blues, but he can sing scat and sing it well. All those years on the stand with the Basie band were not lost on Joe, whose ideas scat-wise are fresh and exciting.

We once appeared together on the Merv Griffin show, this time from Las Vegas. We got into a scatting contest (I forget which tune we sang), and Joe was a killer. He sings "In the Evening" with the same aplomb he exhibits doing "All Right! Okay! You Win!," but his scat singing is relatively unknown and unappreciated. Look out for him! He's something else!

Annie Ross had a breathtaking range and the ability to sing the lyrics of Jon Hendricks at breakneck speed, enunciating them clearly and cleanly. Born in Surrey, England, she was reputedly the daughter of famed musical comedy star Ella Logan (not proved.)

Annie first appeared, at the age of eight, in a Little Rascals short entitled *Our Gang Follies of 1938.* As a young girl, she settled in London, getting work as an actress and as a singer in jazz clubs. It wasn't until 1952 that she made a record, which brought her to the attention of Hendricks and Lambert. The tune was "Twisted," which made some noise, but not before Ross was off and running all over the Continent, recording with this group and that and starring with Anthony Newley in *Cranks* at the Hammersmith theater in London.

When she got back to New York for an engagement at Upstairs at the Downstairs, Lambert and Hendricks were lying in wait for her, and the rest is history.

Through much of their output, she sings wordlessly, in what can be called a scat vein. She is simply wonderful, kicking that incredible range of hers into gear and soaring to the stars.

Certain singers have tried to scat with sometimes disastrous results. They seem to think that scat singing is a matter of spitting out random syllables, with no attention to the chord structure or the melody of any given song. "Skee-deet-n-dat-n" pours out of their mouths, and there is no relationship whatsoever to the essence of the chordal sequence of the tune.

Scat singing is a very specialized craft. It can't be taught; it has to be ingested by each protagonist through some unusual process of musical osmosis: endless listening to jazz, trial and error, courageous ventures into uncharted territory, with mixed results on occasion, strict attention to intonation, made difficult at times by the very nature of that kind of singing—creative, experimental, haphazard.

It is a constant source of wandering into uncharted territory. It is exploratory and sometimes nerve-wracking. But when you get it right—on those nights when you succeed as the alter ego to the instrumentalists—there is nothing in the world like it.

■

AFTERTHOUGHTS – ON SINGING

■ ■ ■

As our former President Richard Nixon once said: let me make this perfectly clear. What follows is not an attempt to pontificate. Nor is it an exercise in pomposity. What I am about to write is STRICTLY my opinion. It isn't carved in granite or written in blood on the walls of the temple. Merely some observations I have made along the way about singing and careers and comportment.

Right! Now that that's settled:

Singing the same song(s) night after night after night can be boring and troublesome. There is a tendency to be thinking of something else while you are spouting the words to a tune you have done so many times, you know it in your sleep.

I know of a certain singer who had a whopping hit record and is saddled with that song for the rest of his professional life. He once confessed to me that, while he is doing the tune, his mind kicks back to that afternoon on the golf course. How, he thinks as he croons his hit, could I have possibly missed that putt on the sixteenth green?

It takes great facility to pull off this kind of mindless singing. I simply don't have it. I am stuck with singing familiar material time and again, and I have a system that helps me through it. There is an imaginary slot in the side of my head, into which I program the tune(s) in question.

The software tells me that there are people in the audience who may be seeing and hearing me for the first time. Pay attention, Mel. Think about what you are singing. For the most part, it works, and I am able to perform these evergreens creditably.

I approach each song I sing, particularly the ballads, as if it were a little playlet. Since acting is an important element in putting over a song, I immerse myself into a game of role playing. I actually try to "be" the man who is singing about his lost love, or newfound love, or what have you.

The result is, it makes for a better, more thoughtful rendition, and it occasionally involves members of the audience, so that the performance becomes a shared experience.

One night, at the Off Broadway, a club in San Francisco, I sang "When the World Was Young," directing my gaze toward a young couple at a front-row table. The girl was beautiful, the guy was good-looking, and they sat there, heads together, holding hands, listening to me sing. Suddenly, the three of us were in a cocoon of music, oblivious to the rest of the audience, transported to France and "summers in Bordeaux, rowing the bateau." They got misty over that song, and I was moved.

There is also a tendency these days to forget about the words and read what is sung off a teleprompter. That's fine for some people, but I am not one of them. First of all, how can you invest feeling and understanding of the lyric into any song when you are involved in the sterile practice of reading those words off a scroll?

For me, the retention of lyrics is not only vital; it's mandatory. We singers are paid ridiculously high fees to go out on the stage and sing from our repertoires. That means having at your beck and call the words to virtually thousands of songs. If a member of the audience calls out something he wants to hear that you recorded fifteen years ago, you should be able to dredge it up in your mind and spew forth with the tune, lyrics and all.

Michael Feinstein and Bobby Short are two artists who have a vast storehouse of the words to songs; that stamps them both as unique performers. Catalogues of every kind of tune are at the root of truly great singers. When the day comes that I have to go out in front of the public and read the lyrics off a screen, I will happily hang up my guns.

There are so many things that go to make up a successful career in the singing game: appearance, publicity, accessibility, resistance to rejection, picking the right tunes to record, and maintaining a good attitude.

Breath control plays a great part in how you sing. The ability to string phrases out, not having to take a breath in the middle of a given line of lyric, means the difference between making sense out of the words or merely singing them as they are written and letting the proverbial chips fall where they may.

Long ago, I devised a way to maintain good breath control. When I know I have to sing a note or a phrase that requires lengthening a held tone within the body of the song, I suck in my stomach (or diaphragm) and continue to do so as I hold the note. When my abdomen is halfway extended (in the middle of the note or phrase), I pull it in again, slowly allowing my breath to come out until I have finished with whatever I am singing. It is my own method, and it may not work for everyone, but it suits me and it suffices.

The "reading" of lyrics is the single most important aspect of singing the popular song. Most songs are written in old-fashioned rhyme, so that the end of a rhyming pattern goes neatly with the next one coming up. To sing songs in this fashion is anathema to me. When I choose a song to do, the lyrics have to have something to say that is meaningful, and they have to contain inner rhymes so the phrases can be broken up and the singing can mirror talking.

I like words to songs that you would say in everyday life. Of course, in "All the Things You Are," we're talking about poetry, a string of words that goes beyond everyday conversation. It is pleasant to hear and to sing that kind of song, but mainly I stick to "conversational" lyrics.

The words to any given song are 99.8 percent of what a song is all about. If the melody is pleasant, that's fine. That's the frosting. But the cake, the meat, of any popular song is the lyric. The only way to communicate pain, love, hurt, joy, and/or hopefulness is through the singing of the lyric.

Songwriters tend to become overly protective of their lyrics. In one case I recall, that protectiveness became ridiculous.

I stood on the soundstage at MGM, preparing to sing "Blue Moon" with the MGM orchestra. Lennie Hayton had written the arrangement, and Richard Rodgers stood close by. When I reached the second stanza of the song, I sang:

Blue Moon
You knew just what I was there for
You heard me saying a prayer (pause)
For someone I really could care for.

"No, no, no!" Rodgers stormed, stopping the session and startling the orchestra. "Don't sing it like that." He beat time with one hand, palm upward, into his other hand, also palm upward.

Blue Moon
You knew just what I was there for
You heard me saying a prayer for
Someone I really could care for.

It was fruitless to try and tell him that I wouldn't say it that way and therefore I resisted singing it that way, sing-song, serving the rhyme and not the meaning of the words. I capitulated and did it his way, but I have always regretted not sticking to my guns and singing the lyric the way good poets read their poems—to express an idea, not merely to make a rhyme.

I choose my songs very, very carefully. Since I write my own arrangements, a time-consuming process that occasionally drives me around the bend, I have to be sure that whatever I am going to sing (and arrange) will have "legs," that it will be performable for a long time to come.

Arranging is a two-edged sword. I love to write, particularly symphony charts. When I stand in front of seventy-five or eighty people, and they play what I put down on manuscript paper, it is the closest thing I can think of to being God.

On a few occasions, I have brought an arrangement to the symphony that, for one reason or other, simply didn't jell. Those moments are devastating to me. All that work down the drain. Mostly, the charts do function well.

The down side of this process is the laboriousness of sitting there, hour after hour, scribbling notes on a large pad of paper. The work is tiring and lonely and tentative. You never know, until you place the parts in front of the orchestra for the first run-down, whether you have succeeded or not in creating something playable. When it clicks, it is a wonderful feeling.

Musicians play a large part in a successful performance. If you become saddled with inferior players, it can mean the difference between success and failure. Most of the musicians I wind up working with are more than competent. My own trio (John Colianni, John Leitham, and Donny Osborne) are superior musicians who breathe with me. It makes for a very comfortable time onstage, and I can relax and be about my business. Those rare periods when the backing by a big band or a symphony is something less than thrilling mean I have to make do, to rely on the trio to come forth, in front of the assembled players, and dominate the performance.

The pursuit of a singing career is fraught with pitfalls. Being a singer means being on the road. That engenders having to live in hotels, travel in limos and airplanes, function in a wide variety of venues, eat in good and bad restaurants, and in general lead a monastic, nomadic kind of life.

For one hour a night, you are in heaven, standing in the spotlight, performing for a crowd of people who came specifically to see you. You work your wiles on the audience, pacing your performance with ballads and "up" tunes, incorporating patter into your set that puts the patrons at ease, makes them laugh, tells them you don't take it all too seriously.

That is one hour of a twenty-four-hour day. The rest of the time, you sleep, read, catch a movie, eat, and sometimes simply stare at the four walls of your hotel suite. Sound glamourous? Believe me, it isn't.

The financial rewards are great, of course. But you pay an exorbitant price for being well paid. I am married. For the most part, my wife stays at home, taking care of the house, doing errands, and making multiple contact with me by phone every day. Telephonic contact, however, isn't like "the real thing," and it creates a feeling of apartness that makes for loneliness in the extreme.

Re: critics. Forget 'em! There are only a handful of critics in this country and abroad who know what the hell they are talking about.

I have been inordinately lucky. Most critics, particularly the qualified ones, like Phil Elwood of the *San Francisco Examiner* and Whitney Balliett, who writes for the *New Yorker*, have been extremely kind to me. That also goes for a smattering of writers around the country who have ears and knowledge where jazz and jazz singing are concerned.

The bulk of the so-called critics, however, are simply incompetent. It seems irresponsible to me that city editors assign hacks to review performers. They make mistakes, criticize for the sheer pleasure of criticizing, and, in some cases, don't even stay for the full performance, preferring to walk out and then "create" a review that makes little sense to those who did stay.

Case in point: a certain critic in the city of Los Angeles. No matter how well you perform, no matter how great an ovation you receive from the audience, he feels it is his duty to make at least one negative comment on your performance. He's a critic; therefore, if his evaluation of your stint on the stage is nothing but glowing, he has betrayed his calling.

Hogwash!

The toughest critic I know, the meanest man when it comes to damning a performance, holding a given evening up to the light and examining it mercilessly or commenting on my singing abilities (or lack of them) is . . . me.

There is no critic in this country who monitors my
engagements as closely and critically as I do. There have
been nights when I walked off a stage to a thunderous
ovation. As I cleared the curtain line, I shook my head
sadly and remarked: "Don't they know what a rotten,
flawed, absolutely terrible performance I just gave?"

At the same time, I have gone out in front of an audience, given my all, sung to the zenith of my ability, and
walked off the stage to minimal applause, thinking:
Where did I go wrong? I sang well tonight. Why didn't
the audience respond?

The point I am making is, right or wrong, the audience and the audience alone gives you your reviews, good
and bad. Your only responsibility is to them, and when
they react enthusiastically, then all the reviews in the
world count for nothing.

I haven't read my press notices in years. Richard Burton once said: "I never read reviews; when they're bad,
they just kill me. When they're good . . . they're never
good enough!"

I love to sing. Being out there, with appreciative people applauding, is one of the great thrills in life. Once in
a while, an interviewer will ask: "When are you going to
retire?" I give them my stock answer.

"Well, there are three reasons I can think of for giving
up the ghost: One, if I walk on the stage, look around and
think, 'This isn't fun anymore' . . . then I'll retire.

"Or, if I walk out on the stage of a venue that holds
2700 people and encounter an audience of 268 . . . I'll
retire.

"Or, if I open my mouth to sing . . . and nothing
comes out . . . I'll retire."

Knock on wood, I seem to be in good health. The critics, to a man, have commented that my voice is stronger
than ever, for which I am deeply grateful. There's an old

saying: if you rest, you rust. I have no intention of resting. As long as the public cares to support my work, I'll be out there, singing and swinging away. Besides, I have a long way to go, learning my craft.

A career should be a "work in progress," a giant "learning curve." At least, that is the way I view my life. There are nights when, after a performance, I walk off the stage and my pianist or bass player will say to me: "Hey, Mel. You sang such and such differently than I ever heard you sing it before."

That kind of comment is rewarding to me. I never ever sing the same song the same way twice. Popular songs are open to interpretation. If they weren't, then we might as well, all of the singers in America, meet in a midnight conclave at Madison Square Garden and elect one person to sing all the songs for all of us. That is why I do not agree with Richard Rodgers. What these are, are popular songs. They are not Holy Writ or the Sermon from the Mount. They are little pieces of experience, jotted down by songwriters for singers to interpret as they see fit.

That's what I do . . . and I am going to keep on doing it till I get it right.

Index of Names and Subjects

Index of Songs and Albums